CYNTHIA FREEMAN

ALWAYS AND FOREVER

JOVE BOOKS, NEW YORK

This Jove Book contains the complete
text of the original hardcover edition.
It has been completely reset in a typeface
designed for easy reading, and was printed
from new film.

ALWAYS AND FOREVER

A Jove Book/published by arrangement with
the author

PRINTING HISTORY
G. P. Putnam's Sons edition published April 1990
Jove edition/July 1991

ISBN: 0-515-10607-0

Jove Books are published by The Berkley Publishing Group,
200 Madison Avenue, New York, New York 10016.
The name "JOVE" and the "J" logo
are trademarks belonging to Jove Publications, Inc.

PRINTED IN THE UNITED STATES OF AMERICA

10 9 8 7 6 5 4 3 2 1

To my own beloved family and to my devoted family of readers.

A portion of the royalties from this book will be donated to the Cynthia Freeman Foundation, which is dedicated to the education of our children, the care of our elderly, and the granting of literary prizes.

ALWAYS AND FOREVER

$=$ Chapter 1

Kathy Ross awakened early one unexpectedly sultry October morning in 1945 with an instant realization that it was to be a landmark day. She lay motionless, and for a few moments her sometimes hazel, sometimes green eyes remained closed. But her thoughts raced forward to nightfall, when she would board an ocean liner en route to Southampton, England, the first stop to her ultimate destination of Hamburg, Germany. For once in her life, she thought with satisfaction, she was about to do something useful.

Every school day of the past four years, when she had climbed down from their apartment above the family's candy store on Thirteenth Avenue in Borough Park, Brooklyn, she had battled guilty feelings over the fact that she was on her way to classes at Barnard when she ought to have been enrolled in the WACS and doing something for her country.

For all her first-generation American patriotism, her mother had been hysterical when Kathy first mentioned joining up. Her father had been speechless with fear. Their baby—their only child—off to fight in the war? Aunt So-

1

phie, the family's Rock of Gibraltar, had persuaded her that it would be more sensible to stay home and earn a college degree, then go to Columbia at night for a master's in social work.

"In the WACS you could be killed," Aunt Sophie had said matter-of-factly, with the faintest trace of a German accent. "This way, even if you quit work at sixty-five, you can contribute over forty years of service to people who'll need you. One thing you have to learn, Kathy," Aunt Sophie had admonished, but with love in her voice, "you must see the whole picture, then decide what to do."

Only Aunt Sophie truly understood why she was sailing tonight with a volunteer group out to help resettle some of those millions just released from such horror spots as Belsen and Auschwitz and Dachau. Aunt Sophie understood Kathy's obsessive need to contribute to the world in which she lived.

For Aunt Sophie the war had evoked a very personal pain. She had been born in Germany and had expected to spend her life there, until her father abruptly moved the family to New York City. And Kathy knew she felt a fierce pride that her grandniece was among those eager to help the victims of Hitler and the Nazis. Somewhere in Germany the Rosses had left behind cousins. How many had died in the concentration camps? Long ago Aunt Sophie had lost touch with family in Germany.

Aunt Sophie—in truth, her great-aunt Sophie—had been part of the immediate family since before she was born. Dad's mother and his Aunt Dora had both died in their early sixties, before Kathy was born. Like herself, Dad had been an only child. Aunt Dora's two daughters had moved to California, and in their newfound prosperity preferred to forget their cousin in Brooklyn who ran a small candy store that dealt in pennies.

Aunt Sophie was, to his knowledge, Dad's only surviving relative other than the California cousins. She had taken care of the apartment and cooked and watched over their only child while Kathy's parents put in the required sixteen hours a day in the candy store. Small and seemingly fragile at seventy-seven, though the years rested lightly on her, she continued to be the family's strength in time of crisis.

Kathy pulled herself up in bed, taking guilty pleasure in sleeping late this morning. She had quit her job as a law office receptionist the week before, in order to allow herself the luxury of a few days off. The leader of their group had been blunt in warning them of the heavy work load that lay ahead.

"You'll see sights that will turn you sick, horrible examples of man's inhumanity to man. Sights we must make sure never come to be again." Brian Holmes had been a war correspondent with the American forces that had liberated the concentration camp at Belsen in April. "You'll work till you drop because there's so much that has to be done."

For a while it had appeared that their project would never get off the ground, but Brian had been persistent. Europe was in chaos. The presence of relief organizations was desperately needed. Finally, he was able to pull the right strings. Bureaucratic red tape was cut. The group acquired passage to Europe, though Kathy had refrained from telling her parents that there was serious concern about the return trip, with every inch of space on ships from Europe to America slated for returning GIs.

Conscious now of the unseasonable heat, of her perspiration-dampened pajama top, Kathy left her bed and crossed the tiny bedroom to head for the shower. Dad had opened the store at six. Mom always joined him an hour later. Only Kathy and Aunt Sophie were in the apartment. They and the voice of WNEW radio, she thought with a flicker of humor. Aunt Sophie was addicted to the radio.

"Kathy?" Her aunt's voice drifted to her above the mid-morning radio news.

"I'm going to shower," Kathy called back, reaching for a cap to cover her lush, dark, shoulder-length hair. "God, what a hot night."

"I've got fresh coffee perking," Sophie reported. "And I'll put up the French toast the minute you tell me you're out of the shower."

"Great."

Kathy loved her aunt the way she loved her parents. Sometimes she felt closer to Aunt Sophie than to them. Despite her age, Kathy thought tenderly while she adjusted the water's temperature, Aunt Sophie was more modern in her thinking than Mom. Even in those long-ago days back in Berlin, Aunt Sophie had argued that women should have the right to vote. And here in New York in 1912 she had marched with other feminists down Fifth Avenue to declare the equality of women with men.

It had not been easy for Mom and Dad to see her through Barnard, even as a day student with a weekend job, Kathy reminded herself. Even though the Depression was over, Mom and Dad's income was more suited to Hunter or City College. Aunt Sophie had argued that she should go to a prestigious school, that good times were ahead and a degree from Barnard would be money in the bank. But Kathy had taken the first job offered to her at graduation because she had known it would be of short duration.

Kathy remembered the Depression. Those frightening times when Dad and Mom were terrified they would lose the store. When Aunt Sophie conjured up new ways to make potatoes and rice and spaghetti more appetizing. She wore the same two blouses and two sweaters through the last three years of elementary school. At first they were all too large, because Mom bought them to "grow into"—then they were embarrassingly small. But Mom had been proud that they never had to go on Home Relief. She had realized times were better, Kathy thought whimsically, when Dad started to bring home lox and bagels on Saturday nights to enjoy with the Sunday *Times*.

Kathy stood under the stinging spray of the shower and remembered how she and Marge—her best friend from Erasmus High—had been fascinated for a while in the late thirties by the fiery street-corner speakers who climbed atop wooden cartons on Thirteenth Avenue and talked about a world where no one went hungry. Once they had taken the subway to Columbus Circle on a Saturday night to blend with the hordes of humanity that roamed about the Circle, listening to first one soapbox orator and then another. It had seemed exciting and idealistic to hear such eloquence on behalf of the segment of the American population that Franklin Delano Roosevelt called "ill-fed, ill-housed, ill-clothed."

They had taken the subway into Manhattan for the May Day parade six years ago when veterans of the Abraham Lincoln Brigade, which had fought against Fascism in Spain, gave the marchers the Popular Front clenched-fist salute. This was one of the rare occasions when she had argued with Aunt Sophie.

"Idealistic fools," Aunt Sophie had said, scoffing at the Americans fighting against Fascism in Spain. "What's the difference, Fascism or Communism? Both are bad," she had said with contemptuous rejection. "The Russians don't like the Jews. I remember the stories I heard back in Berlin about what Czar Alexander III did to the Jews in Russia."

Kathy's father had told her how Aunt Sophie had left a young man she had loved behind in Berlin. He was a student who had fled Russia to save himself from persecution. Aunt Sophie had never married. She was always there to "help the family through a bad time."

Kathy stepped out of the shower when she heard the phone ring. Dripping wet, with a towel draped sarong fashion about her petite, slender body, she raced to respond.

"I'll get it," she called to her aunt and charged into the living room to pick up the phone. "Hello," she said breathlessly.

"I'll pick you up at two o'clock," Marge reported. "I finally convinced Joe he had to let me have the car to drive you to the pier, though he cried bitter tears about how much gas I'd use." Two of Marge's brothers stayed out of the army via defense jobs. The third was 4-F.

"Oh, wonderful. A taxi into town would have cost a fortune." Marge was picking her up at two o'clock, Kathy mentally noted, which would give them time for a long farewell. "I still wish you were going with us."

"I know," Marge sighed. "I gave it a lot of thought. It's not for me. But I'm going to get out of New York as soon as I've saved up enough to take me to San Francisco and to live on until I find a job. I've had all I can take of Mom telling me the only way for me to go is to marry and have eight kids—or to be a nun."

"Start saving, Marge." Kathy knew Marge was determined to escape from the tyranny of her mother and three brothers, all of whom lived in the pleasant three-story O'Hara family house on Fiftieth Street that had been converted in the dark Depression days to a three-apartment house.

"How's the group shaping up?" Marge asked. "Anybody really exciting?"

"If there was," Kathy laughed, "you'd be joining us." Marge had sat in on those first emotion-laden meetings at the West End bar favored by Barnard and Columbia students. The volunteer group was being financed by a syndicate of wealthy American Jews, impatient with delays of the various governments to cope with the problems of those released from the torture chambers of the Nazis. They had campaigned immediately among Columbia-Barnard seniors, known for their liberal leanings. "But they're really dedicated to the cause. Everybody's friendly. Except that one character, who rarely opens his mouth," Kathy conceded. "Probably he's still recovering from his residency at Bellevue." Everybody knew how hard interns and residents worked. Especially at Bellevue. "I think his name is David Kohn."

"Does your mother know?" Marge giggled. "She'd love to see her daughter married to a doctor."

"Marge, I'm not going on this trip in search of a husband. I have no intention of getting married for a long time, if ever. After this I have to settle down to working for my master's."

"I'll settle for a master who's good-looking and sexy and has a terrific job." Marge sighed. "That was what I hated about Hunter. No men. At least at Barnard you had all those Columbia guys."

"Not really. I was a commuter student." Marge had been a commuter at Hunter. "You know what happens. On Thursday or Friday evenings—depending upon class schedules—commuters take off for home. Maybe those in the dorms have some social life with Columbia guys."

"Kathy, breakfast." Sophie appeared in the doorway.

"See you at two," Kathy said hastily. "French toast calls."

Kathy and Marge tried to keep the conversation light, but Kathy knew her aunt was anxious about this trip overseas, even while she was proud of its purpose.

"I know the war's over," Sophie said with an apologetic smile, "but take care of yourself, darling." A tic in her left eyelid betrayed her concern that Kathy was about to put an ocean between them. "God knows how long before we'll see you again."

"Aunt Sophie, we're scheduled to be there four months," Kathy chided. "If I'd gone to college in the West, I would have been away that long between holidays."

"It's going to be a pain in the ass to get a ship home." Only when she was distressed did Sophie allow herself even the mildest profanity. "Look at all the soldiers who are trying to get home. Look at all the war brides who are trying to get here. Sure, it's easy enough going over—"

"Not that easy," Marge reproached. "They had to get priorities."

"Aunt Sophie, I'll get home all right," Kathy soothed and reached to hug her aunt. "And if I have the chance, I'll go to Berlin and say 'hello' for you."

"I could never set foot in Germany again," Sophie said

sharply, all at once looking ten years older. "Not after Hitler. Not after what the Nazis did to the Jews."

"Aunt Sophie, it's over," Kathy said.

"For Jews it will never be over." Sophie's voice trembled. "No Jew must ever forget what happened in Nazi Germany. We must never let it happen again."

"I'd better go down to the store and say good-bye to Mom and Dad." Kathy broke the grim silence that engulfed them for a moment and reached to kiss her aunt with warmth. "They're still upset that I'm going."

"Ach." Sophie shrugged and forced a smile. "They've survived worse." She hesitated for a moment, her eyes over-bright. "If you do get to Berlin, have a cup of tea or coffee at a sidewalk café on the Kurfürstendamm. If any still stand."

Sophie remained still, watching Kathy head down the stairs. Her mind raced back through the years. She was fifteen again and in Berlin where she lived for almost six months. Papa had given up trying to support the family on the farm, and had moved in hopes that big-city medical care would improve Mama's health.

Papa had been so proud that his daughter had gone through the free, country district elementary school. For a year, before they had moved to Berlin, Sophie had worked as a domestic for a wealthy neighboring household. There she had learned a smattering of English. But in Berlin it was her job to take care of the flat and her mother.

Just the week before, two students from the university had moved into the flat across from the one she shared with her parents and two older sisters. From the first sight of one of the pair, a slender blue-eyed boy, she had been drawn to him. Again—in her mind—she was at the landing on their floor as the young men were mounting the stairs. . . .

Her heart pounded when her eyes met those of the blue-eyed young man, and she sensed a similar response in him.

"Excuse us, Fräulein," he said politely and smiled. "We are neighbors, yes?"

"Yes." Her own smile was dazzling.

Alex's friend Sigmund grinned in amusement as Alex introduced them both to Sophie. She was enthralled when Alex asked her to join him later at a nearby beer garden. "I will meet you there," she said shyly.

Bidding the two young men a polite farewell, she hurried down the stairs and out into the street on her shopping mission. She would say nothing at home about meeting Alex Kohn at the beer garden this evening. She was not yet ready to reveal this new friendship to her family. Often in the evenings she went out for a walk, since by then the others were there to look after Mama, so her leaving would not provoke curiosity.

Papa disapproved of the university students because of their liberal attitudes. *"Troublemakers, all of them, with their crazy ideas."* In their flat she never talked about her fascination for the suffragists in England and the United States, who were fighting for the rights of women to vote.

With startling yet glorious swiftness, the romance between Sophie and Alex became the focal point of both their lives. Alex was so handsome, so sweet and gentle. And one day he would be a doctor. That would impress Mama and Papa. But before she could marry, she forced herself to explain to Alex, they would have to wait—in the Jewish tradition—until her older sisters had acquired husbands. When Alex protested, Sophie pointed out that he had much schooling ahead. They were young and had time. They could wait.

Sophie cried in Alex's arms with happiness when he presented her with an exquisite brooch—precious stones in a gold setting designed as a bow—that had belonged to his mother. He told her how his mother had given it to him when he'd had to flee from St. Petersburg because Alexander III had begun to persecute Jews and students, which put him at double risk.

"The pin was created by the jeweler who designed for the czarina. Mama said I was to give it to my wife," he said tenderly. "Keep it close to your heart until the day we can be married."

"Oh Alex, I love you so much," she said with an abandon that would have shocked her the year before. "I live for the day I can be your wife."

But then Sophie's world was shattered. At the supper table in the early summer of 1883 her father told his three daughters that the family was to leave within a week for America.

"Papa, why?" Sophie whispered, pale and shaken.

"For a better life," he said. "My cousin Isaac writes from New York City that work is to be had there. Not just for me, but for Dora and Hannah, too. And in America," he said reverently, "we will find doctors who can help Mama become well again."

"Do we have the money?" Hannah asked doubtfully.

"Isaac has sent us the tickets. We will work hard in America and pay him back."

All at once Hannah and Dora were plying their father with questions. The kitchen was charged with excitement. Sophie saw the glint of hope in her mother's eyes. *Would the doctors in America help her?*

The next morning Sophie waited until Hannah and Dora had left for their jobs to talk to her father.

"We have little time for talk, Sophie," he warned in high spirits. "We must prepare for our journey."

"Papa, I would like to stay here. I—" She hoped she could make him understand about Alex. But her father would hear none of it.

"You'll go to America with the family," he barked at her. "Always, you have crazy ideas."

"But Papa, I have to tell you—"

"I will tell you!" he thundered. "You will go with the family to America. Who else speaks the language there? You will lead us. Where Mama and I go, our children go."

"Papa, there is a young man," she said desperately. "He wishes to marry me."

"You have been carrying on behind our backs?" he demanded, all at once ashen.

"Papa, no!"

"Who is this man who talked to a child about marriage?"

"I'm fifteen. Mama was fifteen when she married you. We—"

"Enough of this. It would break your mother's heart to leave you behind. You have an obligation to take care of the flat and of Mama," he blustered. "You will go with us to America."

Later she sat with Alex at their favorite sidewalk café and told him her father's ultimatum. She fought against tears. How could her whole world have fallen about her shoulders this way? Yet she knew she could not refuse to go with her family. Mama needed her. In a strange new world they would all need her.

"Sophie, this is insane." Alex reached across the table for her hand. "You will marry me and stay in Berlin," he said determinedly. "We have a right to our own lives."

"I have to go with them, Alex." Gently she withdrew her hand. "Our time will come later." She tried to smile. "I'll come back to you." She reached within the neckline of her dress to unpin the jeweled brooch she always wore hidden from all eyes. "I will come back, Alex, and you will give me my pin again. Keep it safe for me. I will come back to you."

Sophie pulled herself back into the present. She had never been able to go back to Alex. Their time had never come.

Downstairs Kathy walked into the cluttered candy store. Assailed by the familiar aromas of chocolate, soda flavorings, and newsprint, she felt an unexpected emotional wrench. She wouldn't see Mom and Dad and Aunt Sophie for almost half a year.

"Bubbeleh—" Her mother emerged from behind the counter with arms outstretched, her eyes moist.

"Mom, just think I'm going to the Catskills to work for the summer," Kathy coaxed. The year between Erasmus and Barnard she had been a waitress at Grossinger's for the summer. Mom and Dad hadn't minded that, though their phone bill for that eight weeks was frightfully high. Still, in an emergency they could drive up in two hours.

"You're going to a foreign country," her mother reminded dramatically. "Germany yet."

"I'll make you an egg cream for the road." Her father strived for nonchalance. "You, too, Marge."

"A little one," Kathy stipulated and Marge nodded.

"You still have your job at Macy's?" Mrs. Ross asked Marge with sudden concern.

"Oh, sure." Marge smiled. She knew Kathy's mother kept predicting women would be losing their jobs now that the soldiers were all coming home from overseas. "I called in sick. Even a trainee can be sick," she drawled. At first enthusiastic about the job that could lead up to being a buyer, Marge was talking privately about quitting to look for something on Seventh Avenue, at the wholesale level.

"Don't be sick too often," Mrs. Ross exhorted.

"My wife still lives in the Depression," her husband chuckled. "So Marge calls in sick. Girls aren't standing in line waiting to grab her job. These are good times."

"Your ship doesn't sail till midnight." Mrs. Ross turned to Kathy accusingly. "So why do you have to leave early in the afternoon?"

"We're having a meeting up near the campus," Kathy fabricated. Mom would feel better if she *had* to go into the city early. In truth, she wanted to roam about Times Square for a nostalgic while with Marge. Then they were going to splurge on an early dinner at Lindy's. It would be her big farewell to the city.

"We should get moving," Marge said and drained the last

of her egg cream in noisy appreciation. "It gets harder and harder to find a place to park in the city."

"Drive carefully," Mr. Ross told Marge when Kathy had exchanged warm embraces with her mother and then himself. Kathy suspected he didn't trust any woman driver. "Crazy drivers on the road these days," he'd always say.

"Kathy, you write home regularly," her mother ordered and Kathy steeled herself to smile in the face of a possible emotional outpouring.

"I'll write twice a week," she promised. "And I'll be fine."

"I won't have a moment of real peace until you come home," her mother declared. "Not a night that I won't lie awake worrying about you."

"The war's over," Mr. Ross reminded his wife. "Kathy'll be safe."

"I'm glad Aunt Sophie made me learn German through the years," said Kathy. "At least, I'll be able to communicate with the people." But she was somber as she remembered that a longtime neighbor had given her the names of family members who had been caught in Hamburg during the Nazi rule in hopes she might look them up. But it was unlikely that she could track them down.

Seated on the front seat of the 1937 Chevy beside Marge, her luggage stashed in the trunk, Kathy considered what lay ahead. It would not be a joyous adventure. She and her group would see what had shocked the world when Allied soldiers had liberated the concentration camps. She suspected how they would react to the kind of atrocities that were difficult to conceive but had been documented by photographs and news stories flashed around the world.

Mom wanted her to stay home, meet a nice man, and get married. Couldn't Mom understand that after what had happened in the last few years she couldn't live with herself if she didn't make an effort, however small, to help the world recover from World War II?

"Kathy," Marge began as she pulled away from the curb

and joined the stream of traffic down Thirteenth Avenue, "how many doctors did you say were in the group?"

"Two," Kathy reported. "The other ten of us are what my English teacher would have called a motley crew. Including a plumber, a psychiatric social worker, and a third-year law student."

"And all of you under thirty," Marge drawled knowingly. "Don't tell me there won't be a lot of partying aboard that ship."

"There won't be any partying in Hamburg," Kathy said with conviction. "I hear the city was one of the worst hit in Europe. And we're traveling with hoards of canned goods because food is hard to come by."

"Two doctors," Marge repeated. Her smile blissful. "And one of them, I gather from what you told me, is the smoldering, moody type. Like Laurence Olivier in *Wuthering Heights.*"

"No," Kathy denied. All at once self-conscious.

Marge clucked in reproach. "What did you say his name was?"

"I forget," Kathy lied.

She had never compared David Kohn to Laurence Olivier, she told herself defensively. She and Marge had had such mad crushes on Olivier their last year at Erasmus. But all at once she recalled David Kohn's brooding good looks. There *was* a kind of resemblance between him and the famous actor.

Chapter 2

As the commuter train from Greenwich chugged into the depths of Grand Central Station, David Kohn reached for the two much-scarred leather valises that had traveled with him from Berlin ten years ago, when his parents had packed him off to school in New York. It was still possible then to send money out of Germany for educational purposes. He could hear his father's voice:

"You'll be far away from home, David; but you won't be alone. My cousin Julius will watch over you. You'll go to school with his son Phillip. You'll be with family—and you'll be safe from this curse that has come over us here in Germany."

He hadn't been back to Europe since the summer of 1937, when, according to his father's instructions, he visited Salzburg. Was he making a mistake in returning to Germany, even for a few months? *Could he handle it?*

All these years later he felt sick when he remembered that strange meeting with Papa on the bridge that connected Salzburg with Germany. The Nazis had allowed Papa to continue operating his private hospital and research cen-

15

ter—which had been his father's before him—because of the
important work on nutrition he was doing in his laboratory.
A special ruling afforded him the privilege. By then, Jews
had been deprived of almost all their rights. Papa had gone
to Munich to deliver a paper on this research, and from
there had traveled to the bridge. David broke into a cold
sweat as he remembered that meeting. . . .

His eyes crept constantly to his watch because the timing
of this meeting was crucial. Papa had insisted that it was
too dangerous for him to travel through Germany under
present conditions. Instead, he had gone from London to
Prague and then to Salzburg.

His gaze clung to the face of his watch as the time of the
meeting approached. His heart pounded. *Now,* he exhorted
himself. Now was the time. Walk toward the bridge. Appear
to be a tourist. The Nazi frontier guards at the barbed wire
must not realize he and Papa knew each other.

There he was. How much older his father looked in the
two years since they had seen each other! Papa said it was
impossible to send money out of Germany anymore. This
was the only way to give him funds to continue on through
college and into medical school. There had never been any
question in either of their minds but that he would become
a doctor like his father and grandfather.

"David, you're taller," his father whispered as they met
at the barbed wire. The Nazi guard fortunately engaged in
conversation with another guard.

"Just filling out, Papa." His eyes clung to his father's face.
"How is Mama?" Why hadn't she come with Papa? "And
my sisters? And Grandma and Grandpa?" His words tumbling over each other in his haste to communicate. Knowing
this meeting must be brief.

"Take this," his father ordered, eyes fastened on the
guards, and thrust a small cloth bag through the barbed-
wire fence. "Hide it quickly."

"Yes, Papa." He took the bag and thrust it into his pocket.

"Don't lose it, David."

"The family?" David asked urgently.

His father's face was anguished.

"David, I know no easy way to tell you. Mama died five weeks ago. Her last words were of you."

David stared at his father, trying to assimilate what had been told to him.

"Why didn't you bring me home?" he reproached with a mixture of grief and anger. "I should have been with her!"

"Mama insisted—" his father began, then suddenly straightened up and became a stranger. "I am sorry, young man. I can't give you a cigarette—I don't smoke."

"Move along," the Nazi guard ordered ominously. "Before I decide to search you. Are you transmitting money into Austria?" he demanded in sudden suspicion.

"Who has money?" Dr. Kohn shrugged with a touch of humor, avoiding a backward glance as David moved away. "Everything costs so much today—"

Later he understood that Papa had sold off what the Nazis allowed him to keep and bought diamonds with the money. Diamonds were small and easy to transport. His father knew his cousin Julius would be able to find a buyer for the gems in New York. It was these diamonds, his family's life savings, that would see him through college and medical school.

David had never seen his father again. The entire family had died in Bergen-Belsen. He felt again the awful pain when word had come through to him of their deaths in the gas chamber. A former patient of his father—a man who had survived Bergen-Belsen—had contacted him through one of the relief agencies just four months ago. Even while he had hoped for their survival, in his heart he had known they were gone.

The train pulled to a stop. Passengers were moving to-

ward the exits. David waited for the others to leave. Though
the limp he had acquired in a skiing accident at fifteen was
barely perceptible—but sufficient to prevent his joining the
American armed forces—David was ever conscious of this
imperfection.

He had gone up to Greenwich for two days before sailing
for Hamburg out of respect for Uncle Julius and Aunt Bella;
they were actually his cousins, but he had been told to regard them as his uncle and aunt. School holidays and summer vacations had been spent with them and their son and
daughters. At boarding school he had shared a room with
his cousin Phil. He had needed that sense of closeness these
years away from home.

He was never entirely comfortable in their ornate Greenwich mansion. Uncle Julius's taste was flamboyant compared to that of his parents. True, the Julius Kohn estate—
as Uncle Julius enjoyed calling it—was only minutes from
the Merritt Parkway in Round Hill, the posh backcountry
of Greenwich, and marvelously peaceful after his back-
breaking tours of duty first as an intern, then resident at
Bellevue Hospital. Julius Kohn was recognized as one of the
most successful furriers in America, yet David suspected
that to his neighbors he was an outsider. David doubted that
any Jew—no matter how wealthy—would be anything but
an outsider in Greenwich, Connecticut.

Emerging in the central area of the terminal, a valise in
each hand, David paused. He had hours on his hands before
boarding the ship. He would call Phil to see if he was at that
little apartment he had rented for himself up on West End
Avenue. Maybe they could have dinner together. Aunt Bella
was upset that Phil had insisted on having a place in town
for himself, but David understood. After two years fighting
a war, Phil wasn't ready to settle down in Greenwich and
go into the fur business with his father.

Phil answered the phone on the second ring.

"Hello." He sounded cautious. Expecting a reproachful
call from his mother, David guessed.

"Hi, it's me," David said. "I've got some time on my hands before the ship sails. Feel like coming downtown for dinner?"

"Sure. Where are you?"

"Grand Central. Where should I—"

"I'll pick you up at the Information Center," Phil interrupted ebulliently. "It's past the rush hour—I can be there in five minutes."

They went to dinner at Toots Shor's. Phil was restless, talking about trying to line up a job as a roving photographer.

"The old man's still on the kick about my coming into the business." He shuddered expressively. "Climbing into the limo with him every morning at five forty-five for the miserable drive into the city. When I got out of uniform, I swore I'd never get up before nine again."

"You're just out of uniform a few weeks," David said soothingly. "He knows you need some time to adjust to civilian life again." He felt guilty that he had never served his adopted country. He was a citizen now. He'd applied for citizenship on his twenty-first birthday. "Thank God for V-J Day."

"You bet." Phil grinned. "Two years in Europe and they had me out in Texas training for the Pacific. I got rescued just before I was to be shipped out again." He was pensive for a moment. "You might just see me in Hamburg. I've got something going with a magazine. A possible photo layout on postwar Germany."

"Great," David approved. The last few days he'd been having reservations about setting foot on German soil again, yet his conscience told him that as a survivor, it was his personal obligation to help those displaced persons in such need. And he had to see for himself the concentration camp where his family had died. Bergen-Belsen was close enough to Hamburg for him to be able to drive there in, perhaps, an hour—provided car and gas were available. Aunt Bella said it was masochistic, but he had to know what they had endured.

"I'd kind of like to see Paris again." Phil intruded on his introspection. "Some of those babes over there, zowie!" He whistled in appreciation. "And didn't they just love American GIs."

David glanced at his watch. He was hardly in the mood, he thought somberly, to be concerned about girls. This was not a vacation in Europe; there was much work to be done.

"Maybe I ought to head for the pier. The traffic can be heavy—I wouldn't want to miss the sailing."

Kathy stood on the deck of the ship with Rhoda Karsh—fresh out of Teachers College at Columbia but in no rush to start her teaching career—and watched the lighted torch of the Statue of Liberty disappear from view.

"My father said he didn't believe the war was truly over until he saw the torch lighted again," Kathy said softly.

"When I was about ten, my parents took me out to Bedloe's Island to see the Statue of Liberty," Rhoda remembered. "To them it was holy. They came here as kids early in the century. On the same boat, would you believe it? Of course, they didn't find that out until they were married."

"My Aunt Sophie was sixteen when her family came here from Berlin. She never talks about it, but she worries about cousins that stayed behind in Germany. She hasn't heard from them in over fifty years—you know how people lose touch. It would be impossible to track them down even if they survived."

"This must be a kind of pilgrimage for David Kohn," Rhoda said, her voice deepening in compassion. "Somebody said his whole family died in the camps."

"How awful for him." She felt a sudden chill, just hearing about it. "I don't think I could go back if something like that had happened to me."

"Wouldn't you think we could have gotten passage on something better than this heap?" Rhoda deliberately redirected the conversation. Soon enough, Kathy thought, they'd come face to face with the atrocities of the camps. "I didn't expect the *Ile de France,* but this is for the birds. Four of us stuffed in a cabin big enough for one!"

"We'll spend most of our time on deck," said Kathy.

"I know. We'll have classes in German every day." Rhoda sighed. "Why didn't I take German in college?"

"Let's go down below and unpack," Kathy suggested.

"I get claustrophobic down there," Rhoda said. "And why unpack? There's nowhere to put anything."

"Unpack pajamas and your toothbrush," Kathy ordered. "And something to read. I have a feeling we won't fall asleep quickly tonight."

"I hope we can get to Paris before we come home," Rhoda said wistfully. "Wouldn't you love to stock up on Chanel No. 5?"

"From what I hear," Kathy laughed, "we won't be able to afford it. Not even in Paris. Inflation's hit Europe like crazy."

Though Brian Holmes tried to keep up the spirits of the group, they heard enough from the crew—familiar with Hamburg—to know that conditions were difficult in that city. On the ship they ate in their own private mess, the food plentiful but bland. Some early talk about the excitement of seeing Europe evaporated when Brian used the idle hours aboard ship to stress what was expected of them.

"Boy, am I glad my mother loaded me up with extra bars of soap," Rhoda giggled on the night before they were to reach Hamburg. "One of the crew told me the only place to buy soap in Hamburg is on the black market."

"Rhoda, we're not going on a vacation," Kathy reminded. But for most of them the glamour of seeing Europe had been an incentive to join the group.

It still amazed Kathy that David Kohn had been born and raised in Berlin. He spoke English as though he'd always lived in America. But wasn't it going to be awful for

him to go back to Germany after losing his family in the
Nazi gas chambers?

Kathy and Rhoda stood at the railing of the deck as their
ship approached the harbor at Hamburg.

"I read somewhere that Hamburg is called 'Germany's
door to the world,' " Rhoda said. "It's one of the most important seaports on the Continent."

"And not far from the concentration camp at Bergen-
Belsen," Kathy said grimly. Their reason for coming to
Hamburg was to help victims brought from Bergen-Belsen
into relief stations here. "I remember the newspaper reports
when the British liberated the camp." Kathy's throat was
tight in recall. "They found over 10,000 unburied bodies
and 40,000 sick and dying prisoners. My Aunt Sophie didn't
stop crying for three days."

"Remember Ed Murrow reporting on Buchenwald? The
way he begged people to believe him when he talked about
what he'd seen? 'I reported what I saw and heard, but only
part of it. For most of it I have no words,' " Rhoda quoted
him. "I think more than anybody else Ed Murrow is responsible for my being here."

Though they had all seen newsreels that showed the devastation of German cities, Kathy—like most of them—was
not prepared for what they saw when they arrived in Hamburg.

"Remember, Hamburg was one of the main targets of the
Allied bombers," Brian said gently, feeling their shock as
they rode through the bombed-out streets. "Over sixty percent of the homes here were destroyed."

"Why are those men chopping down the trees?" Kathy
asked curiously.

"There's no coal to be had," Brian explained. "They're
trying to pile up firewood for the winter ahead. But we're
not concerned with the Germans." All at once he was terse.
"We're here to help their victims."

Quarters had been arranged for them in a flat in one of

the still-standing apartment houses. One double bed and one single occupied most of the space of each of four bedrooms.

"Cozy," one of the men labeled these arrangements. "Reminds me of summer camp."

"We'll have to post a bathroom schedule." Rhoda was determined to be cheerful. "Please, nobody come down with diarrhea."

Almost immediately they joined the relief organization which they were scheduled to assist. Kathy's major skills were her familiarity with German and her typing speed. Before they plunged into the work ahead, they were shown films of the concentration camps at Belsen and Dachau and Auschwitz.

The room where the films were shown was deathly still until two of the girls broke into sobs. Kathy was terrified she was going to be sick. Unconsciously her eyes moved to David Kohn, feeling rather than seeing his anguish. When the lights came up again, she saw him stumble from the room without a word. The others were suddenly vocal in their recriminations against the Nazis.

"I thought I was prepared for anything," Kathy stammered. "But not this. Oh, Rhoda, how could it happen?"

As Brian had warned, they worked long hours, sometimes against impossible odds. Kathy tried to explain to an emaciated, obviously once very pretty young girl—perhaps thirteen or fourteen and slowly being coaxed back to a semblance of health after two years in Bergen-Belsen—that it would be difficult to track down American cousins in the Bronx.

"But you come from New York," Heidi pleaded. "You know about the Bronx. My cousins are there. Before the war when"— she choked back tears—"when my family was alive, they came to spend the summer with us on our farm near Munich."

"We'll try," Kathy soothed. "I promise you."

Heidi had been through so much, Kathy thought in pain, remembering how she had told them about the women who

gave birth and had their babies drowned before their eyes—
and then themselves were carried off to the gas chambers.
"I was so glad I was too young to have a baby."

Because of their fluency in German, Kathy and David
became a team. She was touched by his tenderness, his compassion, yet was awed by his strength. She knew that he saw
the victims of the camp and envisioned what his family had
suffered.

With a growing closeness they walked about the near-
deserted streets of the city to their specific destinations. The
people of Hamburg were unexpectedly friendly. When
Kathy remarked about her surprise at this, David told her
how the British had taken over the city without a shot being
fired.

"That's one of the reasons the German police have been
allowed to keep their guns. You see them," David pointed
out with a chuckle. "They patrol the streets right beside the
British 'Little Red Riding Hoods.' " The British MPs acquired their nickname from their red caps.

Yet despite the friendliness of the Hamburg citizenry,
Kathy thought of this as a dead city. It was possible to walk
for an hour without seeing more than a handful of civil-
ians—shabbily dressed, furtive, unhappy over the city's lack
of food and clothing and coal.

With David—on their off-duty hours—she walked along
the Reeperbahn and flinched at the sight of the desperate
human beings involved in the black market operations—trying to sell what little they had or what they could steal in
order to survive.

"I remember coming here with my family years ago,"
David said softly. "This used to be Hamburg's Broadway."

"You want to sell gloves?" a ragged fourteen-year-old
with a persuasive smile approached David. He'd spied the
pair of gloves David had stuffed into his jacket. "I have four
apples. Very good. See? You will like very much—"

"Take them," David said roughly, reaching into his
pocket. "And keep your apples." He handed over the gloves

to the astonished young teenager and prodded Kathy down the street.

"That was sweet of you, David," she said softly.

"How can we blame him for the concentration camps?" David countered. Now he reached for her hand. "I've been thinking about that girl. The one you've been so upset about—"

"Heidi?" Kathy asked. "The one with cousins in the Bronx?"

"I'll write back to my uncle in New York," David decided. "I know it's a long shot, but I'll ask him to advertise every day for a week in the New York *Daily News.* Maybe a miracle will happen."

"David, it would be so wonderful." Kathy was rapturous.

"You're wonderful," he said, holding her hand in his. "The way you instill hope in people who have seen such pain. I've watched you with them." He hesitated. "I know there's no one left of my family in Berlin, but I want to go there, just for a day. The trains are running again, not too often and they're usually packed, but would you like to go with me? You said your aunt had come from Berlin—"

"Could we go and return the same day?" All at once her heart was pounding. David was someone special. "Won't Brian be upset if we take time off?"

"We'll go on Sunday. It's something I have to do." She remembered the day he had taken off to go to Bergen-Belsen, and had returned gray and in shock. He had not joined them for their usual late dinner, closing himself off in his bedroom until morning.

"Aunt Sophie said to me, just before I left, that if I got to Berlin I must have a cup of coffee at a sidewalk café on the Kurfürstendamm," she told him.

"We'll do that," David promised. "Now do you suppose we could find a café here somewhere for a beer?" With his free hand he pulled the collar of his jacket close about his throat. "It's getting colder."

"I'd like that." She *liked* David Kohn. She had never felt so drawn to any man.

Phil leaned back on the rear seat of the Cadillac limousine while the chauffeur held open the curbside door.

"I called your mother and told her you were coming home with me for dinner," Julius Kohn told his son while he maneuvered his Brooks Brothers–suited bulk into the car. "She was pleased."

"She won't be pleased when she hears I'm headed back overseas."

"She'll carry on." Julius was unperturbed. "For a few minutes. There's no war on now. You tell her about your roving photographer assignment." He smiled smugly. "I knew if I leaned hard enough on the magazine, they'd go along with this. You know what my billing with them amounts to every year?"

"A lot." Phil nodded with the expected air of respect.

"I hope you know what you're doing." Julius inspected his son with some unease. "I'm giving you thirty thousand to buy a pig in a poke."

"It's not a pig in a poke," Phil reproached. "It's like I told you. This French couple with the little house outside of Paris has been hiding these two paintings since the Nazis were run out of the area. Sure, they belonged originally to a museum; but the Nazis took them over. They left in such a rush they forgot to take them along. They're worth close to a million. I can buy them for thirty thousand."

"If they haven't disposed of them already—"

"I told you. They're waiting for me. They trust me. I had a little thing going with the wife when we landed in Paris." He gave his father a knowing wink. "They're holding the paintings for me. They're sure I can get them out of the country."

"Don't go to Paris first," Julius warned. "You've got to handle this just right." His eyes gleamed with anticipation. The old boy was dying to have two old masters to hang in the house up in Greenwich, Phil thought with amusement. Especially if he could brag about what a bargain he got. "Don't give anybody any ideas."

"I'm going to Germany to do a photographic layout on Hamburg," Phil reminded him.

He'd chosen Hamburg because David was there. David might be useful. The two of them could go off to Paris together for three or four days. That was a good cover in case anybody got curious. Two Americans out to play in gay Paree. David wouldn't have to know he was there to dig up two paintings he'd buried in the garden of that creepy little house, where he and Chuck had been billeted for a few days. He and Chuck found the paintings hidden away in the attic; the Nazis had taken off so fast they'd left them behind.

Chuck had come though the war without a scratch only to die in a car smashup on a weekend pass in Texas. So the two old masters belonged to Phil alone. And the old man was handing over thirty thousand for them, he congratulated himself.

"I don't like you walking around with that much cash," Julius complained. "It's dangerous."

"I'm taking it over in traveler's checks," Phil soothed. "No danger at all."

He'd take a couple thousand or so with him for the trip. The rest would go into a New York bank account. His nest egg. The old man would brag about the great deal he'd made, smuggling two old masters out of France. And Paris in peacetime should be a ball.

═ Chapter 3

Hamburg was still wrapped in gray dawn as Kathy dressed in the bathroom in the dank November cold. She relished the scent of David's shaving cream that hung in the air. He'd had first use of the communal bathroom. Rhoda thought she was out of her mind to get up at this ungodly hour to catch a train to Berlin. *"The one morning in the week when we can sleep, Kathy!"*

She was eager to see Berlin, not just because of Aunt Sophie, but because until now she had never been farther away from Brooklyn than Washington, D.C. But often it was painful to move among the German streets and ask herself which of those people she passed had been Nazis. Equally painful was the sight of those who had managed to survive the horrors of Bergen-Belsen.

She started at the faint knock on the door.

"Yes?" She opened the door a crack. She was ready except for brushing her hair.

"Dress warmly," David told her. "It's cold out."

While the others slept in the silent flat, Kathy and David tiptoed down the hall and out the door.

"We may have to stand on the train," he warned as they emerged into the empty street.

"I don't mind." She didn't mind because she was with David. It was hard to believe she'd known him only a month. The meetings in New York, when they were recruited, then briefed, didn't count, she thought conscientiously. How could she feel this way about David so quickly? And she knew he felt something special for her. Under the circumstances she couldn't expect him to put his feelings into words. Berlin was a living nightmare for David.

As they'd expected, they had to wait almost an hour for the train. Miraculously they found seats in the last car. Though the winter had hardly begun, Kathy was ever conscious of the cold. When she hunched her shoulders against the draft that filtered in through a window, David dropped an arm about her shoulders and drew her close.

From habit they spoke in German—one of Brian's rules that was meant to extend their vocabulary. A woman across the aisle smiled, taking David for a German with a foreign girlfriend. German was obviously a second language to Kathy. The people here were all so friendly, Kathy thought with recurrent surprise. Yet for her there was always a wall between them. Whenever she dealt with Germans, all those displaced persons were never far from her thoughts.

By the time the train arrived at the main station in Berlin, the temperature had risen. A bright sun shone down on the city. The city Aunt Sophie had once loved, Kathy remembered nostalgically.

"I haven't been here in ten years." David's voice trembled with emotion. "I want to see my father's hospital. I want to see the house where we lived. If anything remains," he said with sudden intensity. "Let's walk, Kathy." He reached for her arm. "Later we'll take a bus to our house and to Papa's hospital—"

David pointed out the zoo, next to the railroad station.

"When we were little, Mama and Papa would take us there one Sunday every month."

"It must have had a few direct hits," Kathy surmised, inspecting the bedraggled structure.

"Cigarette?" an elderly man approached them hopefully. "A butt?" he asked with an apologetic smile.

"I'm sorry. We don't smoke," David told him.

"You've been away a long time," the man guessed, inspecting their clothes. "But people still come to the zoo, though it looks so bad. And on warm days tea is served on the terrace."

"Frock-coated waiters carrying silver teapots," David guessed, and the man nodded. "I remember from years ago. And music by a Bavarian band."

"Life goes on," the man shrugged. "And with plenty of money you can find a good black market restaurant." His eyes glittered. "But everything is so high." He mentioned the equivalent of $100 for a bottle of "bad beer," $120 for a pound of butter, $50 for a pound of coffee, $25 for a pair of silk stockings.

As they walked, Kathy was conscious of the polyglot of languages spoken around them. Russian, English, French as well as German, plus what David told her were dialects of Soviet Asia. Street signs were all in Russian now. Doctors' and lawyers' offices and even many private residences bore tacked-up notices that translated their names into English or Russian. Proclamations to the Germans, attached to the walls of public buildings, were printed in the four languages of the Western Allies.

They were quick to understand that Berlin today was a city of sharp contrasts. While the center of the city had been badly hit by American and British bombers and Russian shells—the devastation was awesome—large areas around the central city and in the outskirts had been untouched.

"Berlin is not flat on its back," David said, "though at first sight all I could see was the destruction."

Everywhere, it seemed, there were movie houses, hundreds of cafés. The outdoor areas were closed in deference to the weather, but Kathy could visualize them open in a few months and well patronized.

"This is the Kurfürstendamm." Kathy suddenly recognized and heard Aunt Sophie's voice: *"If you do get to Berlin, have a cup of tea or coffee at a sidewalk café on the Kurfürstendamm."*

The next best thing was to have a cup of tea at an indoor café on the Kurfürstendamm, she told herself, and David was happy to oblige.

Life in Berlin appeared far more normal than in Hamburg, Kathy thought.

"We'll take a trolley—" All at once David was unfamiliarly brusque. "I want to see what happened to my father's hospital. And our house was quite near."

They stood in line for forty minutes for a bus, David silent as they rode toward their destination. Kathy knew she must not talk to him. She must not even touch him in sympathy. And then they stood before a pile of rubble that had been the pride of the Kohn family for two generations, the hospital where his father had conducted experiments in nutrition considered valuable by the Nazis—for a while.

She walked in silence beside him till they stood before a sheared-off building that had once been his home.

"That room there," David told Kathy, his voice strangled, "that was Mama's music room. She played the piano with almost professional skill." Only bare, weather-ruined walls stood there now. Looters had taken whatever had remained in the music room. "Let's get out of here." His face was taut with anguish.

David took her to see Unter den Linden—named for the rows of linden trees in the pedestrian island down the middle of the street, 198 feet wide and nearly a mile long. He reached for her hand again as they began to walk.

"When I left here ten years ago, this was the pride of Berlin," he told her. "Elegant jewelry shops, fancy restaurants, luxury hotels, salesrooms for custom-made cars." Now most were no more than shells if not totally destroyed.

"There were always crowds of people walking here and expensive cars and limousines driving down the street. The university is farther down, and the State Opera House, and American, French and Soviet embassies. And the fine hotels like the Adlon and the Bristol." His smile was nostalgic. "We'll have lunch at the Adlon," he decided. "If it's still standing."

The hotel had been badly damaged, though the paved court in the center remained. Entrance was through the back alley earlier used by tradesmen—the front entrance had collapsed. They soon realized that even today the Hotel Adlon was where the fashionable of present-day Berlin met for lunch or afternoon tea.

After a surprisingly adequate lunch they resumed their walking. They realized that the signs they'd seen in other parts of the city, offering to barter such items as shoes and cigarettes and sugar, were everywhere. The stores were almost empty of stock. The tailors' sole occupation was to mend or patch.

Tired from walking, they stopped at a café to sip at watered wine, watched as a crowd of children and three elderly men encircled a man smoking a cigarette.

"They're waiting to pounce on the butt," David said. "Cigarette butts are more desirable than marks."

As dusk fell and the restaurants were brightly lit, the destruction seemed to fade away. A man hovered in the doorway of a pawnshop, seeming hopeful of finding customers among the visitors who came into the city. Out of curiosity—because most shop windows were empty—Kathy paused to inspect the few items on display.

"Oh my God!" David was staring in disbelief at a small brooch, designed in the form of a bow. The setting, the collection of small stones discolored. "Kathy, we're going inside."

The shop owner smiled benignly and gestured for them to enter.

"The brooch in the window," David told him. "May I see it, please?"

"With pleasure, sir." The man rushed to comply.

David held the brooch in his hand as though it was precious beyond imagination. After a moment he turned it over, and Kathy saw the initials there. "F.K." And she saw the tears that glistened in David's eyes.

"How much?" he asked.

The shop owner hesitated, then named a price Kathy was sure was more than he had been asking in the past. The brooch appeared of little worth except, perhaps, for sentimental reasons.

"Wrap it for me, please." Without quibbling David reached into his pocket, though they had learned that in Germany today one bargained over everything.

They walked for almost a block before David explained his purchase.

"That brooch has been in my family for four generations. My great-grandfather had it designed as a wedding present for my great-grandmother. She gave it to my grandfather when he had to run from St. Petersburg because the new czar was a threat to rebellious university students. She told him to give it to his bride," David said softly. "But his first love was taken off to America by her family, and he never saw her again."

"How sad. But how did you come to know of it?" Kathy asked curiously.

"On my grandfather's seventy-fifth birthday—just before I was shipped off to school in America—he gave the brooch to my grandmother. Not telling her how long he'd had it, nor the circumstances. She wore it at my last dinner with the family. That night he told me its history."

"How wonderful that you saw it there in the window." But she knew David agonized over how it came to the pawnshop.

"I wouldn't have seen it if you hadn't stopped to look," David said and reached into his pocket for the small parcel.

"Let me give it to you. Seeing you wear it will be like seeing a bit of home."

"But David, I—" *A brooch that his grandfather was told to give to his future bride?*

"You're very special to me, Kathy. You've made these weeks bearable."

"I'll wear it while we're here in Germany," she agreed. How did David mean this? His eyes were ardent. He *said* she was very special to him. But he wasn't giving the brooch to his prospective bride, she warned herself. She was a close and dear friend. "Then I'll return it to you."

"Wear it now. Please." He unwrapped the parcel, held the brooch for a poignant moment in one hand, then with unsteady fingers pinned it to her lapel. "Even in her seventies Grandma was a beautiful lady. Like you."

"It's a lovely brooch."

She lowered her eyes in fear of betraying her emotions. His own eyes made love to her. But here in Germany, with his grief so close to the surface, he could not bring himself to talk of the future. She could understand that, Kathy told herself.

If Rhoda or the others noticed the brooch, she'd just say it was a souvenir she'd picked up in a pawnshop. When they left Germany, she'd return it to David. Unless by then he could bring himself to talk about a future together. . . .

With Thanksgiving just a week away Kathy was conscious of homesickness. It would be a grim holiday here, she thought, though Brian was plotting an American-style dinner. And he never once allowed the others to express despair about the hordes of displaced people in such desperate need.

"So we'll have Spam with our canned cranberry sauce instead of turkey," Brian said as they gathered for another monotonous dinner prepared from their stock of canned goods. "We're having real American pumpkin pie for dessert."

"We're eating better than most people here in Hamburg,"

David reminded them. Kathy knew he was frustrated that so many potato-fed babies were dying despite the efforts of the relief agencies, and that the TB rate was escalating wildly.

"How do these people go on week after week?" Rhoda asked, but what else could they do? "Sleeping on floors. Six families using one gas stove. I spoke to one woman this morning who gets up at three in the morning so she can cook in peace—what little she has to cook."

Everybody at the makeshift table started at the sound of a sharp knock on the door.

"It can't be the Gestapo," Brian said flippantly. "Somebody go answer." He was busy slicing another chunk of Spam.

"Hi, is this where David Kohn lives?" an ebullient voice demanded at the front door, its owner not visible from the dining room.

"Phil?" David leapt to his feet with a brilliant smile. Kathy remembered he'd mentioned a cousin coming over on some photo assignment.

"Yeah," the voice confirmed.

"Hey, you made it!" David charged down the hall. "Did you have dinner yet?"

"We had dinner aboard ship, such as it was. It wasn't luxury liner chow, but I could handle it."

Kathy looked up from the table to inspect David's cousin, standing in the doorway now with a camera hanging over one shoulder and a duffel bag over the other. He was a couple of inches taller than David, more sturdily built, with rumpled dark hair and magnetic good looks. A definite family resemblance, Kathy decided, though already she knew their personalities were very different.

"Come sit down and have tea with us." David prodded his cousin into the dining room. "If we can find another chair—" Their supply of coffee was rationed, served only at breakfast.

In a rush of activity another chair and a chipped mug was found for Phil, and David made the introductions.

"Maybe it's like bringing coals to Newcastle," Phil drawled, "but I dragged a magnum of great burgundy all the way from New York."

"Well, bring it out!" Rhoda ordered jubilantly. "What we get here is so watered down you can feed it to a six-month-old!"

It was amazing how Phil had brought such vitality into their group these past few days, Kathy thought as the women moved about the kitchen preparing their so-called Thanksgiving dinner—served late in the evening because this was another working day in Hamburg. Phil's magazine had arranged for living quarters for him, but most evenings he found his way to the group's littered, overcrowded flat.

"That damp, dark basement isn't fit for a rotten-tempered dog," he was complaining in the dining room, "but what the hell, I only sleep there."

"How's the assignment going?" David asked.

"It's coming along," Phil said. "I'm taking a million photographs, and I'll have to sort out what's strong enough for the layout."

"What's your bribery for today?" one of the men asked. Each night he arrived with some item in short supply. He had an uncanny talent for dealing on the black market.

"Chocolate bars, that's what," he said in triumph. "And wait till I make my side trip to Paris," he gloated. "Am I going to be popular with the women when I get back! Even in wartime, I'll bet the French kept on making perfumes."

Phil was popular with the women here in the flat, Kathy thought while they settled about the dining table—actually two tables shoved together to accommodate the group. They acted as though he was Clark Gable in person. Sometimes he had a way of looking at *her* that was disconcerting.

"How did you get chocolate bars?" Rhoda demanded. "Let's see them."

"You don't believe me, hunh?" Grinning, he pulled a batch of chocolate bars from his pocket. "Eight of 'em. We'll break them up in squares and share."

Kathy pretended to be unaware of Phil's thigh pressing against hers under the table. He wasn't even conscious of it, she told herself, they were just so crowded together.

"I wish to hell I could be in Paris for that International Women's Congress," Claire, their psychiatric social worker, said wistfully. "I hear they're coming from all over the world."

"Women have to make themselves heard." Kathy was ever conscious of the need for women to stand up for their rights. "Did you know that until a few days ago Frenchwomen were denied cigarette rations? Only men are allowed to smoke." Her voice was scathing.

"You don't smoke," David teased.

"No," Kathy acknowledged, "but I don't want some man—in this case Marshal Pétain—saying men can but women can't."

"I have a hankering to make a run to Paris while I'm over here," Phil said casually. "I was with the American troops that liberated Paris. Wow, did we get a warm welcome!"

"The international trains are running again," Brian conceded, "but it's a long haul these days. From Paris to Nuremberg is thirty hours, sitting up all the way."

"I'm trying for a flight." Phil shrugged. "That's the only way to go now."

"This is not prime flying time," Brian cautioned. "The weather is bad. Too many mountains and too many mist-producing rivers."

"When a plane seat becomes available I'll take it. How about you, David? Come along with me, just for a couple of days? You're not afraid of flying in bad weather?"

"I'm not afraid," David said quietly. "But I'm needed here. Doctors are in short supply."

"If you do go," Rhoda said, "bring me back a bottle of Chanel No. 5. That may be the closest I'll ever get to Paris."

It was weird, Kathy thought, the way the girls in their group were attracted to Phil and not just because he'd been with the First Army when it liberated Paris. Girls back home must have been throwing themselves at him before the war. David must have had plenty of girls after him, too, she told herself defensively. Yet he had a way of retreating into the background when Phil was around.

So many times she'd thought David was about to talk about *their* future, and each time he'd retreated. There were moments when he seemed about to take her into his arms— and she wanted that so much—but each time he backed away. The ghosts of the past had not yet been put to rest.

Knowing her interest in the International Women's Congress in Paris, David combed Hamburg for copies of the Paris newspapers. Along with the other girls, she avidly read the reports.

"How do you like this?" Rhoda said smugly. "This reporter says the Congress had more substance than the Allied male meetings at Yalta, Potsdam, and London. Cornelia Pinchot, wife of the governor of Pennsylvania, was there, and Florence Eldridge—she's not just a terrific actress who happens to be married to Fredric March—and Vivian Mason, of the National Council of Negro Women, were there!"

"Irene Curie-Joliet spoke for the French delegation," Kathy read with pride. "Mme. Curie's daughter."

"It's strange," David remarked, his smile whimsical. "People here in Germany have money but no goods. According to the Paris papers, the Paris shops are loaded with all kinds of fancy gifts for Christmas, but few people have money."

"David, as a man, how do you feel about the Women's Congress?" Claire asked.

"I think it's a fine thing," he said quietly. "They have a right to say, 'Look, we've been through a terrible war. We have a right to be part of what happens in the future.' As participants, not just onlookers."

Kathy glowed as her eyes met his. David had responded just as she had expected. Women went out to work in defense plants, and they joined up to serve in military uniform; but now that the war was over, most men expected them to go back into the kitchen again and stay there. For a truant instant—*just an instant*—she thought, I wouldn't mind staying in the kitchen for David.

Phil sat with David in a dreary tavern not far from the flat.

"David, why can't you take off a couple of days to go with me to Paris?" he argued again. "And don't give me that crap about how badly doctors are needed. You've worked like a dog since you've been here. You have a right to a couple of days off."

"I'm needed, Phil," David insisted. "Even on Sundays I go in for a few hours. We haven't much longer here. Our budget runs out in a few weeks. I want to do as much as I can."

"I think you enjoy being a martyr," Phil taunted. Damn it, he wanted David as a cover when he went digging for those paintings. He couldn't afford any curiosity. He wasn't the only ex-GI trying to smuggle museum paintings out of France. The government *knew*. They just didn't know who or where. "I'd hate chasing around Paris on my own."

"I doubt that," David laughed. "You'll find some French mademoiselle delighted to entertain you."

"It'll feel strange going back alone." Phil tried a fresh tactic. "I told you how it was last time. Chuck and I lived it up like wild, and now he's dead."

"You'll get along," David said calmly. "But I'm sorry about your buddy. That was a rotten deal."

"I'll go," Phil said after a minute. Maybe he'd try to persuade Kathy to go with him. David would be pissed if he did, he thought. It would serve David right. He was mad about Kathy and doing nothing about it except giving her those brooding looks. Kathy was a hot little number, he guessed, if a guy played it right. Maybe she wasn't Betty Grable, but she was damned pretty. And built, he remembered with a familiar stirring. "Hell, I can't go back home without one little fling. I'm beginning to feel like a monk here in Hamburg."

"Whatever happened to that girl you were so overheated about right after Pearl Harbor?" David asked. "Debbie, wasn't it?"

"Oh, we split up." She'd blown a fuse when she discovered she was pregnant. Hell, she always said she knew how to take care of herself. "That's when I enlisted." The timing was right—he knew he'd be drafted in another few weeks anyway. It always got a rise out of women when he pointed out he'd enlisted; he hadn't waited to be drafted. And the old man paid for the abortion when Debbie went screaming to him.

"What are you going to do back home?" David asked. He knew this photography bit was a one-shot situation.

"I'm not sure. The old man keeps trying to shove me into the business. I told him I've spent three years in the army. I need some time to figure out where I want to go. I can't go far on the twenty bucks a week the GI Bill gives me for 52 weeks."

"You could go back to school," David pointed out.

"Are you kidding? I hated school. I never would have finished high school if you hadn't been there sharing my room," he reminded. "All I thought about that last year—when we were together at boarding school—was nookie. And college was a drag."

"I have to go," David said. "I'm working tonight."

"You'll be sorry later that you missed Paris," Phil warned. "I hear the bars and nightclubs are rolling again. But then," he drawled, "you never really appreciated the great things in life."

*   *   *

To Kathy the approach of Hanukkah was unexpectedly poignant here. For how many years had it been impossible to celebrate Hanukkah in Germany? Over half of the group members were Jewish. Kathy knew they shared her feelings about this first Hanukkah since the end of the war. Brian, who was not Jewish, discovered a menorah beneath the rubble of what had once been a Hebrew school. David whittled down candles to fit into the holders, and for eight nights they lit the Hanukkah candles. For Christmas they decorated a tiny pine tree with designs cut from colored construction paper. But ever close to the surface of their minds were the terrible shortages—food, coal, clothing—that plagued the city despite all the relief efforts.

Phil kept up their spirits, Kathy admitted to herself. He charmed everybody. Maybe not Brian, she decided after a moment. Brian was annoyed that most of the girls in their group acted as though Phil had personally liberated Paris.

On Christmas Eve Phil came up with a bottle of champagne after a visit to the crumbling waterfront.

"I won it in a crap game," he reported while someone h___ly unearthed a corkscrew. "A talent I developed in the a___."

He'd also come up with a sprig of mistletoe, which he hung over the kitchen door. Kathy was startled when he reached for her beneath the mistletoe and kissed her. But all at once it wasn't a casual "mistletoe kiss." She was trembling when he released her.

"We'll have to do that again," he whispered. "Why do you keep running away from me?"

"I don't," she stammered. Nobody had ever kissed her like that. Nobody had ever really kissed her, she thought. Just awkward pecks by self-conscious students who hadn't been drafted.

Why hadn't David ever kissed her?

═ Chapter 4

Almost overnight, it seemed to Kathy, Phil was in pursuit. He made it clear to the others that he was intrigued by her. Not Rhoda, or Claire, or the other three girls. She waited for David to show some indication of his own feelings, but he seemed to withdraw into himself. He was relieved, she tormented herself. He hadn't wanted anything more than friendship from her. How could she have been so stupid?

Running from her hurt at David's withdrawal, she found solace in Phil's attentions. At intervals the memory of those heated moments beneath the mistletoe dominated her thoughts. She was disconcerted by the physical arousal she felt in his presence. And Phil made it clear he was attracted to her.

Despite their long working hours Phil contrived to see her alone. They sipped watery beer in a nearby tavern and held hands beneath the table. They managed brief interludes in his dreary basement flat, though only after she made Phil understand nothing would happen beyond passionate kisses and heated touching. And each time she wondered how much longer she could keep saying no to his entreaties. *She didn't really want to stop.*

Then all at once she began to worry that Phil would be leaving before the group began the search for return transportation sometime in February. He kept talking about flying to Paris. Would she ever see Phil back in New York? It was frightening to think that she might never see him again.

Rhoda was having a hectic fling with Frank Collins, the would-be writer from Columbia's School of Journalism.

"Look, we're three thousand miles from home," she said calmly. "Why shouldn't I play? We're careful. I won't get pregnant."

"You hope," Kathy said grimly. So many girls played around during the war years, and everybody just looked the other way. But she couldn't bring herself to sleep with Phil. Her body said "yes," but her heart said "no."

"I know nothing's going to come of it. But ten or twenty years from now, when I'm teaching somewhere in Brooklyn, I'll look back and remember this as the exciting, wild time of my life." Her eyes were quizzical. "I can't figure you out. I thought you and David had something real going on, and now you're all starry-eyed over Phil. Not that everything female in this flat doesn't feel the same way." She giggled reminiscently. "But I'm happy settling for Frank."

"David is a close friend," Kathy said self-consciously. *That's all he wanted to be.* Maybe at first she was just flattered that Phil was interested in her. He made it clear right off that he thought she was attractive and exciting, and he was dying to sleep with her. He had a way of touching her— on the hand or shoulder—that shot off fireworks in her. She'd never known anybody like Phil. What was it Rhoda said the other day? *"That Phil is something. Like a character in a Hollywood movie."*

"If Phil does go to Paris, he'd better come back with six bottles of Chanel No. 5, or he's in big trouble," Rhoda laughed.

Already, they learned, Brian was trying to arrange for return transportation for the group sometime in the latter part of February and encountering problems. They'd hoped that by this time not every transatlantic ship would be commandeered to return GIs to America or to ferry war brides and babies. But again, Kathy gathered, they'd sail home on something less elegant than a commercial liner.

"I hear the *Elizabeth* will be back in normal business in the fall," Brian said humorously. "But our funds will fade away by the end of next month."

On a cold early February night, when their coffee supply had run out, Phil arrived with a pound of Turkish coffee he had acquired at the waterfront. While Rhoda and Claire grabbed the coffee and went out to the kitchen, Phil pulled Kathy off into a corner of the living room. None of the others had arrived home from their assignments yet, but Phil and Kathy knew they'd be coming into the flat at any moment.

"I wangled more than coffee today," he told her with a triumphant smile. "I have plane seats for two to Paris on Saturday morning and return seats on Sunday night."

"This Saturday?" She felt her face grow hot. He'd said *two* seats.

"Day after tomorrow," he confirmed. "Come with me, Kathy. You can't go home without seeing Paris."

"Phil, I can't," she stammered. "I mean, I'll be working Saturday."

"Brian will give you a day off. You've been working harder than anybody—"

"Phil, I can't." She forced herself to meet his eyes.

"Nothing will happen," he promised. "Not unless you want it to. We'll take two rooms in some little *pension*," he teased. "With no connecting door. How can you turn down a side trip to Paris?"

"All right," she said after a moment. Her heart pounding in anticipation. "But only if Brian agrees. And nothing is going to happen," she stipulated. No more than already had.

"Brian will agree." He reached to pull her close. "You know you drive me nuts, Kathy."

The others arrived, and they all gathered around to sample Phil's cache of Turkish coffee. Now he told them about his imminent excursion to Paris.

"I have seats for two," he said casually, and his eyes settled on Kathy. She saw David's startled reaction. For a tense moment she thought he would lash out at Phil. His mouth set in a grim line, he focused on his cup of Turkish coffee. "Brian, you won't object if Kathy takes off to go with me, will you?"

Brian hesitated only a second.

"Not if she wants to go," he said. "She's been working her butt off since the day we arrived."

On Saturday morning—hiding her terror as she remembered Brian's earlier comments about the hazards of flying in winter—she left the flat with Phil while the others struggled into wakefulness. For a moment last night she thought that David was upset that she was going to Paris with Phil. But only for a moment.

"Who can show you Paris better than a GI who helped to liberate it?" he'd said quietly. "Enjoy the trip, Kathy."

Kathy managed to conceal her alarm on the short flight from Hamburg to Paris.

"My family won't believe I've been up in a plane," she told Phil, one hand in his as the pilot began the descent to the airport below. "The closest I've ever been to a plane is when they had one on display in the center of Penn Station when I was a little kid."

"It won't be the old prewar Paris," Phil warned. "I came over with my dad in '37. It was a business trip for him. I was twenty and raring to see everything. The Moulin Rouge, the Folies-Bergère, Maxim's. And we saw it." He grinned reminiscently.

"Not the Paris of Fitzgerald and Hemingway," Kathy guessed. She'd been fascinated by all she'd read of that period. Was that why she'd agreed to come? "But it's Paris," she said reverently. She was impressed by the knowledge that Phil had been here before the war. David, too, she remembered, had talked of school vacations in Paris. But Phil and David had lived in a different world from hers. A monied world.

Kathy was enthralled by everything she saw, even though this was Paris still in the shadows of World War II. The morning was gray and shrouded in mist, the trees bare. The city had suffered little damage during the war years. It rose stately and beautiful around them.

Phil was in high spirits as they roamed through the streets. He pointed out the silhouette of Notre Dame, the old Ile de la Cité—where the great cathedral stands—and the Eiffel Tower.

"I know the Eiffel Tower is not exactly beautiful," he laughed, "but it has a kind of elegant dignity rising through the mist."

Kathy was conscious of a grimness, a confusion in the people they passed. The Parisians had been wildly happy when they greeted the army of liberation, she understood; but now they had to deal with cold and hunger and a shortage of money. Kathy saw men with fishing poles on the bank of the Seine, and understood fishing today was not for sport but to put food on the dinner table.

In the prestigious shops they found French perfumes but no Chanel No. 5. Mme. Chanel had closed up her huge company in 1939.

"We'll make do," Kathy said blithely, though she was shocked at the prices of French perfumes even in Paris.

"With luck we'll be able to find a taxi to take us up the hill to Montmartre," Phil said while they lingered over a meager lunch in a shabby bistro, dimly lit because Paris suffered from a lack of electricity. "It's like climbing the side of a mountain."

Finally, they snared a taxi. The driver was amused by Phil's college French. The Montmartre beneath the chalk-white dome of Sacré-Coeur had lost its bohemian air of earlier days, though it was still home to the poor of Paris. A few painters had set themselves up alongside the curving, cobblestone streets to entice foreigners to buy their wares. On impulse Kathy bought a small painting of a Montmartre street to take home to her parents.

"You know where I'd like to spend the night?" Phil said softly, an arm about her waist.

"Where?" All at once she was tense.

"The small house at the edge of town where Chuck and I were billeted. I don't know who's there now. It had been deserted when we came into the city. The owners had run off without even packing most of their clothes. They may have been collaborators, knowing what would happen to them with liberation."

"But it wouldn't be deserted now," she guessed.

"Let's try to find a taxi to take us there," he said ebulliently. "Maybe we can rent it for the night. Nobody has money in Paris, the way I hear it. We'll ask them to play innkeeper."

Only Phil would dream up something like this, Kathy thought dreamily when they were at last in a taxi and approaching the house. What a romantic way to spend a holiday in Paris!

Kathy stood inspecting the cottage while Phil paid off the driver. It was probably a hundred years old, she guessed, but cared for lovingly. In another few weeks the tiny garden would be beautiful.

People lived here. An older couple appeared at the doorway, curious about the arrival of a taxi. Phil turned from the taxi, slid an arm about her waist, and prodded her toward the couple. They were suspicious of Phil and her; Kathy interpreted, pleased that her own French was sufficient to translate.

"Please forgive our intrusion." Phil smiled charmingly.

"I was billeted here when the Americans arrived to help in the liberation of Paris. I wanted to show my wife where I lived." Kathy saw the woman glance at her hand and smile faintly. "I was wondering—" He hesitated, his eyes apologetic. "Would it be possible for us to rent the house? Just for one night," he pinpointed. "We'll be gone by tomorrow afternoon."

The couple exchanged a startled glance. A pair of crazy Americans, they were thinking, Kathy surmised.

"We have been here just a few months," the man began. "The house belonged to my uncle, who has since died. I am not sure that he would approve of strangers—" *Why was he talking so much?* He paused while Phil pulled a handful of American dollars from a pocket and held them up eloquently. "But for such a fine young couple," he continued with an expansive smile, "I think he would approve."

The woman indicated a small supply of food could be had if they wished; Phil dug up more American dollars.

"I am sorry, we have no coffee or tea," she said wistfully. "But from the man next door we could buy a bottle of decent wine for you." Phil produced more bills. "Edouard, go fetch the wine," she ordered.

When they were alone in the house—the older couple went off to spend the night with friends—Phil reached into the firewood stack beside the living room fireplace, pulled out a chunk of wood, and looked around for newspaper.

"Over here," Kathy said and reached for a sheaf of newspaper from the waiting heap. "A fire will feel great." There was a chill in the house that told her the firewood was meted out grudgingly.

Kathy stood and watched while Phil crumpled up the newspaper, placed it in the grate, then added the chunk of wood.

"Bring in a pair of glasses from the kitchen," he told Kathy while he struck a match and held it to the paper. "We'll have some wine once the wood starts to burn. Along with those fancy English biscuits and the cheese we bought in that shop."

"Coming right up," Kathy said lightly. This was like something from a Hollywood movie.

They waited until the chunk of wood was ignited, then Phil opened the wine bottle, and filled the two glasses. Kathy was opening the box of English biscuits.

"Close the drapes," Phil ordered. "I want to shut out the whole world."

"All right." Kathy hurried to obey. It was a lovely feeling to be alone with Phil in an ancient cottage with a fireplace lighting up the room.

They settled themselves on the floor, using the sofa as a backrest, and gazed in contented silence at the flames while they sipped the rather decent wine and nibbled at the English biscuits and cheese.

"You know what I said to those people about your being my wife?" Phil said softly, his eyes holding hers. "It sounded great to me."

"The woman didn't believe you," Kathy said, her voice uneven.

"How does it sound to you?" he challenged. "Kathy, will you marry me?"

"You're drunk already?" she laughed, but her heart was pounding.

"Only drunk with the pleasure of being with you." He set down his wineglass, took her glass from her hands and put it on the floor. "Kathy, I'm not drunk." He chuckled. "The whole bottle couldn't make me drunk. I want to marry you. I'm not sure of what lies ahead for us; but whatever, I want to share it with you."

"Phil, I'm not sure. I mean, we've known each other only a few weeks." But her heart was saying "Yes!"

"I know how I feel about you. Maybe we can even get married right here in Paris—" His mouth reached for hers. His hands pulled her close.

Kathy's eyes fluttered shut as his hands reached beneath

her sweater and crept around to unhook her bra. She abandoned herself to the passion that welled within her. No turning back now. His mouth clung to hers while his hands fondled the lush spill of her breasts.

She was aware that he was bringing pillows to the floor from the sofa.

"We'll have a bed before the fireplace," he murmured, his mouth at her ear as he manipulated her along the threadbare rug before the hearth.

She waited, devoid of will, caught up in emotions that refused denial. With gentle impatience he helped her out of her clothes, then shucked away his own.

"Cold?" he asked as she shivered faintly.

"No," she whispered.

His mouth found hers again, and he made his way between her slender thighs. She murmured a startled protest for an instant, but her arms tightened about his shoulders in approval, everything forgotten in the joy of this meeting.

Phil rummaged in the closet in the upstairs bedroom and returned to Kathy with a pair of shabby robes.

"Not exactly Coco Chanel," he said humorously, "but why bother dressing?"

In a little while they made love again. Kathy refused to allow herself to think beyond this weekend. Had he meant that about their getting married? Or was it just a pitch to make her stop putting up barriers?

Later, he lounged before the fireplace and listened to squeaky old records on the phonograph while she prepared a Spartan dinner.

"Let's eat in here," he called to her. "It's the only warm place in the house."

"They won't be happy that we're using so much wood," Kathy said uneasily while she brought in a large bowl of noodles and cheese along with a pot of tea.

"I hear most of the French can't stand the sight of noodles," Phil said. "That's what they've been eating for years.

And where did you find tea? I thought the old broad said they had no tea or coffee."

"I always keep a couple of tea bags in my wallet," she told him.

"Don't tell me. I'm acquiring a shrewd little wife."

"I can't believe this is happening." Her eyes glowed. *He'd meant it about their getting married.* "Three months ago I didn't know you existed."

"I don't suppose we could get married here in Paris this weekend," he said wryly. "I have reservations about being married in Germany."

"I'd hate a cold civil ceremony." Kathy flinched in distaste. "I want my parents and Aunt Sophie there—and your parents and your sisters."

"Oh God, I can just hear my father and mother going at it again," Phil said groaning. "When my sisters got married, you'd think they were planning a royal wedding."

"We'll insist on something quiet. Just family," Kathy decreed. "And let's don't say anything to the others. Not until we're on our way home."

"I should have reservations for myself in eight days," he told her and her eyes widened in surprise. "The magazine is arranging it," he explained. "I'll be waiting for you in New York. But don't keep me waiting too long."

Phil lay naked beneath the pile of comforters on the bed. He listened to the faint sound of Kathy's regular breathing. Yeah, she was asleep, he told himself confidently. Hell, she ought to be, the way they'd made love. He felt a smug approval that she had been so responsive.

Wouldn't David be pissed when he realized that his cousin had moved in where he had never made it! David was such a loser. He wouldn't have to say anything to David. David would understand just from seeing them together.

He knew when he asked Kathy to come with him to Paris that he'd propose. She was beautiful and bright and hot. After two years of fighting a war he wanted a steady woman in his life. No more having to chase after girls—he'd have a woman of his own. Chuck and he had talked a lot about that.

He waited another few moments, just to make sure Kathy was asleep for the night, then slid from under the comforters with a silent oath as he emerged into the dank cold. Swiftly he dressed, with constant glances at the bed to make sure Kathy was asleep.

He walked down the stairs, out through the kitchen into the backyard. He'd find a shovel in the toolshed. It was almost as though the calendar had swung backward and he was heading with Chuck to bury the paintings. Only that had been a scorching night in August and they'd worried about being seen in the spill of moonlight.

The paintings had to be here, he thought with sudden apprehension as he found a shovel. Who else knew about them? He counted off paces from the back steps, then began to dig, no longer cold with the physical effort required of him. Damn, how far down had they planted the canvases? Then the shovel hit the metal lid of the oversized toolbox in which they had cached their secret treasure.

Gloating in relief, he brought out the box and opened it. The paintings had not suffered through the course of being buried. He could take the art and bury the box again, cover it up. Nobody would know he'd been digging out here. And if they got curious, so what? Nobody knew who he was. By tomorrow afternoon Kathy and he would be heading back to Hamburg. Just an ex-GI and his girlfriend out for a weekend in Paree.

He'd have Kathy bring in the paintings, he decided as he made his way back into the house. He'd just ask her to stuff a box of film into one of her valises. The box would be sealed up; she wouldn't bother trying to open it.

"I've got so damn much film I can't squeeze this batch into my luggage. Bring it in for me, honey."

*   *   *

David watched in private torment while Phil presented each of the girls of the group with a bottle of French perfume.

"A gift," Phil stressed with an air of gallantry.

It wasn't the perfume that upset David. He knew from the glint in Phil's eyes, from the possessive way he dropped an arm about Kathy's shoulders, that his cousin had made yet another conquest. *How could Kathy fall for that line of shit that Phil spread around?*

"I'll be sailing out of here in about eight days," Phil told them. "Provided, of course, my magazine gets the ticket here in time. You know the problem we're having with mail these days," he reminded grimly.

"Take my place on the group's return trip, Phil." David turned to Brian. "That'll be okay, won't it?"

"What about you, David?" Brian seemed troubled.

"I'm going on to Berlin," he said. "I'll probably stay there."

"You mean for good?" Rhoda asked.

"For good," David acknowledged. "I'd like to pick up where my father left off." He made a point of avoiding Kathy's eyes. *Why did she look so shocked?*

"Why don't you come back home with us and give it some thought?" Brian urged. "It's a serious decision."

"I know," David said quietly. "It's what I have to do. Thanks for bringing me over, Brian. This has been a very special time for me."

Later, when the others had gone off to bed, David sat alone in the living room. When had he lost out with Kathy? When Phil arrived, he taunted himself. But then Phil always had that way of moving in and taking any girl that appeared interested in him. It was a weird kind of competition, but it had never disturbed him until now.

"David—"

He glanced up with a start as Kathy came into the night-cold room. She wore a maroon flannel robe over her pajamas.

"I thought you'd be fast asleep by now after a weekend in Paris." He managed a light chuckle.

"I can't believe you're not going back with us."

"I'd been thinking about it for weeks," he lied. "I can be useful to those who're trying to pick up their lives again in Berlin."

"Everything will be hectic from now on," Kathy said slowly. She was reaching for something beneath the lapel of her robe. "Let me give you this back before I forget about it." She unpinned the bow-shaped brooch, closed the pin again, and handed it to him.

"Keep it," he said, almost brusque. "As a souvenir of our time in Germany."

"David, I can't do that," she said. "It's too important to you. A piece of home, you said—"

She held out the brooch with an air of finality. Reluctantly he took it from her. No woman would ever wear it, he vowed. He would love no other woman.

"Be happy, Kathy," he said with unexpected intensity. "You're a very special lady."

═ Chapter 5

As February approached its end, Brian and his group grew apprehensive about transportation back to New York. Phil, too, reported that the magazine was encountering problems about his passage home. Kathy was touched when she inadvertently discovered that Phil had received reservations on a west-bound liner and was concealing this. He was uneasy about leaving her behind in Hamburg, she interpreted, when he knew their funds were running out.

Then Brian managed to cut through bureaucratic red tape to acquire reservations for the group but with only forty-eight hours' notice before sailing.

"I won't even be able to tell my folks I'm coming home," Kathy told Phil while he helped her pack. He was apologetic about asking her to find a place in her luggage for batches of his film because his own was overstuffed, and it was impossible to buy luggage in Hamburg. Nor was there time to try to secure any using the barter system.

"I'll just walk in on them," said Kathy, her thoughts still with her family. She felt a rush of excitement at the prospect of seeing them all again. She had never been away so long.

"I cabled my folks," Phil said casually. They grew up in such different worlds, Kathy thought again. "Would you like me to send a cable to your family?"

"No," she said quickly and laughed. "They'd be terrified before they opened it and saw it wasn't some awful message—like I'd died or was badly hurt."

"We're traveling like cattle," he warned. "The next time we cross the Atlantic it'll be on the likes of the *Normandie* or the *Queen Elizabeth.*"

Kathy started at the light knock on the open door, and turned to face David.

"Kathy, I thought you'd like to know," he said with a shy smile. "I heard from my uncle in New York. Phil's father—"

"What's up?" Phil demanded, one eyebrow lifted in curiosity.

"I had your father run an ad in the *Daily News* to try to locate somebody in the Bronx. A cousin to a teenager Kathy and I were working with."

"Are you kidding?" Phil clucked in skepticism. "People read the three front pages, the sporting news, and the columnists. Who's going to notice a personals ad?"

"Heidi's cousin did," David shot back, his face triumphant. He turned to Kathy. "The cousin's been in touch with the relief agencies. She and her husband want to bring Heidi to live with them."

"Oh, David, how wonderful!" She darted across the room and threw her arms about him. "Did you tell her yet?"

"She knows." David nodded while Kathy self-consciously took a step back.

"Phil, this is such great news." She turned to him, surprised by his lack of enthusiasm. "Heidi has nobody else in the world but her cousins in the Bronx."

"Some luck." Now Phil acknowledged his approval.

"I'm glad it happened while we're here. I wanted so much to see Heidi with family. It was a fine thing for you to have accomplished, David." Why wasn't David going back to

New York with them, Kathy asked herself for the dozenth time. Why must he sentence himself to stay in Germany? New York was his home now, he hadn't lived in Berlin since he was a teenager.

"I'm happy for Heidi." All at once David was unfamiliarly formal. "It's what she wanted."

At dinner David announced he was leaving for Berlin late that evening. Kathy was startled. She'd thought he'd stay until the group sailed tomorrow night.

"Our work is done here," he said quietly. "I'm anxious to find out how I begin to operate in Berlin."

"It may take a while," Phil told him, "but you'll collect a fortune in reparations from the German government. Keep your eyes open, old boy."

"The German government can never repay for the lives they took." David's face was etched with rekindled rage. "The world must never forget."

"There's probably a frightful shortage of doctors in Berlin," Rhoda said softly. "They'll be fighting for your services."

After dinner David shook hands with the men, kissed each of the girls on the cheek—Kathy last of all—and with valise in hand walked down the hall and out the door. Kathy was conscious of a painful sense of loss. David was Phil's cousin and her close friend. She had expected to see him when they were back in New York. She had thought that of all those in the group David and Rhoda would remain part of her life after Hamburg.

"David couldn't bear to stand at the harbor and see you leave," Rhoda said sentimentally when they were alone in the kitchen on dishwashing duty.

"You're way off base," Kathy said defensively. "David and I were close friends. There was nothing romantic between us."

"David was mad about you. We all knew that."

"He never said a word to me." He'd never even tried to kiss her. He'd asked her to wear the brooch because—she sought for his words and then remembered—*"Seeing you wear it will be like seeing a bit of home."*

"Hey, Kathy—" Phil hovered in the doorway. "What about a refill on that Turkish coffee? Is there enough left for one more pot?"

Again, the group crossed the Atlantic in primitive quarters. The days seemed to drag for all of them, though Phil labored to create a sense of conviviality. On their last evening before arriving at their port, Kathy stood at the railing with Phil and gazed at the spill of moonlight on the water. She was eager to see her family, yet apprehensive about telling them about Phil. She should have given them some warning.

"Why don't we both stay over tomorrow night at my place in town?" Phil said, an arm about her waist. "I feel so deprived."

"You'll make up." She lifted her face to his.

"This is such a teaser," he reproached but kissed her with passionate promise. "What about staying over?" he tried again.

"I'd feel so guilty at not going right home," she confessed.

"Okay." He sighed and slid a hand around to the curve of her breast. He laughed as she glanced around in instant alarm. "Nobody can see us." He pulled her around to face him, moved with her in arousal. "So when's the wedding?"

"As soon as my parents can make the arrangements." Her voice was unsteady. "They don't even know you exist—"

"We go home tomorrow night, but the next night," he said firmly, "I show you my place." He chuckled with pleasurable anticipation. "Among other things."

"Why not? But I can't stay all night." Even knowing she was marrying Phil, Mom and Dad would be horrified if they thought she had spent the night with him.

"My folks won't believe it." Phil was amused. "They've been trying to marry me off since I finished college. And here I'm bringing home a nice Jewish girl. Mother was sure I'd marry a *shiksa*. Dad figured I'd play the field forever."

How would his parents feel about his marrying a girl whose father ran a candy store in Brooklyn, Kathy asked herself. At intervals she worried about his parents' reaction. She'd grown up in an apartment above the candy store. Phil was raised in a mansion in Greenwich.

Aunt Sophie had said it was important for her to go to a prestigious college—translation, where the students came from rich homes. If she hadn't gone to Barnard, she wouldn't have been part of the group that went to Hamburg. She wouldn't have met Phil. She wouldn't have met David, she thought involuntarily.

Their ship docked early in the afternoon. Their group exchanged fervent good-byes and promises to stay in touch. Duffel bag over one shoulder, Phil insisted they find a cab to take them to Lindy's for a late lunch before she headed for Brooklyn and he went to his father's office and a ride to Greenwich.

"Oh, let me get my film out of your valise before we eat," she said as they climbed out of the taxi and the driver circled to the trunk to bring out their luggage.

"Phil, you're opening my valise right here on Broadway?" she reproached with laughter while he reached for the valise that contained his package.

"Why not?" he shrugged, ignoring the curious glances of passersby. "Here it is." He withdrew the package and closed the valise again, shoving the package into his duffel bag. "We could go to a hotel—" He managed an appealing grin. "Walking into Lindy's with all this gear could be awkward."

"I hadn't thought of that." She was too excited over being home to think straight about anything, she admitted subconsciously.

"We'll go over to Seventh Avenue to the Taft," he decided, his eyes amorous. "We'll make love, then call room

service for thick roast beef sandwiches and real coffee. I dare
you to say no."

"Roast beef and real coffee?" She pretended to be weigh-
ing this. "Now how could I turn down an offer like that?"
So she'd arrive in Borough Park two hours later.

At shortly before 5 P.M., Phil put Kathy into a taxi and gave
the driver instructions to take her to her address.

"In Brooklyn," he repeated, and erased the driver's gri-
mace with the bill he dropped onto the seat.

"Drive carefully," he ordered. "This is my bride-to-be."

He watched the taxi pull away from the curb, then
flagged down another to take him down Seventh Avenue
to his father's office. He hated that drab area, the ugly manufacturing loft that was set up around his father's lushly furnished oversized office, plus the loft on the floor above
where the furs were dressed and dyed. All the worktables
and machines were set up around the old man's office like
a colony of peons around an exalted master, he thought with
a touch of humor.

He'd heard a million times about how his grandfath[er]
Peter had come to America from Russia back in 1881 t[o]
build a fur empire, as his father and uncle had done in Russia. *"Your great-grandfather Nathan was furrier to the czarina herself, as well as to the Royal Court,"* his father loved
to brag. *"Your grandfather on my side came to New York,
he learned the place to trade was Alaska—and he went there
and bought raw furs from the natives on the mainland. That
was the beginning of the Kohn Fur Company. And I don't
do so bad myself. Look at the movie stars who come to Julius
Kohn."* It became Julius Kohn Furs at the death of his
grandfather.

His duffel bag over one shoulder in the image of the returning GI, Phil walked into the elevator in the turn-of-the-
century building where his father had moved the manufacturing section of the firm twenty years ago. The Kohn Furs
retail store was a huge expanse of lush decor up on Madison

Avenue, but the old man spent most of his time here, though he made a habit of summoning favored models from the store to his office. "To model the new styles for me" was the way he put it, Phil recalled. Most of their modeling was on the maroon velvet sofa that dominated one wall of his office.

Riding up in the ancient elevator, Phil remembered how his father had brought him into the ostentatiously furnished office on his sixteenth birthday and pointed to a tall, rather flat-chested young model sitting on the sofa with her legs crossed so high he could see velvety white skin between stocking top and lace-edged panties.

"Phil, this is Daisy," he'd said with a wink. "Daisy, my son. It's his birthday—be good to him."

Dad didn't know that he'd been pulling up skirts since he was fourteen. Still, it was fun to do it with a high-class model ten years older than he was. She'd been surprised that he wasn't exactly inexperienced.

He walked from the elevator onto the huge floor, deserted now because the workday was over. As far back as he could remember, Dad made a point of bringing him into the work area three or four times a year, showing off "my only son."

For a moment he hesitated before the closed door to the office. Was he interrupting a little something? Then with a shrug he lifted a hand and knocked.

"Come in." Expectancy in his father's voice. He opened the door and walked inside. "What took you so long?" Julius Kohn reproached, but he was on his feet and rushing to embrace his son. "I thought you'd be here this morning."

"I didn't say what time," Phil reminded, always uncomfortable when his father kissed him. "We just docked. You know what traffic is like this time of day."

"I told Wally to hang around at the garage until I called him to come and get us." He dropped an arm about Phil's shoulders and prodded him toward the sofa. "Well?" he asked with a sly grin. "You brought back my paintings?"

"Right in here." While his father watched, he reached

into his duffel bag and brought out the tightly wrapped parcel.

"Thirty thousand bucks and I don't even get frames?" Julius lifted his eyebrows questioningly.

"Dad, you didn't expect me to smuggle them out of the country in the frames?" he demanded. "These are two old masters. If I'd been caught, you'd have one hell of a time bailing me out."

For a few moments they were silent while Phil ripped open the parcel, brought out the two canvases, then spread them on the floor.

"That's worth close to a million?" Julius was dubious.

"In ten years they'll be worth more," Phil surmised. "When the museum realizes it's lost for good. You can't brag about them all over town," he warned.

"I just want to hang them in the house," Julius soothed. "And show them to a few neighbors."

"If it ever comes out that you have them," Phil pointed out, "you'll have to pretend to believe they're copies. You bought them from some refugee who came into the shop," he said, instructing him.

"It'll be worth thirty thousand to show some of our bastardly neighbors," Julius said complacently.

"Did you tell Mother about them?" Phil asked.

"Am I nuts? She'd be worried to death that you'd be caught and thrown into jail. We'll tell her tonight after dinner."

On the drive toward Greenwich Phil debated about the best time to tell his father about Kathy. Meanwhile he listened to the latest Greenwich gossip.

"You wouldn't believe the housing boom out here. Houses that went begging at $7,500 five years ago are selling for $20,000 now. Everybody who can afford it wants to live in Greenwich and commute to Manhattan."

"What's happening with that United Nations deal?" he asked. The little while he was home between coming back from camp in Texas and leaving for Germany, everybody seemed to be talking for or against bringing part of the United Nations organization to Greenwich.

"People voted against bringing it here." Julius frowned. "They're scared to death it'll bring a lot of Jews into the community. I don't know why they think it'll be mostly Jews coming in, but you know the thinking out there. I ran into Bert Baldwin in town. He was sure that Sound Beach Avenue would be a lineup of hot-dog stands. " 'Another Coney Island,' " he mimicked caustically.

"Dad, I have some news," he began tentatively.

"You didn't come home with the clap?" Julius demanded—his smile belying such suspicion—and slapped Phil on one thigh.

"I met a girl in Hamburg—"

"Wherever you go, you meet girls." But his eyes narrowed in speculation.

"I mean to marry this one."

"So fast, Phil? What's the matter, no nookie over there?"

"Plenty for the taking," Phil assured his father. "But this girl's something. David was drooling over her."

"But you got there first?"

"David didn't have a chance once I campaigned," he said nonchalantly.

"What's she like?"

"Small, features like a Hollywood starlet. Built."

"Jewish?" Julius appeared self-conscious at this question.

"Yeah." He grinned. "That'll please the old lady." He paused. "She graduated from Barnard last June."

"What about the family?" Julius pursued. "From New York?"

"Brooklyn." Phil paused. "Her father runs a candy store in Borough Park."

"She knows about the business?" All at once Julius was suspicious. "She knows your father owns Julius Kohn Furs?"

"She may," Phil evaded. "I didn't talk about it with her."

"So a smart little girl from Borough Park meets the rich

son of Julius Kohn in Hamburg." He was grim. "She figures she's marrying into a lot of money."

"Nothing like that," Phil rejected.

"She's a hot little number?"

"From all indications. I didn't sleep with her, Dad. I'm marrying this one."

"So she won't let you in," he pinpointed in triumph, "and you're so overheated you're ready to marry her."

"Dad, I'll be twenty-eight in a few weeks. I thought you'd be glad to see me settle down."

"You're coming into the business?" He saw the cagey glint in his father's eyes. "How else are you going to support a wife?"

"I'm taking a flier in the theater. Give myself a year to see if I can make it as an actor." He had a bankroll—most of that thirty thousand from the old man. He didn't have to settle for the fur business just yet. Coming over on the ship he'd thought about theater. He had the looks for it. He'd take some classes. It ought to be fun for a while.

"Because you did a couple of plays in college?" His father's mouth dropped open in disbelief. "Who makes a living as an actor?"

"Clark Gable, Tyrone Power, Errol Flynn—"

"They're in the movies," Julius pointed out.

"First you do a play, then Hollywood takes you out there."

"You're *meshuggeh*. This some idea you got from that little broad?"

"She doesn't know about it. But if I want to do it," he predicted, "she'll go along."

"Your mother won't be happy," Julius warned.

"Mother won't be happy unless I marry Princess Elizabeth," Phil chuckled. "And she's not my type."

"Your mother wouldn't be happy if you married Princess Elizabeth." Julius grinned. "*Maybe* if she converted."

= Chapter 6

By the time the cab approached Thirteenth Avenue, night had settled over Brooklyn. Kathy gazed avidly out the window, absorbing familiar sights, impatient now to see her parents and Aunt Sophie. Her heart pounded as she tried to frame the words to tell them about Phil.

She glanced at her watch. Mom and Dad would both be at the store. First, Dad would go upstairs to have dinner, then Mom would go up and eat with Aunt Sophie. The only time they all sat down to dinner together was on a holiday.

The driver slowed up, searching for numbers.

"It's two doors past the fish store," she told him, excitement surging in her. "Right here!"

While the cabdriver brought her two valises from the trunk, she saw her mother hurrying from inside the store. Dad was making a soda for a customer.

"Kathy! Oh, baby, it's wonderful to see you!" Her mother reached eagerly to embrace her. "We had no idea you were arriving today."

"We had only forty-eight hours' notice. With the mails the way they are, I knew we'd get home before a letter."

Clinging to her mother, Kathy saw her father hurry from behind the counter and across the sidewalk. "Daddy—" She opened her arms to him. "Every day on the ship seemed to drag forever."

"I'll take your luggage upstairs. Edie, watch the store." His eyes bright with love, he reached for the two valises.

"How's Aunt Sophie?" Kathy asked as they walked up the stairs to the flat.

"You know Aunt Sophie." He chuckled affectionately. "She's full of dire predictions about the Russians now that the war is over. And every day she cut out items in the newspapers about how terrible things were in Europe. She was afraid you were going hungry."

"Adam?" The door to their apartment opened and Sophie gazed out inquiringly. "Kathy! You're home!" she shrieked in delight. "*Bubbeleh!* You didn't give me any warning." She clutched at Kathy and rocked her. "Why didn't you let us know? I would have made brisket for dinner. You always love my brisket."

"Aunt Sophie, whatever you make is terrific!" She reveled in the presence of family.

"I'll go down and send your mother up," her father told her. "Later we'll talk."

Not until her father closed the store for the night and the four of them were gathered around the table over a freshly baked coffee cake and tea did Kathy begin to talk about Phil.

"Kohn?" Her aunt gazed earnestly at her. "From Germany?" She paused. "From Berlin?"

"No, Aunt Sophie, his family is from Russia. They've been here for three generations, I think. Phil came to Hamburg to do a photo layout for a magazine. You know, shots of the concentration camps and the survivors." Kathy saw the swift exchange of a pleased glance between her parents.

"He's Jewish?" Aunt Sophie asked, although she'd already made that clear.

"Yes, Aunt Sophie."

"Kathy, are you serious about him?" Her mother was trying hard to appear casual. Kathy intercepted a furtive glance at her ring finger.

"Very serious." Kathy sensed her father was having difficulty accepting this. To Dad she was still his "little girl."

"So fast?" her father said warily.

"I've known Phil almost four months, Dad. And over in Germany," she managed a humorous smile, "that's like a year."

"What does he do for a living?" Sophie was ever practical.

"Well, he's just out of the army," Kathy explained. "But I know his father wants him to come into the family business." Not that Phil was ready to do that. She wasn't sure what he meant to do, she suddenly realized. He'd said the magazine job was just something he did "for a fast buck."

"What's the family business?" her father asked.

"Wholesale and retail furs." She paused, knowing they would be impressed. "Phil's father is Julius Kohn, the furrier."

"A wealthy family—" Edie Ross broke the sudden silence. Her expression was respectful.

"So when do we meet this young man?"

Her father cleared his throat self-consciously. "You'll bring him home for some Friday night dinner," he decided before Kathy could reply. "I'll have Mannie come in and cover the store for me." Mannie was a retired garment worker who took over running the store on rare occasions: a funeral or the wedding of a child of close friends or a son's bar mitzvah.

"Next Friday," Kathy said with a brilliant smile. Her gaze moving from one to the other. "We want to have a very short engagement."

"Kathy, you want to marry him?" Edie Ross was ecstatic. "If you picked him, my darling, we'll love him, too."

"So how long have we got before we have to plan a wedding?" Sophie asked, her eyes bright with sentimental tears. "You don't arrange a wedding without a lot of plans."

"We'll talk about it when Phil comes over for dinner."

"I can't believe it!" Adam Ross shook his head. "She goes away my little girl, and she comes home a few weeks later and she's ready to get married."

"A few months later, Dad," Kathy corrected tenderly.

"Adam, bring out the bottle of schnapps," Sophie ordered.

Bella Kohn stared in disbelief at her son, a forkful of porterhouse suspended in midair.

"You want to marry some girl you met in Hamburg?" Her voice was shrill.

"She's from New York," Phil said. "She was working with that group David was with. She just graduated from Barnard last June."

"She comes from Brooklyn, Bella." Phil knew his father was in a needling mood. His mother was born and raised in Bensonhurst, though she preferred to forget that now. "Her father runs a candy store on Thirteenth Avenue in Borough Park."

"What difference does that make?" Phil demanded. Christ, couldn't they ever sit down to a meal without needling each other? "I'm marrying Kathy, not her family."

"And how do you plan on supporting a wife?" his mother asked, grim but polite now.

"I'll get a job. We both will. I thought you'd be thrilled that I'm getting married," Phil reproached. "You keep telling me I ought to settle down."

"Bring her out to the house for dinner," Bella ordered. "Later we'll meet the family."

"What do you know, Bella? This wedding's not on me." Julius grinned. "The father of the bride foots the bills."

On Friday evening Phil arrived for dinner. Sophie had been cooking for two days. Her mother had taken time off from the store to buy a new dress at Klein's. *"I saw the same thing in Saks for three times the price."* Her father wore his good suit. The table was festively laid; Friday candles were still burning when they sat down.

They liked Phil, Kathy told herself in relief. He was going all out to charm them. They hung on his every word about what he'd seen in Germany.

"Kathy, did you ever get to Berlin?" Sophie asked as she brought in an oven-hot coffee cake. "Did you have a cup of tea or coffee in a café on the Kurfürstendamm?"

"Yes!" Kathy's face lighted in tender recall. "I made a day trip to Berlin." She saw Phil lift an eyebrow in surprise. She hadn't mentioned the trip to Berlin—that was before he arrived in Hamburg. "We had tea at an indoor café on the Kurfürstendamm." All at once she visualized herself and David in that café, herself and David at the pawnshop where he discovered what he called "the secret pin." Was he all right? He was always so vulnerable. "Berlin was very different from Hamburg. A lot of destruction," she conceded, "but people there seemed in better spirits. More able to go on with their lives."

Now both she and Phil were plied with questions about both Hamburg and Berlin. Everything was going well, she told herself. Let it go as well tomorrow night, when Phil took her to meet his parents in Greenwich. Because Phil knew her parents were up before 6 A.M. to open the store, he said good night at an early hour.

"I'll walk with you to the car," Kathy told him. He'd borrowed his mother's white Cadillac convertible for the drive down from Greenwich and out to Brooklyn.

"You wouldn't consider driving into the city with me?" he whispered. "I'd send you back home in a taxi."

"Not a chance," she flipped. "You're going to wait for me now."

"The chauffeur will pick you up tomorrow at five," he said after he'd kissed her good night in the dark shadows of the car and reluctantly released her. "Watch for a maroon Cadillac limo."

"Around here I can't miss it," she laughed, hiding her

disappointment that Phil was sending a chauffeur for her instead of coming himself. It was a long drive both ways, she reproached herself. When the family had a chauffeur, why should Phil have to make that long trip? The rich knew how to live.

They wouldn't live in Greenwich, would they? Phil had kept his little apartment on West End while he was in Germany. It would be big enough for the two of them, she surmised. So many things Phil and she must talk about!

When she walked into the living room again, she discovered the others had gone out to the kitchen. The kitchen was where they held serious discussions. The voices were low, sounding almost somber. Had she been wrong? *Didn't they like Phil?*

Her mother looked up with a smile when she came into the kitchen.

"We were talking about the wedding," she told Kathy. "We've managed to put aside a little money. But I don't know what Phil's parents expect in the way of a wedding." Her voice was troubled. "We can't afford a fancy wedding at the Plaza or the Hampshire House."

"Mom, we'd both hate a splashy wedding," Kathy insisted. "Phil said his sisters' weddings were like royal affairs. He wouldn't want to go through something like that." They were anxious about not being able to spend a fortune on a wedding, she thought tenderly. "Just family and a handful of friends," she emphasized. Marge for her maid of honor, Rhoda as bridesmaid.

"You set a date," her mother said. "I'll start calling the caterers. But you'll wear a white gown and veil," Edie Ross insisted. "I've always dreamt of the day I'd see you walking down the aisle in a bridal gown."

She had been awed when the chauffeur turned into the park-like grounds of the Kohn house, a modern Tudor-style gray cut-stone residence with gabled roof set far back on five acres. Phil had come out immediately to welcome her. His mother was not yet downstairs. He and his father showed her through the lower floor.

There was a two-story beamed entrance hall with fireplace, a gallery at the upper level, a huge living room and formal dining room—both darkly beamed and paneled—a library, a smaller family dining room, a spacious breakfast room, powder room, and a complete kitchen wing. On the second floor, Julius told her, there was a two-bedroom master suite plus five additional bedrooms, all with their own tinted tile bathrooms. The servants' quarters were on the third floor.

The furniture was baroque, richly carved, upholstered in elegant damasks and velvets, its scale appropriate to the dimensions of the rooms. But to live here, Kathy thought, would be like living in a minor museum.

Kathy sat beside Phil on a gray velvet sofa in the Kohns' almost oppressively ornate Louis Quatorze living room and listened with a show of polite interest while Phil's father talked about the founding of the Kohn fortune. Obviously bored, Bella Kohn flipped through a copy of *Town & Country*. Kathy was grateful that Phil's two sisters and their husbands had been unable to come to dinner on such short notice. It was enough to have to deal with his parents.

In the course of a tour she'd been startled to see a collection of family photographs that included David as a teenager. She could not imagine David living comfortably in such surroundings. For a poignant moment she remembered that day in Berlin when she had stood beside David while he gazed agonizedly at a sheared-off house and pointed out what had once been his mother's music room. How could he bear living in Berlin again?

"I know you both want a May wedding"— Bella's voice brought Kathy back into the conversation— "but you must realize there's so much to be done. I'm afraid your mother will have a dreadful time locating an available room on such short notice."

"You'll need a large place," Julius said expansively. "Our guest list will be about two hundred."

"We're planning a very small wedding." Kathy tensed, anticipating a battle. "Just immediate family and a handful of friends."

"Out of the question." Julius waved a hand in rejection. "My two daughters were both married at—"

"Dad, Kathy and I don't want that," Phil said, reaching for Kathy's hand. "It's a bore."

"Phil, we have obligations." His father bristled. "It's expected that you'll have a large wedding."

"It's a financial impossibility for my parents." Let there be no pretense, Kathy told herself defiantly. "And even if it were not," she continued, polite but firm, "Phil and I prefer just family and a few friends."

Kathy saw the swift exchange between Julius and Bella Kohn. Phil's mother was not above offering to pay. His father balked. Thank God for that. She couldn't have allowed Phil's parents to pay for their wedding. Mom and Dad would have been humiliated.

"Only our immediate family will attend." Julius made no attempt to hide his anger, but Kathy sensed a reluctant respect on the part of his wife. Kathy realized she'd made an enemy of Phil's father. He wasn't accustomed to being crossed. What an awful beginning for her marriage, she thought in dismay. But she wasn't marrying Phil's parents, she reminded herself defensively. Phil understood. "My wife and myself, our two daughters and their husbands." Julius made it seem an unpleasant obligation. "There will, under the circumstances, be no announcement in the newspapers." Did he consider that a punishment, Kathy mocked in silence. So his publicist wouldn't get the item into the *Times*.

"Where do you plan on living after you're married?" Bella gazed from Kathy to Phil.

"At my place on West End," Phil said after a moment. "For now."

Kathy remembered that Julius Kohn had given a home

in Greenwich to each of his daughters upon their marriage. Had Phil been expecting the same? She wouldn't want to live out here. She'd feel herself in exile. And given the chance, she suspected, Phil's father would try to rule their lives.

Three days after she had met Phil's parents, he presented her with a minuscule diamond engagement ring.

"The old man says it isn't legal without the ring," he told her with a teasing grin. "So he sprang for this. It'll do for now." He was amused by the modesty of the engagement ring. "I'll buy you a real one later."

"Phil, it's beautiful," she insisted. "And it fits perfectly."

"Your mother sneaked out your high school class ring. I told her to keep her mouth shut until I had it cut down to size."

"She didn't say a word," Kathy said softly.

Despite Phil's objections and that of her parents, Kathy decided to look for a job immediately. She had abandoned all thoughts of a master's in social work. She was disturbed by Phil's lack of concern about their future income. He had intention of going into his father's business. He talked andly about finding a part in a Broadway play. He sat around some Times Square drugstore, she gathered, and read a newspaper called *Show Business*. And he "made rounds."

When she tried to pin him down even about the rent of his apartment, he brushed this aside. *"Sweetie, it's a steal."* From her mother and Aunt Sophie she had learned the need to budget. Now Phil was complaining about the difficulty in buying a car. They weren't coming off the assembly line fast enough to satisfy prospective buyers. *Could they afford a car?*

As an English major she tried for a job in publishing. The first job offered her was at a record company. She accepted it, with the stipulation she could take off two weeks in May for her wedding and honeymoon. Marge was working on Seventh Avenue as a cutting assistant. She declared she finally knew what she wanted to do with her life. *"I want to be part of the fashion world, Kathy—forget the master's in social work."* Rhoda was working as a receptionist in a law office. In September she would begin to teach at an expensive private school.

Kathy tried not to be caught up in the details of the wedding. Her mother and Aunt Sophie argued with the caterers about what was to be served as the main course, about the wedding cake. They worked out the small guest list, insisted on a room that was big enough but not too big. They talked to the rabbi and the florist and the woman who would play the organ at the chapel.

On a bright Sunday morning Kathy went with Marge and Rhoda to the bridal shops on the Lower East Side. The three girls were shocked at the inflationary prices even down here. But they quickly found a bridal gown that elicited squeals of approval not only from Marge and Rhoda and the saleswoman but other shoppers. Before they headed to Ratner's for a celebratory lunch, they shopped for dresses for Marge and Rhoda as well.

"I'd better not eat too much at Ratner's," Rhoda sighed, "or I'll never get into that dress, but, oh, those blintzes and the onion rolls!"

In a grandiose gesture, Julius Kohn told Phil that he would pay for the honeymoon—ten days at The Cloister in Sea Island, Georgia. He made the announcement at a family dinner at the Greenwich house, where Kathy met his younger daughter Brenda and her accountant husband Eli and his older daughter Gail and her shirt manufacturer husband Milton.

"That's where the Thomas Deweys went after he lost the election in '44," Brenda said with a hint of envy. Kathy recalled that Phil said Greenwich was a Republican stronghold. He said they'd even voted against Roosevelt two to one. "Eli and I had five days in Palm Beach."

"You were married a week after Pearl Harbor. Eli had to report to his reserve unit," her father reminded her.

Eli had spent the war years working for Naval Intelligence on lower Broad Street, Phil had told Kathy with the contempt of men who had seen active service. Milton had worked for his father's shirt manufacturing firm, thanks to his 4-F status. Their wives, like Bella Kohn, had put in the requisite hours as Red Cross volunteers.

Kathy went through her wedding day in a euphoric haze. She ignored the coolness of her father-in-law, reveled in her parents' happiness, tossed the bridal bouquet to Aunt Sophie. Late in the afternoon she and Phil left for the airport for their flight south. She was Mrs. Phillip Kohn, Kathy thought joyously. Life was wonderful.

Kathy adored the quiet beauty of Sea Island, warmed by the Gulf Stream but with cool off-shore breezes to assure comfort. She admired the tall palm trees, the live oaks and pines. She enjoyed the quiet elegance of The Cloister, the exquisite beauty of the beach. The little girl who'd helped out on Saturdays behind the counter at her father's candy store had come a long way.

In Phil's arms she could forget his father's hostility, the hint of arrogance she felt in his mother and sisters. She was obsessed by her husband, she thought in glorious abandon. She posed radiantly with Phil for the traditional honeymoon photograph, to be added to the albums on display in an alcove off the hotel lobby.

But back in New York, in what she called "the real world," Kathy worried about their future. When she tried to discuss their financial situation, Phil brushed away her questions.

"Kathy, don't be a worrier," he scolded. "I saved most of my money from that magazine assignment. By the time it's gone I'll have a part in a play." *But he never told her how much money they had from the Hamburg assignment.*

Phil's father might be rich, but they were not. They had to live within their means. She was a Depression child—she could remember her parents' fears about tomorrow. Of her own volition she assumed the responsibility of paying for their daily expenses. Phil paid the rent, utilities, and the car loan. She would have liked to redecorate the apartment but was wary of such an outlay of cash. They could live for now with the hand-me-down furnishings plucked from the attic of the Greenwich house when Phil moved into his Manhattan apartment.

One night a week they drove to Borough Park for dinner with her family. The evening was always a warm, joyous occasion. At intervals Phil announced they were driving up to Greenwich for dinner. He was quick to say how much he hated Manhattan in the summer—the stretches of steamy heat meagerly relieved by electric fans. He was annoyed, too, that he had not been able to find a job in summer stock.

"But it's just as well," he bounced back, "because I'll be here in town when they start casting for fall productions."

In July Phil's mother and two sisters took up residence in their summer house in Maine. His father and two brothers-in-law flew up for weekends, then went up for two weeks in early August when Julius Kohn Furs—except f the Madison Avenue retail store—closed for vacation.

"We'll drive up to Greenwich for the weekend," Phil decided on a sultry August night when they deserted the apartment for a bench on Riverside Drive. "We'll have the whole house to ourselves." For a moment his face tightened. "I don't know why the hell we haven't been invited up to the Maine house for a couple of weeks."

"I couldn't go, Phil. I took off two weeks in May."

His family was punishing Phil for marrying her, she reasoned. They held it against her that she wasn't from an affluent family, that her father wasn't rich and successful. A disconcerting fear took root in her. Was Phil beginning to regret having married her?

= Chapter 7

Kathy was increasingly involved in her job with the record company, which produced records for young children. Her boss was delighted when she took some of the public relations work upon herself, and arranged for promotion gimmicks that worked out well. When actors were being ... to appear on their latest releases, she contrived for ...il to audition for a small part.

The evening after his audition, Kathy rushed home jubilantly with the news that he had been hired.

"It's crap," he told her. "A shitty five lines on a kids' record."

"Phil, it's a job," she said earnestly. "It means you're a professional."

"Don't tell the family," he ordered her. "They'd never stop kidding me, and no pun intended."

"You said you were going to start taking classes this fall." She was concerned by his restlessness, his anger that he was making no headway. With her he was restless and angry, she pinpointed. When they met with his "round-making" friends once or twice a week for a cheap Chinese or Italian dinner, he radiated optimism. There was always some producer, he intimated, becoming interested in his potential.

"You said the others all take classes," Kathy pursued.

"For Chrissake, Kathy, stop nagging me!" he flared. "You work for a children's record company, so now you're an authority about acting!"

They went to Greenwich for Thanksgiving dinner, though Kathy would have preferred going to her parents' home. Phil's father called and told them—he didn't ask— that they were expected for the holiday dinner. It would be the first time since the wedding that Kathy and Phil would be seeing Brenda and Gail and their husbands.

Kathy was disappointed that Phil's four nieces didn't come to dinner. All under five, they were relegated to the care of nursemaids. She had brought along a batch of records for the little girls and had to settle for giving them to their mothers.

"So when are you going to stop playing games and come into the business?" Julius demanded of Phil as a maid brought in the traditional pumpkin pie, and Kathy thou~~~ involuntarily of last Thanksgiving in Hamburg.

How different that Thanksgiving had been from this on~~~ in the ostentatiously formal dining room with a crystal chandelier hovering over the table like an oversized diamond on an overdressed matron. At Thanksgiving dinner in Hamburg she'd felt part of a family. Here she was an outsider—accepted but hardly welcome.

"Dad, I'm not the furrier type," Phil drawled and grinned. "I don't have the girth for it."

"That'll come," his mother said drily. "Along with a regular salary." Kathy knew her mother-in-law frowned on Phil's unemployment at a time when jobs were so available. Nor was Bella Kohn comfortable in the knowledge that Phil was out of work while his wife held down a job.

"I had a letter from David," Julius said, and Kathy turned to him with a glow of pleasure. At intervals she thought about David, wondered how he was faring. "He wrote to give us his address in Berlin, but after that we heard nothing until now. He's all steamed up over some research project in Berlin."

"That's David." Phil smiled indulgently. "The perennial do-gooder."

"David felt he could be useful to the Jewish survivors in Berlin. And he was hoping to pursue his father's research on nutrition," Kathy told them. "He said that before World War II the Germans were convinced they'd lost World War I because their soldiers were not properly nourished. He was hoping that his father's research had been saved by the government."

"David should worry about the nutrition of the Germans?" Bella asked scornfully. "When his family died in the camps?"

"I suspect he's thinking in terms of world nutrition," Kathy said. All at once Hamburg seemed so close. Yet David still seemed far away.

"I sent him an invitation to the wedding, of course," Bella said, "but we knew he couldn't make the trip."

Kathy felt suddenly cold. David knew she had married Phil. She should have realized that. Why did she feel this sense of guilt? David and she had just been close friends. He'd shown no interest in making it anything more.

"David sent his best wishes to you and Kathy," Julius broke into her thoughts. "Better he should have sent you a wedding gift."

"I doubt that David has money for that." Faint rebuke crept into her voice.

"David's a *schmuck.*" Julius ignored his wife's low sound of annoyance at his Yiddish vulgarity. "He's an American citizen. He could make a lot of money here in this country. Why does he waste his time in Berlin?"

Gail turned to her mother after a scathing glance at her father. "Are you going to Palm Beach with Brenda and me in January?" she asked. "We have to make reservations within the next few days if we're to have decent accommodations."

"The Breakers is already booked for all of January," Brenda sulked.

"I'd been thinking about running over to Paris the end of January," Bella said with a covert glance at Julius. "Geraldine tells me she's going over to see the collections. Christian Dior—who's done such marvelous things for Lucien Lelong—is opening up his own house. Geraldine says his first collection is sure to be sensational."

"Like his prices," Julius said grimly. "Geraldine Somers's husband has Texas oil wells. I sell furs."

Now Bella and her daughters dominated the table talk. Kathy gathered Bella had been pressuring her husband to approve the Paris jaunt. She guessed that he would.

Kathy was relieved when Phil insisted—against his mother's objections—that they leave early. The talk of David had been oddly disturbing. And she'd fought to stay awake during after-dinner conversation. Tomorrow was not a day off for her, though Phil said nobody would be making rounds. Phil slept till ten every day. He said nothing happened in theatrical offices before eleven or twelve.

Fighting yawns, Kathy prepared for bed. Phil was listening to the news on the bedroom radio.

"Hey, baby," he scolded, "what's taking you so long?" He switched off the radio and came into the bathroom, where she stood before the mirror brushing her hair into the silken sheen that he loved. "My sisters hate you for having such a great figure," he said complacently, sliding his arms about her waist as his body nestled against hers. "Prettiest little rump, most gorgeous boobs in all New York," he crooned, and maneuvered one hand down the neckline of her black chiffon nightie, a shower present from Marge.

The one time when she felt secure in her marriage was when they made love, Kathy thought, while Phil lifted her off her feet and carried her to their bed. Then life seemed so glorious for them. In Phil's arms, blending into one with him, she could forget all her apprehensions about their future.

A few days later—still fighting constant drowsiness and now aware of a faint morning queasiness—Kathy guessed that she was pregnant. She was alternately ecstatic and anxious. She could work for a while, yes, but what about when she had to stop? Phil would never discuss the details of their financial situation though they both knew that, like all his actor friends, most of whom worked at side jobs, they couldn't count on the theater for a living at this point.

First, she told Marge when they met for lunch. Then, in a phone call from the office, she told her mother that she suspected she was pregnant. Her mother was joyous and tender.

"Phil must be so excited!"

"I haven't told him yet," Kathy confessed. "I just realized it this morning, and he was asleep when I left." She visualized her mother's almost imperceptible frown. Mom thought Phil ought to look for a real job, she surmised, but she'd never say that. "I'll tell him tonight."

Kathy meant to wait for a romantic moment to tell Phil, but the words spilled out as she slid a steaming plate of spaghetti before him.

"Phil, I'm pregnant."

He stared at her in disbelief.

"You're sure?" he asked after a moment that seemed endless.

"I'm sure." She nodded. Her face was aglow with joy. She tried for casualness, but her heart was pounding.

"I thought you always took care of that."

"Nothing's a hundred percent safe except abstinence," she said lightly. "And that's not our style." He looked shocked, she thought with sudden unease. But that was natural. And he was worried about the money situation when she had to stop working. "Phil, are you upset about the baby?"

"Honey, no!" With a reassuring smile he reached for her

hand. "I'm just—just surprised. I figured we'd wait three or four years. The folks will be pleased. One more chance for a grandson. Brenda and Gloria insist they've closed up shop. We'll manage," he said. "I'll just have to land a part before you quit work, that's all."

After an obstetrician had confirmed Kathy's suspicions, Phil telephoned his father to say that they would be near Greenwich on Sunday and would drop by in the afternoon.

"Come for dinner," his father ordered. "I want to show Kathy the sable coat I had made up for your mother." He chuckled knowingly. "She'll be like Brenda and Gail. Drooling. I want my competition to know my wife wears only the best."

The old man didn't suspect why they were coming up, Phil told himself, pleased. Tell him face to face. If Kathy delivered a boy, their stock would rise sky-high. Maybe now Julius would give them a house. Give him a house, Phil amended mentally. Gail and Brenda held the deeds to their houses in their names only. No in-laws sharing. Phil remembered his father's explanation. *"Look, if there's a divorce, I want to be sure the houses stay in the family. Why should I let those two* schmucks *get something for nothing?"*

Dinner on this occasion was without the usual bickering between Julius and Bella. Phil understood. His father was feeling smug because he'd given his wife a coat fit for royalty. She was smug because she would be the envy of other wives in the neighborhood. In Greenwich mink was as common as mouton lamb in Brooklyn, but sable said your husband was *very* rich.

Phil waited until Bella took Kathy upstairs to show off the sable coat, then told his father that he was to be a grandfather once again. Immediately the atmosphere was supercharged.

"A boy this time, Phil!" Julius made it sound like a command. "If it's a boy, I'm giving you a house up here." His eyes narrowed. "But now when you're going to be a parent, how do you plan on supporting your family?"

"I've got a couple of hot leads," Phil lied. "And Kathy can work for another three or four months." Damn, why hadn't she been more careful? What was the rush in starting a family?

"Phil, stop shitting around. Trying to land a job on Broadway is playing Russian roulette. It's time to be a *mensch.* You come into the business with me."

"Dad, I'm not cut out for business," he interrupted.

"Stop throwing the crap," Julius shot back. "You need a paycheck every week. You come in with me. You learn from the ground up. But fast," he said quickly before Phil could utter a complaint. "In five years—if you play your cards right—I'll bring you in as a partner." He smiled in triumph. "What more can you want?"

"I'll come in part-time," Phil hedged. *A partnership meant a big salary.* Money was going so fast. And he was fed up with living in a lousy three-room apartment, eating in cheap restaurants because that was all his theater friends could afford. "I'll come in part-time," he repeated, "and make rounds in the afternoon. If I land a part, I take it."

"You come in at eight A.M. and work till noon," his father agreed. The old bastard looked so pleased with himself, Phil thought. "If you don't have a theater job by March, you come in full-time. You said you were giving yourself a year to make it in the theater. March will be a year. When I'm gone, Julius Kohn Furs goes to you," he added with a flourish. "Provided you're working in the business. Let the girls carry on all they want—I didn't break my back so their husbands can run the business into the ground."

"Dad, you'll still be haggling with the suppliers when you're ninety-five," Phil joshed. *And still chasing women.*

"You start tomorrow," his father decreed. "You've got a wife and child to support." He pushed back his chair. "Let's go have a drink. I don't become a prospective grandfather every day in the week. And this time, Phil, it had better be a boy."

Kathy was delighted that Phil was working for his father, even on a part-time basis. He complained about the need to be on the southbound IRT by 7:40. *"Damn, it's like being in the army again!"* He complained that his father was trying to run his life for him. Yet despite his gripes Kathy sensed he was finding a certain challenge in the job. He was moving from one phase of the business to another with lightning speed, often remaining for a full day rather than his scheduled four hours. Kathy sensed he had abandoned making rounds. He had stopped poring over the current edition of *Show Business.*

Meeting Marge for lunch on a blustery March day soon after she had quit her job, Kathy reported that Phil had officially gone to work for his father full-time.

"He won't admit it," Kathy said, her eyes tender, "but I think he enjoys showing his father he can do well. There's a crazy—but good—competition there."

"Let him not do as well as his father with the Julius Kohn Fur models," Marge said drily.

"What do you mean?" Kathy was instantly defensive.

"Julius Kohn has a reputation for being the biggest wolf on Seventh Avenue. He has the fastest turnover in models in the business. Jobs aren't that tough to find these days— they don't all have to lie down for him."

"Phil doesn't fool around." Kathy stared at her in reproach.

"Kathy, I didn't mean that." Marge was contrite. "I was just gossiping about the old bastard. You know there're no secrets on Seventh Avenue."

"How're you doing on the new job?" She knew Marge was excited about being promoted to assistant designer.

"I love it!" Marge was radiant. "If I could just make Mom understand that if I move into my own apartment, it doesn't mean I'm shacking up with a guy or selling it on the street. I hate that long *schlep* from Borough Park every day."

"Marge, she can't stop you from moving into your own place," Kathy reasoned. "If you can find anything these days. You practically have to read the obits to locate a vacant apartment."

"I haven't changed my mind about San Francisco," Marge said softly. "When I have enough cash stashed away to handle the situation, plus I feel I've learned enough to land a job as a full-time designer, I'm blowing this town."

For her this was a happy time, Kathy thought sentimentally, though Phil still griped about his father's failure to come through with financial help beyond his salary.

"Damn, why can't he give us a house now instead of waiting until the baby's born?" Phil was convinced his father would give them a house in Greenwich whether the baby was a boy or a girl, though Julius good-humoredly repeated his condition that his latest grandchild be a grandson.

"We're better off here in Manhattan," Kathy soothed. "You'd hate coming in from Greenwich every day." She resented the way her father-in-law played this game with them. They didn't need a house in Greenwich. They could manage on Phil's salary if they stuck to a budget.

"I'll bet the old buzzard already has the house picked out," Phil surmised. "In Round Hill, close to the family house." Wouldn't *they* have anything to say about the kind of house? Kathy wondered.

It would be exciting to have a house of their own, Kathy conceded inwardly. She'd talked about it with Mom. A lot of returning GIs were buying houses, with government help. But did it have to be in Greenwich? Mom said having a house with a yard for the baby would be like owning a piece of Eden. Yet she was uneasy at the thought of living within a few minutes of her in-laws.

With Kathy enormous late in her eighth month, Phil came home to announce they were to go up to Greenwich in the morning to spend the weekend.

"Phil, do we have to?" The June heat wave left her exhausted. And she was nervous at being so far from the hospital this late in her pregnancy.

"We have to," he said jubilantly. "Mother tipped me off. Dad is buying a house in Greenwich about a quarter-mile down from theirs. He's telling us we can live there rent free once he closes on the house. If the baby is a boy, the house is ours."

"Phil, that's awful!" Kathy flinched in anger.

"It's awful to give us a house?"

"The way he does it! If the baby's a girl, we're supposed to drown her?"

"Kathy, have you any idea what a house in Greenwich is worth?" he flared. "He's not talking about a $7,000 Levittown house. And Dad may grumble, but he'll give us the house—boy or girl—just like he did with Brenda and Gail."

"We're all pawns on your father's chessboard. My father doesn't try to run our lives. Why should he?"

"Your father isn't giving us a house in Greenwich," Phil shot back. "So the old man makes a lot of noise," he reminded with a conciliatory smile. "We'll go out to Greenwich for the weekend. It'll do you good to get out of the city. And we'll pretend we know nothing about the house."

Two hours later Kathy felt her first labor pain. For a moment she sat transfixed, silent, saying nothing to Phil, who sprawled on the sofa listening to a radio newscast. Maybe she was wrong, she told herself, but her heart was pounding in anticipation. A few minutes later she felt the same knot tightening in her stomach. *No mistake about this one.*

"Phil—"

"Yeah?"

"I think I'm in labor."

"You're not due for two weeks." But he switched off the radio and leapt to his feet.

"The baby says differently. Let's time the contractions." She tried to sound matter-of-fact. *Her baby was about to make his way into the world.*

They sat together now on the sofa, hand in hand. Phil's eyes fastened to his watch.

"They're coming fast," he said nervously after forty minutes. "I'm calling the doctor."

"Phil, it'll be a long time yet," she said calmly, but before she could say another word, she was seized by yet another contraction. "Maybe you'd better call—"

The obstetrician ordered Kathy to head for the hospital. While Phil went down to bring the car to the front of the house, she phoned home.

"Darling, you're going to be fine," her mother said briskly. Kathy sensed her excitement and anxiety. "We're coming right over to the hospital."

"Mom, come tomorrow morning. You know a first baby takes a long time."

"Daddy and I are coming into the city right now," Edie insisted. She laughed shakily. "I can't believe I'm going to be a grandmother!"

"Mom," Kathy said slowly, "are you hoping for a boy or a girl?"

"I'm wishing for a grandchild." Her voice was tender in anticipation. "What difference does it make, boy or girl? Let the baby be healthy, that's all I ask of God."

Fifteen hours later—after a difficult labor—Kathy gave birth to a six-pound, three-ounce son. At last allowed to see her, Phil kissed her with an awed tenderness.

"Did you see him?" Kathy asked, exhausted yet exhilarated. He was fine, the doctor said.

"He's terrific," Phil told her. "Looks just like you."

"Is Mom here?" she asked.

"Your mother, your father, and Aunt Sophie were here all night." He chuckled. "They didn't go back to Borough Park to open up the store yet. For them this is like a national holiday."

Kathy was relieved that the heat wave had broken in time for the baby's *bris* and the reception that followed. Even with the small apartment crowded this way everyone was comfortable. In addition to family, the guests included Marge, Rhoda, Brian, a pair of Phil's actor friends, and a dozen longtime family friends. Gail and Brenda and their husbands were not here. They'd left last night on a cruise.

Mom and Sophie had prepared a feast. Everyone was making frequent trips to the buffet. Right now—with Jesse in her arms—Mom was holding court across the room. She and Dad and Aunt Sophie were so proud of him!

This was the first time that Phil's parents and hers were meeting since the wedding, Kathy thought. They'd done little more than exchange greetings. She gathered her father-in-law was annoyed that the baby would be called Jesse—after her paternal grandfather—rather than Peter, the middle name given in honor of his own father. Still, it was clear that Julius Kohn was jubilant at having a grandson.

"Kathy, I'm going to steal him," Rhoda bubbled, crossing to her side with one of Aunt Sophie's miniature knishes in her hand. "He is so precious." She dropped her voice. "That actor friend of Phil's—Derek Williams—just asked me out for dinner on his night off from the theater." Derek had a two-line part in a new Broadway hit.

"You said 'yes'?"

"Am I crazy? Of course I said 'yes.' "

Bella had crossed the room to coo over Jesse again, but Kathy intercepted her furtive glances at her diamond-studded wristwatch. Julius was drawing Phil off into a corner. Kathy saw him hand a manila envelope to his son. She suspected the envelope contained the deed to the house in Greenwich that he had promised them.

She ought to be madly happy, Kathy reproached herself. A house in Greenwich was an impressive chunk of security for Phil and herself and the baby. *Why did she feel she was caught in a terrible trap?*

Chapter 8

Kathy had been wrong about the manila envelope that exchanged hands at the baby's *bris*. It had been a thousand-dollar savings bond for Jesse Peter Kohn. Now Phil waited impatiently for his father to fulfill his promise. What would they do about furniture if he gave them a house, Kathy asked herself. Phil's salary was too small for them to have put aside any savings. They lived from check to check, and she had such a fear of buying on time.

When the baby was one month old, Julius summoned Phil into his office in midafternoon.

"I want you to come up to the house on Saturday morning. Bring Jesse and Kathy with you," he said with a sly grin. "I've got a surprise. I'm flying to the house in Maine after an early lunch." Julius was proud of having made a deal with a charter service to fly him and his sons-in-law to the Maine house and back every summer weekend. "But you stay for the weekend."

"Okay," Phil agreed, his stomach churning in excitement. Here it came, he thought exultantly. The house in Greenwich. "What time shall we be there?"

"Be there by eleven. That'll give us plenty of time to talk and have lunch before I have to leave."

"Dad, what about shifting me over to the store for a while?" he asked casually. He'd been building up to this for a week. He didn't want to wait five years for a partnership. He wanted to sell the old man on bringing him in within a year. "I think we're missing the boat on our retail sales."

"What do you mean?" Julius demanded with a hint of belligerence. "Where are we missing the boat?"

Dad had his back up, Phil warned himself. Take it easy. He resented having his business skill questioned.

"I mean, Dad—" He leaned forward, exuding filial charm. "I mean, we could expand our sales, build up our image if we bring in a famous dress designer. I—"

"We're known as the furrier of the Hollywood stars," Julius bristled. "I spend a shitload of money to keep up that image."

"We should be catering to society women as well," Phil pursued. "There are a hell of a lot more of them than there are Hollywood stars, and they're not impressed by Hollywood names. Listen to Mother and the girls when they start talking clothes." Phil felt a surge of excitement at this fresh approach for Julius Kohn Furs. It was time the fur industry recognized the value of name designers. "Whose names do they mention? Jacques Fath, Balenciaga, and that new designer—the one who caused all the excitement with his 'New Look.' " Phil snapped his fingers in recall. "Christian Dior."

"Who do you think buys our furs at the Madison Avenue store?" Julius demanded. "Rich women. Who else can afford them?"

"Wouldn't you like to see a Julius Kohn fur on the back of every important society woman in America?" Phil replied. "They're the real fashion leaders, not Hollywood stars. And they spend much moolah on clothes. What they buy, the rich wives across America will buy. We need to bring high fashion into the fur industry. Give furs more pizzazz." He was conscious of an enthusiasm for the business he had never expected to feel.

"We'll talk about it when I get back from Maine," Julius hedged. "All of a sudden movie stars don't count? With half the people in America sitting in a movie theater on Saturday nights watching Joan Crawford and Ava Gardner and Loretta Young, you think I have to worry about society broads?" he derided. Yet Phil knew he'd planted a seed in his father's thinking. He could sense the wheels turning in the old man's head.

"The world's changing, Dad. A lot of people came out of the war with more money than they ever dreamed of having. They see themselves moving up in the world, and that means socially. Read the tabloid gossip columns," he challenged. "They're full of society names. Parties in Palm Beach and Bar Harbor and Southampton."

"Don't mention Southampton to me," his father grunted in irritation. "All your mother's been talking about the past three weeks is about getting rid of the house in Maine and buying something in Southampton."

"Because it's the smart place to go in the summer," Phil pounced. "It might even be a good business move for you to have a place out there."

"Our neighbors on both sides have summer houses in Southampton, so your mother has to have one, too," Julius grumbled, then squinted in thought. "I'll talk to the publicity woman. Maybe you're right. She might be able to get some mileage out of 'the Julius Kohn place at Southampton.' "

"Dad, put me in the store for a while," said Phil trying a second time. "Let me get a feel for the retail trade." And a feel of that gorgeous blond model he saw when he went into the store last week to check on inventory. He couldn't get her out of his mind. "Not as a salesman," he stipulated. "As a consultant." He'd struggled for ten days to come up with a title that pleased him. "Look, rich women are no different from others. They love flattery. I'll have them try on

several coats or jackets, then decide one makes them look
like Vivien Leigh or Joan Fontaine. 'Ah, but this one is for
you,' " he improvised. " 'I won't allow you to consider any
other.' And then I'll beckon to the saleswoman to take
over."

"You'd make a sensational gigolo," Julius chuckled.

"I'll host our fashion show," Phil offered. He saw his father's eyebrows shoot upward like a pair of frightened swal-
lows. "When you decide we'll have an annual fashion
show."

"You don't decide to have a fashion show and do it the
next month," Julius pointed out.

"I know," Phil agreed. "You start six months ahead. I'm
looking toward 1948." He saw his father's smug reaction.
So Phil plans on staying with the business, the old man was
thinking.

Phil was looking toward a partnership. A partner drew
a bundle in salary plus a chunk of the profits. "Make it a
charitable event, Dad," he continued. "Bring in the top debutantes of the season to model. Give a percentage of the
sales of the day to a designated charity. It'll be easy enough
to push up the sales prices so we don't feel the contribution."

"That'll bring in newspaper and magazine coverage." Julius was contemplative.

"Even television. A big spread in *Women's Wear Daily,*
a story in the *Times,* " he expanded enticingly.

"All right," Julius capitulated. "Monday morning you'll
be reassigned to the store. We'll think about the fashion
show in early September of next year, when everybody's
back from the resorts. We might even send a show on the
road to hit major stores in key cities." Now he was beaming.
"You gave me a lot of gray hairs, worrying about your future. But you're coming through with real class now. No
doubt about it, Phil, by the time I decide to retire, you'll
be able to take over. You're a chip off the old block."

*　　*　　*

Kathy talked to her mother briefly on the phone while Phil did last-minute packing and Jesse slept in his crib.

"Phil's sure his father is bringing us up to give us the house," Kathy reported without enthusiasm.

"Kathy, your own home," her mother said reverently. "It's like a dream."

"A lot of returning GIs are buying homes now," Kathy reminded.

"Tiny crackerboxes out in Levittown," her mother scoffed. "You'll be living in Connecticut in a beautiful house. Julius Kohn is an awful show-off," she reminded. "He'll want to brag to his friends about his son's fine new house."

"Kathy, it's getting late," Phil called. "Let's get ready to shove off."

"Mom, I have to go. I'll call you when we get back on Monday," Kathy said. "Bye."

Phil carried their valises and the baby paraphernalia. Kathy held Jesse—still sleeping—in her arms. It was weird, she thought, while they waited for the elevator. They'd probably be moving into the house in Greenwich any week now. And Phil would be driving into New York every day with his father. What he'd sworn he'd never do. But he was in high spirits. He didn't seem upset at all at the prospect.

They were following the pattern set by Phil's parents, Kathy told herself, and felt alarm signals pop up in her mind. She and Phil mustn't allow their marriage to become a replica of his parents' marriage. They wouldn't, she promised herself. She and Phil loved each other too much for that. They'd always work things out.

They arrived at the Greenwich house to find Julius sprawled on a chaise on the elegant veranda. He jumped up to greet them, called to a servant inside the house to take care of their luggage. He played the fatuous grandfather for a few moments, then herded them toward the limousine, parked in the drive with Wally at the wheel.

"We're just going about a quarter-mile down the road,"

he told them in high spirits with an air of mystery, which they pretended to respect.

As Phil anticipated, his father was at last making official the gift of a house. To *Phil,* Kathy understood. Not to Phil and his wife. She was just an onlooker, she thought in silent rage. Julius was behaving as though she wasn't present.

"There she is." Julius smiled in approval as Wally turned into a circular driveway before a pretentious, freshly painted, white colonial set on an acre of manicured lawn. "Eleven rooms, three baths, and a two-car garage."

"Looks sensational, Dad," Phil said. "But what about the taxes? Are we going to be clobbered?"

Wally hurried around to open the car door and Kathy emerged with Jesse. *Who was going to clean those eleven rooms? Who was going to mow the lawn and trim the hedges?* Phil and his father were involved in lively discussion about the features of the house. It would be like living on a movie set, Kathy thought rebelliously.

"Well, Kathy?" Julius turned to her when he had shown them through the three floors of the house. "How do you like it?" He spoke to her but he looked at Phil.

"It's a lovely house," she said politely. She would have preferred one of the new casual, comfortable ranch houses that were mushrooming all over. "Thank you."

She never knew how to address Phil's parents. Nobody had set the ground rules. She would have been self-conscious calling them "Dad" and "Mother." She suspected they would balk at "Julius" and "Bella."

Three weeks later Kathy, Phil, and tiny Jesse moved into their new home. The furniture from the West End Avenue apartment was inadequate and incongruous. For now much of the house would be closed off.

At precisely 5:50 A.M. each morning, Phil left the house to join his father in the backseat of the limo for the drive into Manhattan. On their first morning in the house he had encouraged Kathy to remain in bed when he arose, since he would have only coffee and juice at this hour. He'd have breakfast in the city. But she insisted on getting up with him. Jesse always awoke at 6 A.M. for a bottle.

Later in the morning—because it took her an hour to go back to sleep after Jesse's 2 A.M. feeding—she would nap while he slept. She must learn to drive, she told herself repeatedly. Otherwise, she'd be a prisoner in this house. Phil seemed unenthusiastic about her driving, but she'd have to make him understand.

She had been worried that Phil's mother and sisters, living so near, would be popping in often with advice about caring for Jesse. Instinctively she knew their ideas of child-raising would clash with her own. Phil and his sisters had been raised by nursemaids, as Phil's nieces were being raised now. But Phil and she might have lived a continent away from his family, she quickly realized.

Phil's father picked him up in the morning in the chauffeured limo, and brought him home at night. Once or twice a week Julius came into the house for a few minutes to fuss over Jesse. Phil's sisters sent lavish, impractical gifts from Saks but never bothered to call. His mother came by for ten minutes one afternoon between a luncheon party and a garden club meeting to stand beside the crib for a few moments. *"He looks just like Phil at that age."* He didn't. He looked like the Ross side.

The Kohn women were more concerned about their volunteer activities and social organizations and prospective trips than about Phil's son. But Jesse could survive without the attention of the Kohn family. He had an adoring grandmother, grandfather, and great-great-aunt on her side.

Kathy talked regularly with her mother and father and Aunt Sophie by phone. Mom was always anxious about their talking too long. *"Darling, you'll run up such a big bill."* They developed a routine. One time Mom would call, the next time she would call. Except for phone calls to and from her family and Marge and Rhoda, she was living in isolation, Kathy thought wryly after a refreshingly long call from Rhoda.

On their third Sunday in the house, Kathy's parents and Aunt Sophie were coming out for a midday dinner. Eager to see them, she went with Phil to the station to pick them up. She felt a poignant rush of love as the familiar figures emerged from the train.

"I'll take Jesse," Phil said, standing beside the car. "Go meet them."

It was as though they'd been apart for months, Kathy thought affectionately as the three women settled on the rear seat and her father joined Phil on the front. Jesse nestled in her mother's arms.

"I made a batch of *rugelach* and a *challah,*" Aunt Sophie said, patting the parcel on her lap. "Jesse will have to wait a while before I make him cookies. Precious little sweetheart—"

While Phil was showing them through the house, Kathy went into the kitchen to put up dinner. As Mom had insisted, she'd prepared a simple menu. They'd have to be heading back to the station in four hours so Dad could relieve his helper at the store.

"It's a beautiful house, Kathy." Her mother appeared in the doorway, her smile sympathetic. Mom understood she didn't feel comfortable here. Not in this house. Not in Greenwich. "You'll feel better here when you have more of it furnished." She hesitated. "Dad and I want you to come into town and choose a table and chairs for your breakfast room. Our housewarming gift," she said with a bright smile.

"Mom, you and Dad have done enough," Kathy protested. "I know what the wedding cost you."

"It's our pleasure, darling. You'll come into New York as soon as it's convenient, and we'll go shopping. Such a lovely breakfast room. You should be able to enjoy it."

Chapter 9

At Phil's insistence Kathy arranged to go into New York the following Saturday to shop with her mother for the breakfast room furniture.

"I'll phone when I get into Grand Central," she told Phil while they waited for the train at the Greenwich station. "If you're having any problems, I'll just turn around and come back." He'd never taken care of Jesse on his own before today. At the moment, Jesse slept contentedly in the car-bed.

"Honey, relax. Jesse and I will have a high old time. If I have any problems, I'll buzz my mother." He reflected on this a moment. "Or I'll ask Clara to drive over and give us a hand." Clara had come to the Kohn family as a teenager and worked her way up from maid to housekeeper in thirty-one years, the one member of the domestic staff who remained in place. "Clara changed a lot of diapers for me and gave me a lot of bottles," he said whimsically. "Even then, Mother was all involved with charities and garden clubs."

"Here's the train—" Kathy felt a disconcerting wrench

at the prospect of putting so many miles between Jesse and herself even for the afternoon.

"Try to find something that's available for fast delivery," Phil encouraged. "Maybe a floor sample if it's in good shape."

"I will," she promised, reaching for the car door. "Don't forget to burp Jesse after his bottle."

Kathy was shocked when Phil announced—the night he arrived home to find the charming country maple table and four captain's chairs sitting in their spacious breakfast room—that he was inviting his mother and father over for brunch the following Saturday.

"It'll be no extra work for you," he soothed. "I'll bring up a slab of nova and a bagful of bagels from the city Friday night. There's nothing the old man likes more than lox and eggs and onions. He'll be in a great mood."

"You're going to taunt him with my parents' housewarming present," she accused in sudden comprehension. "Phil, they've given us the house!"

"They can afford it," he shrugged. "Dad's got an accountant who knows every tax shelter on the books. I remember the fancy furniture they gave Gail and Brenda the first year they were married. Hey, I'm their only son."

On Saturday morning Julius and Bella Kohn arrived for brunch. Kathy watched them tense and exchange a meaningful glance when Phil—seemingly ingenuous—showed off the "great breakfast room furniture Kathy's parents gave us." Early the following week Phil came home to announce that *his* parents had ordered formal dining room and living room furniture for them, plus a TV set with the much-coveted fourteen-inch screen.

"We'll have to wait three months before it all arrives," Phil said blithely while Kathy seethed. Her father-in-law had probably ordered the furniture over the phone, no doubt through some "inside connection" that guaranteed a discount price. How could Phil's parents know what *they* would like?

Kathy's life revolved around the baby. Jesse was her sole companion from the time Phil left the house at 5:50 A.M. until he came home around 7 P.M. In their area of expensive estates she found no opportunity to make friends. She yearned for the camaraderie of young wives and mothers that she would have found in a less affluent suburb.

She adored Jesse. She enjoyed fulfilling all his needs, hearing his laughter, soothing his tears as the first tooth began to push its way through tender gum. But she felt with painful frequency that she was living in exile. Phil came home from the city tired from the long commute and hectic hours in the business. By 9:30 he was falling asleep.

On Saturdays Phil slept late. After breakfast he drove her to the supermarket to shop for the week. On Saturday nights—with Jesse comfortably asleep in the car-bed—they went to one of the new drive-in movies that eliminated the need for a baby-sitter. Saturday night became their night for making love. Phil referred to this as the Saturday night national pastime. One Sunday each month they went to Phil's parents' house for dinner. Another Sunday they drove into the city to have dinner with her family. On Thanksgiving they would go to her family in Borough Park.

Phil appeared to be enjoying his job. He talked with pride about his father's new respect for his abilities. Early in December he came home from the city with a box of Kathy's favorite chocolates.

"Dad's giving me a raise," he announced triumphantly. "I won't have to wait five years for a partnership," he predicted.

"Phil, that's wonderful! How much of a raise?"

"Don't worry your head about that, baby. It's enough so we can spend more freely." He went grocery shopping with her and paid the bill. He paid all the bills. She rarely had more than ten dollars in her wallet. "Maybe we'll have a few people up for New Year's Eve and to sleep over. You'd like that, wouldn't you?"

"We don't have beds for them," she reminded reluctantly. The dining room and living room furniture that Phil's parents had ordered for them had at last arrived. Far too elaborate for her taste, but she mustn't say that even to Phil, she'd warned herself. "It would have been fun."

"There's a place where we can rent beds. I'll take care of it. We won't have a big crowd. Six guests," he decided. "Our first party in our own house!"

Coffee cup in hand, Phil stood by the breakfast room window and stared up at the still night-dark winter sky.

"I hope Wally put the snow tires on the car," he told Kathy while she warmed Jesse's morning bottle on the electric range. "I don't care if it is only mid-December. We're in for a heavy snow this morning."

"Maybe you ought to take the train in."

"Ugh." He shuddered eloquently. "I can't face that at this hour. So it'll take us longer if the snow begins to fall along the way."

"If the roads are bad, Phil, take the train tonight," Kathy urged.

"There's the car—" He swigged down the rest of the coffee, kissed her, and headed down the hall toward the door.

As usual, he and his father both dozed much of the way into the city. By the time they'd turned off the Merritt Parkway, silver dollar–sized flakes had begun to fall. When Wally pulled up before the restaurant where they went each morning for breakfast, the roads and sidewalks were white.

"Go sleep at your mother's place," Julius told Wally. "I won't be needing the car this morning." Wally's mother and sister lived in a walk-up in Hell's Kitchen. "I may even cancel my lunch meeting. I'll phone around eleven to let you know."

Phil and his father hurried into the restaurant, already filling up with the regular morning customers. They relished the rush of warmth that greeted them. Savory aromas of fresh coffee, bacon sizzling on the grill, toast popping up provided a cozy welcome. They settled themselves at the rear booth, always held available for them at this hour.

"Early in the year for snow." Julius appeared unperturbed, however. "If it keeps up like this, we'll stay in town for the night. I don't like driving on icy roads." All at once his voice seemed guarded. "I can sack out in my office. The sofa's not great, but it'll do for one night. You got a place to stay in town? If you haven't, call a hotel by noon. It gets to be a rat race in this weather if you wait until late in the afternoon."

"Yeah, I can stay with one of the guys for a night," Phil said. The old man wouldn't be sacked out on the sofa, he surmised in amusement. He'd be screwing that *zaftig* little bookkeeper that just came to work for the company. "If the snow keeps up."

After breakfast Phil went up to the office for the customary conference with his father and whatever staff members Julius Kohn chose to call in that morning. Phil was pleased that they were already planning on a charity fashion show for next September. Negotiations were going well with a top designer to work with them on the new line.

"Phil, you've spent enough time in the store," Julius said, while a secretary rounded up those called in for the conference. "Maybe you should go on the road for a while. Fuck the wholesalers—let's set up some concessions in key stores in big cities." This had been *his* most recent suggestion, Phil remembered complacently. "Only the best, most expensive stores," Julius stipulated. He squinted speculatively at Phil. "Is Kathy going to be mad if you're out of town a lot for a while?"

"Look, it's business," Phil said calmly. "She'll understand."

At the store he phoned for a weather report. The snow was expected to continue through the day and into the evening. He whistled in approval. He'd have to stay in the city tonight.

He waited for Leila to arrive. She had replaced the iceberg who made it clear she didn't "mess around with married men, not even the boss's son." Leila had not rejected his quick grabs at opportune moments in the dressing room. She was tall, slim, sultry. He suspected she entertained some of their visiting buyers from time to time. This might be just the time to expand their own relationship.

Christ, he hadn't slept with another woman since he met Kathy. The old man was screwing somebody else on his honeymoon. Like Dad said, what the wives didn't know couldn't hurt them.

By noon—when the major topic of conversation around town was the snowstorm—Phil confided to Leila at a private moment that there was no way he was going up to Greenwich tonight.

"That's a long haul," Leila sympathized. "I'm one express stop on the subway."

"I suppose I ought to start calling around for a hotel room." His eyes were boldly speculative.

"I suppose—" Her smile was provocative.

Phil glanced around to make sure no one was approaching. He slid a hand down the sharp cleavage of her white crepe blouse.

"Would you join me if I can book a room?"

"No," she said. "But you can stay at my place if you like."

"I'd like that very much." His hand found its way beneath her bra and fondled a hard nipple.

"I'll meet you at the restaurant." She reached to pull his hand away. "Let's don't advertise to the others. I like to keep my personal life private."

"What restaurant?" he asked, impatient for night to arrive.

"There's a great little French place in the West Fifties." She told him the name and address. Expensive, he noted. But he was avoiding the cost of a hotel room.

"What time?"

"Early," she said. "Six-thirty. Before the mobs descend."

Now she shot a brilliant smile to someone behind him. "Jean, that cape is gorgeous."

A little past five Phil phoned Kathy to explain that he and his father were staying in town for the night.

"Where will you be?" He heard a wistful note in her voice.

"Gee, I'm not sure. Dad had his secretary make reservations for us. But I'll call you later and let you know."

"You don't have to do that. It's just for the night."

"This has developed into a real blizzard. You all right out there?" he asked solicitously.

"I'm fine," Kathy assured him.

"Give Jesse a big hug and kiss for me," he ordered. "I'll miss you, honey."

"I'll miss you, too. But I'm glad you decided not to drive."

"Call and ask Clara if she can baby-sit Jesse tomorrow night," he said amorously. "I'll take my old lady out to dinner."

Julius decided to let the office staff and the workers leave at four o'clock because of the storm. When Phil came in to say good night, he noticed the *zaftig* little bookkeeper was lingering over a ledger. He'd been right, Phil told himself. The old man had plans.

"I'm taking off, Dad," he said casually.

"Where you staying?" Julius asked.

"Up in the West Eighties with this guy I know from my theater days. He has a small part in a Broadway play." He saw his father's supercilious smile. A Broadway star Julius Kohn respected. An actor in a small part was nobody. "I called him up earlier." He hesitated a moment. "Look, Dad, if Kathy happens to bring it up, just say I went to the Taft with you."

"Hun-hunh." Julius grinned. "You're going to the Taft with a hot little number."

"Not the Taft." He exchanged a loaded glance with his father. "See you for breakfast as usual?"

"Skip breakfast," Julius said. "I'll talk to you later in the day." He winked knowingly. "Don't do anything I wouldn't do."

"That gives me a lot of leeway. See you tomorrow, Dad."

Leila was waiting for him in the restaurant vestibule.

"I reserved a table for us in the name of Phillips," she told him, moving insinuatingly close for a moment. "Just in case the blizzard brought a rush of business."

The softly lit, attractive restaurant was empty except for two other couples. Their table was in a private corner, as Leila had requested. Right away he knew she was one of those women who liked to linger over dinner. He would have been happier to rush through it and head for her apartment. They'd have a devil of a time finding a cab. Maybe he should have booked a room at a nearby hotel.

They had a cocktail before dinner and white wine with their meal. He was conscious of a heady pleasure at being here with Leila, knowing what was to come. This one would be game for anything, he told himself.

"I know a lot of people are staying in town tonight, but maybe we could get a hotel room close by," he said over dessert. "It'll be a bitch to find a cab in this weather."

"Slum with me," Leila taunted. "We'll take a subway. I like my own place. All cozy and comfortable."

"So we'll take the subway," he agreed.

Leila lived in a graystone on West Seventieth, close to West End. Once it must have been an elegant town house. Now it was slightly shabby, struggling to keep up pretenses of its earlier status. Leila's third floor walk-up apartment consisted of a square living room with a Pullman kitchenette and a tiny bedroom and bath.

"Take off your wet shoes and relax," she told him as she headed for the bedroom.

Phil kicked off his shoes, walked across the thick gray shag rug to a window. Only an occasional car crept along on the street below. Parked cars were blobs of white, not likely to be moved tonight. God, he felt like a kid again. It was great.

"If you'd like wine," Leila called from behind the partially closed door, "there's a bottle of Chianti in the fridge."

"You trying to get me drunk?" he joshed.

"You wouldn't dare," she said with a throaty laugh. "I have other plans."

Heat was pouring into the apartment. It was beginning to feel like a tropical jungle, he thought. He pulled off his jacket and loosened his tie. Why were New York apartments either overheated or freezing?

Leila emerged from the bedroom. She'd brushed her blond pageboy into a silken wildness that fell about her shoulders. Her sheer black negligé over an equally sheer black nightie—displaying small breasts, huge nipples—reminded him of a bordello he'd visited in Paris; her perfume was a blatant aphrodisiac.

"Sensational window dressing," he drawled. "You ought to be starring on Broadway in that. Every man in the audience would have an erection."

"Do you know people in the theater?" All at once her face was luminous with excitement.

"A few," he said casually. He might have known. A model with stage aspirations. "We'll talk about it. Later."

In a sudden surge of passion he reached to pull her close. She lifted her mouth—already open in welcome—to his. For a few moments they were satisfied with a mouth-to-mouth duel while their bodies nuzzled in sensuous invitation.

"Take off your clothes," he said when their mouths separated with mutual reluctance, and she clucked in reproach.

"Don't be like an overheated college boy," she taunted. "Persuade me."

"Honey, you'll never be persuaded better," he boasted and with deliberate slowness began to strip away his own clothes. "Me first, you next."

For a moment her eyes followed his progress, then with

the same slowness she slid the black negligé from her shoulders and allowed it to fall to the floor. She pushed aside the pencil-thin straps of the nightie from her shoulders, coaxed it over milk-white breasts, past narrow hips and thighs, to join the negligé on the floor. They stood naked and flexed for action, like gladiators in an arena. Her mouth parted as her eyes watched him harden in arousal.

"Don't move," she ordered, her smile dazzling, and dropped to her knees before him.

"I'm all yours, Leila," he murmured hotly. "Show me how good you are."

He gloried in her manipulations, murmuring passionate encouragement while his hands cradled her head. And then with sudden urgency he ordered her to her feet.

"Let's get this show on the road, baby." He pulled her tightly against him for a moment, then prodded her back toward the sofa. This was going to be a long night, he promised himself. A great night.

═ Chapter 10

Kathy enjoyed their small New Year's Eve house party. Rhoda and Brian from the Hamburg group were there, which lent a special poignancy because the three of them remembered New Year's Eve in Germany and the sense of hopelessness among many of those they tried to help. She remembered David spending most of New Year's Day—officially a day off for them—with a despairing Bergen-Belsen survivor who had attempted suicide the night before.

Rhoda had come with Derek Williams—Phil's friend—who had a tiny part in a current Broadway hit. Rhoda said he was talking about their getting married in the summer. *"No ring yet because he's working for Equity minimum, but who needs a ring?"*

Brian was leaving for Greece in three weeks on a magazine assignment. He said if conditions were as bad in Greece as reports claimed, he'd remain there for a while. Marge was hoping to leave for San Francisco in late spring. Kathy felt herself caught in a vacuum in Greenwich. The phone was her lifeline to the outside world.

An instant later she was filled with guilt. How could she

envy Brian and Marge when she had Phil and Jesse in her life? So many girls in her graduating class at Barnard would love to be in her shoes! When the weather was better, she'd get into the city more often. And they'd have friends up for spring weekends, she promised herself. She'd stop feeling this awful loneliness.

A week later Phil came home, excited about new plans for his role in the business. Over dinner he elaborated in detail, growing apologetic when he talked about an imminent two-week trip through the Midwest.

"I know it's going to be tough on you, baby, but this pushes me closer to that partnership!" he gloated. "And the traveling won't begin until late March. We need time to formulate the setup."

Kathy was silent for a few moments as she tried to assimilate what lay ahead.

"Kathy?" Phil was solicitous.

"It sounds wonderful." She forced a smile. "But I'll have to learn to drive. I can't be alone here for two weeks without being able to get around."

"You need something, just call over to the house. Clara drives. You tell her what you need and she'll get it for you."

"No." Kathy smiled, but she was firm. She would *not* be stranded in Greenwich with a young baby. Even Clara, his parents' housekeeper, drove. "I know you're busy so I'll arrange to take lessons." Marge had warned her never to ask Phil to teach her to drive. *"No family—I went through hell with my brother teaching me. Spend a few bucks and take lessons."*

"I don't know why you have to drive," Phil balked. His face flushed. "I don't want to have to worry about you when I'm away."

"You don't have to worry about me." All at once her heart was pounding. She and Phil had never had a real fight, but the atmosphere now was heavy with his hostility. "Millions of women drive." His mother had been driving for over thirty years, she'd said once when Julius complained she'd dented the fender of her new Cadillac convertible. *"Once in thirty-eight years, Julius—that's a good record."*

"We'll talk about it," Phil hedged. "Any more of that pot roast?"

"I'll bring it to the table."

Phil was not going to stop her from learning to drive, she promised herself. If she had to, she'd borrow the money for lessons from the emergency fund Phil kept hidden away in a garment bag. Several hundred dollars had been sitting there, she remembered, since they moved into the house. *This was an emergency.* She had to have a driver's license before Phil left. Suppose Phil was away and, God forbid, something happened to Jesse? She had to know she was mobile. She couldn't depend upon his family or their servants.

The following morning Kathy called a nearby driving school. With Jesse in a car-bed on the rear seat she took her first lesson.

"I have to be driving by the end of March," she told her instructor. "I mean, I have to have a license by then."

"It'll be a snap," he said good-humoredly. "Let's schedule the lessons. And I'll put in for a road test in mid-March. How's that?"

"That's great." Her smile was convivial, but she dreaded the confrontation with Phil when she told him that she'd borrowed from their emergency fund—and that she was a licensed driver.

Early in February Phil came home to announce that they were invited to a dinner party the following month.

"It's the old man's sixtieth birthday," Phil told Kathy in high spirits. "Mother and the girls decided the big six-O deserved a real bash. You'll need an evening dress. Something splashy."

"Where will it be?" Already she felt tense at the prospect of meeting a lot of strangers.

"At the house," he told her while they walked toward the nursery. "All of a sudden Dad's on an art collection kick. He's dying to show off two old masters he managed to buy from some German refugee who smuggled them into the country. The caterers will handle the dinner. Gail will handle the music and the flowers."

"I'll go into the city one Saturday to shop," Kathy said tentatively.

"I'll open a charge for you at Saks," Phil told her. "Don't look at price tags. Just choose something that'll make you look like a movie star. My wife will be the best-looking broad at the party," he said amorously and paused in the hallway to pull her close. "I don't hear any sounds from Jesse. Is he asleep?"

"He had a rough afternoon, poor baby. The new tooth is finally coming through. He fell asleep a few minutes ago."

"I had a rough afternoon, too," he teased and nuzzled her ear for a moment. A sure sign that he was aroused. "Can dinner wait a while?"

"Sure thing." Most week nights Phil just wanted dinner, an hour of television, and then he was ready for sleep. He always laughed and said Saturday was their night to howl.

Hand in hand they walked into the dark bedroom. Kathy left the door ajar, though she doubted that Jesse would awaken. Phil crossed the room to close the drapes at the two windows, then reached for her.

"I thought we'd never get off the parkway tonight," he murmured, swaying with her. "I couldn't wait to get home to you."

"Don't you think you ought to get out of your suit?" she joshed.

"I'm popping out of it already." He brought her hand to his crotch. "How's that?"

"First class," she approved.

In mutual silence they hurried to undress. Phil pulled her down on the bed beside him and began the sensuous exploring that shot off rockets in her. And then—while his mouth caught one nipple between his teeth—she saw in the ribbon of light from the hallway the long, blond hair that lay across his shoulder.

All at once all her senses seemed to sharpen. She saw the long, blond hair, and she caught the scent of pungent perfume. A woman's perfume. No, she reproached herself. She mustn't be one of those suspicious wives. Phil worked around women. A blond hair could fall across his shoulder.

His naked shoulder? Beneath his shirt? And that perfume. Her throat grew tight as she struggled to cope with this. There was a logical explanation, she told herself. From time to time even now he was at the store. He was doing his usual *shtick,* as he liked to call it, and paving the way for a saleswoman to sell an expensive fur. Somehow, that blond hair made its way beneath his collar. The woman wore too much perfume. When he held the coat for her, some of the scent clung to him. *She mustn't become one of those suspicious wives who made a big thing out of nothing.*

"Kathy?" He paused.

"I thought I heard Jesse—" she fabricated.

"Relax. He's fast asleep. This is fun time, baby."

The following Saturday—though the day was gray and bitterly cold—Kathy prepared to go into New York to buy a dress for Julius's birthday party. Grumbling mildly at having to wake up early on a weekend, Phil drove her to the Greenwich station in time to catch an early train and then headed with Jesse for his parents' home. Sitting in the train as it pulled out of the station, she strained for a last view of Phil and Jesse in the car.

She felt guilty at her eager anticipation of a day in the city on her own. She'd go out to Borough Park from Grand Central and spend some time with the family. At three she was to meet Marge inside the Fifth Avenue entrance to Saks. At five she and Marge would meet Rhoda, who was treating them to tea at the Plaza. How wonderful that Marge and Rhoda had become instant friends, too.

Rhoda had been mysterious about the reason for the

super-extravagance of tea at the Plaza, Kathy remembered. Hardly a routine part of a schoolteacher's budget. Marge suspected Rhoda was having this little celebration to announce her official engagement to Derek. With the school spring vacation just ahead, maybe they'd get married then. Rhoda's parents would be upset. They didn't consider an actor a responsible provider.

Kathy was glad that on this dreary Saturday few people were bound for Manhattan. She dozed much of the way into the city. At Grand Central she left the train for the shuttle to Times Square, then headed for the Brooklyn-bound BMT. One thing she didn't miss was the New York subway system, she thought humorously. All those years of chasing back and forth between home and Barnard! Marge teased her about getting spoiled now that she had married "into the rich Kohn family."

She was hardly leading the rich life, Kathy analyzed, other than living in a half-furnished, half-closed-off house in Greenwich. Phil's sisters both had full-time domestic help, drove Cadillac convertibles, wore shockingly expensive clothes, vacationed at Palm Beach in the winter and Maine in the summer, and took cruises at frequent intervals. She recalled that Phil said his father was talking to brokers now about a house in Southampton.

She left the train at the 50th Street station in Brooklyn and headed for the apartment. She paused before the store for a moment. Her father was in absorbed conversation with a longtime customer while he simultaneously made a soda. They'd be arguing about politics as usual, she thought affectionately. Oh, it felt good to be standing here again!

"Kathy!" He'd seen her. "I'll be right there." He hurried from behind the counter with outstretched arms. "Mom went upstairs a few minutes ago. You'll have lunch with her and Aunt Sophie, then Mom will come down and I'll come up. And how's Jesse?" His face lighted with love.

"Oh, he's fine. He's got another tooth coming in. And last night he tried to pull himself up in the crib."

"In such a rush to walk. Like you, Kathy." His face lighted in reminiscence. "But go on upstairs. I'll see you later."

Aunt Sophie had lunch ready on the gas range. For a few minutes they were caught up in greetings, then the two older women were plying her with questions about Jesse.

"Such an angel!" Aunt Sophie glowed. "I tell the neighbors. They've never seen a baby like Jesse."

Mom never said anything that reflected badly on Julius and Bella, yet Kathy sensed her mother's disapproval. Mom knew Phil's parents were not the normal, doting grandparents. For a man who was so anxious for a grandson, Kathy thought bitterly, Julius was a cold grandfather. Even with his granddaughters he was cold. For the business he had warmth.

Feeling herself enriched with their love—but mindful of the time—Kathy left her mother and Aunt Sophie a little past two, and stopped by the store again for a final embrace from her father. For a moment she considered calling Phil, then dismissed the thought. He'd be at his parents' house with Jesse. Clara would have taken over by now. From little things that Phil said now and then she surmised that Clara had been more of a parent to Phil than either his mother or father.

Marge was waiting for her at Saks.

"Remember when we were too intimidated even to go beyond the first floor of Saks?" Marge reminisced. "We've come up in the world since the Depression."

Shuddering at the price tags, Kathy debated between two dresses. With Marge's approval—and she regarded Marge's clothes sense as impeccable—she chose the ivory brocade, with tiny nipped-in waist and the billowing skirt of Dior's New Look.

"Kathy, you look sensational," Marge approved. "Phil's sisters will hate you."

"I can't believe I'm spending so much money," she whispered, while they waited for the saleswoman to return with her charge slip. At Marge's suggestion she had instructed that the dress be sent to Greenwich. The ultimate touch of luxury, she thought with giddy pleasure.

With an eye to the time, they lingered briefly on the first floor, and on impulse Kathy bought the perfect small evening bag to accompany the dress.

"You have a flair for clothes," Marge decided as they left the store to walk north to the Plaza to meet Rhoda. "The two of us should open a shop someday. An expensive shop."

"Is that what you plan to do when you go out to San Francisco?" Kathy asked wistfully. She hated to think of a whole continent between the two of them.

"If I could find somebody to back me up," Marge drawled. "You think Julius Kohn would be interested?"

"Only if he could collect in your bed," Kathy guessed. "You said he was the worst wolf on Seventh Avenue." At disconcerting intervals she remembered the long blond hair she'd discovered on Phil's shoulder, and the scent of sultry perfume. But Phil wasn't his father. It was ridiculous of her to worry that he was sleeping around. "We'd better walk faster, Marge." She tried to dismiss the troublesome vision of Phil in bed with a beautiful blond model. "We don't want to be late."

"I'm so bloody cold," Marge complained. "If I ever strike it rich, the first thing I'll buy is a mink coat."

"You gave up on your muskrat?" Kathy joshed.

"It gave up on me. I wear it, and I look like an oversized dead rat." Marge was speculative for a moment. "When's your father-in-law going to loosen up and give you a mink coat?"

"Marge, he gave us a house and living room and dining room furniture—and the TV set."

"That was for Phil's benefit," Marge said bluntly.

"If I could afford the price, he'd probably sell me a mink wholesale," Kathy laughed. "But I'm not sure I want a fur coat."

"Are you kidding?" Marge pulled the collar of her black

cloth coat more closely about her throat. "Every woman loves furs."

"I'm not sure I do. Oh, furs are gorgeous," Kathy conceded. "But the thought of walking around with furs that used to be on some wild animals' backs bothers me."

"Let Julius Kohn present you with a gorgeous mink, and you'll change your mind," Marge predicted. "There's something so sexy about a mink coat."

Rhoda was waiting for them with an air of frenetic gaiety and prodded them into the Palm Court. All three relished the elegance of their surroundings. Not until the waiter left with their orders did Rhoda abandon her convivial smile.

"Rhoda, is something wrong?" Kathy asked solicitously.

"Oh, something is wrong," she conceded. "Wrong with my thinking."

"You had a fight with Derek," Marge guessed. "Honey, you know actors are temperamental."

"He's been offered a Hollywood contract," Rhoda told them. "He's given notice to the producer, and he's heading west in three weeks. We're all washed up. 'I don't think this is the time for me to tie myself down,' " she mimicked caustically.

"Oh, Rhoda." Kathy was cold with shock.

"Why do so many women fall in love with the wrong men? Maybe it isn't love," Rhoda said after a moment. "Maybe it's just old-fashioned lust."

"It's not the first time you've broken off with a man," Kathy reminded. "You'll hurt for a while, but somebody else will come along."

"I had a crush for a while on David," Rhoda reminisced. "But, of course, he couldn't see anybody but you."

Kathy tensed, her face growing hot. She didn't want to remember those beautiful weeks with David, before Phil came to Hamburg.

"I seem to recall your having a great time with Frank. You snap back fast," Kathy reminded with a cajoling smile.

"Frank was fun," Kathy admitted. "But we both knew

that was just a fling." She squinted in thought. "Where was Frank going after Hamburg?"

"To Alaska, I think," Kathy said. "He wanted to write a series of articles about wildlife reserves."

"You see?" Rhoda's laughter was mixed with irony. "Every man I go for runs off into the wild blue yonder."

On the long train ride back to Greenwich Kathy's thoughts focused on what Rhoda had said. *"Why do so many women fall in love with the wrong men? Maybe it isn't love. Maybe it's just lust."*

She'd convinced herself she was in love with Phil. Later, she'd laughed and said she was obsessed by him. Had it been just loneliness and frustration? And lust?

She'd wanted David to make love to her. His eyes had said so much, but he'd never touched her. And then, when Phil arrived in Hamburg, he seemed to back away as though in relief.

She'd been flattered by Phil's attentions, she analyzed. And, yes, he excited her physically. All she thought about after that weekend in Paris was how wonderful it was in bed with him. But that was *all* they had together. And now— these last months—something had gone out of their love-making. It was just part of their Saturday ritual.

David and she had met at the wrong time in their lives.

== Chapter 11

David stood on the deck of the New York–bound, newly refurbished *Queen Mary* and tried to gear himself for this brief return to the United States. He would linger in New York for two days, then head for Boston, where he had been invited to read a paper on his nutrition research before a prestigious gathering. He'd endured several sleepless nights before he agreed to accept the invitation.

He'd never felt comfortable in Berlin during these two years since Hamburg, he admitted to himself. How could he when he was constantly assaulted by memories? Always that sense of guilt that he was alive when the rest of the family had perished. He was surviving by burying himself in research. Thank God, so much of his father's research had been preserved. And he had been welcomed by the research community. A crucial problem in postwar Europe was malnutrition.

Sometimes he asked himself if it was wrong to spend so many long hours in the laboratory and only a few hours each night in his gratuitous medical practice, geared to Jews returning from exile. And always he remembered the agonizing hours when he had toured Bergen-Belsen. The good memories were the weeks he had spent with the Hamburg group, because Kathy had been part of that.

So often he thought about Kathy. Worried about her because he knew Phil so well. It had been a terrible mistake to back off when Phil arrived. Kathy was the only woman he'd ever love. But he had been too caught up in grief to say what he should have said.

It had been a painful shock when Aunt Bella sent him the invitation to Phil and Kathy's wedding. He hadn't expected that. And now there was a baby. He'd have to see the family while in the States. Would he see Kathy? The possibility was both exhilarating and terrifying.

"Our last night aboard," said a friendly male voice, intruding on his thoughts. David turned to face a fellow passenger with whom he'd spent many hours in discussion about the Cold War. "There's always something sad about that to me."

"The days and nights aboard ship are like an escape from reality," David mused. His whole life these last two years was an escape from reality. "We hit land, and we have to face the real world."

When the ship docked, David went directly to a small hotel on the Upper West Side where he knew an inexpensive room was being held for him. He felt at home here, more than he ever did in Berlin. Were Kathy and Phil living in Manhattan or up in Greenwich? All at once the months in Hamburg seemed just behind him. *Was it truly two years since he had seen Kathy?*

In the morning he awoke early and went to a Broadway cafeteria for breakfast. David marveled at the abundance of food after the scarcity and long lines in Berlin. Because his working schedule—between the lab and his after-hours practice—was so hectic, he'd never got around to writing home of his arrival. He'd call Uncle Julius in half an hour, he decided, enjoying the luxury of a second cup of coffee in the cafeteria. In Berlin, he remembered, a pound of coffee could cost 600 marks on the black market—two months' salary for a white-collar worker.

"David! Where are you?" Julius asked in surprised welcome when the switchboard put him through. David had forgotten his private number.

"In New York, Uncle Julius. Just for a couple of days. I'm on my way to Boston to read a paper on nutrition."

"You'll come home with me. You arrived just in time for my sixtieth birthday. Bella's throwing a big party tonight. Hey, you'll need a tux," he remembered. "The party's at the house, but it's formal. You can rent one at—"

"It's all right, I have a tux with me," David told him. "There's a formal dinner in Boston—"

"You'll stay at the house for a few days," Julius said. "We'll—"

"I'll have to leave for Boston tomorrow," David apologized. "I'm on a tight schedule."

"If you came all the way to this country to deliver a paper, you must be doing all right, David," Julius joshed.

"I'm pleased with the research. No money in sight," he laughed. Knowing that money was what commanded respect from Julius Kohn.

"I'll call Bella and tell her the news. Don't worry about this being a last-minute deal," he said anticipating David's thought. "Bella will handle table arrangements. And you know we always have guest rooms ready. And wait till you see my grandson," he boasted. "He's going to be a real lady-killer."

They talked a few moments more, until the switchboard operator broke in to say that Julius had a long-distance call.

"Be here at five, David. You'll drive up to Greenwich with Phil and me."

Nude beneath her robe—because the elegant designer evening dress that lay across the bed had a built-in corset to cinch in the waist and push up the bosom—Kathy carefully applied the final touches to her makeup. Clara had arrived early to bathe Jesse and put him to bed. As usual on special occasions, she would baby-sit.

Kathy sighed in relief when she heard the car pull up before the house. Bella was worried that Phil and Julius might be delayed in Friday night traffic. Dinner was to be served at 8 P.M. sharp.

"Kathy!" Phil yelled exuberantly as he strode toward their bedroom. "You'll never guess who's in town!"

"Who's in town?" She turned around from the mirror to face him.

"Wow! You look sensational."

"Who's in town?" she asked again, holding up her face for the routine homecoming kiss.

"I'm not going to spoil all that," he demurred, then continued. "David's here. He drove out with Dad and me. He'll be at the party."

"What's he doing in this country?" *She'd see David tonight.* Her mind shot back to that night when he'd said good-bye in Hamburg. She'd felt such a sense of loss, knowing he wouldn't be a part of her life anymore. "Is he moving back to New York?"

"He's just here for a few days. He's reading a paper at some medical convention in Boston." Phil began to undress. His tux was already laid out across the bed. "He'll stay out here till late tomorrow morning, then head for Boston. After that, it's back to Berlin."

"His research must be going well if he was invited to read a paper at a medical convention. How exciting for him, Phil!" Now she was ambivalent about seeing David. Part of her was eager to see him, to talk with him. Part of her was fearful of seeing him. She was wary of recalling those early weeks in Hamburg, before Phil had invaded their lives.

"You know David," Phil drawled, a hint of condescension in his voice. "Always so bloody serious about his work." He paused in his dressing to gaze quizzically at Kathy. "I always suspected he had a thing for you."

"Phil, he and I were a team." Kathy forced herself to appear amused. "Both of us were terribly involved in what we were doing in Hamburg."

"Get into your dress and let's move," he said in high spirits. "I want to give Dad his present before the bash begins."

"What are you giving him?" Kathy asked curiously.

"Something he'll appreciate." Phil grinned. "Remember when you bought a painting in Montmartre?"

"That scene of a sidewalk in Montmartre," she remembered. It hung in her parents' bedroom.

"I bought a canvas—I could pack it easier without a frame. It's been lying in my knapsack ever since we got back. The old man will love it. He'll be sure it's an unknown masterpiece." He chuckled. "You know Dad."

"Phil, don't hint that it is," she scolded.

"He'll have fun with it." He brushed aside her misgivings. "Oh, wear that perfume my folks gave you for our anniversary," he said.

"I'm wearing it," she told him. Miss Dior.

Chilly in her long black velvet cape over her ivory brocade gown, Kathy ran from house to car.

"I'll turn the heat on in a couple of minutes," Phil said with a frown as he reached for the ignition. She knew he was annoyed that his father had not presented her with a Kohn fur. Didn't Phil understand his father disliked her?

As Phil planned, they arrived at the house before any of the guests. Only his father was downstairs. In what Bella referred to as the family sitting room but Julius called the library—with a pair of bookcases displaying exquisitely bound books that were never read, to judge by their spines— the two men exchanged ribald jokes about Julius's sixtieth birthday, and then Phil presented his birthday gift.

"From your Paris trip?" Julius asked cagily, squinting at the illegible signature.

Phil nodded.

"I was saving it for a special occasion," he bragged. "I can't say it's an old masterpiece, but one of these days it could be very valuable."

Now Julius turned his attention to Kathy.

"Terrific dress," he approved. "Classy."

"It should be for what it cost me." Phil dropped an arm about her waist. Where was David, Kathy wondered. Her eyes strayed at intervals to the doorway. "I told her, go to Saks and buy a designer dress."

"Ah, here's David," Julius said expansively. "The family intellectual."

Kathy lifted her face with a smile of welcome. How handsome he looked in evening dress. And so distinguished, though barely thirty.

"David, how wonderful to see you!" Impulsively she held her arms out to him.

"Beautiful as ever," he said quietly and kissed her on the cheek.

"You two knew each other in Hamburg," Julius recalled. "If not for you, David, Phil wouldn't have met Kathy."

"That's right," Phil murmured.

Kathy intercepted a silent, smug exchange between Phil and his father. And with sudden clarity she understood. Phil had told his father that David had been interested in her. Everybody in the group had thought so, but David never uttered one word to indicate that. Even his asking her to wear the jeweled brooch had been out of nostalgia for home. *Was that why Phil had chased after her?* To show he could take her away from David? No, she rebuked herself. She was being melodramatic.

"David! Oh, how good it is to see you!" Bella strode into the room with outstretched arms, her black velvet dinner dress perfectly setting off the magnificent diamond necklace she wore.

"Aunt Bella, you look marvelous." David and she exchanged an affectionate embrace. The obvious warmth between them surprised Kathy.

Now Bella turned to her husband.

"Julius, did you tell Wally to exchange the bottles of

champagne on the tables?" She continued without waiting for his answer. "We can't serve that swill at a dinner party."

"I should waste our fine champagne on a party?" Julius gestured his disdain with one pudgy hand.

"I've told Wally to replace them." Her eyes dared him to fight her on this. "That's all right for your Christmas party at the business."

"David, I want to show you my paintings." Julius brought a hand to David's elbow. "I bought them from a German refugee who smuggled them into the country. They used to hang in a famous museum."

"I don't know why the girls haven't arrived," Bella said when she and Kathy were alone. "I want them to check out everything before the others arrive."

"I'm sure everything is fine." Kathy smiled in encouragement. "And your necklace is exquisite."

"I never really enjoy wearing it." Bella sat on the burgundy velvet sofa. "Julius had it made up from diamonds he'd bought. Again," she said drily, "from German refugees. Some family who managed to escape before Hitler closed in on them. Julius was happy because he bought them for a fraction of their worth."

"At least they escaped with their lives."

"I never wear the necklace without thinking about them." This was a Bella whom Kathy had never seen. She would not have expected this sensitivity. "It was the summer of 1937, when Jews had been deprived of all their rights. Julius said the family had sold their possessions secretly, then bought diamonds because they were the most easily smuggled out of the country."

All at once Kathy was hearing David's voice, talking about how at a barbed-wire fence in Salzburg his father had slipped a bag of diamonds to him while the border guards were in private conversation. Everything the family still owned had been sold to buy those diamonds. The money had put David through medical school.

Julius had told David he sold the diamonds to acquaintances, who had paid top-price, and David had been so grateful for his efforts. But Bella just said *"Julius was happy because he bought them for a fraction of their worth."* No doubt in Kathy's mind that the diamonds Bella wore about her throat were those that David's father had given him. *Julius Kohn had cheated his own cousin.*

Within twenty minutes the lower floor of the senior Kohns' home was alive with conviviality. The women were expensively dressed; most of the men wore tuxes under duress. Few of the guests resided in Greenwich, Kathy noted, and remembered Bella's remark at a family dinner that the town was integrated until 5 P.M., when non-Jews and Jews went their separate ways. It was fine for all Greenwich ladies to share in volunteer work, garden parties, benefit luncheons, and teas. After 5 P.M. the fraternization ceased.

The formal dining room, rarely used more than once a year and capable of seating thirty-six, had been dismantled for the occasion. Five tables, each accommodating eight diners, had been brought in early in the day. An extra setting for David had been laid at the family table.

Now waiters bustled about the tables, serving the elaborate meal the caterer had devised. The scent of pink, white, and red roses was almost sickeningly sweet. A quartet of musicians played in the background, in no way interfering with the lively conversation. Sitting between Phil and David, Kathy spoke little, ever conscious of David's nearness.

"American soldiers' wives are managing," David said in response to a question from Bella. "But believe me," he smiled whimsically, "without a sense of humor they'd never make it. No one can say that the Americans are welcome in Berlin."

"In the two years since we were there, David," Kathy asked, "has there been much rebuilding?"

"Somebody described the Unter den Linden as a mile-long coffin," he recalled. For an electric instant his eyes met hers, and she knew he was remembering their day in Berlin.

"There are efforts to rebuild, but it's a long, drawn-out process."

"What about the people?" Brenda's husband Eli—the accountant—asked. "Has the war changed their thinking?"

"Most Germans consider themselves martyrs." Bitterness colored David's voice. "They don't feel humiliated, as you'd expect. As they're the first to admit, they still 'think brown'—*Braunchaus* or Nazi. Except, of course, for returning Jews and a small anti-Fascist group that always hated Hitler. They're forever complaining," David continued with distaste, "about all they've lost. Never for a moment thinking of what anguish they inflicted on others. Maybe a later generation will understand. Not this one. This one says 'that was the war, this is the peace'—and blames the Allies for everything that goes wrong."

"What about inflation, David?" Julius asked.

"It's so wild that Berlin doctors have gotten together to ask for a change in the German penal code regarding abortion. Right now it's illegal, but we want to make it legal during the first three months of pregnancy because so many women are too malnourished to be able to nurse their babies when they're born."

"What about the schools?" Brenda asked with a touch of arrogance. "Are German children being taught about the war?"

"Not at all. Whatever is taught would have to be approved by all four Allied *Kommandaturen.* And nobody agrees. And talking about inflation," David pinpointed, "it's so bad. School books cost a fortune—one book can cost 150 marks. At the university level most students skip classes at least twice a week to work on the black market—the only way they can survive."

"Anything great available on the black market?" Julius's eyes lighted.

"Most Berliners who've come through the war with anything good—and unbroken—are selling it piece by piece just to buy food. Biedermeier furniture, fine white Meissen porcelain—"

"Can you pick up some of that and ship it to us?" Julius asked avidly.

"Julius, no," Bella objected. "I couldn't live with it."

Kathy looked upon her mother-in-law with fresh comprehension. She remembered Marge's remark that Julius Kohn "has a reputation for being the biggest wolf on Seventh Avenue." Bella Kohn—early in her marriage, Kathy suspected—knew about her husband's infidelities. She had built a shallow little world that allowed her to survive in that marriage.

"My wife's so delicate," Julius said with sarcasm and for an instant hostility threatened to break through the veneer both cultivated.

"What about theater in Berlin?" Kathy rushed to brush away the awkward moment. "I read somewhere that *Three Men on a Horse* is a big hit in the U.S. sector."

"It's been running for months," David said. "A lot of plays are running, though the quality of acting isn't always good. I go occasionally. It's interesting how so many nationalities—German, Russian, American, French, British, Brazilian—can sit side by side in the theater and be so friendly. That's not the usual scene in Berlin."

"What's this business with Russia and Czechoslovakia?" Milton—Gail's husband—asked David.

"You know what has just happened." David smiled ruefully. "Stalin has taken over Czechoslovakia. The Communists won 114 of 300 seats in the national assembly almost two years ago—now the Commies have revolted. Stalin rules."

"The Russians are out to take over the world," Milton said gloomily. "The handwriting is on the wall."

"Berlin is in for bad times," David predicted. "Stalin is paranoid about a rebuilding of Germany. He'd do anything to stop its recovery."

"Enough of politics," Bella decreed. "This is a birthday

party. Don't you all think Gail did a beautiful job with the flowers?"

While guests lingered over coffee, Phil brought out the latest collection of snapshots of Jesse to pass around the table. When they reached David, Kathy involuntarily turned to him. She basked in the warmth and tenderness she saw on his face as he slowly inspected each snapshot.

"You must be very happy." David's eyes moved from Kathy to Phil.

"Yes," Kathy lied. Phil dropped an arm about her shoulders in a gesture of possession. For a while they were happy. What happened—what was happening—to their marriage?

"Come over to the house tomorrow before you head for Boston and see the little character," Phil invited. "He's something."

"I'd like that very much," David said softly.

Sunlight poured into the first-floor room designated "Jesse's playroom." While Jesse embraced his latest stuffed animal ordered from F.A.O. Schwarz by Julius, Kathy folded diapers and tried to stifle yawns. Though they had not arrived home until past 1 A.M., she had known Jesse would be wide awake and eager for breakfast in five hours. Phil would sleep till noon.

Kathy paused as she saw a limousine turn into the driveway. That was Wally driving David over to see Jesse, she thought. Her heart began to pound.

"I'll be right back, Jesse," she soothed and darted from the room and down the hall to the front door. She'd been waiting subconsciously all morning for David to appear. She'd discarded three blouses before she chose the tailored gray cotton that went so well with her gray slacks. Fighting for poise when she was a shambles inside, she reached to open the door. "I wasn't sure you'd wake up in time to come over," she said as David approached.

"I couldn't leave Greenwich without seeing your son,"

he chided. Behind that casual facade he was tense, Kathy knew. "Great party last night."

"Yes, it was." Small talk because there was so much they could not allow themselves to say. But as always David's eyes spoke with such eloquence. "You chose the right time to arrive."

"I almost didn't come," he said, and his face softened at the baby sounds that filtered down the hall. "Almost didn't come to the States," he emphasized as they walked toward the playroom. "There's so much to do in Berlin. But the Boston convention seemed important."

"I'm glad you came, David," she said. "And here's Jesse." With a surge of maternal love she reached to scoop him up in her arms.

"You looked like this at his age," David said after a moment. "The same bone structure, the same eyes, the same mouth."

"He's the image of my father. Of course, everybody says I look just like Dad." Her parents and Aunt Sophie would like David, she thought. She always felt a kind of wariness in them toward Phil, despite his potent charm.

"Would he come to me?" David asked, almost shyly.

"Of course." This was unreal, to be standing here with David this way. "Jesse, this is your Uncle David—"

David reached to take Jesse in his arms. Gently so as not to frighten him. The atmosphere in the room suddenly was unbearably tense. Without David's saying a word she knew his thoughts. This could have been his child. Their child. But, she told herself yet again, the timing for them had been all wrong.

"I imagine Phil's still asleep." David chuckled. "He was always a great one for sleeping late."

"He's never up before noon on Saturdays." Kathy fought an urge to reach out and touch David. "I could wake him—"

"No, let him sleep. I have to leave in a few moments. Wally's waiting to drive me to Stamford to catch my train."

David hugged Jesse for a moment, then handed him back to Kathy. "Enjoy and cherish him. Nothing is so important as family."

With Jesse in her arms, Kathy stood at the window and watched David walk back to the car and climb inside. Tears blurred her vision as the limousine moved down the driveway and out onto the road. She felt that a part of her had just died.

= Chapter 12

As Phil's trip through the Midwest grew close, Kathy realized that the business monopolized his thinking. Their conversation in the brief time they shared during the week was always one-sided: Phil reported on his latest confrontation with his father about some new approach for the business. With astonishing frequency Phil was winning. There was no need for her to contribute to the talk, she thought. All Phil wanted was an audience.

Now on weekends Phil would disappear for hours to huddle with his father. He always came home exhilarated. He was the little boy who was showing his father how great he could be.

Occasionally Kathy asked herself if Phil *was* with his father. She was too proud—too guilty at such thoughts—to check this out.

"As soon as I finish the swing through the Midwest," he told her on a mid-March night when the threat of snow hung over the area, "we'll start thinking in terms of a trunk show. Probably in early September, right after the New York fashion show. It works for the garment industry. Why not for furs?" It was a rhetorical question. No reply was expected of her.

She had given up trying to persuade him to postpone the trip. She worried about his flying in the sometimes treacherous March weather. But he was impatient to be out in the field. It was as though he had to show his father what an asset he was to Julius Kohn Furs.

"Remember the charity dinner tomorrow night," she said as she brought dessert to the table. "If we do get snow, maybe you should start out early from the city. Your father and mother are going, too."

"I doubt that I can make it." He had forgotten the dinner, Kathy understood. "I'll be working late with the publicity team tomorrow night." At intervals now he remained in the city to work well into the evening, taking the train to Greenwich and coming home from the station by cab. He'd always said he'd move back to Manhattan if he had to travel by train. "Dad and Mother will go. They never miss one of those bashes."

"I'll call and cancel the baby-sitter." Occasionally Clara would sit, but she admitted the years were catching up with her and she was tired the next morning.

"You can go with my parents." All at once Phil seemed self-conscious. "They'll pick you up and bring you home."

"I'd just as soon not." She debated for a moment about telling him tonight that she'd taken her road test. No, wait and see if she'd passed.

He pushed back his chair and yawned broadly.

"I'm beat. I'll watch a half-hour of TV and hit the sack."

While Phil went into the living room, she carried the dishes into the kitchen, washed them, and stacked them in the rack to dry. She debated about running a mop across the kitchen floor, then decided to leave it until tomorrow. On Fridays now Lottie Mae came in to clean. She smiled, remembering how Bella had brought this about. *"Phil, Kathy needs a woman in to clean once a week. I'll line someone up for her."* Her mother-in-law was accepting her. Not

Julius—he still resented her facing up to him about a big wedding.

In the living room she walked over to turn off the TV. Phil was sprawled across the sofa, asleep.

"Phil—" She frowned at the glass on the floor beside the sofa. Like his father, he'd begun to take a straight shot of Scotch after dinner. It was beginning to show in that tiny roll around his waist. "Phil, wake up and go to bed—"

Later, lying awake while Phil snored beside her, Kathy worried about the road test. It would be awful if she didn't pass. Mom, too, said she had to learn to drive. It wasn't good to be alone in the house with Jesse without a car. Living in Greenwich wasn't like living in Levittown. She had never exchanged more than a few words about the weather with any of the neighbors.

The following morning her driver's license appeared in the mail. She was jubilant, yet dreading the confrontation with Phil. She'd worry about that later, she decided in a surge of pleasure. She phoned home and told Aunt Sophie she had her license.

"Good," Sophie approved. "Twenty years ago I told your mother she should know how to drive. Why is it always the man who sits behind the wheel?" Not that the Ross family had owned a car since Dad's secondhand Chevy collapsed of old age in the early days of the Depression.

Ten minutes later her mother called to congratulate Kathy.

"Now you won't be stuck in the house so much," her mother comforted. She'd never complained about that, Kathy thought, but Mom understood. "You'll make friends out there."

She phoned Marge, in her last week on the job before heading for San Francisco, and on impulse invited her to come out to stay for a couple of days before leaving town.

"In the middle of the week?" Marge asked, and Kathy understood she'd prefer avoiding Phil for most of the time.

"Great. I'll pick you up at the station," she said blithely.

"We need some time together before you leave town. I'm going to miss you like hell."

While Jesse sprawled contentedly in the playpen—installed now in a corner of the kitchen—she prepared a dinner that featured Phil's favorite dishes. She'd set up the card table, and they'd eat before a roaring fire. She remembered the first time she and Phil had made love—before a fireplace in that little house at the edge of Paris. *What had happened to the magic she'd felt then?*

She breathed a sigh of relief when she heard the car pull up in front of the house. The roast would have been overdone if Phil had not come home on time tonight. But he'd worked late last night, and he didn't do that two days in a row.

Phil came into the house and down the hall to the kitchen. After the routine kiss and comment about the traffic on the Merritt Parkway, he scooped up sleeper-clad Jesse from the playpen and headed upstairs for the nursery. Kathy hurried into the living room to set up the card table before the fireplace, lit the crumpled newspaper that laced the chunks of log and kindling wood in the grate. Phil would roughhouse with Jesse for a few minutes until Jesse's eyes would begin to flutter in drowsiness. Then he would put him in his crib and come downstairs for dinner.

Kathy waited until they'd eaten and she'd taken the dishes out to the kitchen to tell Phil her news.

"I wanted it to be a surprise for you," she told him. "I was scared I'd fail the test. So many people fail the first one." *Why was she rattling on this way?* "But I passed it. My driver's license arrived in the morning's mail."

"Who taught you to drive?" He was staring at her as though she'd committed some monstrous act.

"The driving school." She hesitated. "I borrowed the money from the emergency fund. I wanted to surprise you," she stammered.

"You took money from my emergency fund?"

"I thought it was *our* emergency fund." All at once anger

welled in her. Why did she have to apologize to her husband this way?

Phil reached into his pocket, pulled out his car keys. "I have another set in the car." Now he was taking money from his wallet. "Here, you buy the groceries this week. You don't need to drag me over to the supermarket anymore." Radiating hostility, he tossed bills onto the coffee table, pushed back his chair and crossed to the television set. He ignored her completely for the next few hours until he sullenly went to bed.

Kathy was happy that Bella was taking more interest in her grandson. Two or three afternoons a week she drove over to spend an hour with Kathy and Jesse. Now she made an effort to bring Kathy into some of the local socializing, though Brenda and Gail continued to ignore her.

Late in the spring Bella announced that she and Julius were driving out to Southampton on Saturdays to look at houses.

"If we find a place and buy it, we'll expect you and Jesse to come out for the summer along with the girls and their kids. Julius and Phil can commute from Southampton."

Three weekends later Julius gave a binder on a fifteen-room house right on the ocean at Southampton. Now he behaved, Kathy thought, as though the Southampton house was his own idea. He ordered Bella to hire a decorator to furnish the house. Kathy gathered from Phil that this had been at the persuasion of their new public relations woman, who hoped for a magazine spread built around "the charming Kohn estate at Southampton."

Kathy was pleased that she had persuaded her father to put his longtime friend Mannie in charge of the store one Sunday every month so that he could bring her mother and aunt out to the house for the day. On Sundays Phil slept till noon. After Sunday brunch he would drive to Julius's to spend much of the afternoon in conference with his father. Kathy explained to her family that Phil was pushing toward the partnership his father had promised him. She enjoyed having most of the day alone with her father and mother and aunt.

Rhoda came up for the Memorial Day weekend. Her depression over the breakup with Derek had receded. Now she was enthusiastic about having bumped into Frank at the Times Square BMT station. She was seeing him again.

"Just for fun," she told Kathy. "Remember what a great time I had with Frank in Hamburg?"

On impulse Kathy invited Rhoda to come up to Greenwich with Frank the following weekend. Why not? Phil would be flying to the Coast early Saturday morning to discuss a concession in a prestigious San Francisco store. It would be good to spend time with Rhoda and Frank. It would be like reliving those days in Hamburg, she thought sentimentally. But David was in Berlin.

Phil enjoyed these trips around the country, Kathy thought while she saw him off from the local airport for the flight to New York. He enjoyed flying around the country, entertaining important merchandising people out of town. It gave him a sense of power.

She waited until his plane lifted off the ground, then slid behind the wheel of the new Cadillac that Julius had presented to Phil as a "company car." She had hoped to inherit the old one as her very own—because she lived in fear of even the smallest dent on the Cadillac—but Julius had taken it to give as a bonus to his publicity woman.

Kathy drove away from the airport with a guilty sense of freedom. For eight days Phil would be away from Greenwich. And in an hour she'd be picking up Rhoda and Frank at the station.

At Idlewild Phil checked his luggage, then jumped into a taxi and headed for the city. He was taking a westbound flight tomorrow morning. Kathy wouldn't phone the Mark Hopkins to see if he'd arrived, he told himself with confidence. She'd be all wrapped up in her stupid houseguests.

Leila was still in bed when he used his key to let himself into the apartment.

"Hi," she drawled, naked beneath the blanket, sure Phil would be ready to jump into bed the moment he arrived.

"Any coffee?" he asked, shedding his jacket.

"Now?" she pouted.

"Now," he said. "Go on, don't be so lazy."

"All right," she said aggrievedly and tossed aside the blanket. Phil swatted her across the rump as she headed toward the closet kitchenette.

Leila had been a great lay at first, he thought while he watched her move with deliberate provocativeness about the kitchenette, a minuscule apron making a parody of her nakedness. Now she was beginning to irritate him with that constant yammering about introducing her to people in theater. He'd told her that Derek was his main connection, and right now Derek was out in Hollywood.

He undressed and sprawled on the bed, still warm from her body, exuding the heavy scent she favored. He'd leave the keys here today, seemingly accidental. He'd phone from San Francisco and tell the old man to fire her while he was away. Dad was trying so hard to get into the new publicity gal's pants. Maybe he could do what the old man couldn't.

"Coffee, sir," Leila flipped.

Phil reached for the cup, took a few sips, then set it down on the night table. Just thinking about that sexy publicity gal got him hot.

"Come on, baby. Show me how good you are."

On June 24th the civilized world was alarmed to learn that Stalin had imposed a blockade on Berlin. Earlier the Communist nation had tried to induce inflation in the western zone of Germany in an effort to thwart recovery. The Russians had interrupted rail traffic between Berlin and West Germany for two days, stopped highway bridge traffic, and now this.

"Phil, what's going to happen now?" Kathy asked him

anxiously when he came home from the city that evening. *How would this affect David?*

"Truman will be afraid to make a move," Phil guessed. "He doesn't want to start another war."

"But if Berlin is blockaded, how will the people get food? How long can the city survive?"

"They'll find a way to fly in food." Phil was impatient with her. "West Berlin has two airports. It may be tough, but the Allies will figure a way out."

Two days later all the Kohns moved into the spectacular fifteen-room house in Southampton for the summer. Bella had insisted that the decorator be given a free hand, and Kathy was enchanted by the results.

Brenda and Gail's older daughters went off to camp. A summer nursemaid was hired to take care of the two younger daughters and Jesse, though Kathy took on most of his care. Jesse was the focal point of her existence, the source of her joy in life. Her reason for being, she told herself.

Kathy relished her early morning strolls along the beach while the others slept. To her the ocean was mesmerizing, to be worshipped afresh each day. It was as though, for a little while, she walked alone with God, she thought.

Julius was furious when he discovered that, despite his space-grabbing publicity woman and the prestige of Julius Kohn Furs, he was not likely to be invited to join the choice clubs. The anti-Semitism of earlier resort society still lingered in Southampton's "Old Society." Families that had reluctantly survived without footmen during World War II and recognized that it would be impossible to replace them in the postwar era had not opened their minds—or their homes—to Jewish arrivals. A Pulitzer, a Belmont, an Otto Kahn might be welcomed in their sacred enclaves. Not a Julius Kohn.

When the Southampton household assembled on their third Saturday for what was becoming a ritual brunch, Brenda and Gail announced that they were taking off for

Europe for three weeks. Their husbands exchanged a glance of resignation. They'd obviously fought a losing battle.

"We'll arrive in Paris in time for the couture shows." Brenda's usual petulance had given way to a glow of triumph. Brenda and Gail would have been attractive if they weren't forever sulking over some grievance, real or imagined, Kathy thought. "Our travel agent managed to get us reservations at the Ritz. Then we'll spend some time in Cannes. At the Carlton. They have an exciting summer season there now."

"How do you expect to spend time in Paris and Cannes?" Phil challenged. "Each way by ship will—"

"We're flying," Gail announced. "We've never flown to Europe before. Everybody's flying these days," she forestalled her mother's objections. "Air France has nine flights a week between New York and Paris. We're taking the Golden Comet—it's an all-sleeper flight that leaves every Saturday."

"We make way-stops at Gander, Newfoundland, and Shannon, Ireland," Brenda picked up. "Then we'll fly from Paris to Nice. It's much more chic than spending the summer here."

At Phil's advice—derived from a sarcastic remark about Southampton anti-Semitism made by Kathy—Julius ordered Bella to give one of the most extravagant parties of the season. Phil realized—as Kathy had said—that "Old Society" might not come calling, but monied café society would rush to socialize where champagne and caviar were lavishly offered them. Already Phil was negotiating through their publicity woman with post-debutantes to model in the fall charity show.

Julius viewed the horde of expensively garbed guests with savage pleasure. He was especially pleased by the presence of syndicated columnist "Cholly Knickerbocker"—in private life Igor Cassini—which meant a column item about the party. A chauffeured limousine had been sent to bring the columnist to Southampton and to return him to Manhattan. Roz had arranged this coup. Their publicity gal was a smart little bitch, even if she was a *gonif*. Every month he flinched at her expense account billing.

Kathy would have liked to invite her parents and Aunt Sophie to spend a weekend at the Southampton house, but there was no communication between her family and Phil's. Instead, she took Jesse and went to Borough Park for a weekend in early August. She had forgotten how oppressively hot the city could be; but Jesse didn't seem to mind, she realized gratefully. He was fascinated by the train, the bustle of the city, their taxi ride from Grand Central to Borough Park. And he adored being fussed over by her family.

"So," Aunt Sophie demanded as they settled at the table for Friday dinner while Jesse slept in Kathy's old room in the crib kept for such times. "What do you think of Southampton?"

"The beach, the ocean, they're breathtaking," Kathy's face reflected her love. "The house is like a movie set."

"Good movie set or bad?" her father asked.

"Beautiful," she emphasized. "I'm sure Julius is disappointed, though. For what he spent he probably expected a replica of the palace at Versailles."

"What about anti-Semitism?" Aunt Sophie's smile was wry. "Has that changed on the fancy resort circuit?"

"Not in what is known as 'Old Society,'" Kathy told her aunt, for whom she knew this was ever a vital issue. "And Jews are not welcome at the Beach Club or the Meadow Club. But some very socially important—very wealthy—people came to Bella's party. I know she was nervous that it would be a fiasco."

"Free food, free liquor?" Her father chuckled. "They come. But we all know the other side." Now he was serious. "The private clubs all over the country. Right here in New York, in Minneapolis, Dallas, Atlanta, San Francisco—all over." He waved a hand in contempt. "Kathy, you've heard the stories about Saratoga and Palm Beach and other fancy resorts where Jews are not welcome in certain hotels. I always say, 'Who needs them?' "

"You love the ocean," Aunt Sophie said. "Forget about the Beach Club and the Meadow Club. Walk on the beach, swim in the ocean. Enjoy, darling." She glanced about the table with an air of satisfaction. "We watched while you built sand castles at Coney Island. Now Jesse will learn to build sand castles on Southampton Beach."

= Chapter 13

Immediately after Labor Day the company presented its first designer furs collection at a lavish fashion show, where the models were last season's top debutantes and three expected to be the top debutantes of the coming season. Phil gloried in hosting the event. Kathy was unable to attend because Jesse was down with a bad cold. She refused to leave him in the care of a baby-sitter.

Phil's stock with his father was riding high. Now he was away from home more than he was there. Reluctantly Julius agreed to heavy advertising, but was pleased when he saw this bear results. For Christmas Phil received a huge bonus, which he immediately spent on furniture for the house. Kathy went with him on shopping expeditions, but it quickly became clear that *he* would make the decisions.

In the beginning of the new year—again at Bella's insistence—Julius gave Phil a raise that permitted the hiring of a live-in nursemaid for Jesse.

"How does it look to the neighbors to see Kathy with so little domestic help?" Bella had reproached her husband in Phil and Kathy's presence, knowing this approach would elicit results. "Do you want them to think you're too cheap to pay your son a decent salary?"

Marge flew home for a week in March. Kathy was impatient to see her. She invited her to come out for a weekend and then extended the same invitation to Rhoda and Frank. Two of the bedrooms had been furnished as guest rooms. Twin beds in one of them—Marge and Rhoda could share. Phil would be out of town so there had been no need to consult him.

Kathy arrived at the Greenwich station twenty minutes early in her eagerness to see the arriving trio. By the time they were at the house, Alice would have put Jesse to bed, she realized as she waited in the car. But they'd see him in the morning.

Then the train was pulling into the station. Kathy hurried from the car. In moments she was exchanging warm embraces with Marge and Rhoda and Frank. Oh, it was good to have them here!

"Look at that car!" Frank whistled in approval. "We'll live in style this weekend."

Now they were caught up in a lively discussion of Marge's job in San Francisco. It was a stopgap, Marge admitted; but she felt she was learning.

"One of these days I'll have my own collection," she bubbled. "It may take a while, but all good things take time."

Kathy had prepared dinner earlier in the evening, and it was being kept warm in the oven. A log was crackling in the fireplace of the recently furnished den. Of all the rooms in the house this was Kathy's favorite because of its casual air, in such contrast to the ornate decor of the rest of the house. Tonight, Kathy thought as they sat down at the dining room table, the house was alive with friendship and affection.

Inevitably table conversation turned to reminiscences about Hamburg. While Marge had not been there, she'd heard much about it. Like Kathy, Rhoda and Frank had lost touch with other members of the group except for

Brian, who always sent greeting cards on every holiday and included a gossipy letter about his latest activities.

"What about David?" Frank asked when they had transferred themselves into the den for coffee and liqueurs. "You ever hear from him, Kathy?"

"Not since he was here last February." *It seemed so long ago.* "He drops a note to my in-laws a couple of times a year. He seems all wrapped up in his research."

"Even with the airlift, it can't be too comfortable living in West Berlin," Rhoda said somberly.

"The first months of the blockade must have been awful." Kathy remembered her anxiety as the newspapers reported on the city's lack of food, the prospect of starvation hanging over the heads of West Berliners. Electricity, she recalled, had been rationed to two hours a day, and the population worried that the rain-filled summer would give way to an autumn and winter without fuel. "My mother-in-law told me David wrote that the airlift is preventing starvation, but there's still much malnutrition despite the food that gets through."

"It's a miracle how the airlift has built up," Frank said with infinite respect. "The Commies have to know they're beaten." He left the burgundy leather club chair to put another chunk of wood into the grate. "The end of the blockade can't be far off."

"It's incredible how the Russians are dominating our lives." Sharing the matching leather sofa with Kathy, Rhoda kicked off her shoes and tucked her legs beneath her. "Our Air Force, the RAF, and French fliers are all involved in frustrating the Russian blockade. And here in this country it's the House Un-American Activities Committee craziness. To listen to them, half the Hollywood actors and writers are Commies, intent on overthrowing our government."

"It's going to get worse before it gets better," Frank predicted.

"Frank, tell Kathy and Marge about your new job," Rhoda persuaded.

"It's not mine yet," he hedged, then grinned. "Well, it's mine except that some minor details have to be ironed out. I'm leaving the ranks of free-lance writers to become an editor." He paused, mockingly dramatic, then named a prestigious national magazine. "With a weekly paycheck."

"Frank, that's great!" Kathy turned to Marge. "Now we'll have to subscribe."

"He'll still find time to write an article now and then," Rhoda said encouragingly.

Kathy sensed that something lasting was building between Rhoda and Frank, and she was pleased. They would have some problems to work out—Rhoda was Jewish and Frank, Catholic—but they had something special going for them.

On an unseasonably warm June afternoon, Phil sat in his father's lushly furnished office with one leg thrown over a chair and listened while Roz Masters—their attractive and ambitious publicity woman—tried to make Julius understand that to tie in with a top-name French designer would cost high but would pay off.

"You've been working with a name designer, sure, but he's not one of the six 'greats,' " she pursued. "That'll put Julius Kohn Furs on a level with *haute couture,* but you'll be selling to a mass market. In *volume,* " she stressed.

"Why should I pay a royalty to this hot-shot French designer after I've paid for the design?" Julius was belligerent, but Phil knew he was weakening.

"Because that's the only way you can get him," Phil said bluntly.

"I can wangle a lot of newspaper and magazine space on the strength of that kind of tie-in," Roz said. "Even some radio and television time. Phil's good-looking and knows how to handle himself." Phil suppressed a smile. The old man didn't know *he* had got into Roz's bed. "He's a definite

asset. And while we're talking about assets, let's move Phil
and his wife into the Manhattan social scene. We'll zero in
on you and Bella on the charity circuit," she said diplomati-
cally to Julius. "Kathy's a beautiful girl. Good figure. Not
tall enough to be a model, but send her out with Phil, wearing a succession of Julius Kohn furs. Let Phil and Kathy
be your ambassadors."

Before they ended the meeting, Phil knew the business
was entering a new era. Roz was sharp. Kathy might have
been raised in Borough Park, but she had that Park Avenue
gentility that his sisters strived for but never quite achieved.
Roz would work with her. She'd be great.

His father was silent on much of the drive to Greenwich.
Phil knew not to disturb him. The old man was savoring
their new image. Instinct told him they wouldn't battle on
this.

"Phil, I want you to put out some feelers to a top-notch
French designer." Julius finally broke the silence. "Through
his business manager or lawyer or whatever. We'll sit down
with Roz and figure out who's our best bet, and if he says
'no,' move on to the next on the list. You'll go to Paris to
work out a deal," he plotted. "Take Kathy with you. Your
grandfather might turn over in his grave if he knew what
this was costing, but he'd be damn proud to have a guy at
the top of the heap designing for us."

"I'll give it top priority," Phil said briskly.

Damn! The old man was already thinking of it as *his* idea.
The great Julius Kohn hadn't come up with a fresh idea in
twenty years—he still ran the business on his father's blue-
prints. But the time for change was here. Dad was sharp
enough to realize that.

Again—at the end of June—the family moved en masse
to the Southampton house. Mollified by the success of their
mother's party the previous season and reciprocal invitations, Gail and Brenda planned to remain in residence until
early September. Kathy looked forward to relaxed early
morning walks along the beach, magnificent sunsets, lovely

sessions of sand castle efforts with Jesse. She was resigned to the endless chatter of her sisters-in-law that focused on clothes, cosmetics, and cruises.

She was astonished when Phil announced—as they prepared for bed on their second evening at the Southampton house—that he was making arrangements for the two of them to fly to Paris late the following month.

"We'll be there for the collections. I'll talk with the designer we hope to sign up after he presents his collection," Phil said nonchalantly, but he exuded excitement. "Our passports haven't expired, thank God. That's one less thing to deal with."

"Phil, I can't leave Jesse—" While the prospect of seeing Paris again had initially entranced her, she focused now on reality.

"Why not? Alice is great with him, and my mother will drop by to see him every day."

"Phil, he's a baby. He's two years old. He'd be terrified if I suddenly disappeared from his life!" Phil, of course, was often away for ten days at a time.

"Okay," Phil said after a moment. "We'll take him with us—and Alice." He seemed amused by the vision of traveling with a small entourage. "Talk to Alice in the morning. The office will push through passports for her and Jesse in a hurry and arrange for additional seating on the plane and a two-bedroom suite for us at the hotel in Paris."

"It sounds exciting." *Phil wanted her with him in Paris!* He'd never asked her to go with him on any business trip before. Maybe in Paris they'd find the magic of their early days together. "Remember the last time we were in Paris?"

"Yeah—" Phil began to sing the opening bars of Hammerstein and Kern's "The Last Time I Saw Paris."

"That wasn't the Paris we saw," she reminded. But in Paris he had asked her to marry him. Her whole world had become suddenly beautiful. For a little while.

"You'll see a different Paris this time," he promised, an amorous glint in his eyes. She knew he'd make love to her tonight. Even though it wasn't Saturday, she told herself mockingly. "Roz says it's gay Paree again."

"Are we really going to fly?" she asked, remembering how terrified she'd been in that awful little plane that had taken them from Hamburg to Paris.

"Kathy, it's the only way to travel." She caught a hint of condescension in his voice. "We'll take an overnight flight, be in Paris for breakfast the next morning."

When Phil made a major deal of helping her choose her wardrobe for the trip to Paris, Kathy understood that she was playing a role in a Phil Kohn production. He arranged for Roz to accompany the two of them on the second frenzied buying trip in town. Afterward, Phil escorted Roz and her to a late luncheon at the Stork.

All at once, she thought, Phil was intrigued by the café society circuit. Last night he'd talked about taking his parents to the Colony for their wedding anniversary. Last year it had been Billy Rose's Diamond Horseshoe.

In the Cub Room—paintings of *Cosmopolitan* cover girls smiling down upon them from the walls—they concentrated for a few moments on ordering. Kathy was trying not to be dazzled by lunching at the Stork. Marge would want to know every minor detail: what they ate, what celebrities they saw, what the women were wearing.

When the waiter disappeared, Phil and Roz embarked on business talk. Twice Roz interrupted Phil to say, sotto voce, that a celebrity had just arrived, and he would shoot a covert glance in the indicated direction. Kathy sat at the table with a polite show of interest, but her mind wandered into private reverie.

She understood what was happening in their lives now. It wasn't enough for Phil that his father was very rich. He was out to become part of the café society world, which created celebrities via such columnists as Winchell and Sullivan and Cholly Knickerbocker. The Kohns—Jews—would never make it into the Social Register. They could make it into café society. And Julius Kohn was willing to pay the bill.

"Kathy, you wear clothes so well," Roz interrupted her straying thoughts. "That's a gift."

"Thank you." She was wary of compliments from Roz. The few times they'd met she'd felt almost gauche beside Roz's glossy sophistication.

"How's your French?" Phil asked Kathy in sudden curiosity. "I only passed high school French because David tutored me. I took German in college."

"I managed when we were in Paris last," Kathy reminded and saw Roz lift one eyebrow in surprise. She detected the intimate exchange between Roz and Phil. It was as though Roz was reproaching him for not having mentioned seeing Paris with Kathy.

Was Phil having an affair with Roz? She remembered the nights when Phil stayed late in Manhattan "to work with our publicity team." She must stop this, she reproached herself. She hated those wives who suspected their husbands of having affairs with every attractive woman who was part of their lives.

A few days before their flight to Paris Kathy went out to Borough Park with Jesse. She felt self-conscious at arriving in the chauffeured limousine, but Phil had insisted. Tomorrow afternoon Wally would pick them up for the return trip to Southampton.

"I know it's expensive," her mother said, "but cable me when you arrive in Paris. I'm so nervous about you flying."

"We'll be fine, Mom," Kathy comforted her. "I don't know how much Jesse will remember, but it'll be nice to be able to say that he was in Paris when he was two."

"Don't let him forget his grandparents and his aunt in Brooklyn," Sophie teased. "We don't have money, but we're rich in love."

Kathy relished this brief time with family. Jesse enjoyed all the spoiling, she thought tenderly. Bella loved him, but she'd never learned to display affection. To Julius he was a toy, an entertainment at certain moments. When he was home, she acknowledged, Phil fussed over Jesse. But he was so wrapped up in business, and away so much.

The day before they were to leave for Paris, Kathy phoned Marge in San Francisco.

"Oh, baby, do I envy you," Marge admitted. "Buy me something mad in Paris. Like a black lace-trimmed garter belt or a sexy pair of black panties. Not that I've found anybody to wear them for, but I can dream."

"Phil says we're staying at the Ritz," Kathy reported. She knew that Roz had suggested this. "And he's promised to take me to dinner at Maxim's."

"So romantic," Marge drawled. "Why can't I find a man who wants to take *me* to Paris and to dinner at Maxim's?"

Kathy waited for Phil to say that they would take a side trip to Berlin. The Russian blockade had ended in May—it was now possible to visit Berlin. *They could see David.* But Phil never made the suggestion.

While they waited for takeoff at the airport, Kathy remembered the excitement of sailing from New York for Hamburg. She remembered standing on the deck of their ship with Rhoda as the Statue of Liberty disappeared from view. She remembered David.

They'd be so close to Berlin. Wasn't it natural to think that they might fly there for a quick visit with David? Phil made a pretense of being close to his only cousin on his father's side—but in truth, she thought, Phil was close to no one except maybe to his father and even then only in a false fashion.

"Hey, Jesse, how do you like the big planes?" Phil joshed, taking his son from Alice and lifting him onto his shoulders. "Let's go over for a better look." Phil was playing to an audience again. Waiting fellow passengers were sending him admiring glances. Phil was forever onstage.

This was different from the trip to Hamburg, Kathy analyzed. She had gone to Hamburg on a mission. Incredible that it was not quite four years ago. She felt fifteen years older now. For Phil this was a business trip. She meant to enjoy it as a tourist.

She had never felt entirely comfortable in Germany, faced by constant reminders of the Holocaust. How did David survive in Berlin when he must face ghosts every waking moment? He could have become involved in research in the United States just as easily. But he'd been able to locate his father's research, and he was building on that. There had never been room in David's life for anything but his research.

"My sisters can't believe I'm going to Paris." Alice brought her back to the moment. "That we're going by *plane.*"

Only minutes before their plane landed at Orly, Phil told Kathy that a Peugeot would be waiting for them at the airport.

"You rented a Peugeot?"

"I bought it through the Renault agency in New York," he told her with a smug smile. "It'll be there with license and all the necessary papers. We'll use it in Paris and have it shipped back to New York. You'll have my old Caddy for yourself."

"I thought it was a company car—" She gazed at him in surprise.

"No more," he said indulgently. "Mother, Gail, and Brenda drive their own Cadillacs. Why shouldn't my wife?"

"Thank you, Phil." He realized, she thought, that their marriage needed bolstering. *He cared.* That was why he'd brought her along on this trip. How cynical of her to think he had done it for business reasons! And now he was giving her the Caddy to patch up that old wound about her driving. They would make this a *fine* marriage. They'd both work at it.

She sat beside Phil on the front seat of the Peugeot while Alice sat in the back with Jesse. Phil pointed out historic sites as they arrived in the city. She had forgotten that Phil knew Paris from prewar days as well as when he was in service.

"Roz was over last summer. She gave me the addresses of some great little bistros."

"How nice."

Why did Roz's name come into so much of their conversation these past few months? But she was immediately ashamed of this fresh wave of suspicion. Here Phil was making an obvious effort to mend their marriage, and she kept jumping to ugly conclusions.

Kathy was enthralled by their suite at the Ritz, which overlooked the Place Vendôme: the furniture elegant, the walls upholstered with lovely fabrics, tall French windows adorned by velvet drapes.

"We're having dinner tonight at the house of our prospective new designer." For the first time Phil mentioned the designer by name, and Kathy's eyes widened with respect. Now she understood Phil's excitement about bringing off this deal. "He wants to meet me socially before we sit down with the lawyers. Wear the white chiffon dinner dress from Bergdorf's. It's classy." These days Phil only liked what he labeled "classy."

To her astonishment Kathy enjoyed their dinner on the balcony of their host's eighteenth-century town house. While he was multilingual, at times he was lost for a word in English and she was able to interpret for him. She felt warmed by Phil's glow of pride.

"Hey, we make a pretty good team," he told her while they prepared for bed. His success had made him amorous, she thought. She willed herself to respond.

The days in Paris passed in a euphoric haze, except for those intrusive moments when she remembered how close they were to Berlin. While Phil involved himself in business, she embarked on sight-seeing, sometimes with Jesse and Alice, sometimes on her own. She moved in a dream through expeditions to the Louvre, the Luxembourg Gardens, Notre Dame, the Eiffel Tower.

In the evenings she and Phil dined at romantic places. She was dazzled by dinner at Maxim's, refurbished now to mirror its 1900s elegance—red velvet everywhere, calla-lily lighting fixtures, baroque mirrors, murals featuring nude beauties. They dined at the Ritz and at Lapérouse and Grand Vefour. For luncheons when Phil was not involved with business and could join her, they sought out the bistros recommended by Roz.

She was intrigued by the ground-floor boutiques of the great couture houses, where the prices were less astronomical. At Molyneux she bought deliciously naughty lingerie for Marge and Rhoda; from Vedrenne, elegant and lovely umbrellas for her mother and Aunt Sophie. For her father and Frank she bought exquisite silk ties at the shop where Phil had bought shirts for his father and himself.

Boarding their flight for the return trip to New York, she felt wistful that they had not managed a quick flight to Berlin to see David. Rhoda and Frank had assumed that they would.

Family fondness and loyalty among the Kohns, she realized, only existed on David's side.

Chapter 14

Again in September, Julius Kohn Furs presented their fashion show with debutantes appearing as models and a portion of the proceeds of the day's sales going to charity. On Friday evenings now—she had overcome her fear of venturing so far behind the wheel—Kathy drove into New York to meet Phil for an evening on the town. They limited their dining to the Stork, El Morocco, "21," and the Colony—the stamping grounds of café society, and Roz managed occasional mention by the columnists.

Early in the new year Julius announced he'd bought a two-bedroom apartment in the East Sixties. *"A company apartment. A tax write-off."* At Phil's insistence—Kathy was upset at being away from Jesse for any extended period—the two of them stayed in the company apartment on Friday evenings, not returning to Greenwich until late Saturday night. They were joined on occasion by Julius and Bella. This year—with Phil so active in the business—Julius went with Bella and his daughters to Palm Beach for three weeks. Phil said he was on the phone with the office at least once a day.

Uneasy about driving in Manhattan rush-hour traffic, Kathy made a point of arriving in the city no later than 4 P.M. This allowed her to meet with Rhoda for coffee and conversation on Fridays. Once a month her parents and Aunt Sophie came out to spend Sunday in Greenwich. Mannie and a helper managed the candy store. Phil slept most of the day, emerging only in time to sit down to dinner with his in-laws.

At Passover—which went unobserved in the senior Kohns' house except for the presence of a plate of matzoh on the table for each of the eight days—Kathy took Jesse and went to Borough Park for the first seder, remaining overnight to Jesse's joy. Spending this precious parcel of time with her parents and her aunt, Kathy realized how bored she was with her life.

Bella had dragged her into the charity luncheon and tea circuit, which was so important to Gail and Brenda. She'd succumbed after much prodding and played canasta two afternoons a week—the Argentine rummy game that was sweeping across the country. And there were the nights of socializing in Manhattan, when she felt as though she was playing a role in a stage play.

Late in May she went into New York to be a witness at the City Hall wedding of Rhoda and Frank. Both families had created such an uproar that they decided upon a civil ceremony with only Kathy and Frank's longtime best friend in attendance. In a burst of exuberance—and the knowledge that this could be charged to Phil—Kathy took them to a wedding luncheon at "21." The others were impressed that the waiters knew her.

At the end of June, along with the rest of the family, Kathy took up residence at the Southampton house. There were no trips into Manhattan now. The café society that Phil courted was out here in the Hamptons or at Newport or Bar Harbor—or in Europe. Except for Kathy and the nursemaids, the women of the household slept until ten or eleven, and by noon were sprawled on chaises on the beach.

Lunch parties were frequent, as was canasta playing before the cocktail hour.

In mid-July, battling boredom, Kathy adopted a habit of going into Manhattan once a week despite the sultry heat that so often assaulted the city. She spent two or three hours out in Borough Park, then left to meet with Rhoda. She made a point of being on a train that would bring her home in time to read to Jesse at bedtime.

On a rainy Wednesday morning in August, with a thunderstorm predicted, Kathy received a phone call from Rhoda.

"I realize this is a last-minute thing, but Frank just called to say he's been offered a pair of tickets for today's matinee of *South Pacific*. You know how impossible it is to get seats—"

"Are you inviting me to go with you?" Kathy interrupted blithely. "Because if you are, the answer is 'yes'!" She dreaded a day cooped up here in the house. "When is curtain time?"

They arranged to meet at the theater. With luck she'd be out in time to catch a ride home with Phil and his father, Kathy noted.

She phoned for the schedule of trains into Penn Station, dressed for the city, played with Jesse and his Tinkertoys for twenty minutes, then drove to the station. She wouldn't even mind the hot train ride into town, she thought with a delicious sense of freedom.

By the time she arrived at the Southampton station, the rain was coming down in torrents. She left the car and ran for shelter. On the train—sparsely populated at this hour—she kicked off her shoes and dozed. At Penn Station she debated about calling her family in Borough Park. She decided to call later, when she'd have more time. Phone the office, she thought belatedly, and tell Phil she was in town.

Phil was out of the office. Probably at lunch, she guessed. All right, she'd call him later. She pushed her way through the vacation crowds that milled about Penn Station, and walked out into the street to find a taxi. She glanced at her watch, anxious about the time. She'd forgotten how difficult it was to get a cab in Manhattan on a rainy day.

Finally—her summer sandals drenched from the rain— she settled herself in a taxi and gave the driver the address of the theater. Rhoda would never forgive her if she was late. She tensed at the delay in traffic as the taxi crept uptown.

She spied Rhoda waiting anxiously under the marquee. Most of the others had gone inside already. She overtipped the driver and hurried out of the taxi to Rhoda.

"I was scared your train was late," Rhoda said, relieved at her appearance. "Let's go on inside."

They were so enchanted by the music, by the unexpected, last-moment pleasure of being able to see the musical, that they remained in their seats between acts, content to talk.

"What do you hear from Marge?" Rhoda asked after she'd reported on her own activities and Frank's since they'd last talked.

"I think she'd like to come back to New York—after all, Seventh Avenue is where most of the designing goes on— but she says she's learning a lot. Still dying to open up her own shop, though she'd feel better doing that with an active partner. If I wasn't otherwise engaged, I'd love to join her."

Rhoda knew how bored she was much of the time. Not the mothering hours each day, she thought guiltily. She loved being with Jesse, but Alice freed her from the nonsense, *boring* hours. There was never a moment in Hamburg when she had been bored, because she'd been doing something she believed in, something that was useful.

After the performance they fought their way through the euphoric audience to the ladies' room. Kathy tried to reach Phil again. There was no answer on his private line, and the switchboard was shut for the night. She'd have to take the train.

"You couldn't get Phil?" Rhoda asked sympathetically when she emerged from the phone booth.

"He must have left for the day. Let me drop you off by cab—if we can find one—then I'll go on over to the apartment, call Mom and talk comfortably for a while. I'll miss the rush-hour madness on the train that way."

"Would you like to come over for an early dinner?" Rhoda asked. "Nothing fancy, just—"

"That would get me home too late. Thanks anyway. Now let's try for a taxi." She'd call out to Southampton and explain to Jesse—guilty that she might not be home in time to read to him tonight.

They left the theater and walked over to Eighth Avenue because the lineup for taxis was horrendous. At Eighth they finally signaled an empty taxi and began the slow crawl uptown.

"Frank's getting nervous about this Korean situation," Rhoda said somberly. "He's scared to death we'll be drawn into another war. Everybody's so afraid of Communism. Look what's happening with that awful book, *Red Channels*. Innocent people are going to have their lives ruined."

"I remember back in high-school days, when Marge and I used to hang out on Saturday nights on Thirteenth Avenue and listen to the young Communists climb up on their soapboxes and talk about how nobody should go hungry or homeless. We knew nothing about Stalin and what was going on inside Russia—"

"Back in the thirties Frank's father and mother worked hard for the Spanish Loyalists. His father went over with the Abraham Lincoln Brigade. Afterward, Frank said, his father was disillusioned about the whole deal in Spain."

"Sometimes I feel as though I'm living in outer space somewhere. In Greenwich or Southampton—it doesn't matter where we are—all I hear is talk about the fur trade. I don't understand how Phil could have fought in World War II and not give a thought to what's happening in the world now. His father's the same way."

"They're one breed and you're another, baby," Rhoda said. "But don't knock it—you're living well."

The taxi pulled up at the curb before the West Seventies brownstone where Rhoda and Frank lived.

"I'll talk to you soon." Kathy exchanged a hasty kiss with Rhoda, and Rhoda sprinted across the sidewalk. The rain was coming down heavily again.

The driver cut through Central Park—a glorious, shimmering green in the summer rain—and emerged on Fifth Avenue. Within minutes Kathy was at her destination. She fumbled impatiently for her keys to the entrance of the building. Usually so demanding of services, Julius had bought an apartment in a building without doormen or elevator operators.

She crossed the carpeted lobby to the immaculately maintained elevators. In moments she was gliding in admirable smoothness to the twelfth floor. In her mind she tabulated the inventory of clothes she kept in the apartment. She'd change into a pair of dry shoes, she decided in relief. She'd sat through the performance with rain-sodden shoes removed and now was intensely aware of discomfort.

Call Southampton first and talk to Jesse, she instructed herself. Then call Mom. Maybe she'd make herself a cup of Earl Grey to sip while they talked.

She left the elevator and hurried down the hall to the apartment in an oddly relaxed mood, she realized. Continuous rain had a lulling effect. And the play had been a delight. Now she anticipated a long talk with Mom, then she'd talk with Aunt Sophie and Dad.

She unlocked the door and walked into the foyer, conscious of a pleasant silence. She started down the carpeted hallway that led to the pair of bedrooms, then froze in shock. Her eyes focused on a trail of fragile material that littered the hallway. Sheer nylons in a discarded heap. A few feet beyond—gossamer black panties. Near the door to the first bedroom a matching bra and a black, lace-trimmed garter belt.

Before she followed the trail that led into the bedroom she shared with Phil, she knew what she would find. The nude bodies of Phil and Roz lay in a tangle on the oversized bed. Both Phil and Roz asleep. Phil always fell asleep after they made love, she remembered subconsciously.

For an agonized instant she closed her eyes against the tableau before her. Dizzy with shock, she felt her whole world crumble around her. Then in a blend of anguish and rage she spun around and walked down the hall, across the foyer and out of the apartment.

In a daze she went to Penn Station, arriving just in time to board a train for Southampton, forgetting to phone ahead to talk to Jesse or to call her family in Borough Park. Wanting to blot out the memory of Phil and Roz, lying in satiated slumber on the bed she'd shared with Phil, yet perversely clinging to that image.

How many times she had scolded herself for being suspicious of Phil! *And it had all been true.* Not just Roz. That blond hair she'd found on Phil's shoulder had belonged to one of his bedmates. How many others had shared his hotel beds during those trips around the country? Phil was a carbon copy of his father.

The trip to Southampton seemed endless tonight. Her mind was in chaos. Why had she married Phil? She hadn't been in love with him—she had been obsessed by him. Again she remembered Rhoda's words when Derek had walked out on her: *"Why do so many women fall in love with the wrong men? Maybe it isn't love. Maybe it's just old-fashioned lust."*

She'd pack a bag for herself and Jesse and take the train back to New York. For tonight they'd stay at a hotel. In the morning they'd go out to Borough Park. Mom and Dad would be upset, but they'd understand.

The rain had at last subsided by the time she left the train. She hurried across the parking area to the waiting Cadillac, and slid behind the wheel with painful urgency. She would take Jesse and leave Phil and his world behind her.

Driving up the long entranceway to the house, she saw the lower floor was dark except for the foyer, and remembered that Gail and Brenda and their husbands were at some affair tonight. Bella had elected to remain home because Julius had flown out to Cleveland on business. Whose bed was Julius in tonight, Kathy asked herself bitterly. It didn't matter how old they were if they were rich enough.

She let herself into the quiet house and headed up the stairs. The nursery was dark. Jesse must be asleep, like Phil's small nieces. How awful to wake him, she thought; but they must be out of the house before Phil returned. The prospect of facing him after what she'd seen this afternoon was intolerable.

At the upstairs landing she heard the muffled sound of television filtering from Bella's room. She'd have to tell Bella she was leaving Phil.

"Kathy?" With one hand on the knob of the nursery door she turned to face Bella.

"Yes—" Her heart was pounding now.

"Phil called a little after seven to say he'll stay at the apartment tonight. He's tied up with an out-of-town buyer and—"

"Oh, he was tied up all right," Kathy broke in with a fresh surge of rage and humiliation. "I walked into the apartment and found him. He was asleep, in bed with Roz Masters. They didn't even know I was there."

Bella flinched, then closed her eyes for a moment.

"He's his father's son."

"How do you stay married to a man like that?" Kathy demanded.

"I didn't know until after Gail and Brenda were born. I didn't want to know. But I couldn't walk out on the security he offered the girls. And then later there was Phil. What could I give them?"

"Integrity. Love. Self-respect." Kathy's eyes smoldered with contempt for her husband.

"Integrity, love, and self-respect don't pay the rent. They don't buy food and clothes. They don't pay doctor bills."

"I'm leaving Phil. I never want to see him again."

"Kathy, don't do this," Bella pleaded. "I know how you're hurting, but there's too much at stake to throw away your marriage. Oh yes, I hurt. God, did I hurt! But I know that I and my children and my grandchildren will have everything we need in life."

"I'm divorcing Phil. I could never live with him again after what I saw this afternoon." Tears stung her eyes as she remembered all the times she'd upbraided herself for being suspicious of him.

"Phil will fight you every step of the way," Bella warned. "He'll drag you into the dirt. You'll claim you found them in bed together, but who will corroborate that? Did anybody see them come into the building, go to the apartment? Did anybody see you?" she challenged and smiled bitterly as Kathy remained silent. "Why do you think Julius bought an apartment in a building without doormen or elevator men? *Because it's discreet.*"

"I was there," Kathy said stubbornly. "I saw them."

"That's not good enough. And Phil will find people who'll vouch for being with him every moment of this day and evening. He'll claim you married him for the Kohn money, that you're just after heavy alimony payments."

"I don't want Phil's money—or his father's," Kathy shot back. "I'll work and support Jesse. I don't need Phil!"

"You need him," Bella insisted. "You have no real job experience—how much could you earn? Who'll take care of Jesse while you're working?"

"I'll find a way—" But fear was clutching her throat.

"You can't expect your Aunt Sophie to raise him for you," Bella pointed out. "Not at her age. And you know what nursemaids cost. Be practical, Kathy. As I was. Make a life for yourself, as I have, and let Jesse have all the advantages that money can provide."

"It's wrong," Kathy defied. But doubts began to erode her determination. How would she raise Jesse alone? "It's not fair."

"Much is not fair in this world. We do what we must to

survive." But Kathy saw the compassion in her mother-in-law's eyes. "You'll be brighter with Jesse than I was with my three. I built myself this protective shell and hid behind it. My children were raised by nursemaids and boarding schools and summer camps because I was afraid to love and be hurt again." She smiled at Kathy's startled expression. "Oh, I was madly in love with Julius in the first two years of our marriage. Did you think I married him because he was the son of the rich Peter Kohn?"

"No," Kathy stammered. She *had* suspected that. At intervals Julius dropped snide remarks about his wife's years as the only child of poor Russian immigrants.

"You don't know Julius as he was in those early days. Oh, he was a charmer! I thought I was so lucky when he chose me. Probably," she said with bitter humor, "because I was the only girl who'd ever said no to him."

"Bella, I don't know—" It was the first time she had ever called her mother-in-law by name. "I feel used. Degraded—"

"I know." Bella's eyes and her voice reflected remembered pain. "Let's go downstairs and make a pot of tea. We'll talk some more. Phil doesn't have to know you were in that apartment. It's better he shouldn't know. And you'll learn to build a life for yourself. I've watched you. You're stronger than I was. You won't make my mistakes."

Kathy and Bella sat in the kitchen, talking as women have talked through the centuries about philandering husbands. Thank God that Phil was staying in the city tonight, Kathy thought in shaky relief. She wouldn't have to face him until tomorrow night.

In her night-darkened bedroom Kathy lay sleepless under the light coverlet required by Southampton nights. The sound of the waves lapping at the shore normally lulled her to sleep, but tonight the sound had lost its magic. Her mind was too active and tormented.

Was Phil still there in the apartment with Roz? Were they

making love right this minute? For a little while she'd convinced herself that she and Phil would make something fine of their marriage, despite its shaky status. They'd both work at it, she'd thought.

Was she doing the right thing to stay with Phil? How could she let him make love to her, knowing what she knew? She felt sick at the prospect. Yet she realized that Bella was right. Phil wouldn't agree to a divorce. His pride wouldn't allow that. Divorces could be expensive and messy—and she had no money.

Without alimony and child support she'd live in constant uncertainty. If she worked, she'd have to leave Jesse in a nursery for long hours every day. She wouldn't be able to afford to hire a woman to come in to take care of him.

Where would she live? Everybody knew how rents in the city kept escalating. *What would she be able to afford?* She couldn't move back in with her family. Her bedroom had been an oversized closet. She remembered how cramped it was those occasional times she'd slept over with Jesse. She had to manipulate to get past the crib to her bed. Jesse needed space.

Of course, other women without husbands managed to raise children. But did she want to subject Jesse to denial when it could be avoided? *The important thing at stake was Jesse.* She must do what would be good for him.

At last she fell into troubled sleep, to awake at sunrise, instantly conscious of the emotional turmoil of the past dozen hours. She got out of bed with a searing need to leave the house behind her, showered quickly, dressed in slacks and a warm sweater because the beach would be chilly at this hour. She hurried from her bedroom, down the stairs of the silent house, and out into the sea-scented morning air.

Fog hung over the beach. A host of gulls cawed a jubilant welcome to the new day as she trudged over the damp white sand, as yet untouched by footprints except for those of an adventurous dog. She was grimly aware that she must gear herself to face Phil.

The time would come, she vowed, when she would free herself of this mock-marriage. But until Jesse was safely launched in life she must play the game. Nothing must be spoiled for her precious child.

By the time she returned to the house, the sun was breaking through the fog. Yesterday's rain was a memory. Somehow, the sunlight was an affront to her.

Each hour of the day dragged. Normally, Kathy loved these days when daylight reigned until close to nine in the evening. Now she longed for night to put an end to the exuberance of day.

Late in the afternoon—when the other women were lounging on the ocean-facing deck and dissecting an earlier cocktail party—Kathy went out to the kitchen. Perched on his knees on a chair, Jesse was deep in contemplation as he considered the puzzle on the table before him. How sweet and warm and beautiful he was! Dad was so pleased, she remembered, that Jesse was enraptured by the puzzles that had been part of the third-birthday gifts.

"I'll give Jesse his dinner and get him ready for bed, Alice. It's a marvelous evening. Why don't you go for a walk on the beach?"

"That would be nice." Alice smiled in appreciation. "My hips need that walking. Everything I eat seems to be settling there."

Jesse was finishing up his dinner when Kathy heard a car drive up to the house. That would be Phil and his father, she guessed, and was instantly tense. Moments later she heard their voices as they talked with the women on the deck. Through a kitchen window she saw Phil stroll into the house.

"Mommie, I want to do the puzzle again," Jesse said with a determination to delay going upstairs to the nursery and soon to bed. "I can do it all by myself," he reminded triumphantly.

"Hey, what's my boy been up to today?" Phil swept into the kitchen, gave Kathy a perfunctory kiss and settled at the kitchen table. "Behaving yourself?"

"I made a sand castle with Alice. A big one," Jesse reported.

"Wow, I wish I could have seen it!" This was the period each day that Phil played the affectionate father, Kathy thought.

"You didn't come home last night," Jesse said accusingly. "You promised to read me a story." Jesse's choice delaying tactic at bedtime.

"I'll read you one tonight," Phil cajoled. "We don't have anything lined up later, do we?" he asked Kathy.

"No, you turned down the Jacksons' dinner. I phoned and said you'd be out of town." *How can I talk this way with Phil after last night?*

"They're nobodies," Phil shrugged. "We'd be bored to death."

"I want a ride on your shoulders," Jesse said imperiously. "And *two* stories tonight because you didn't read me one last night."

She could see this through, Kathy told herself grimly while Phil swooped Jesse from his chair. She would not deprive Jesse of the life the Kohn money could give him. She wouldn't deprive him of those moments each day when Phil played the affectionate father. Being part of a family was important to a child.

She would pretend last night had never happened. But it was etched forever on her brain.

═ Chapter 15

As usual, shortly after Labor Day the Kohn entourage left Southampton and returned to Greenwich. On the surface, Kathy thought, nothing had changed in her relationship with Phil. He was too egotistical, too smug, to suspect that she knew about his affair with Roz. He seemed not to notice a change in her response to his lovemaking, though that had lost its magic long before the night she found him in bed with Roz.

To Phil she was a convenient outlet for those nights when he was aroused and Roz—or whomever else he was seeing—was not available. She had to force herself not to flinch each time he reached for her, feeling herself no more than a high-priced call girl. But for Jesse she could go through with this travesty.

Phil and his father remained away from the business for only two Jewish holidays—Rosh Hashanah, the New Year, and Yom Kippur, the Day of Atonement. If the weather was suitable, they played golf. But on this Rosh Hashanah Phil came downstairs shortly before ten to announce he was going to his father's house for a conference.

"On Rosh Hashanah?" Kathy frowned in mild reproach. "Can't you forget business today?"

"This is a personal deal." He grinned, clearly pleased with himself. "How would you feel about our moving back into Manhattan?"

Kathy stared for a moment in amazement.

"I'd love it," she told him. Joyous anticipation charging through her. "But what about the house?"

"It'll be our second home. We'll come out some weekends, throw an occasional house party. I'm sick of these long hauls between Greenwich and the city." He grimaced in distaste. "Of course, I have to convince the old man the move is necessary for business. More time for socializing, all that shit."

"What about the company apartment?" Her mind ordered caution. "Won't your father suggest we stay over in the city part of the week?" But that wouldn't work. Jesse had just started nursery school—they couldn't drag him back and forth.

"The company apartment will be for him and my mother. And we'll put up management from the stores when they come into town. We should have been doing that all along."

The company apartment would be there for Phil and Julius to take their women, Kathy thought with bitter humor. And it was a tax write-off, she mentally mimicked her father-in-law. Julius Kohn took such pleasure in charging expensive items off to the business.

"Are you having breakfast here or with your father?" she asked politely. *It would be so wonderful to be back in the city.* She could see the family more often. She could spend more time with Rhoda and Frank.

"Over there," Phil said. "We made a date."

Three hours later Phil returned to the house. His father had put up a battle, he reported, but he'd made his point.

"I want you to go into the city and start looking at apartments. Something on Park or Fifth—we need a classy address. And while you're apartment hunting," he said in soaring high spirits, "start buying more clothes. We'll be going out several nights a week. I'll open more charge accounts for you."

"Open a checking account, too," Kathy said casually. "It's ridiculous the way I have to run to you all the time when I need cash."

For a moment she thought he was going to argue about this, then he shrugged and nodded.

"Yeah. You pay the bills for the house and your charge accounts—save me wasting time on that crap. Oh, a news bulletin," he said with plotted nonchalance. "As of the first of the month I'm president of the Out-of-Town Stores Division. Dad will head up the wholesale operation and the New York store. And my salary goes up again."

"Congratulations." She contrived to sound admiring.

"Your old man's doing okay," he boasted. "Dad realizes what I'm bringing to the business. And he loves those column items! I'm making Julius Kohn Furs a household name."

Kathy began immediately to search for an apartment. By the end of the month she had located a spacious, charming apartment on Fifth Avenue overlooking Central Park, with sufficient space for themselves and domestic help. A high floor that, she surmised, would assure them quiet.

She arranged for Phil to see the apartment one morning. He called from the city to say he'd be signing a lease as soon as the broker had drawn it up.

"We're renting with an option to buy," he said ebulliently. "Hire an interior decorator. I want to move in as soon as possible."

"I'd rather handle everything myself," she told him. "I know what's best for our life-style."

"Hey, you're becoming real independent." Phil's voice carried an aura of surprise. "That's what comes of taking you into the outside world," he joshed. "Okay, I gotta run. Start looking for whatever it takes to make that apartment classy."

"I'll get right on it," Kathy promised. *Didn't he know another description besides "classy"?*

Phil had wanted to give a New Year's Eve party in their new apartment but the celebrating had to wait until late February. Kathy was pleased with the apartment. She had consulted endless interior decorating magazines and books until she could visualize each room down to the most minute detail. She'd searched the city for the right chandelier for the living room, the perfect paneling for the den. She'd been glad to be involved in a project that was so consuming.

Even Julius—who had been given a preview before tonight's housewarming—reluctantly admired her efforts.

"I hate to see the bills," he'd told Phil in her presence, "but you could invite the Duke and Duchess of Windsor here."

Phil was in the living room now with Julius, who'd changed into evening wear at the company apartment and had come over early. Wally had driven back to Greenwich to bring Bella into the city. Brenda and Gail and their husbands were off on another cruise.

Kathy had insisted that they keep the list small. *"That makes it more important."* Neither her parents and Aunt Sophie nor Rhoda and Frank would be here tonight. This was their café society "inner circle"—including Roz Masters. While Phil was out of town last week, she'd had family and Rhoda and Frank to a preview dinner. Mom and Aunt Sophie had been so delighted with the apartment. Zipping up the back of her white chiffon evening dress, over which she would wear a black silk tight-fitting jacket, Kathy remembered Aunt Sophie's remark: *"Kathy, it's like I'd died and gone to heaven. It's the most beautiful apartment I've ever seen."*

She heard Bella being welcomed in the foyer as she left the master bedroom. Bella would want to look in on Jesse, even though he was asleep. Kathy hurried down the hall to the living room.

"Darling, you look beautiful," Bella greeted her with a kiss. "Now can I look in on Jesse? I promise not to awaken him."

"Of course." Kathy linked an arm through her mother-in-law's.

The party was a huge success, but Kathy was ever conscious of Roz's presence. She caught the secret small exchanges between Roz and Phil. She heard Phil's low expression of approval of Roz's red velvet evening dress, cut daringly low. How long before he left Roz for someone new?

"It was a marvelous party," Bella told her as she and Julius took their departure—the last of the guests to leave. "But make Phil buy you some spectacular jewelry," she ordered, loudly enough for the two Kohn men to hear. "Nothing advertises a man's success like the jewelry his wife wears."

Kathy managed a show of enthusiasm when Phil arrived at the apartment a week later with a diamond and sapphire necklace that she knew must have cost a small fortune.

"Don't wear it until I have the insurance policy taken care of," he admonished.

"I won't," she agreed. *The necklace was hers.* Also, a small but growing savings account in her name. Rhoda had prodded her into managing this.

Their lives were falling into a pattern. Four nights a week they played on the café society circuit. One night a week Phil would call to say he wouldn't be home for dinner. *"I'm tied up at the office, baby."* Kathy understood this to mean that he was holed up at the company apartment with Roz. She always knew when this happened. The next night Phil always brought her flowers.

On alternate weekends they went up to the Greenwich house. Usually there was a small house party. Phil relished playing the genial host. Kathy contrived to hide her boredom. These people spent their waking hours seeking amusement. She was concerned about the Korean War and the possibility of World War III. Their conversations revolved around the "in" vacation spots, the newest splashy musical on Broadway, who was sleeping with whom. Kathy came alive in intense discussion with Rhoda and Frank about the ignominious Red-baiting through *Red Channels* that was infecting the country.

To fill the empty hours, Kathy focused on building an exquisite wardrobe. She signed up for a class in fashion design. And she found pleasure in shopping for small but luxurious gifts for her parents and Aunt Sophie—conveniently charged to her account at one of the Fifth Avenue stores.

On Alice's midweek day off she waited downstairs for Jesse to be delivered home from nursery school, took him upstairs for lunch, then off to Borough Park. Business was good in the candy store. Her father had arranged for Mannie to come in on a regular basis, which allowed her mother some free hours.

She was delighted when her father told her at the Passover seder that in August he and her mother and Aunt Sophie were taking a week's vacation—for the first time in Kathy's memory.

"Mannie and his friend will run the store," her father said with elaborate casualness. "We'll go to the Catskills. Not to Grossinger's or the Concord," he said humorously. "A smaller, less expensive place. But for a week Aunt Sophie and Mom won't cook and clean. Mom and I won't stand fourteen hours a day in the store. We're learning to live, Kathy."

She could survive, Kathy thought tenderly, because of the hours here with the family, and the hours with Rhoda and Frank, when Phil was out of town on his constant trips or was "otherwise engaged."

Phil sat with his legs crossed and one expensively shod foot jiggling impatiently as his father talked on the phone with an out-of-town supplier. At last Julius put down the phone.

"Let's shake a leg, Dad. If we're not at the bridge by four, you know what traffic's going to be like getting to the

Hamptons." The city had been like a steambath the past three days. When the hell was this August heat wave going to break?

"Wally's downstairs with the car," Julius told him. "Bring along those reports from the Dallas store. We can go over them on the way out." He glanced sidewise at his son with a sly grin. "You see that red-haired temp that came over from the agency this morning?"

"I didn't notice," Phil said.

"This one you'd notice. Even at my age she gives me that urge."

"I'll let you know. Let's get this show on the road."

The two men left the office and headed down the hall to the elevators. En route they passed the small office shared by the bookkeeper, the office manager, and a pair of secretaries.

"There she is—" Julius poked Phil in the ribs.

Phil managed a fast glance into the room. Normally he wasn't turned on by girls with no tits, but this one exuded sex. Tall and skinny, four-inch heels, with a curvaceous rump and a baby-doll face.

"How long is she going to be here?" Phil asked while they waited for an elevator.

"As long as Maisie needs her. Two or three days," Julius guessed.

The next morning Phil contrived to meet the new temp. Her name was Carol Graham, she was fresh out of Northwestern with a degree in drama, and she shared an apartment with another girl in the West Seventies. By late afternoon he'd asked her out for dinner, and she'd accepted. He called the Southampton house to tell Kathy he was staying in New York.

"I've got a buyer from the Dallas store that I have to take out to dinner," he lied. "See you tomorrow night."

He was whistling when he got off the phone. Roz was becoming a pain in the ass with all the hints she'd been dropping lately. Where did she get the nerve to think he'd dump

Kathy and marry her? He had a good thing going—why should he change it? The trouble with Roz, she was all shook up at hitting thirty and no rich husband in sight.

As prearranged, he met Carol at the soda fountain around the corner. She was sipping a Coke and carrying on a conversation with a male-model type behind the counter.

"That soda-jerk has a walk-on in a TV show next month," she said wistfully when they were on the sidewalk. "That's a start."

Phil took her to dinner at an Italian place down in Greenwich Village, where they were unlikely to encounter anyone he knew. She was twenty-two and dying to make it big in theater.

"Oh sure, TV is okay," she said with mild condescension, "but theater is the real action."

"I took a flier in theater for a while." All at once Phil felt ten years younger. *Free.* "I was in a couple of shows that closed before they even came into town," he lied offhandedly. "That's when I went into the business with my old man."

"Are you sorry you walked out on theater?" she asked, making no effort to remove her knee when it collided with his under the table.

"Now and then. I still have a few contacts." He saw her eyes light up. "Everybody I know is away for the summer, but I'll put in a good word for you when they come back."

"Just looking at you, I guessed you'd been involved in theater somewhere along the line. You've got that look." Under the table her knee jiggled against his.

When he took her home to the brownstone apartment on West 73rd that she shared with another recent Northwestern graduate, he discreetly left her at her door after a goodnight kiss that told him Carol Graham was a girl worth cultivating. He promised himself he'd make it into her bed within a week. She made him feel like a kid again. This could be a fun summer.

Phil was disappointed when Maisie dropped Carol after

three days. Still, he was taking her to some weird downtown theater to see a play on Friday night. He'd stay over in the city, go out to Southampton on Saturday. He'd invite her up to the apartment. The company apartment, he reminded himself. No need for her to know where he lived.

On Friday he met her at the same drugstore as the last time. She was there waiting for him.

"Where'd you work today?" he asked, sliding an arm about her waist as they left the drugstore to look for a cab. They were heading downtown to a pre-theater dinner.

"Oh, I don't go out on a regular basis," Carol explained. "Just when my cash flow is bad. My folks give me money for the basics; but when I want something else, I go out for a few days."

At Carol's suggestion Phil instructed the driver to take them down to Rappaport's on Second Avenue.

"It's real close to the theater," she'd pointed out.

"How do you know Rappaport's?" Phil asked curiously.

"It's where my father always takes my grandmother on special occasions," Carol told him. "I'm from Irvington, up in Westchester."

"What does your father do?"

"He's an orthodontist. My name's really Garfinkel, but I thought Graham would look better on a marquee."

"I can buy that." Phil nodded in approval.

While they ate blintzes and sour cream, Carol talked about the new little theaters popping up not only in Greenwich Village but farther east.

"I mean, nobody makes any money in these crummy little playhouses, but you have a showcase. You can invite agents to come down and see you."

"You're something to see," he teased, aware that several male diners agreed with him.

"We're just around the corner from the playhouse," she told him later while she debated between ordering strawberry shortcake or apple strudel. "We've got plenty of time."

The playhouse—a converted store—was drab, tiny, and miserably hot. The cast varied from fair to awful. The play was pretentious drivel. When the lights came up for intermission, they discovered that a chunk of the small audience had crept out during the first act.

"It's so bloody hot," Phil complained as they rose in their seats. "Do we have to stay?"

"No. It was terrible. I'm glad I didn't bother to try out for a part."

"Let's go somewhere for something cold to drink. I've got a better idea," he said, trying to make it seem spontaneous. "Why don't we run up to the company apartment and have some chilled wine and great air-conditioning?"

She gazed at him for a moment as though in deliberation.

"I know this is when I should look you straight in the eye and say 'no.' But I'll say 'yes' if you remember this is only the second time we've been out together and I'm not popping into bed with you." But the ingenuous smile was accompanied by a seductive glint in her artfully made-up hazel eyes.

"A little romance on the sofa?" he coaxed with the potent Phil Kohn charm.

"Yeah. Within limits."

Okay, so she wasn't going to make it easy for him. In time he'd get there. And this little babe was worth waiting for.

Early in the fall Bella called Kathy to tell her that David would be in New York in two weeks.

"He'll stay up here at the house for a couple of nights before he flies out to California for some medical convention. Why don't you and Phil plan to stay with us, too? Phil can drive in to the city with Julius in the morning, like in the old days."

"I'd love that, Bella." Kathy tried to mask her joyous reaction. *David would be here in New York.* She hadn't seen him in three years! "By then the leaves will be changing color—it's such a beautiful time in Greenwich."

"You know David—he never boasts—but I suspect he must be making a name for himself in his field. They wouldn't ask him to come all the way from West Berlin to San Francisco unless he has an important contribution to make."

"I'll tell Phil about it tonight," Kathy promised.

They talked awhile until Bella realized it was time to leave for one of her volunteer meetings.

"I feel so guilty," Kathy said. "I'm not involved actively in anything here in New York."

"Some of the committees!" Bella grunted in distaste. "The women aren't concerned about raising money for charities. They fight over who's to get credit for pulling it off. But I'd better run now. I loathe being late."

Kathy put down the phone and crossed to a window to look down on Central Park. She was glad she'd persuaded Phil that Fifth Avenue was more elegant than Park. That glorious sweep of open land down there filled her with such a sense of peace most times. But not today. All she could think about was that David would be in the city in two weeks.

Every six months or so Bella said they had a letter from him. He hadn't said anything about being married. As always, she thought tenderly, he was all wrapped up in his work.

The September sun was dropping low in the sky as David waited restlessly for the weekday rush-hour traffic to begin to crawl again. He was tense behind the wheel of the vintage Mercedes that the Institute put at his disposal from time to time in recognition of his work. He'd hoped that a few hours in the Grunewald—walking along the bank of the Havel, breathing in the fresh greenery-scented air—would ease the taut muscles between his shoulder blades, drive away the dull pain at the back of his skull.

He'd been like this ever since he had accepted the invitation to the San Francisco medical conference. Not because of anxiety at reading his paper before the conference. Because he knew he'd be seeing Kathy. In every life there was a crucial turn in the road, and he had taken the wrong turn.

"This was a beautiful day for a picnic." Gretchen's low, musical voice tugged him back to the present. "Aren't you glad I said we should take the afternoon off after working ourselves ragged over the weekend?"

"It was great." His eyes swung to meet hers. Gretchen had been invaluable in these four months that she had been his lab assistant. She was pretty, intelligent, and dedicated to her job. He brushed aside the suspicion that she was eager to expand their relationship to a personal one. "We both needed a few hours away."

"You must be looking forward to the trip. Berlin is such a grim city. Everybody working endless hours. At least, those who have jobs," she added with ironic humor because unemployment was distressingly high.

"I know I overwork you, Gretchen," he said apologetically. "I—"

"I didn't mean us," she broke in. "I'm fascinated by what we're doing. But most people in the city—even in the Western Sector—seem to live such frenetic lives."

"It isn't easy for any of us to put the past behind us." The traffic was beginning to move again. "And we never quite forget that we're encircled by the Communists. Are you sorry you didn't stay in England?" Like himself, just before war broke out Gretchen had been sent out of the country to study. She had gone through the war years at school in London.

"I had to come back," she told him. "I've told you how I tracked my mother and sister down after V-E Day. They were the only ones in the family to survive Buchenwald. I brought them back to Berlin and tried to make a home for them. Except for them I would never have set foot on German soil again."

"I'll drop you off at your flat and go back to the laboratory for a little while," he decided. "I'd like to review some notes tonight." He had not meant to return to Berlin after those months in Hamburg. But seeing the survivors, he'd known he must go back to help those who returned from the camps. And he was haunted by the possibility that he might be lucky enough to locate his father's papers—as he had.

"David, you drive yourself too hard," Gretchen scolded.

"I won't stay long," he promised. "I like to be by my home phone in case I'm needed." His improvised clinic in the flat usually served at least two or three patients after his laboratory hours.

He left Gretchen at her flat, and returned briefly to the Institute. His head still ached. A walk would help, he decided. Tonight he was drawn to Potsdamer Platz—the symbol of divided Berlin. It was at the Platz that East and West met and vied for the other's loyalty, and was on occasion the site of violence between residents of the two sectors of the city.

By the time he arrived at Potsdamer Platz, the area was in its usual evening chaos, with pedestrians darting to avoid the onrush of trolleys, bicycles, and trucks taking workers to their homes. The Western Sector's 90-foot electric sign—it reminded him of Times Square in New York—was flashing out in five-foot letters the latest news, living up to its heading of "the Free Berlin Press Reports." The gray-uniformed police of the West and the blue-uniformed "Vopos" of the East exchanged glances across the square.

David paused to buy a newspaper at the booth on the Western side. The varied offering of West German newspapers, books, and magazines brought East Berliners across the invisible line between the Eastern and Western sectors. From where he stood David could see the queue before the Soviet food store just beyond, and he was conscious—again—of the difference in the quality of life between the two sectors.

In the Western Sector life was almost normal again. In the Eastern Sector there were painful food and housing shortages because, unlike in West Berlin, construction focused on public buildings rather than housing. Every day people streamed from the East to shop in the Western Sector—those who had money to spend.

Restless, David began to walk away from the Platz. Tonight his mind focused on the day almost six years ago that he'd spent with Kathy in Berlin. She would be amazed at the way the Kurfürstendamm had been rebuilt, its shops stocked with luxury goods that many West Berliners relished inspecting even though few could buy. The Kurfürstendamm was like a blend of Fifth Avenue and Broadway in Manhattan, he mused.

Unter den Linden—where he and Kathy had walked in the sharp November cold—was in the Eastern Sector now, one of its "show window" streets. Here the Russians were constructing buildings to house government agencies for the most part. The enormous new white-marble Russian embassy was mocked by West Berliners as being wedding-cake ornate.

He remembered lunching with Kathy at the Hotel Adlon. After lunch they had walked endlessly, and then they'd stopped at the pawnshop window and he saw the family brooch. His throat tightened as he recalled the moment when he asked Kathy to wear it. *"Seeing you wear it will be like seeing a bit of home."*

How stupid he had been. He should have said, "Wear it because I love you, and once this madness has faded into memory I want to be your husband." That was the moment, and he had thrown it away. No one else would ever wear the brooch—because he would never love another woman.

= Chapter 16

Wearing a delicately printed silk with the new princess line decreed by Dior, Kathy sat with her two sisters-in-law in the living room in the senior Kohns' Greenwich house. She had come up yesterday afternoon with Jesse and Alice so that the three Kohn men—Phil, Julius, and David— could drive up in masculine solitude this evening. Bella was in the kitchen conferring with the cook about dinner.

"I can't understand why David keeps staying in Berlin," Brenda was saying, "when we keep hearing such awful things about the Communist zone."

"Professionally he's doing so well," Gail pointed out. "He has to be good if they're bringing him all the way from Berlin to San Francisco. Don't you think so, Kathy?"

"I'm sure David's doing wonderfully with his work," Kathy agreed.

She was ambivalent about tonight's family dinner party. Part of her tingled with anticipation of seeing David. Part of her flinched at the imminent encounter. *One little mistake*—turning to Phil because David had been slow in declaring himself—and her whole life had been wrecked.

No, she reproached herself. How could she say that? Her marriage to Phil had given her Jesse. Her son would fill her life.

"Oh, they'll talk business all evening," Gail predicted, puncturing Kathy's introspection. "Dad and Phil will be all keyed up over tomorrow night's fashion show."

"I don't know why Dad couldn't have insisted that we model in the show," Brenda sulked. "Why does it always have to be all debutantes?"

"We're a teensy bit heavier than ten years ago," Gail reminded her sister, wistful for a moment. "What about running out to Maine Chance for a week? I hear it's marvelous. All the movie stars go there."

"Milty will scream I'm driving him into the poorhouse," Gail predicted.

"In a late model Mercedes," Brenda said drily. "You can persuade him to let you go. I'll call tomorrow and make reservations."

Then they heard the limousine turning into the driveway, and Bella was hurrying down the hall and into the entrance foyer. Kathy willed herself to remain seated with Gail and Brenda in the living room, but at the sound of David's voice she abandoned casualness to rush out to join Bella in welcoming him.

"Kathy, you look wonderful," he said softly when they had exchanged a chaste, familial kiss. "And how's Jesse?"

"He seems to be coming down with a cold—he's sleeping already. But you'll see him in the morning."

A few minutes later Eli and Milton arrived. For a while they all settled themselves in the living room with pre-dinner martinis for everyone except Kathy and Bella, who were served their customary white wine. David inquired with sincere interest about Gail and Brenda's daughters, whose names and ages he remembered, though at his last visit they had not been part of the family gatherings. In the same situation, Kathy thought, Phil would not have asked about them, he'd probably not remember they existed.

Kathy made a point of not focusing on David, though she was gloriously yet painfully aware of his presence every moment. She was relieved that the table conversation required little of her. The men seemed avid for word from an insider about conditions in Berlin.

"You say the East Berliners cross over into the Western Sector to do their shopping," Eli pinpointed. "What about vice versa?"

"Oh yes, that happens, too." David nodded, chuckling. "Of course, loyal West Berliners consider this *Schimpf und Schande.*"

"A burning shame," Kathy interpreted.

"Why would West Berliners cross over to shop?" Eli persisted.

"Because groceries—particularly bread and potatoes— are cheaper there," David explained. "Because of that, reports say, thirty percent of West Berlin bakers are out of work. The same goes for barbers because haircuts are much cheaper on the Soviet side."

"David, what's happened to the Tiergarten?" Kathy asked on impulse. "I remember they were cutting down those lovely old trees for firewood."

"We saw only the beginning of that," David said grimly. "That first winter after the war was bitterly cold. The Tiergarten had to be stripped of most of its big trees. The Germans didn't want to take down the trees that had been growing for a century, but it was that or freeze. Then during the winter of the blockade and airlift the stumps and roots were dug out of the ground to feed the stoves and fireplaces again. But now over two million little trees have been brought in from West Germany and planted."

"Marshall Plan money paid for that," Julius guessed with distaste. "We had to pay for two million trees for the Nazis."

"Dad, what time do we have to be in New York for the fashion show?" Gail asked. His sisters had a habit of ignoring Phil's position in the business, Kathy remembered.

"They'll be in early," Eli said before Julius could reply. "If they go to New York, they have to go to the shops. It'll cost me plenty."

The evening was brought to an early conclusion since Julius and Phil would be in the car in the morning no later than 6 A.M. Family affairs were always guided by the requirements of the business.

"You don't have to come in for the show," Julius told David. "Relax here at the house. We'll be home for a late supper. Bella, drive him over for lunch at that new restaurant you found."

In the morning Kathy knew that this year she would again miss the fashion show. Jesse was definitely coming down with a cold. She guessed that Phil would not be upset by her absence. He'd feel less constricted; he'd be able to flirt with the socialite models without first glancing over his shoulder to check on her whereabouts.

At the insistence of both Bella and Alice she agreed to go out to lunch with her mother-in-law and David.

"Jesse'll be fine with Alice," Bella comforted, sensing Kathy's ambivalence as they walked to the white Early American house that had been converted into a chic restaurant. "He was already drifting off to sleep when we left."

The restaurant was set up in a series of rooms on the lower floor. It was almost like dining in a private house, Kathy thought, while David and Bella exchanged reminiscences about his years of residence at his cousins' home. Brief periods, she realized, because most of the time David and Phil were at boarding school or college. Still, she felt a warmth between Bella and David that had escaped her on his last visit to Greenwich.

Early in the afternoon Wally arrived back at the house to drive Bella into town for the fashion show.

"I'll dress at the company apartment," Bella told Kathy while Wally carried her valise out to the car. David was upstairs in his room, allowing himself the luxury of a post-luncheon nap. "Dinner will be served for you and David at seven. Julius and Phil and I will have dinner in the city and then drive home. We should be here around eleven."

"I doubt that Phil will come back with you tonight," Kathy said. "He'd just be able to grab five hours' sleep and have to climb into the car again."

"But he'll want to see David," Bella protested. David was scheduled to leave on an afternoon flight tomorrow. "Phil will come home," she said confidently.

Phil wouldn't go out of his way for anybody but Phil, Kathy thought. She rechanneled the conversation: "Bella, wear your diamond necklace, you'll look beautiful." Subconsciously she remembered what Bella had told her about the diamond necklace. It had been made up of the diamonds David's father had given him to smuggle out of Germany, and bought by Julius for a fraction of their worth. *Had David never guessed that?*

"I don't dare show up without my necklace. The Kohn crown jewels," Bella chuckled, but Kathy saw the cynical glint in her eyes. "Julius has to let his society customers know his wife wears expensive jewelry, too."

"Enjoy the fashion show," Kathy urged and kissed Bella good-bye.

"Phil, you didn't rent enough chairs!" Julius complained, wiping his forehead with an expensive Brooks Brothers handkerchief, though the air-conditioning was more than adequate.

"Dad, relax. We've got a chair for every ticket the women sold."

Handsome in white dinner jacket that highlighted his Southampton tan, he glanced about the spacious, gray-carpeted showroom with satisfaction. The small gilt chairs were neatly lined on either side of the runway. The flowers were exquisite. In ten minutes—before the first guests arrived at 5 P.M.—the string ensemble would begin to play.

"I don't know why it's not enough to donate the money

from the tickets," Julius grumbled. "We've got to give them a percentage of the evening's sales as well."

"We raised the prices of every fur in inventory," Phil reminded.

"You're sure we'll get film footage decent enough to show in the out-of-town stores?" Julius watched with obvious skepticism as the light men made their final check.

"We'll have great footage," Phil promised. Hell, it was a sensational idea to film the whole deal, he congratulated himself. "I'm going to check on the models."

Bella, then Gail and Brenda—whom their brother called the Siamese twins—arrived and surrounded Julius. The musicians began to play. Right on schedule the guests—who in the name of charity had paid high for their tickets—began to pour into the showroom. For a moment of drama the music stopped. With a scintillating smile Phil emerged from behind the array of screens that doubled as theater curtain.

"Welcome to Julius Kohn Furs. . . ."

Striving to conceal her anxiety, because Phil kept saying she was paranoid about the polio epidemic this summer, Kathy leaned over Jesse and felt his forehead.

"Alice, find the thermometer, please. I think he may be running a fever."

"It's right here." Alice reached inside a dresser drawer. "But he was normal an hour ago."

"His face looks flushed now," Kathy worried.

She waited while Alice took his temperature, awakening him in the process.

"Go 'way." He protested the invasion of the thermometer. "Don't want it."

"Just lie still, darling," Kathy pleaded. "It'll be over in a minute."

"It's a little over 100 degrees," Alice said. "That's nothing."

"I'm going to ask David to have a look at him," Kathy decided.

She found David sitting in the library listening to a TV report on the fighting in Korea. She told him about Jesse's slightly elevated temperature.

"I know it's probably nothing," she apologized, "but would you run up and have a look at him, David?"

"Of course, Kathy.

"Your mommie tells me you have a cold, Jesse," David said while he placed a gentle hand on Jesse's forehead. How tender he was, Kathy thought. "Do you feel sleepy?"

"Wanna drink of water," Jesse told him with a frown. "Want it now."

"I'll get it, Jesse." Alice hurried from the bedroom.

"Do you know if any of his friends have come down with colds, too?" David asked.

"I don't know about the children at his nursery school." Her eyes searched David's. "But he plays every day with one little boy and a little girl. The nursemaids have formed a kind of clique. Alice would know—"

"Could you call their homes and ask if they have colds?"

"David, can polio start with a cold?" She was dizzy with alarm.

"Kathy, don't jump to a diagnosis," he chided. "I'd just like to reassure myself that they're both all right. It's just a precautionary inquiry."

"I don't know the families personally, but I'm sure I can phone and ask."

Within five minutes she had learned from servants in the children's homes that neither was suffering from a cold. Kathy felt relieved. This was probably nothing more than an early fall cold. She hurried back to Jesse's bedroom. He was sipping water through a straw while Alice held the glass for him.

"Neither of the children has a cold," Kathy told David. "They're both fine."

"Good. Let's go downstairs and have a cup of coffee." His smile was reassuring. "We'll check his temperature again in an hour."

"Call me, Alice, if Jesse wants me," Kathy said, though he was already dozing off again.

Over coffee in the den David talked earnestly about his research. He was trying to distract her from worrying about Jesse, Kathy thought while she made a pretense of being deeply involved in what he was saying. When he'd asked her to check with the other children, he hadn't been concerned about colds, she decided with sudden apprehension. He was anxious about Jesse's exposure to polio.

They'd lingered in the den for almost an hour when David suggested they look in on Jesse again.

"As long as we're here, let's check on his temperature. You remember me," he said with a chuckle. "Always over-precautious." In Hamburg the other doctors in their group had ribbed David about this. "And Jesse's a very special patient."

The thermometer in one hand, Alice looked up from Jesse's bedside.

"I was just coming downstairs to tell you. I took his temperature. It's up to 102."

"It's probably some minor infection," David said, leaning over Jesse. "I'd like to see some tests done. Now don't be alarmed, Kathy. This is just to be sure. But the tests have to be done in the hospital." He hesitated. "I think we should take him over right away. Is there a car available?"

"Yes." Kathy fought against panic. "Bella's car is in the garage; the keys are always in a drawer in a foyer cabinet. I'll bring the car out front."

She hurried out of the room, down the hall, down the stairs, and through a side door to the garage. By the time she pulled up before the house, Alice stood there with Jesse, swathed in a blanket in her arms and querulous. David was trying to soothe him. Now David moved forward to open the door for Alice.

"I'll drive," he told Kathy compassionately and swung around to the other side of the car. "All right, point me in the right direction," he said when he was settled behind the wheel.

"I thought with the hot weather over we'd come through another summer without trouble," she said with an anxious glance toward Jesse. He was lethargic now. She was more frightened by this than if he had been crying.

"Kathy, this is probably nothing," David told her. "I just want to play it safe. Thank God, there appears to be some breakthrough on polio research. It may take years, but one day we'll have a vaccine. There's a Dr. Salk who's working on something right now, I hear."

"I've tried to be so careful, David." *This was a nightmare.*

"It's most likely just some minor infection," David reiterated.

At the hospital Kathy waited with Alice while David disappeared behind doors with Jesse. Thank God for David, she thought.

"I ought to be with Jesse," she protested to Alice when they'd sat waiting for almost fifteen minutes. "Why are they keeping me out here?"

"He's in good hands," Alice comforted. "He's going to be all right." But Kathy knew that Alice, too, was anxious.

David emerged at last, accompanied by a pediatrics resident.

"We'd like to admit Jesse," the resident explained after he and Kathy had been introduced. "There's nothing conclusive, but his symptoms bear watching."

"I want to stay here with him," Kathy said, her voice warning against refusal. *He was so little. He'd be so frightened in a strange hospital room.*

"I'm sure that can be arranged," the resident said gently. "Right now we need some statistics."

At last Jesse was settled in a private room, where a bed would be brought in for Kathy.

"You'll be needing some things for the night," Alice reminded her. "Why don't you go home, pack a valise, have dinner, and then come back? I'll be here with Jesse. If they'll let me, I'll go along with him when he has the tests."

"Want Teddy," Jesse complained. "Mommie, bring me Teddy."

"All right, darling." Kathy reached to squeeze his hand. "Alice will stay here with you. I'll be back soon."

Again, David settled himself behind the wheel of the car, Kathy grateful for his presence. She would have been terrified if she had to go through this alone.

"Remember, Kathy, these tests are just a precautionary measure." He took one hand from the wheel and rested it on hers for a moment. "And they won't be frightening."

"But the symptoms suggest polio?" she challenged.

"Suggest." David was matter-of-fact, but she sensed his concern. "And most cases last only a few days. With no permanent damage," he emphasized. "We hear only about the bad ones." He hesitated. "Shouldn't you call Phil?"

"Not until after the fashion show." Bitterness crept into her voice. "Phil takes the phones off the hook until it's over."

"What time will that be?"

"About 7:30 or 8," she surmised. "Phil will probably go off to dinner with a group afterward. There's no way I can reach him."

David left the car in front of the house, and he and Kathy went inside. The housekeeper came down the hall at the sound of their voices.

"It's well past seven," she said aggrievedly. "Mrs. Kohn told me to send dinner in at seven sharp."

"I'm sorry," Kathy apologized. "We've just come back from having Jesse admitted to the hospital."

"Oh, my!" It seemed to Kathy that the housekeeper inched away from them. When a child was sick this ghastly summer, everyone suspected polio. "I hope it's nothing serious."

"We're fairly certain it isn't," David told her. But Kathy

knew he wasn't certain at all. They wouldn't know until after the tests.

"I'll have Madeline serve dinner," the housekeeper said. "Oh, your husband called about five minutes ago. He said to tell you he'd be staying in the city tonight."

"Thank you." Why did the woman look so scared, Kathy asked herself in anger. But then adults, too, came down with polio. "I'll try to reach Phil at the apartment," she told David. "Later."

"Oh, the fashion show was so exciting, Phil!" Carol glowed as the taxi carried them from the usual Village restaurant toward the company apartment. "And afterward the champagne and the smoked salmon and the other stuff, mmm."

"The show's great for the business." Phil's smile was complacent. He'd known Carol since August and this was late September. They'd been out seven or eight times and he still hadn't got in. But tonight was their night. He'd known that the minute she told him—right after the fashion show—that she was going to a backers' audition next week and wanted to take him. She wanted something from him, and was willing to pay.

"It was sweet of you to get me a ticket," Carol purred, the skirt of her black chiffon cocktail dress riding perilously high as she leaned against him. "You never know whom you'll meet at that kind of bash."

"That's a great dress." His eyes clung to her cleavage. "I can't wait to take it off."

"Phil, you talk so awful," she scolded. "I charged it to my mother's account at Bergdorf's," she chattered on. "I want to wear it to the backers' audition next week. I've got this tiny little part to read. If it goes on Broadway, I've got a chance at playing it."

"Is it a comedy?" Phil asked. He understood what Carol was implying. If she brought in an investor—him—then the part would be hers. So tonight there'd be no red lights.

"No, it's serious theater," Carol said with pride. "The

producer's hoping to persuade Lee Strasberg to come in to direct. He wants it to be a true Method acting production. He'd love to get Marlon Brando for the lead, but Brando's all tied up with films."

Phil had heard, in boring detail, about Carol's acting classes with a Method teacher. He was cynical about how "being a tomato"—Carol's last class assignment—would make her another Garbo, but he listened to all her outpourings about motivation and "real-life" experiences because Method had become so "in" these days. He liked appearing knowledgeable about the theater scene.

"Phil, you *are* coming to the audition with me?" she prodded when he'd paid the driver and they were headed for the entrance to the apartment house.

"You bet," he said breezily, reaching into his pocket for the keys. No stop signs tonight, he reminded himself. He was never comfortable making love—doing everything "but"—in her apartment, even though her roommate made a point of being out. He wanted nobody around to say, "Sure, I saw them in bed together." He opened the door and drew her into the lobby with him.

"Great building," Carol approved while they waited for the elevator.

"I've got something else great for you," he promised, nuzzling suggestively against her pelvis.

As Phil slid the key into the lock of the apartment door, the phone began to ring. It continued to ring. He pushed the door open, switched on the foyer lamp, and ushered Carol inside.

"Aren't you going to answer the phone?" she asked curiously.

"It's probably a wrong number." He shrugged and locked the door behind them.

"It would drive me crazy not to answer." She giggled as he slid a hand down the neckline of her dress.

"You drive me crazy," he reproached. "All through the show I kept thinking about you. About us—"

He pulled her close, confident that the backers' audition was the key to the room he'd never entered.

"Oh Phil, you are *so* passionate," she drawled while he shoved her dress away from her shoulders, down the undulating length of her body to the floor.

It was going to be one hell of a night, he promised himself while he stripped away the rest of her clothes and ran his hands over her delectable twenty-two-year-old nudity.

"Okay, Carol," he ordered, his voice husky with anticipation, "let's get this show on the road!"

Half an hour later—while he lay tired but exultant above her, triumphant in the knowledge that in a few moments he'd be ready for the second round—the phone rang again.

"Phil?" Carol lifted an eyebrow questioningly.

"Let it ring. I've got other things on my mind."

═ Chapter 17

Before 7 A.M. Kathy was fully awake, after a night of broken sleep. While she sipped at a steaming cup of coffee—brought to her by a compassionate nurse—she received the first phone call of the morning.

"Any word yet?" Bella asked anxiously. Bella and Julius had come to the hospital last night, with David, at close to midnight. Bella was anxious about Jesse and Julius, Kathy suspected, nervous about the contagion aspect of polio. "Are the test reports in?"

"I have to wait until they're all in," Kathy explained. "We should have the results sometime this morning."

"Have you talked to Phil yet?"

"I couldn't reach him." Despite her determination to be casual about this, Kathy heard the angry edge in her voice. "I kept trying until past one this morning. I'll try him at the office around nine. He should be in by then." Julius was taking the day off, but Phil was scheduled to go in to the office.

She had not called home to tell her parents. What was the point in upsetting them when they weren't sure what the diagnosis was? They would have insisted on coming right out.

At 7:30 Alice walked into Jesse's hospital room.

"I'll stay here with him," Alice said firmly and handed Bella's car keys to Kathy. "Mrs. Kohn says you're to drive home to shower and have breakfast."

"But the reports may come in," Kathy stalled.

"I'll tell them to call you at the house. You'll feel better after you've showered and had a decent breakfast."

Reluctantly Kathy went to her in-laws' house. David was at the breakfast table when she came downstairs after her shower. He'd already talked to the hospital office.

"They'll have word on the tests within an hour," he said soothingly.

Kathy was en route to the car when the hospital called. She rushed back into the house, breathless with anxiety.

"Jesse tested positive," the pediatrician at the hospital told her gently. "But all indications are that it'll be a mild case."

"Thank you, doctor." But her heart was pounding. He thought it was a mild case. *Suppose it wasn't?*

"What did he say?" She put down the phone to find David at her elbow.

"Positive. He thinks it'll be a mild case."

"Jesse is going to be all right." David's voice was forceful. "There's not likely to be any permanent damage."

"But we don't know for sure." Kathy was trembling, remembering the children in iron lungs at the hospital.

"The odds are on Jesse's side," David said. He hesitated. "I have to fly out to San Francisco this afternoon, but I'll keep in touch. I'll return as soon as my share of the conference is over. Jesse is going to be all right."

"I'm so scared," she whispered.

"I know," David said compassionately, and pulled her into his arms in comfort. "Just keep remembering that eighty percent of polio cases are mild. Jesse is going to be all right."

Before she returned to the hospital, Kathy phoned her family in Borough Park.

"Jesse's going to be fine," her mother insisted in that calm voice that always covered extreme anxiety. In less serious moments, Kathy thought, Mom was vocally emotional. "Dad'll call Mannie to come to the store. I'll check with Grand Central about schedules. We'll take a taxi from the Greenwich station to the hospital."

"Mom, you don't have to come out," Kathy protested.

"Our grandson's in the hospital. Of course, we want to be there." She paused for a moment, and Kathy heard Aunt Sophie's voice in the background. "Aunt Sophie's coming with us."

Kathy returned to the hospital. She waited until shortly after 9 A.M. to phone Phil at the office, phoning from Jesse's room while he slept. She told Phil that Jesse was in the hospital for tests.

"The tests have come back, Phil," she said. "Jesse has polio. But—"

"What do you mean, he has polio?" Phil's voice crackled with shock.

"He has a case of polio," Kathy reiterated, striving to sound calm, "but it appears to be very mild. Thank God, David was suspicious and got him into the hospital quickly. Of course, we can't be sure for a few days, but the doctors are hopeful that there'll be no permanent damage." She hesitated. "I tried to reach you last night. I called our apartment and the company apartment—"

"I went out to dinner with people," Phil said. His voice sounded strained. "I had a few drinks. I came home and was out cold in ten minutes. A bomb couldn't have awakened me. If there's any change, call me right away. Otherwise, I'll be home by seven. No," he corrected himself. "I'll tell Wally to take me directly to the hospital."

The next few days were agonizing for Kathy. She slept in Jesse's room, hurrying back each time she went to the house. Phil stopped by the hospital each morning before driving into the city, and again on his return to Greenwich. He was upset, but not so upset that he'd stay away from the office, Kathy thought in silent rage. Her family had come all the way up from the city as soon as she told them about Jesse. Mom was staying here at the house, spending most of the day with her at Jesse's bedside.

Bella came to the hospital twice a day, called regularly to comfort her, but Jesse's father was too involved in business to stay at his son's bedside in these critical days. The business would survive if he was away for a few days. God knows, he was on the road often enough. Phil wasn't just a rotten husband. He was a rotten father, too.

David phoned twice a day from San Francisco, always after speaking with the doctors.

"Jesse is going to be all right," he reiterated each time.

"I'm scared," Kathy confessed. "David, I'm so scared!"

Seventy-two hours after he'd flown out to San Francisco, David called to say he was en route to New York.

"He'll be here tonight," Bella told Kathy while they sat together in Jesse's room. "He'll stay until we're sure that Jesse's all right. And he will be," she emphasized gently.

"It just seems to be dragging on so long." Kathy closed her eyes for a moment. "This is one long nightmare."

"Kathy, you're exhausted," Bella said. "I want you to go home and sleep for a few hours. I'll stay here with Jesse. If there's any word about his condition, I'll call you immediately."

"Bella, I can't leave—"

"You can," Bella insisted. "You're just drained. What good will you be to Jesse if you collapse? Go home, sleep for a while, shower, have dinner, and come back."

"I shouldn't," Kathy wavered, her eyes on Jesse, sound asleep on his hospital bed.

"Go, Kathy. I won't leave his side," Bella promised.

Leaving the car in the garage, Kathy realized the house was empty except for the housekeeper. The other servants were off today. Wally was in town with Julius, who was staying at the apartment tonight because he and Phil were entertaining out-of-town store executives. Probably Phil, too, would remain in the city, she thought with contempt. He would call and ask about Jesse, then dash off to that business life that was of more concern to him than his family.

Kathy walked into the house—the front door was never locked until evening—and up the stairs to the room she shared with Phil. She was so tired, she thought, though she'd done nothing for days except sit by Jesse's bed. Bella was right; she needed to rest, for Jesse's sake. She was too exhausted even to think clearly.

She undressed, pulled on one of her white silk mousseline nightgowns—the matching, lined negligé draped across the foot of the bed. In moments she was asleep, caught up in disturbing dreams that revolved about Jesse.

She came awake slowly, reluctantly, then all at once she was wide awake. That was David's voice calling to her from the other side of her bedroom door.

"I'll be right there, David." Trembling, she reached for her negligé, and pulled it on as she crossed the room to the door.

"Kathy, everything's all right," he told her, his face alight with relief. "I called the hospital the moment I arrived here. They were just about to call you. Bella said to let you sleep, but I had to tell you. Jesse is all right. And there'll be no side effects from the polio."

"Oh David, thank God. And thank you for being here," she said shakily. "I don't know how I would have seen this through without your standing by with me."

"You and Jesse are both very precious to me—" David drew her to him in a gesture of mutual relief that Jesse had come through this ordeal.

"And you're precious to us—" Kathy was conscious of her heart pounding wildly. His face close to hers. "I've missed you so much through these years, David—"

Then all at once his mouth was seeking hers, and everything was forgotten in the joyous release of emotions long hidden.

"Kathy, this is wrong," he said in quiet torment after a moment.

"Don't say anything, David," she whispered. "Just hold me."

Again, his mouth found hers, and she knew there would be no holding back now. His hands swept away her negligé while his mouth burrowed in the hollow between her breasts. It was as though, she thought in exquisite pleasure, this was the first time a man had ever made love to her.

They lay together on the bed, touching, kissing with a long denied hunger. A different kind of love, she thought in soaring delight as he sought his way within her. *Let her make this as good for David as it was for her.*

David sat at the side of the bed, his face revealing his pain.

"How could I have allowed this to happen, Kathy? You're Phil's wife. *I was out of my mind.* Can you ever forgive me?"

"There's nothing to forgive, David. I'm just as much to blame as you. It was just that we were both so relieved that Jesse's all right." She was stammering, searching for the right words. David would never allow this to happen again. He'd forever be on guard. "We'll forget it ever happened." She was his cousin's wife, there could never be anything more for them. She drew the silken sheet about her. The wonderful parcel of time with David was over.

"I'm sorry, Kathy—"

"Don't be," she urged. "This mustn't stand between us. You'll always be my very dear friend."

"I couldn't bear losing that," he said quietly.

"You never will," she promised.

David left her to return to his own room while she called the hospital and talked to Bella.

"It's so wonderful!" Kathy said. "The whole world looks wonderful now. Tell Jesse I'll be there in twenty minutes."

"Have dinner with David, before you come to the hospital," Bella ordered. "He was so happy when I told him about Jesse."

"We'll have dinner," Kathy agreed.

Only for the first few minutes at dinner did she feel an uneasy self-consciousness with David. This was David, whom she loved—and who loved her.

"I hope you'll take yourself off for a week or two," David said gently. "Away from familiar scenes."

"I'll take Jesse and run out to California for a while." Maybe Phil had not been lying when he said he'd gone out to dinner with friends and drank too much to hear the phone when she'd called. Maybe. But she knew she must put distance between herself and Phil for a while if their marriage was to survive.

She'd call Marge and say she'd be out in a month or so. Phil couldn't object to that. He might even be pleased.

David slept little on the flight across the Atlantic. Being with Kathy for those days, seeing her with Jesse, had emphasized his loneliness, his aching need for family. The concentration camp had robbed him of that. Perhaps the time had come to think about building another family. A memorial to those he had lost. But he couldn't let himself think of Kathy. Never again would he lose his self-control like that, no matter how much he yearned for her still. He would have to search elsewhere, he told himself. Either that or remain alone.

He wasn't in love with Gretchen, but they had much in common. She was pretty, bright, compassionate. Not right away, he stalled, but he would think about pursuing her. Instinct told him he would not have to pursue very hard.

Not every marriage was based on love. That would come later. He dreaded the empty nights in his drab apartment. He'd told himself that work would fill his life—but seeing Kathy, making love with her, seeing her with Jesse, told him that work was a pale substitute for family.

He would ask Gretchen out for dinner in a few days. He wouldn't rush her—they both must be sure that a relationship would work for them. He doubted that Kathy's marriage was a good one. Too many poignant indications that she was unhappy. Yet she was his cousin's wife, and he had no right to intrude on their marriage.

Late in October Kathy flew with Jesse and Alice to San Francisco. Marge met them at the airport, accompanied them in the taxi that was taking them now to the elegant Hotel Fairmont, where Kathy had reserved a suite.

"God, you live in style," Marge said with uninhibited candor. "Don't you feel absolutely decadent, with a suite at the Hotel Fairmont?"

"I'm learning to enjoy it," Kathy said, feeling herself out of prison. "Bella's teaching me."

"You're hitting it off well with your mother-in-law?"

"We're close, Marge. In the beginning I didn't expect it to be that way." She was intrigued now by the salt-scented fog that hung over the road, lending an eerie air to the landscape. "But tell me about your job," she ordered.

While they drove from the outskirts of San Francisco into the city itself—up and down endless hills—Marge talked about her continuing affair with designing, her determination to open her own shop one day. Self-conscious at first, Kathy admitted to the exhilarating satisfaction she was finding in the classes she was taking at F.I.T.—the Fashion Institute of Technology.

Then they were pulling up beneath the huge portecochère of the square-block Fairmont. While Alice supervised the transferral of their luggage into the hands of hotel personnel, Kathy and Marge walked into the palatial lobby.

"I come here when I'm depressed," Marge confided laughingly. "Just to walk over these miles of gorgeous carpet and to see the marble staircases, those marble pillars, and the mirrors. I can't afford to stay here, like some people," she teased, "but once in a while I get taken to the Top

of the Mark—you know, on the top of the Mark Hopkins—
for a drink at sunset. We'll go there for sure," Marge promised exuberantly.

Not until they were in the posh suite at the Fairmont—
atop Nob Hill and across the street from the equally famous
Mark Hopkins—did Kathy confess to boredom with her so-
called good life.

"One of these days I'll break out of my prison," Kathy
warned. "I'll do something more exciting with my life than
being a semi-parasite."

"I wish you were living out here," Marge sighed. "And
that we had a shop of our own. Selling mostly casual sportswear," she pinpointed.

"That's going to be the big market in the years ahead,"
Kathy predicted. "It's the kind of clothes that fit in with
suburban life, and let's face it, Americans are rushing to the
suburbs."

"Mommie—" Jesse returned from his tour of the suite
with Alice. "Alice says those funny trains down in the street
are cable cars. Can we go on one?"

"You bet, Jesse," Marge answered for her. "And we're
going to the zoo and Golden Gate Park and, oh, lots of
places."

Marge took two days off from her job to show them San
Francisco. After that Kathy roamed about the city with
Jesse and Alice. Jesse was fascinated by the cable cars,
though Alice good-humoredly admitted to some trepidation
about this fanciful mode of transportation.

Each evening—once Jesse was settled in for the night and
Alice chose her television fare—Kathy met Marge for dinner and a walk about the city. Each night Marge chose a
different restaurant, delighted that Kathy insisted on picking up every check and that they dine in the best San Francisco restaurants.

Not until their third night—when Marge took her to the
glass-domed, multi-chandeliered Garden Court in the his-

toric Palace Hotel—did Kathy talk with candor about her
marriage.

"I was sure it wasn't the ideal marriage," Marge confessed, her beef pie *bourguignonne* ignored now. "I know
you too well not to recognize that."

"I'm not sorry I married Phil," Kathy said slowly. "I
wouldn't have Jesse if I hadn't, and I love him so much,
Marge. But once Jesse is eighteen and in college, I'm leaving
Phil. Of course, I'll be—what? Forty-one," she calculated
and laughed. "Still, I'll be a free forty-one."

"It doesn't seem fair for you to have to waste all those
years," Marge rebelled.

"I have to do it for Jesse," Kathy insisted. "There's no
way that Phil would give me a divorce. He'd fight me—fight
me dirty—to gain custody of Jesse. I'm Jesse's mother—he
belongs with me."

"You can fight dirty, too," Marge pointed out. "Hire a
detective to get evidence of adultery."

"I couldn't bear an ugly divorce. I don't want Jesse to
know, ever, about Phil's chasing after other women. I want
him to believe he's had a normal childhood."

"My mother always pretended my father was a devoted
husband. She never guessed my brothers and I knew about
the string of floozies that kept him away from the house a
couple of nights a week almost to the day he died. She still
doesn't know."

"Jesse won't know," Kathy vowed. "I'll make sure of
that. He'll think that his father works very hard at his business, and some nights he can't come home. *I'll* always be
there for him. But once he's off to college, I'm off to a life
of my own."

"I hope you're squirreling away money," Marge said
bluntly.

"Some," Kathy conceded. "And once Jesse's in school
full time, I mean to move out into the business world. Phil
can carry on all he likes. I'll try for a job."

"On Seventh Avenue," Marge guessed. "That's why you're taking classes."

"At first I just signed up for a course to fill my time. Then I knew it was what I wanted to do. I got the bug from you, Marge," she scolded affectionately. "But I'm glad."

Julius stared at Phil over a steak at Toots Shor's.

"Why the hell should I invest in a Broadway play? Because of some slut you want to *shtup?* She'll get a part in the play if I put up money?"

"It's a sharp move, Dad." Phil ignored his father's jibe. He'd been to three auditions of the play already. Carol wasn't bad. And she had every guy in the room overheated. "If it's a hit, you make a bundle. If it folds, then you have a tax write-off. And you're moving in the right circles."

"I'll talk to the accountants," Julius said after a moment. He liked the idea of being an investor, Phil guessed.

"He'll tell you this is a no-lose deal. You win either way. And it'll be fun. We'll go to the opening when the play comes into town, wait for the reviews at Sardi's. And you'll meet some gorgeous broads."

"I said I'll talk to the accountants," Julius repeated. "When's Kathy and the kid due back from San Francisco?"

"Tomorrow night."

"Your mother wants Kathy to go with her to Palm Beach in January," Julius told him. "The girls are going down to Cuernavaca this year."

"She'll want to take Jesse," Phil warned.

"So she'll take Jesse." Julius shrugged and inspected his son through narrowed eyes. "When are you going to have a second kid?"

"We've never discussed it." Phil was startled by the question. "Why do we need another kid?"

"It pays to keep the little woman occupied with children. They don't get the wrong ideas in their heads." He grinned. "You were born when your mother started to look at me with a weird glint in her eyes."

"To tell you the truth, I think Kathy's so wrapped up in Jesse she doesn't want another kid." He squinted in thought. He wasn't crazy about the image of himself as the father of two.

"She's at the stage now when she turns her back to you in bed," Julius guessed. "Wives—they're all alike. The first year or two, before you get 'em pregnant, they're always ready. After that, it's the part of the marriage they're happy to forget about. I remember your old lady—I used to call her Miss Ironpants. But we understood each other. She has what she wants, and I have what I want."

"Don't wait too long about investing in the play," Phil warned. "They've already got half the money up."

The next morning over breakfast at their usual restaurant Julius told Phil he'd invest in the play.

"My accountant says go ahead. It's like the Income Tax Bureau is financing the theater. When do you want the money? And when do *I* see a backers' audition?"

"Tomorrow night there's another," Phil told him. He'd see Carol, of course, and get the message. But so what? Dad wasn't running to tell Kathy. Any more than he told Mother about the *zaftig* little bookkeeper Dad had been screwing for the last four years. "We'll run over here for dinner, then I'll take you down."

The second week in January, Kathy flew to Palm Beach with Bella, Jesse, and Alice. They were to stay until the end of the month at the "cottage" of Bella's friend, Genevieve, who was sunning herself in Nice before going on to the couturier showings in Paris, the "cottage" being a fourteen-room villa directly on the beach.

Kathy relished the seclusion of the beach house, with a staff of servants who made themselves almost invisible. Here there was none of the constant comings and goings of the beach house at Southampton. Bella and she lounged on the deck alone, reading or engaging in lazy conversation, while Jesse played on the sand under the watchful eyes of Alice, at intervals playing with a small neighbor, also in the care of a nursemaid. Their meals were served on the deck, with the ocean lulling Kathy's tense nerves into a semblance of relaxation.

Some afternoons Kathy and Bella were driven down to Worth Avenue to roam among the magnificent shops. Bella was candid about the pleasure of buying clothes.

"You can always tell when I've had a fight with Julius," Bella confided. "I shop like mad. I'm giving myself treats because he's been a bastard about one thing or another. I don't even care about his parade of floozies anymore. It's the petty little fights, when he makes his snide remarks to me. I've done all right for the little stenographer from the Bronx whose folks thought the height of luxury would be to live in an apartment on the Grand Concourse."

It was amazing, Kathy thought, how close she had become to Bella. After all these years Gail and Brenda were little more than strangers. She enjoyed Bella's turning to her for advice about clothes. Bella said she had a real sense of style, she remembered with satisfaction.

In another two years she'd find out how good that sense of style really was. The day Jesse started the first grade would be the day she moved into the outside business world. She'd have to start at the bottom, she conceded, but she'd build herself a career. She wouldn't allow Phil to stand in her way.

On their return from Palm Beach, Wally met them at the airport with the limousine.

"Mr. Phil said you two ladies were to meet him and his father for dinner at Le Pavillon at eight o'clock. He's made reservations."

"Thank you, Wally." Bella sighed. "The circus begins again."

In an exquisitely simple black crepe dinner dress with a pleated wraparound bodice and skirt—a line-for-line copy of a Dior—Kathy sat between Phil and Julius while the two men argued over the new contract drawn up for their world-class designer. Julius, as to be expected, was outraged at the designer's demands.

Bella turned to Kathy with a sigh of impatience that on their first evening back from Palm Beach, over dinner at Le Pavillon, the two men had to talk business.

"How clever of you to wear black here," Bella complimented Kathy. "It's so dramatic against all this cerise upholstery. And of course, the red roses look as though they'd been ordered just for you."

"Isn't it a beautiful room!" Kathy gazed about with pleasure. "Everything is so perfect." The tab would be enormous, she thought, but it would show up on either Phil's expense account or his father's.

"We're going to a Broadway opening tomorrow night," Julius announced with a complacent grin. "I own a piece of the show."

"You invested in a play?" Bella was astonished. "You've always said that was for suckers."

"That was until our accountant explained the facts of life to Dad." Phil exchanged a knowing glance with his father. "It's a smart move, business-wise. Theater people are always in the news. You travel with them—you're part of that."

"Is it a musical?" Bella asked.

"No." Now Julius appeared slightly self-conscious. "It's serious theater. They wanted Lee Strasberg to direct, but he was otherwise involved. But it's that kind of play."

"Julius, if it's opening tomorrow night, you must have invested months ago. Now you tell me?" Bella shook her head in annoyance.

"What's to tell? It's another investment." Julius shrugged and turned to Phil. "Make sure we have reservations at Sardi's for after the performance."

"They're made," Phil told him.

Instinctively Kathy guessed that Phil had prodded his father into putting money into the play. What pushed Phil back into the theater scene, she wondered curiously. The answer came quickly. Some sexy young actress looking for a break.

"Take home that sable cape for Kathy to wear to the opening," Julius ordered. "Kathy, phone Roz and ask what you should wear with the cape."

"I'll know what to wear," Kathy said with strained politeness. Under the surface there was always this aura of hostility between herself and her father-in-law, she thought. He still hadn't forgiven her for refusing to have a big wedding. And she'd rejected his suggestion about having Jesse's *bris* at the Hampshire House.

"What are we celebrating tonight?" Bella asked. Kathy noted she was wearing her diamond necklace, no doubt at Julius's orders.

"Roz wants us here." Julius glanced toward the entrance. "She and the publicity man for the play are working on a column item. Why didn't you wear your diamond and sapphire necklace, Kathy?"

"I loaned it to Alice tonight," she murmured.

For a moment Julius stared at her in shock, then broke into laughter.

"You mean, to wear to the Firemen's Ball."

"Here comes Roz," Phil whispered. "Smile pretty, ladies."

Even now—and she was sure the affair between Roz and Phil was over—Kathy tensed in Roz Masters's presence. Who in tomorrow night's play had replaced Roz?

Kathy made a pretense of being involved in the opening night excitement. Phil and his father saw the Kohn entourage—Brenda and Gail and their husbands—to their seats, then disappeared until a moment before curtain time. The instant Carol made her entrance—even before she had delivered her five lines—Kathy knew this was Phil's latest fling.

By the end of the second act Kathy was sure the play would close within a week, though the opening-night audience circulating in the lobby between the first and second acts had made the expected laudatory pronouncements. The cast was brought back for several curtain calls, but this was an audience of friends, Kathy realized.

After the show, Julius herded his party from the theater to Sardi's, where Phil had made reservations in the wood-paneled Belasco Room, a favorite site for more intimate theater wakes.

"We'll wait for the reviews," Julius said firmly, though Kathy suspected even he realized this investment would be a tax write-off.

Gail and Brenda dissected the clothes worn by the actresses in the company. Bella said bluntly that the play was dull and that the critics would probably rip it to shreds.

"They should have brought in a Hollywood star," Julius complained. "That's always good box-office."

"The director wanted John Garfield," Phil told him.

"Garfield's a bloody Commie," Julius scoffed. "The whole world knows that."

"Because *Counterattack* and books like *Red Channels* say so?" Kathy challenged.

"We have to protect ourselves against those creeps," Julius blustered, color flooding his face. "They're out to destroy the world."

"During the Depression a lot of loyal Americans were drawn into the Communist Party." Kathy ignored Bella's pantomimed plea to redirect the conversation. It infuriated Julius to be contradicted by anyone in the family, particularly a woman. "Look at all the Americans who fought with the Loyalists in Spain." Frank's father, Kathy recalled, had driven an ambulance with the Abraham Lincoln Brigade. "But they got out."

"A bunch of *schmucks,*" Julius scoffed.

"Look, this is not a period to make waves." Phil shot a warning glance at Kathy.

"Just to ruin careers and lives," Kathy said sweetly.

"Here comes the cast." Bella was intent on diverting the table talk into less controversial areas. "This must be a nerve-wracking time for them."

The two Kohn daughters and their husbands remained for the usual lavish spread of lasagna, seafood Newburgh, salads, macédoine of fruit, and French pastries and then took off for Greenwich. Phil and Julius had made it clear they meant to remain until the early morning reviews came through. The company press agent put on an Academy Award performance, but most of those present knew the reviews would be bad.

Kathy was aware of the secret exchanges between Phil and Carol Graham, who sat at the next table with others in the cast. She heard Carol's squeal of delight that the reviewers—when at last the newspapers were brought into the Belasco Room—had singled her out as "a promising young actress," though the reviews in general were so bad that Phil said closing notices would be posted the following day.

As the Kohn party prepared to leave, Kathy saw Phil contrive to talk for a moment with Carol Graham. His drinking tonight had made him careless. She heard Carol's response to an obviously amorous question.

"Phil, I can't," Carol trilled. "I'm having supper tomorrow night with this man I met who's sure he can get me into Actors Studio, and you know how much that means to me!"

Who would replace Carol Graham, Kathy asked herself. Why did it still hurt, when she knew her marriage was dead? Pride, she taunted herself. Did people around Seventh Avenue talk about Phil the way they talked about his father?

Chapter 18

Kathy was delighted when Marge wrote in March that she would be in New York in April—"with terrific news." She put aside the letter, inspected the clock, and reached for the telephone. With the difference in time it was almost 7 A.M. in San Francisco. Feeling deliciously close to Marge, she phoned, suspecting she would replace Marge's alarm clock this morning.

"Hello—" Marge sounded vaguely awake.

"I just got your letter," Kathy said. "How do you expect me to wait until April for your 'terrific news'?"

"Kathy! It isn't all really set yet, which is why I stalled. But it looks like I'm going to open my own shop!"

"Here in New York?" Kathy asked hopefully.

"In San Francisco," Marge apologized. "I met this rich elderly couple who offered to back me. I gather they've got more money than Fort Knox, and they like to see young 'entrepreneurs' —to use his word—move up in the world. His wife's a steady customer in the shop where I'm working."

"Marge, that's wonderful! That means you'll be selling some of your own designs?"

"I'm sure as hell going to try. Anyhow, I'll be in for a week, staying with Mom in Brooklyn and listening to her complain because I'm not married and not providing her with grandchildren. But I'll be in the city every day. We'll have a ball!"

Kathy waited restlessly for Marge to arrive. She was eager to talk over her own plans to move into the business world. One year from this coming June, she thought with heady anticipation, Jesse would be six. That September he would start first grade. Emancipation day for her.

Kathy arranged a small dinner party for Marge on her second evening in New York. That same morning Phil phoned from the office to say he was flying to Palm Beach early in the afternoon to discuss a lease on a shop on Worth Avenue.

"I'll be down there just for three days. Sorry to mess up your seating arrangements tonight," he apologized. "I'll bring you something pretty from Palm Beach."

"I don't worry about seating arrangements. It's not Noah's Ark," Kathy said casually. In a way it would be a relief not to have Phil there. The guests were all *her* friends. Phil knew Rhoda and Frank, of course, but they had nothing in common. "Shall I pack a bag for you?"

"I'll be home in twenty minutes to pack. I suppose Jesse is at nursery school?"

"Yes."

"Then tell him I'll bring him a present from Palm Beach."

To Phil a present made up for missed storytelling sessions, which were frequent. Probably he'd have his secretary pick up something at F.A.O. Schwarz on her lunch hour, and he'd present it as a souvenir from Palm Beach.

Marge arrived early, as planned, kicked off her shoes and settled on the sofa for ebullient conversation.

"I love Mom, but she does drive me nuts," Marge said

good-humoredly. "You know the routine. Here I am twenty-eight years old and still single. She keeps telling me how I have to go out and join things—political clubs are her main *shtick* now. I should join the Democratic Club and meet young lawyers on the way up. I should take tennis lessons because she thinks I look good in tennis shorts. Maybe," Marge sighed, "I'd look good in shorts if I dumped the fifteen pounds I've picked up from eating sourdough bread lathered with butter."

"Tell me about the shop," Kathy ordered. "I'm dying to know every little detail."

When Jesse arrived, he was instantly the focus of their attention.

"I tell you, if anything could persuade me that marriage is great, it would be Jesse. He's such a love."

"He's what keeps me with Phil," Kathy admitted. "I want him to have the best of everything."

Then the others arrived, and the apartment seemed to radiate high spirits. Here the conversation jumped from subject to subject, erupting regularly into good-humored argument. They lingered around the dinner table talking about the coming Republican and Democratic conventions.

"As much as I'd love to see Stevenson run for president, I think he'd be nuts to do it," Frank declared. "Who the hell can win against Eisenhower?"

They dissected the question of who was winning in Korea and talked with anguish about the red-baiting that was destroying so many of the country's creative talents. Kathy gloried in the stimulation that seemed to ricochet about the apartment. This was her real life—the hours spent among old friends with something on their minds besides the fur industry and making money. This and the hours in Borough Park, with Mom and Dad and Aunt Sophie.

Reluctantly the guests began to leave.

"Tomorrow's a workday," Rhoda reminded while Frank went to bring their coats from Kathy's bedroom. She and Frank were the last to leave. "But it's been such fun."

"Phil's flying to Denver in ten days for business," Kathy remembered. "He'll be away for the weekend. Why don't you and Frank go up to the Greenwich house with me that Friday evening? We can come back into town sometime Sunday."

"I don't think it'll be a good idea," Rhoda said uneasily.

"Why not?" Kathy was puzzled.

"Frank and I are becoming active in a new group that's fighting against the trapping of wild animals by fur traders."

"You?" Kathy broke into laughter. "Rhoda, you're the one who joined Marge in poking fun at me when I'd say I wasn't comfortable walking around with furs that used to be on some wild animals' backs. Marge said—and you agreed with her—'Let Julius Kohn present you with a gorgeous mink, and you'll change your mind.' "

"Frank converted me," Rhoda admitted. "He read me the most heartbreaking plea—written back in the last century by Minnie Madden Fiske—for women to stop wearing furs because of the pain inflicted by the traps. For what? So we can prance around in those poor little animals' skins."

"Oh, you're on the soapbox," Frank chuckled as he approached them with Rhoda's coat. "Nothing like a woman who's been converted to spread the word."

"I've never felt comfortable being a clotheshorse for Julius Kohn furs." Kathy's smile was rueful. "I keep telling myself, I don't own a fur coat or jacket or cape or whatever—"

"No mink-lined bathrobe or car robe?" Frank twitted.

"That has nothing to do with my invitation to come up to the house with me for the weekend," Kathy said resolutely. "Phil won't be there. And if he was, we'd just avoid discussing the subject. Like I never fight with him or his father about the House Un-American Activities Committee and Joe McCarthy. They have their opinions, and I have mine. I always warn my father not to discuss politics with Phil. On those rare occasions when they spend more than two minutes together," she added derisively.

"Then we'd love to go up with you," Rhoda said. "Okay, Frank?"

"Sure, I'd love to slum for a weekend in Greenwich," Frank joked, and kissed her. "Take care, Kathy."

Again, the Kohn entourage prepared to settle at the South-ampton house for the summer. Kathy promised herself she would go into Manhattan twice a week for summer classes, and she'd take advantage of this escape to visit in Borough Park and to meet Rhoda for lunch. Gail and Brenda were heading for Bar Harbor for the month of July, once the little girls were off to camp; and she anticipated a quiet time alone with Bella and Jesse.

At dinner at Kathy and Phil's apartment shortly before the exodus to the Hamptons, Julius announced that he and Phil had just scheduled a business trip to London and Paris at the end of July.

"Good," Bella said casually. "Kathy and I will go with you."

"What do you mean, you'll go with us?" Julius stared belligerently at her.

"Kathy and I will accompany our husbands to Paris. I think the words are self-explanatory." Bella refused to be ruffled. Kathy tensed, dreading another ugly battle between them.

"We'll talk about it later." Julius turned to Phil. "Did you bring those reports from the real estate people in Atlanta?" Kathy knew an Atlanta store was under consideration.

"Yeah. We can go over them after dinner."

At intervals Bella alluded to the forthcoming European jaunt. Julius was sullen but refrained from further argument. By the time the chocolate mousse was served he had capitulated.

"You'll be on your own most of the time," Julius warned. "We've got some difficult contracts to iron out in London and Paris. It'll be business meetings day and night."

"Fine," Bella accepted. "Kathy and I will be able to entertain ourselves."

"Bella, I can't leave Jesse," Kathy reminded anxiously when the men went off to the den, presumably to discuss Atlanta real estate, though she and Bella immediately heard the raucous sounds of the night baseball game being shown on local television.

"You can, but you won't," Bella corrected lovingly. "Jesse will come along with us. Alice adores traveling with you. We'll be in Paris in time for the shows. We'll buy like crazy." Bella's eyes glinted with satisfaction. Kathy knew that Bella had just discovered her husband's longtime affair with his bookkeeper, which probably motivated his capitulation on the London-Paris trip, she surmised. "Julius will scream when he sees the bills. Phil will scream. But somehow, they'll manage to write them off as business expenses. The rich find ways not to pay taxes, Kathy."

After the ball game the two men joined Kathy and Bella in the living room for cups of espresso. Julius seemed more relaxed now. He figured Bella would not rock the boat—or bed—that he shared with his bookkeeper, Kathy assumed. Ever anxious to have Phil understand who was boss, Julius rejected his son's suggestion that they stay at the Dorchester in London.

"We'll stay at the Savoy," he announced. "Their bathtubs are six feet long."

"Julius, you're five feet four," Bella said drily. "Be careful you don't drown."

"During World War II General Eisenhower sent his laundry to the Savoy," Julius told them. "It went there in special aluminum containers."

"Make it the Ritz in Paris," Phil urged. "Kathy and I stayed there last time. It was great."

"Okay," Julius conceded. "In Paris we stay at the Ritz."

Would there be a reunion in Paris with David, Kathy wondered wistfully. It was a short flight from Berlin to Paris. Bella would never set foot on German soil, she'd been eloquent about that on several occasions. *"How could I go to a country where six million Jews were murdered?"* But maybe Bella would persuade David to join them in Paris for a day.

Though Kathy had slept little on the overseas flight, she was delighted when Bella suggested on their arrival at the Savoy that the two of them shower, change into comfortable "tourist clothes," and begin to see London.

"Julius and Phil will conk out for a couple of hours' sleep, then start their round of appointments. We may see them for dinner," Bella said with mild sarcasm. "Do you know, Kathy, I haven't been in London for twenty-four years. Oh, I've been to Paris a dozen times in that period," she conceded. "Going to Paris means spending a fortune on new dresses, and driving Julius into a frenzy. My mother—may she rest in peace—used to call my troubles with Julius 'silken troubles.' She couldn't understand why I was unable to sit back and enjoy all the things the Kohn money could buy for me. But in time I learned," she said with a conviction Kathy didn't entirely believe. "Do you know how many women in this world would sell their souls to be in our places?"

"I stay with Phil for Jesse's sake." Kathy was always candid with Bella. "If the day ever comes when I think it's not good for Jesse, I'll walk out."

"I used to tell myself that once the children were grown, I'd sue Julius for a divorce and demand a big cash settlement plus fancy alimony. But by then I was too lazy to move out into a life of my own. Or maybe too afraid," she acknowledged. "So I look the other way when I see Julius making an old fool of himself—and I shop. That's survival for a lot of women in this world, Kathy. You might say," Bella chuckled, "that we help keep the economy healthy."

"I've made a list of places we must see." Enthusiasm began to well in Kathy. "We're only going to be here five days, so let's don't waste a minute."

The next four days sped past. Kathy and Bella, with Jesse and Alice, visited the Tower of London. They were enthralled by the display of the Crown Jewels and by their climb up the Bloody Tower. Like other American tourists, they dallied at Westminster Abbey, St. Paul's Cathedral, Trafalgar Square, the British Museum, the National Gallery. They were at Buckingham Palace to witness the Changing of the Guard.

Their first three evenings in London—exhausted from the miles they'd walked during the day—they dined with Jesse and Alice in the comfort of Bella and Julius's suite. Both men dined with business associates, they claimed. Bella was dubious but philosophical. The fourth night Bella decreed that the men arrive at the Savoy in time to escort them to dinner. They dined in the elegant Main Restaurant, a jewel of the hotel and reached via an imposing double staircase.

Over dinner, which included fresh Beluga caviar, Bella suggested that Julius call David in Berlin and ask him to join them in Paris for a day or two.

"You've got nothing to do. You call David," Julius ordered. "Tell him we'll arrange for a room for him at the Ritz. I don't think David's bankroll is up to that." His chuckle held a condescending note that infuriated Kathy.

The following morning Bella arrived as usual for breakfast with Kathy, Jesse, and Alice in their suite.

"How's my precious this morning?" Bella crooned over Jesse.

"We're going to fly a kite in the park," Jesse reported happily. "And then Alice said I can feed the ducks in a pond there."

"You'll have a wonderful time, darling," Bella promised. "God, at his age I thought the big treat was a day on the beach at Coney Island!"

"Did you call David?" Kathy asked. He wouldn't let that encounter between them at the Greenwich house affect their relationship, would he? They'd promised themselves to pretend it never happened. Phil—the family—would never know. "Is he meeting us?"

"He'll fly to Paris for the day," Bella said. "I couldn't persuade him to take more time off. I gather he and his lab assistant are involved in some important project. He says he just can't be away for more than a day."

"It'll be great to see him." Kathy's heart was singing. *In four days she'd see David.*

"He asked about you and Jesse. I told him both of you were here, too. Oh, it's going to be wonderful to see him." Bella's eyes brightened with anticipation. "There were times when he seemed more my son than Phil. You know David. So warm and compassionate. He always remembered my birthday—even when the others forgot."

Kathy was glad that today Bella had decreed they would shop. Little would be required of her other than to help make decisions about which blouse to buy, which purse would please "the girls." Today she was obsessed by the knowledge that she would soon see David.

On the flight to Paris Phil talked to Julius about the business ahead. Bella dozed. Kathy encouraged Jesse to complete one of the puzzles they'd brought along for diversion while in a secret corner of her mind she recalled the first time she had seen Paris. With Phil. That was when he had asked her to marry him. The second time was when Jesse was two, and she was still able to convince herself that Phil and she had a real marriage.

It had been frightening to hear Bella say that when her children were grown she was "too lazy" to move out on her own. Too afraid of the outside world, Kathy thought compassionately. Feeling—as she sometimes felt—that *she* had in some way been lacking because her husband sought out other women.

Kathy sensed a fresh serenity in Bella as they began their Paris stay. Here—with her liberal spending at the couturiers—she was treated with all the charm and solicitude and pampering accorded rich American women. For a little while Bella felt coddled and important.

In Paris Bella was concerned mainly with shopping. Remembering Kathy's success with their designer, Phil arranged for the two women to be included in the dinner party with the designer on their second evening in the capital. The designer insisted that in Paris *he* would be the host and sent his chauffeured Rolls to bring them to his newly acquired château at the edge of the city.

Impressed by the grandeur of the eighteenth-century château set on magnificently landscaped grounds, Julius seemed less arrogant than normal, Kathy thought. She sensed that Phil was nervous that his father's vulgarity—though always masked by Savile Row suits and custom-made shirts—would offend their host. But the evening was a huge success. At intervals her mind escaped from the casual conversation to dwell on the fact that in the morning David would be heading for the airport for his flight to Paris.

In high spirits over the cordial meeting with the designer, Julius insisted on their return to the hotel that they go into the Ritz Bar for a drink.

"This is one town I've always liked," he said expansively, the short, thick fingers of one hand wrapped around his Scotch-and-soda glass. "What about you two?" he turned from Kathy to Bella. "Been seeing all the museums?"

"My favorite museum is the House of Dior," Bella said with a taunting smile.

"Hey, Phil, you think maybe your friends here might come up with some more old masterpieces like those two hanging in the Greenwich house?" Julius asked.

"I doubt it." Phil smiled self-consciously. "That was a wartime deal."

"I thought you bought those from a German refugee." Bella lifted one eyebrow in surprise.

"That's the story I figured sounded safest," Julius admitted. "Phil bought them from a couple of old Frenchmen here in Paris. That photography assignment was a cover for him to make the deal. You took long enough," he ribbed Phil. Kathy froze, her mind hurtling back in time. Phil had acquired the paintings when they were in Paris? *When?* "Then he brought them in—without the frames—disguised as a batch of film. They're worth close to a million. Phil got them for thirty thousand."

Kathy was cold with shock, Julius's words echoing in her mind. Phil's story about having been billeted in that house with his wartime buddy had been a lie. The paintings had been hidden somewhere in that house. *By Phil.*

"Julius, were you crazy?" Bella stared at him in disbelief and rage. "You allowed Phil to smuggle museum paintings out of Europe? He could have gone to jail!" *She could have gone to jail, Kathy told herself.* "I think you were both insane to take such a chance!"

"It was a snap." Phil smiled as though in amusement, but Kathy saw his furtive glance in her direction. "I'd worked out all the little details, took my time."

The whole point of the trip to Paris was to recover the paintings he'd hidden at that little house. Kathy was stunned by the realization. He'd brought them out of France, but *she* had brought them out of Germany and across the Atlantic and into New York. *How could he have exposed her to such chances?*

"Let's call it a night," Bella said, her face again its usual inscrutable mask. "I'm tired."

Conscious only of the pleasure of being in David's company, Kathy was relieved that there had been no awkwardness between them. She sat with Bella and David in the Ritz dining room—where the lighting is ingenuously designed to flatter feminine diners—and listened to their reminiscences about his first year in New York. At intervals his eyes met hers in mutual pleasure at this brief reunion.

"David, do you ever think of coming back to New York?" Bella asked. "I mean, to live?"

"I feel more American than German," he confessed after a moment. "I'm an American citizen," he reminded them with pride. "At times I've thought about returning to New York. If ever my research would benefit by the move, then I'd go like a shot. But for now my work is in Berlin."

"Is life easier in Berlin now?" Kathy asked softly.

"It'll be a long time before West Berliners enjoy the luxuries Americans take for granted," he conceded with a wry smile. "Central heating and central hot water are not for the average family. And elevators are still only in luxury buildings."

"Are East Berliners still defecting to the West?" Bella inquired.

"Each day there are more—most of them under forty-five and with talents West Berlin welcomes. Many of the defectors are students just graduated from the university in East Berlin."

"Who can blame them?" Kathy said earnestly. "They want to be free." She wanted to be free, but she didn't have that option.

"It's not as simple as it was before that incident in April, when a Soviet jet fighter shot at an Air France passenger plane in the Berlin Air Corridor. Most of the streets leading from East Berlin to West Berlin have since been sealed off. East Berlin seized property and businesses, even bank accounts, owned by West Berliners—a problem that doesn't affect me." His voice deepened in amusement.

"David, where would you like to go this afternoon?" Bella asked when they dallied over coffee. "Montmartre, the Champs-Elysées, the Louvre?"

"The Louvre." David's face all at once exuded anguish. "I was last there eighteen years ago, on a holiday with my father and mother and two sisters."

"We'll spend the afternoon there," Bella said gently. "Then we're meeting Julius and Phil for dinner at Maxim's."

"That's Uncle Julius." David tried to escape painful recall. "Nothing but the best. Wouldn't he have loved living in Paris in La Belle Epoque?" Suddenly he frowned. "Aunt Bella, I didn't bring a dinner jacket with me," he said apologetically.

"No need for that," Bella reassured him. "These days it's only on Friday nights that men *must* were dinner jackets and women evening dress. And this time of year most Parisians are away—there'll be more tourists than anyone else there this evening."

The three spent a pleasant afternoon roaming about the Louvre, its forty-nine acres of grounds a verdant masterpiece on the right bank of the Seine. It was as though life were standing still for these few hours, Kathy thought, so that she could be with David. They walked along the 900-foot Grand Gallery, lingering long before the *Mona Lisa,* saying little, enjoying the presence of one another.

Then a casual remark by an American tourist—*"I wonder how many paintings were stolen during the war and smuggled out of the country?"*—booted Kathy out of her euphoria. Phil had smuggled paintings out of the country. No doubt paintings that the Nazis had stolen from some museum and left behind in their rush to escape when the Allies arrived. And he had taken thirty thousand dollars from his father for them. But then, she thought cynically, did Julius deserve any better?

Before joining Julius and Phil at Maxim's, they returned to Kathy's suite so that David could spend a little time with Jesse.

"Jesse, how you've grown," he said with the proper amount of admiration. "You were such a little boy the last time I saw you." During that awful polio scare, Kathy remembered, and tears of gratitude filled her eyes. Thank God for David's presence during those awful days.

Usually shy with strangers, Jesse warmed up instantly to David. He told David about his afternoon at the Tuileries gardens and his passion for flying kites. Kathy was touched by David's tenderness with Jesse. It was that tenderness as well as his professional skills that had made him so valuable in Hamburg, she thought.

Now she and Bella excused themselves to change for dinner, leaving David and Jesse to entertain each other. In her exquisite Louis XV bedroom—with the voices of David and Jesse providing a serene background—Kathy changed into her new Dior rosebud-printed chiffon with a strapless, draped bodice, then slipped over it a tiny matching tie-on jacket. She inspected her reflection in the mirror, and was pleased by what she saw. The dress was summery and festive, though not evening length.

At the appointed time she, Bella, and David joined Julius and Phil in the "back room" at Maxim's, where Julius had used his designer's office to secure them a table. Maxim's was as opulent as she remembered, Kathy thought, her eyes sweeping about the room. Lush red velvet everywhere, the same calla-lily lighting fixtures, the same baroque mirrors, the famous murals she recalled from her first visit.

She accepted Phil's ostentatious embrace while Julius extended a demonstrative welcome to David.

"It's great to see you, Uncle Julius," David said with a sincere show of pleasure. "It's three years since I was in the States."

It irritated her that David showed such affection, such deference to Julius. What had his "Uncle Julius" ever done for him? He'd lived with the family in those short periods of time when he wasn't away at school or camp. Julius had cheated him on the diamonds his father had managed to smuggle to him out of Nazi Germany. Julius had boasted about that to Bella, she remembered with contempt, though to this day Bella didn't know the diamonds he'd bought "at a fraction of their value" had been David's inheritance from his family. *And David felt so grateful.*

"I'll bet you didn't eat back here the last time you were in Paris with Phil," Julius challenged Kathy.

"We sat in the smaller front room," Kathy recalled. She'd been enthralled at dining at the famous Maxim's.

"That's for tourists and ordinary people," Julius said expansively. "This is where the celebrities come, and the super-rich, the very fashionable, and nobility."

"I think we could have gotten in without pull tonight," Phil laughed. "Kathy would have pulled it off for us." She lifted an eyebrow in bewilderment. "You're young, beautiful, and you're wearing a $1,000 Dior. You're an ornament to the room. That makes you and your party eligible."

"I hate to think what I paid for Bella's dress," Julius grumbled, but he was in too high spirits tonight to continue on this track. Oddly, Kathy thought, Phil liked her to buy expensive clothes—to him it was an indication of his success to see her in designer dresses.

"I understand the table over there—Number 16," Phil said with an air of authority, "is reserved for big celebrities like the Duke and Duchess of Windsor and Princess Margaret—or maybe Marlene Dietrich or Noel Coward."

"And where did you learn all this?" Bella derided.

"Don't forget, I've been coming over every year for the business," Phil reminded his mother. Kathy wondered now who had been his companion on those trips when she had remained behind. Roz? That was the kind of information Roz Masters would provide.

"Isn't that Ari Onassis over there?" Julius pantomimed a whisper, but the result was more a hiss, eliciting a frown of reproach from Bella. "This is summer. Not many important people are in town."

"It's Onassis," David confirmed in a low voice.

Now Julius made a major production of choosing a bottle of champagne to be served with dinner, deciding on the most expensive on the wine list. He meant to impress the sommelier, Kathy thought. At private parties Bella had to make sure he didn't see to it that the cheapest of champagnes were brought out. At the charity fashion show only the best was served, of course, because he understood there would be those among the guests who would know.

"So, David," Julius said with a jovial glint in his eyes, "when are you going to settle down and get married?"

"I'm—I'm very tied up in my research," David stammered.

"Work's not enough," Julius chided, his eyes moving about the table. "A man needs a wife and children." *Did David know about Julius's philandering? Did he remember how little time Julius had for his children?* "A man's real wealth is his family. That's his immortality." *He was a sanctimonious hypocrite!*

"It's lonely, yes." David's gaze focused on the tablecloth. "I've been spending an occasional evening with my lab assistant. She—she's good company."

Kathy felt suddenly cold. She didn't want to think about David spending evenings with his lab assistant. She didn't want to think of him as married.

"Well, that's good news," Bella said affectionately. "See more of her. You need somebody to spoil you, David."

How awful of her to feel this way, Kathy reproached herself. Bella was right. David should have a wife to look after him. He should have children. Look how wonderful he was with Jesse. Yet she was conscious of an agonizing sense of loss.

"You're almost thirty-four," Phil clucked. "Get married before you're an old fart and the girls are looking around for somebody younger."

"David can have his pick of women," Bella declared. "Look at him. He's handsome, intelligent, charming. He's not letting himself go like you, Phil. Talk to him and Julius, David. Tell them to watch their weight. Even you, Phil," his mother said resolutely. "I see the pounds creeping up on you. Four years ago you didn't have that little paunch. You—"

"Okay, Bella, we'll start playing golf again," Julius interrupted. "One martini before dinner, no more. Satisfied?" He exchanged an indulgent smile with Phil. "You get married,

David, and we'll come to Berlin for the wedding. Even
Bella, who swore she'd never set foot on German territory."

The remainder of the evening was a nightmare for Kathy.
She was shocked and shamed by her reaction to David's admission that he was seeing someone. If David was seeing
a girl, he meant to marry her. He wouldn't have said as
much if he had not already made up his mind. He was slow
and cautious, and that girl was patiently waiting. *Why
hadn't she waited?*

Now she chastised herself for feeling this awful sense of
loss. How could she be so selfish as to wish that David remain unmarried, without a family? No man was more de-
serving of a happy marriage than David. No man would be
a better father.

There could be nothing for David and her beyond a warm
and cherished friendship. They must forever live their separate lives.

Chapter 19

On their return to the Southampton house Kathy found herself battling restlessness. She was sleeping poorly, blaming her awakening at absurdly early hours on the sunlight that streamed into the bedroom despite the closed drapes. Inwardly she understood her insomnia and restlessness. She couldn't erase from her mind the knowledge that David— lonely and yearning for a family—might be marrying.

At times she was consumed by fresh rage that Phil had used her to smuggle two paintings out of Europe, *exposing her to a possible prison sentence.* And she was ever conscious of his infidelities. Bella had willed herself to accept Julius's women. She suspected many wives closed their eyes. She felt betrayed, cheapened by Phil's affairs.

Gail and Brenda and their husbands were in full-time residence the last two weeks of August. Kathy loathed their constant, self-centered chatter. Milton and Eli were concerned only about the activities on Wall Street and their golf scores. Gail and Brenda—as always—were involved in clothes and the latest acquisition of furniture. The four of them were ever resentful of the not-so-latent anti-Semitism that was part of the Southampton social structure. Kathy, too, found this distasteful but refused to allow it to affect her love for the Southampton sunrises and sunsets and for the magnificent stretch of beach.

It was a relief to Kathy that most nights "the girls" and their husbands were off to dinner parties or on the restaurant circuit. By the approach of Labor Day she was plotting an escape from the family scene. Alice was going on a two-week vacation on their return to the city. She'd take Jesse and fly out to San Francisco for a visit with Marge, and to see the shop, she decided. They'd be back in time for Jesse to start kindergarten.

On the Friday morning before the big Labor Day weekend—when Southampton became an endless party—Kathy sat on the deck with Bella at breakfast. Brenda and Gail and their husbands had just left for Bar Harbor. Alice had taken Jesse to play on the beach with a little girl who had been a classmate at his posh nursery school. Kathy enjoyed the air of serenity that enveloped Bella and herself. The quiet before the weekend explosion.

"I'm rather glad that the girls decided to go to Bar Harbor," Bella confessed to Kathy. "More and more they resent Phil's success in the business. They bicker so with Julius because of that."

"Brenda can't understand why Julius won't use Eli as the company accountant," Kathy said, faintly sympathetic.

"Oh, Julius made that clear before they were married. He said he didn't want Eli knowing every cent he made. But he has sent Eli important clients." Unexpectedly she chuckled. "When Gail was first married to Milton, Julius always bought his shirts from him. Wholesale, of course. But then I insisted he go to a custom shirtmaker when he kept putting on the pounds. I gave up long ago trying to make him stop eating like a pig."

"Phil keeps saying he's going to join a gym and work out regularly, but somehow I doubt it." Phil's favorite workout, she thought in distaste, was in the bed of some woman other than his wife.

"I did an awful job of raising my children." It was Bella's frequent lament. "People are dying every day in Korea, but Gail and Brenda sulk over some imagined slight. They spend hours every day talking about lowering or raising their hemlines or whether Dior's new Profile line is truly flattering, while that man McCarthy is ruining American lives for no reason except his paranoia."

"I'm thinking about going out to San Francisco while Alice is on vacation," Kathy said. "Just for about ten days. We'll be back in time for Jesse to start kindergarten." She'd miss the first class of her new course at F.I.T., she realized guiltily, but she'd make it up.

"It'll do you good," Bella approved. "But try to be back in time for this year's fashion show and my Children's Charity Dance." Kathy served on most of Bella's committees, which now included Manhattan charities as well as those in Greenwich, only begging off when one interfered with her classes. "You've become a real business asset. Even Julius admits that."

"Yes." Kathy's smile was sardonic. "Roz does manage to grab column space for Phil and me." Which meant publicity for Julius Kohn Furs.

"You're a Beautiful Couple," Bella said softly. "And you've got a real sense of style. The columnists like that." She hesitated. "Are you serious about finding a job on Seventh Avenue? I mean, all the classes you're taking—"

"I'm very serious. In another year, when Jesse goes into the first grade, I'm going to be out there job-hunting. This is one time I'll fight Phil."

"Good for you, baby." Bella's smile was both approving and wistful. "The time is coming when more and more women won't let marriage stand in the way of their having careers. During World War II they went out and handled jobs men never dreamt they could handle."

"They saw the other side of the door, and a lot of them, like me, want to move into that outside world."

In the course of the weekend Kathy told Phil she'd like to fly out to visit with Marge while Alice was on vacation.

"No problem," he said casually. "I can play the bachelor for a couple of weeks. Call Linda at the office and have her make all your reservations. Charge everything to the company. It'll be a business expense."

As on her last trip to San Francisco, Kathy had a suite reserved at the Fairmont. She went with Jesse by taxi directly to the hotel. Marge would meet them there as soon as she closed the shop.

"Mommie, you said we could go to the zoo," Jesse reminded while she began to unpack in the bedroom.

"Yes, darling. But tomorrow. It's too late now." Too late, too, to take him up for the view from the Top of the Mark. After 5:30 P.M. no one under twenty-one was allowed because of the bar. "Why don't you take a little nap before dinner?" she soothed. Already he was fighting yawns. "Or maybe you'd like to have your dinner now while we wait for Marge?"

"Can I have a hamburger and fries?" he asked hopefully.

"I'll call room service and find out."

Within half an hour Jesse had consumed an elegantly served hamburger, toyed with the fries, had drunk half a glass of milk, and was changing into his pajamas. He was triumphant because his mother agreed to skipping his bath for tonight, whereas Alice would never have permitted this.

The phone rang, piercing the comfortable quiet of the room. Kathy darted to answer.

"I'm in the lobby," Marge said effervescently. "Shall I come up or are you coming down?"

"Come up," Kathy ordered, suffused with a feeling of well-being. "I can't wait to see you!"

For the first ten minutes of their joyous reunion Jesse fought against sleep. Then his eyelids began to droop.

"All right, Jesse. Bedtime." Kathy scooped him up lovingly.

"You won't go away?" But already he dropped his head to her shoulder.

"I'll be right here," she promised.

With Jesse settled in bed Kathy conferred with room service about dinner for Marge and herself.

"I talked with my neighbor, Lee Moses, and she'll be happy to baby-sit Jesse any night you like. She's a widow living on a pension, and she welcomes whatever baby-sitting jobs come up. She's a darling—you'll like her. So will Jesse."

Now talk focused on Marge's new shop.

"Of course, I've only been open five weeks," Marge conceded, "but I'm so pinched for money. This elderly couple that are backing the shop—Cleo and Fred McIntosh—are always after me to cut corners. He worked hard to make his millions, I gather. He figures it won't be right if I don't sweat over every penny."

"I have a little money stashed away," Kathy told her. "I can—"

"No," Marge broke in. "You hold on to that for an emergency." Kathy knew Marge still believed that one day she'd walk out on Phil. "I'll hang on one way or another. But I want your input on a few things. You're my 'board of directors.'"

Kathy relished every moment of the evening. Being with Marge, thrashing out business problems, provided a kind of exhilaration long absent in her life. When Kathy began to yawn, Marge insisted, despite her protests, on calling it a night.

"It may be 9:30 P.M. here, but back in New York it's half an hour past midnight. You're still on Eastern time."

"Shall I phone Mrs. Moses or will you arrange for sitting tomorrow night? And every night that I'm here!" Kathy decided impulsively. She'd spend all his waking hours with Jesse, then she'd have precious evening hours with Marge.

"I'll tell her. And call her Lee," Marge ordered. "She'll

be sixty next month, but at heart she's twenty-six. And she'll be thrilled at all that baby-sitting loot."

The days—and evenings—sped past. Kathy and Marge fell into the habit of going back to the shop every night after they'd had dinner. Marge was eager for Kathy's opinions of styles she was ordering for the fall. At the same time Kathy encouraged Marge to have some of her own designs made up.

"You know what I think, Marge?" Kathy squinted in concentration over dinner at Jack's on Sacramento Street. "I think you could build up something really solid by showing just casual sportswear. Why not just sweaters and slacks and shirts and shorts? The 4-S's," she said exuberantly. "How's that for a name?"

"I like it!" Marge pulled a notebook from her purse and began to experiment with lettering.

"Keep the lettering simple," Kathy cautioned. "Easy to read in advertising."

"I don't think Cleo and Fred are going to spring for advertising," Marge sighed. "But the more I envision what you have in mind, Kathy, the more I like it. We're living in an era when casual clothes—sweaters, slacks, shirts, shorts—make up the major portion of a woman's wardrobe. Maybe not for high society," she said good-humoredly, "but for the rest of us."

"You could feature your own designs, Marge. You don't need your own factory—you can give the manufacturing out to a contractor. I can see this building up into a nation-wide chain in time." Kathy radiated enthusiasm. "It's right for the age."

Reluctantly Kathy left San Francisco with Jesse on schedule. She was excited about the potential of Marge's shop. Maybe—just maybe—she could persuade Phil to talk to his father about financing a similar shop in New York once Marge made a success of the one in San Francisco. She

would manage it. Julius had a sharp eye for business. If she could prove the shop could make money, he'd be interested.
Oh yes, she wanted to get out into the business world.

On this December day—with Berlin still wary about a shortage of coal—David was so engrossed in his work that he was unconscious of the dank chill of the laboratory. Earlier Gretchen had brought him the sweater he kept on a hook on the door for chilly days and at her quiet insistence he had pulled it on.

Now Gretchen was bringing him a mug of coffee. He accepted it with a grateful smile.

"You look tired," she said. "What time did you leave here last night?"

"It was morning. I couldn't break off in the middle of that last experiment. Thanks for staying so late." He'd forgotten the time until Gretchen began to yawn. When he was on to something, he was never aware of time. "You must have been here past ten," he said.

"It was close to midnight. I didn't mind that. But I worry about you, the way you keep robbing yourself of sleep."

"I'm all right. It's exciting when I begin to see results close at hand." He felt guilty sometimes about the way he allowed Gretchen to put in so many extra hours on the job. Taking her out to supper now and then wasn't enough to make up for all she gave him of her time. At intervals he forced himself to recognize that she was hoping for more than a professional relationship. Why did he hold back this way? Gretchen had so much to offer a man.

"Tonight's the first night of Hanukkah," she said nostalgically. "When my family was alive, we always made a big thing of it." He knew her mother and sister had died within two years after their release from Buchenwald. "Would you like to come up to my flat for the lighting of the first candle and for supper? Hanukkah's supposed to be a happy occasion," she reminded.

David hesitated a moment. He was remembering Hanukkah of '45, in Hamburg. For so many years it had been impossible to celebrate Hanukkah in Germany. Half of their group had been Jewish—but for all of them, Hanukkah 1945 was a major occasion because it meant the world was at peace again. Brian—who was not Jewish—had discovered a menorah beneath the rubble of what had once been a Hebrew school. Kathy bought candles, and he had whittled them down to fit into the holders, and for eight nights they lit the Hanukkah candles.

"Thank you, Gretchen. I'd like that very much."

He knew when he walked into the dreary entrance to Gretchen's building that tonight would not be like other nights with her. He had been in her apartment only twice, along with others from their research team. She had made a shabby two-room apartment seem warm and comfortable.

He and Gretchen had much in common, he analyzed as he walked—clutching a bottle of wine—up the dark, narrow stairway: their work, their background, their loneliness. The trip to Paris—seeing Kathy, seeing her with Jesse—had been a private torment for him. For so many years he'd lived half a life. With Gretchen perhaps he could become whole again.

Though the night was cold, he felt a rush of warm air as Gretchen opened the door to admit him. She'd nurtured the coals in the fireplace grate into a heat-throwing redness.

"I brought a little something to go with supper," he said, almost shyly. "I remembered you like sherry."

She'd set up a table before the fireplace. He sniffed the appetizing aromas of supper cooking on the range. He *could* build a life with Gretchen, he told himself with a surge of hope.

After supper—with muted music from Gretchen's radio as a background—he took her in his arms. It seemed natural to make love to her. This was good for both of them, he thought afterward while they lay beneath a mound of blankets on her bed and she told him with ingratiating candor how she had prayed for this to happen.

"Stay tonight," she pleaded.

"I couldn't bear to leave," he said and reached for her again, willing himself to believe this was Kathy in his arms.

He began to spend at least two nights a week in Gretchen's apartment. In the spring, he told himself, he'd ask her to marry him. For now it was enough they were together this way. No fancy wedding, he thought in silent amusement. Just the two of them and a handful of friends from the Institute, and the rabbi who would marry them.

Like Uncle Julius said, a man's wealth was his family. He was over thirty-four. What was he waiting for? He wanted a home and a family. He was so tired of coming back to an empty flat, so laden with bitter memories. With Gretchen he would share a whole new world.

= Chapter 20

In late February Kathy felt as though she were a schoolgirl playing hooky. Bella had gone off with Gail and Brenda for two weeks in the Caribbean. Phil was on a trip to the Midwest and West Coast stores. She could abandon the New York social circuit, the obligatory four or five nights a week of dinner at the spots beloved by the columnists, the luncheons at the Colony or the Stork at Phil's whim or with Julius and Bella at her father-in-law's orders, the parade of charity events that could be avoided by a wife whose husband was detained by business.

On the first evening—Alice's midweek day off, when she went to her sister's in Levittown—Kathy told the housekeeper not to bother preparing dinner. She took Jesse off to the Times Square Automat, where he was enthralled by the procedure of dropping coins into a slot and having a door miraculously open to such Automat favorites as chicken pot pie and baked beans.

Jesse was fascinated by the electric signs and the brilliantly lighted theater marquees. He lived in Manhattan, she thought with a rush of love, but for what he saw of the magic of the city he might still be living full-time in Greenwich. With great reluctance he allowed himself to be prodded into a taxi for the ride back up to the Fifth Avenue apartment.

When Jesse was asleep, Kathy called her mother and arranged an impromptu dinner at the apartment the following evening. It was always so good to have them at the apartment because she knew that to her parents, she was living far beyond their fondest dreams for her.

"If it's too short notice, Mom, we can make it a few days later." She didn't mention that Phil was away on another trip—Mom knew. In the last year Phil was never home— either away on a trip or on fabricated business in town— when they came for dinner.

"No, darling, it's fine," Edie said joyously. "Dad has things worked out so well with Mannie and his friend now. They come in to cover whenever Dad asks. And how's my little darling?" she asked tenderly.

Off the phone with her mother, Kathy called Rhoda to arrange to meet her for coffee tomorrow at Tip Toe Inn on Broadway. Now—checking her watch for the time—she phoned Marge in San Francisco to discuss her latest ideas for the shop.

The next afternoon, at 3:30 P.M. sharp, she arrived at Tip Toe Inn. Moments later Rhoda entered the restaurant.

"God, it's getting cold!" Rhoda shivered good-humoredly as she slid out of her coat and settled down at the table. "And me, sworn never to wear furs."

"You're looking smug today." Was Rhoda pregnant? She and Frank were so anxious to have a baby, and each month Rhoda was disappointed. "What's brought that glint into your eyes?" Kathy joshed.

"Frank's just been promoted. I am now married to an editor-in-chief!"

"Oh, Rhoda, that's terrific!"

"Not much more money," Rhoda said with a sigh. "But Frank says he'll have a much freer hand. He's hoping to reshape the magazine's image."

"What about his writing?" Kathy asked, serious now. She knew how important this was to Frank.

"Oh God, he'll still be bringing work home every night and over the weekend. But he swears that once he has everything in place, he'll find time to write again. He's writing the newsletter every month for our animal rights group. He'd really like to do a book on the subject. Now tell me about Jesse. Is he all excited about going into the first grade in September?"

They talked about Jesse and then about Marge and the shop.

"What do you hear from David?" Rhoda asked while they awaited refills of coffee.

Kathy knew Rhoda meant: What did Bella and Julius hear?

"We saw him in Paris in July," Kathy reminded. "And he always sends cards at Rosh Hashanah. I don't think Bella and Julius have heard from him since." She was silent for a moment, her heart pounding. "He's seeing some girl in Berlin. I suspect the next communication will be a wedding invitation." *Why couldn't she accept that?*

"I remember the way he used to look at you in Hamburg. The rest of us were sure you two were serious."

"The timing was all off for us," Kathy said slowly. No use pretending with Rhoda. "I hope he'll be happy. There's nobody who deserves that more than David."

They talked until both women recognized that their packet of free time was over. Rhoda had to run home to prepare dinner for Frank and herself. Kathy would set a festive table for her small family dinner party and—with dinner ready to be served—dismiss her housekeeper for the evening.

By the time Kathy reached the apartment, Alice was putting out dinner for Jesse. Tonight he'd be allowed to stay up half an hour later than usual so as to visit with his grandparents and Aunt Sophie.

"When are they coming?" Jesse clamored as she walked into the kitchen. "Are they bringing me presents?"

"Jesse, don't expect Grandma and Grandpa to bring you presents every time they see you," she scolded. But she knew they always brought some small gift for Jesse.

Right on schedule the grandparents and Aunt Sophie arrived. It seemed to Kathy that the apartment became alive with their presence. There was the usual effort of Jesse to prolong his time with them.

"Mom, you spoil him rotten," Kathy laughed when her mother pleaded that he be allowed to stay up another fifteen minutes.

"After all, a boy who's going into the first grade in September—" Her father exuded pride and love.

At last Alice took Jesse off to prepare for bed. Aunt Sophie insisted on helping Kathy bring dinner to the table while Edie and Adam pored over the latest batch of snapshots of Jesse. Kathy felt loved and cherished here in the midst of her family.

"All right," Aunt Sophie ordered. "Everybody to the table."

Over dinner her mother asked about Marge and her progress with the shop.

"She's running into all kinds of problems," Kathy reported, "but she'll make it. We talk at least twice a week about the latest developments. I wish she was here in New York, and I could help her."

"Kathy—" All at once her mother appeared anxious. "Are you serious about finding a job when Jesse starts first grade?"

"I can't wait," Kathy said softly.

"How does Phil feel about this?" her mother pursued. She spoke casually, but her eyes betrayed her concern.

"I don't know if he even hears me." Kathy stared at her plate. Edie—who, of necessity, had worked all of her adult life—found it inconceivable that any woman would want to go out to a job if she wasn't forced to do this. "But this is my decision to make."

"I read somewhere that Eleanor Roosevelt said that more and more women will go out to work in the years ahead," Adam recalled.

"I read that, too." Edie was faintly defiant. "But she said that was because we live in a two-pocketbook era. That it takes two wage-earners to support a family today. Kathy doesn't have that problem."

"She has other problems, like other women, too." Sophie nodded in comprehension. "They won't starve if they don't go out to work, but for them it's not enough to stay at home, raise kids, wash their husbands' socks—"

"Aunt Sophie, Kathy doesn't wash Phil's socks." Edie laughed.

"Women have a right to do something with their lives," Sophie insisted. "So the floors are dusty and the chrome needs polishing, but their minds are healthy. If Kathy wants a job she should have it."

"In time, Aunt Sophie," Kathy said affectionately, "we'll have a quiet revolution. A feminine revolution. But it'll be good for everybody."

David was grateful for the approach of spring. He loathed the cold, gray winters in Berlin. He always felt himself living in exile in Berlin—more so than ever in winter.

He ought to feel good, he reproached himself in the midst of a lonely dinner at a crowded café, though like himself many dined alone. This café, mercifully, didn't smell of boiled cabbage and cigars. His work was going well, he considered. The prospect for world peace seemed bright with Stalin dead, though he worried about the red-baiting plague that infested the United States. He'd feel less pessimistic tomorrow night. Tomorrow he'd have dinner at Gretchen's apartment and spend the night.

Tomorrow night he'd ask Gretchen to marry him. The moment had come, he thought in sudden decision. Hadn't he said he'd do this when spring arrived? Spring was almost here. There would be no more depressing, solitary dinners. No more nights of lying alone and fighting insomnia. He would make his peace with the past.

As always, the next morning he was the first to arrive at the Institute. He knew there were those who resented the long hours he spent at work, who made snide remarks behind his back about his traveling to Paris and London and the United States to share the results of his experiments. But medical research was international—it belonged to the world.

Gretchen arrived and went immediately to put up coffee. She scolded him for being a caffeine addict, but she always brought him a mug of fresh coffee minutes after she walked into the lab.

"I got up very early today to go to the butcher shop," Gretchen told him with a satisfied smile. "Before the East Berliners come in to shop. We're having wiener schnitzel for supper." Though for most Germans the midday dinner was the largest meal of the day, dedicated workers at the Institute settled for a lighter midday meal and allowed themselves the early evening American-style dinner. "I'll leave the lab early today."

"I heard birds singing this morning," David told her. "That's a sure sign spring is in the air." He remembered a favorite saying of his mother's—all those years ago before he was sent to New York. *"Spring is a new beginning. It should be the beginning of each new year—not a cold and dreary time like Berlin Januarys."*

"Will you have clinic hours tonight?" she asked.

"I have help now," he reminded her. For the past two months a pair of young doctors had been sharing his unpaid practice. "I'm taking off. I'll be at your place by 7:30."

All through the day at odd moments he remembered his decision to propose to Gretchen tonight. It was both an ending and a beginning, he told himself. An end to an impractical dream—*how could he ever think that one day he might have a life with Kathy?*—and the beginning of a realistic new life. Mama and Papa would want him to marry, to start a new family.

After Gretchen left for the day, he worked with an eye on the clock. Tonight he wouldn't be an hour late to dinner, he vowed, though Gretchen was understanding and forgiving when he did this. He would be there on schedule, with a pound of coffee—which Gretchen would appreciate—and *Himbeertorten* from the bakery.

As he had promised himself, he appeared at the apartment at 7:30 sharp. Even before Gretchen opened the door, he was conscious of the appetizing aromas of dinner on the range.

"David, coffee!" she said and lifted her face to his. Coffee was expensive and not always available in the stores. "And raspberry tortes. You remember that I love them."

Over dinner they talked about the new American president; Gretchen was fascinated by everything American.

"Eisenhower is the first Republican president in twenty-four years," David told her, while in a corner of his mind he considered the best moment to ask Gretchen to marry him. He suspected that others in the Institute assumed this would happen in time. "It'll be interesting to see how he handles the Cold War."

Inevitably they talked about the way East Berliners were sneaking into West Berlin for the free food packages being supplied by the Americans.

"Rumors are that soon the packages will be given out on a monthly basis," Gretchen told David. "Right now they're serving 20,000 to 30,000 people a day."

"And do you know what each package offers?" David said, faintly derisive. "A pound and a half of lard, two tins of condensed milk, one pound of powdered milk, and a package of lentil beans and a pound of flour or rice. This is supposed to be nutritionally sufficient for one person for a week."

"And they—the ones who come to distribution centers—

receive this once a month." She hesitated. "I know it sounds callous of me, but I find it hard to feel compassionate toward hungry Germans when I remember the concentration camps."

"I know," David confessed. "There are moments when I want to scream out to all those people around the world who're so touched by the way the Berliners hang on—that these are the people who allowed their countrymen to kill six million Jews."

"But they're fighting Communism," Gretchen said bitterly, "and that's like a Holy War. Forget the concentration camps."

"I heard an English journalist say the other day that West Berlin is the cheapest atom bomb, and a fairly peaceful one at that. West Berlin keeps the Communists in check."

"It still amazes me that we both came back to Berlin after the war," Gretchen said in an effort to dispel the suddenly somber mood. "I was waiting for you to arrive."

"Gretchen, will you marry me?" he asked softly. "I'd meant to wait until *after* dinner to ask—" He managed a self-mocking chuckle.

"How can I say no to a man who brings me coffee and raspberry tortes?" Her face was luminous. "Oh, David, yes. Yes!"

"Quietly?" It was almost a plea. "Just a few of the crew from the Institute. And the rabbi."

"Yes, we'll want the rabbi."

"Right now could I have more of the wiener schnitzel?" His hand reached across the table to cover hers for a moment. "You're not only lovely and bright—you're a terrific cook."

The evening ended as he knew it would—with their making love. Tonight there was a special intensity, he thought while they lay tangled together beneath the comfort of the blankets in the cold bedroom. For a moment he considered giving Gretchen the jeweled pin that remained hidden away in a dresser drawer in his tiny apartment, but almost imme-

diately he discarded this idea. Gretchen was sentimental—
she would wear it constantly. He knew he couldn't bear to
see any woman but Kathy wear that delicately fashioned
jeweled bow. Perhaps years later, when they were grandparents, he'd give it to Gretchen. But not now.

"Let me set the alarm." Gretchen reached for the clock
on the night table when he began to yawn. "You'll never
forgive me if I let you oversleep."

"It's ridiculous for us to go to sleep so early," he protested.

"No," she rejected with a gentle smile. "You work like
a madman. You need to sleep."

It was absurd to spend his life pining for what he couldn't
have, David scolded himself. Tonight he had eaten well,
loved well. What more should a man demand of life?

Eventually he fell asleep. He awoke knowing instantly
that it wasn't morning, a moment later conscious of his surroundings. Seeking comfort he turned on his side and
reached an arm out to Gretchen. But she wasn't there. Now
his eyes—growing accustomed to the darkness—saw her
standing by the window, staring out into the night.

"Gretchen?" He was anxious without knowing why.
"Can't you sleep?"

"I was too excited," she said and walked back to the bed.
Standing at the edge. "David, who is Kathy?"

"A girl I knew in Hamburg." He was bewildered by the
questions. "One of our group. We were a team—"

"You talked about her in your sleep." She paused. "I
think you love her very much."

"That was a long time ago—" David pulled himself into
a sitting position. He was shaken by Gretchen's statement.
"She's married to my cousin in New York." He'd never told
anyone that he loved Kathy. In sleep his mind betrayed him.
"That was a long time ago," he repeated.

"I think it would be wrong for us to marry." Her voice
was strained but firm. "She would be forever in the bed with
us."

"Gretchen, that's all over."

"It's not over, David," she said gently. "But we can go on as before for now. Even half a loaf is better than none. But I want you to understand that—that whatever we have is of the moment. If someone else comes along, if I feel I can be the only one in his life and he wants the things I want of life, then it's over."

"Gretchen, I'm sorry." He was torn by anguish. He'd thought he could be whole again, but part of him forever belonged to Kathy. "I'm sorry—"

= Chapter 21

Again, the Kohn clan took up residence at the Southampton house for the summer. Kathy provided herself with
weekly escapes into Manhattan. She said nothing to Phil
about her plans to start the job search right after school
opened. She would tell him, of course, she reasoned, but not
yet. He would hardly be aware if she was working, she
thought bitterly.

She was gaining much self-confidence because of her involvement with Marge's shop. Marge welcomed—and
adopted—her suggestions. She knew her mother worried
about Phil's reactions, but Bella approved.

This year she faced the summer in higher spirits because
she saw the proverbial light at the end of the tunnel. She
would have to start low on the totem pole, she warned herself. But by the time Jesse started college, she would have
an established career. And on the day she saw Jesse enter
his freshman year at college, she was leaving Phil.

Early in the summer Kathy realized that Phil was off on
a new affair. He was not bright enough to hide his trail, she
thought with scorn.

Using his sisters' constant entertaining at the house as an excuse, she insisted on renting a house at the beach in Maine for three weeks. Her mother and father and Aunt Sophie would come for a week, she plotted, and Rhoda and Frank for the next two weeks.

"Jesus, Kathy, we've got the big house here at Southampton," Phil complained.

"Gail and Brenda are constantly having parties." Phil knew they were making frantic efforts to push themselves into the upper echelon of Southampton society. It should have been obvious to them, Kathy thought, that they'd never break through. "I need some quiet time. Jesse needs it. And I wouldn't want to spend the summer back at the apartment," she said pointedly. She knew that on those nights when Phil said he was staying in New York at the apartment he wasn't staying alone.

"Nothing expensive," he warned. "Dad's slow with the bonuses right now, though there's no need for his hysteria." Julius was upset about the group that was fighting the fur industry in fear that some wild animals would soon become extinct and in outrage over the painful trap deaths inflicted on these animals—the group with which Rhoda and Frank were deeply involved—but Phil didn't know that.

"It won't be an expensive cottage," Kathy said sweetly. "I'm not talking Bar Harbor."

With record speed—helped by Rhoda and Frank—she rented a cottage right on the beach at an unfashionable area just above Ogunquit. Frank knew the town and the beach. *"You'll love it, Kathy. No crowds, marvelous beach."* Both Alice and the housekeeper would go on vacation. The real estate broker assured her that a daily cleaning woman available, and she planned to do the cooking herself, though she knew the week that Sophie and her parents would be there, her aunt would insist on cooking. At eighty-five Sophie was still mentally sharp and physically active.

On an early Monday morning Kathy drove her small entourage out of Manhattan and headed for Maine, Dad beside her on the front seat, Mom and Aunt Sophie in the rear with Jesse. This was going to be a good time, she told herself joyously.

It was one of the most relaxing periods she could remember, Kathy thought on the last day of her family's vacation time with her. No pretenses, no playing games. And Frank had been right. She loved this part of Maine. Most mornings she watched the sun rise. The sunsets were glorious.

The woman who came to clean was happy to baby-sit in the evenings so that Kathy was able to take her family out to some of the charming restaurants within comfortable driving distance. On two nights they saw summer theater productions.

The day her family left, Rhoda and Frank came up. The following morning, while Jesse, lulled by the sea air, still slept, Frank insisted on making breakfast for himself and the two women and serving it on the deck.

"Oh God, there's something so wonderful about sitting here and watching the waves hit the beach," Rhoda said rapturously. "Frank, you'll finish that article out here for sure."

"I saw him bring in the typewriter," Kathy joshed. "He wasn't fooling me when he said he'd collapse on a chaise and sleep away these two weeks."

"Tell her, Frank," Rhoda ordered.

"Tell me what?" Kathy demanded. *Was Rhoda pregnant?*

"Well, first, let me tell you that I may be pregnant." Rhoda glowed. "I know, I've been late before. But this time I've a premonition it's real."

"Rhoda, how wonderful!" Kathy leaned forward to hug Rhoda exuberantly, almost spilling a cup of coffee.

"Hey, I sweated over a hot stove making that coffee," Frank kidded. "Take it easy."

"Rhoda, I'm so happy for you." She knew how desperately Rhoda and Frank wanted a child.

"I figure I'll be able to work most of the first term," Rhoda said, "then go on maternity leave. My salary goes into the bank toward that little weekend house we want to buy up in Putnam or Dutchess County."

"We both love Manhattan," Frank conceded, "but five days a week of the hassle is enough. We want to be able to get in the car and take off Friday evenings and come back Sunday nights. You like to get out to Greenwich for weekends. I know, you see Central Park trees from your windows in the apartment, but it's not like the country—"

"Frank, tell her the other thing," Rhoda prodded.

"I'm doing a series for the magazine about the agony of animals who're being trapped for furs. And I hope to expand the series into a book. I have a publisher interested." Frank was trying to sound casual, but Kathy knew how much this meant to him.

"That's great, Frank. When will the first of the series come out?" Phil and his father would be livid, Kathy thought uneasily.

"It'll be in the issue hitting the newsstands right after Labor Day," Frank told her.

"That's great timing, hunh?" Rhoda's smile was dazzling. "Just at the time when women start thinking about buying fur coats."

"I don't want to run into Phil when the series starts appearing," Frank said, grinning. "The fur industry is going to be in an uproar."

"I don't think it'll be hard to avoid Phil. When was the last time you saw him?" Phil had a way of being tied up on business the nights Rhoda and Frank came to dinner, or when they were scheduled to go to Rhoda and Frank's apartment.

"We both feel very strongly about this," Frank said seriously.

"I know," Kathy said. "I think it's terrific that you're doing the series, and that it may be a book."

"It's funny," Rhoda reminisced. "Back in Hamburg I never suspected Frank would be anything more than a fling for me."

"And I thought you were just a great lay," Frank teased.

"Oh, shut up," Rhoda scolded good-humoredly. "You're talking to the woman who may be carrying your child." She turned to Kathy. "I wanted to go for the rabbit test, but Frank said, 'Why kill the poor rabbit? In another few days you'll know for sure, anyway.'"

All at once Kathy was mentally hurtling back through the years to Hamburg. To David. If Phil hadn't appeared on the scene, her life would have been so different. *She would have waited for David.* Was it this way with everybody? Could everybody look back to that one critical moment in their lives when they made the wrong move?

Was David married yet? He'd suffered such a terrible loss. He was a warm, compassionate man who shouldn't be deprived of a home and family. *Let him be happy.*

Immediately after Labor Day Kathy and Phil—with Jesse and Alice—returned to the New York apartment. The Southampton house suddenly seemed too small for the Kohn clan when Bella and Julius's four granddaughters— spoiled and demanding their own bedrooms—came out to the beach house at the end of the camp season.

"My nieces are four prize Jewish Princesses," Phil said disdainfully while they sat in the post–Labor Day Tuesday morning traffic. "Why do we have to go into the city a week early so they don't have to share two bedrooms?"

"We'd be coming into town in another ten days anyway," Kathy pointed out.

"Next weekend we'll go out to the Greenwich house," he decided. "It'll be hot as hell in town. I'll take Friday off and we'll drive up in the morning."

"Okay," Kathy agreed. It would be a quiet weekend with just Phil and herself and Jesse at the house. For a moment she toyed with the thought of inviting her family up to Greenwich. No, Phil would be annoyed if she asked them. He liked to think of them as living on another planet.

"I'll play golf," he told her as traffic began to inch along. "Maybe next summer we'll put in a pool."

"We're out at Southampton in the summers," Kathy reminded, turning to check on Jesse on the backseat with Alice. He was fast asleep. In just two weeks, she thought with recurrent satisfaction, he'd be starting the first grade. The first step toward her emancipation.

"We can swim in the pool right through September. I talked to Dad about it. Maybe we'll make it an enclosed heated pool, then we can use it year-round. Swimming's top-grade physical exercise."

Phil meant that they would put in a pool, Kathy interpreted, but his father would pay the bill. It would probably be written off as another business expense. Part of entertaining out-of-town personnel who came into New York for business conferences. "Writing off to taxes" was a way of life for Phil and his father.

On the following Friday morning Kathy waited with Jesse and Alice for Phil to bring the car around to the front of the house. He'd had dinner with his father last night, or so he claimed, and she'd been asleep when he came home. This morning he'd been in a foul mood. She'd told him not to yell at Jesse the way he did this morning. Too often lately, she remembered uneasily, he took his bad temper out by yelling at Jesse and her.

"There's Daddy now," Alice told Jesse—restless with the waiting—as the Peugeot approached. "As soon as we're on the highway we'll play our license plate game."

Phil pulled up at the curb, then left the car to put the luggage into the trunk.

"Get in the car," he said tersely. *What was bugging him this morning?*

Kathy slid into the front seat while Jesse and Alice took their customary places in the rear. Alice was going out with them to Greenwich and would leave tomorrow afternoon to go to her sister's in Levittown for the weekend. Phil had objected to her giving Alice the long weekend off. *"Let her come up with us and leave after lunch on Saturday. Christ, you spoil her the way Gail and Brenda spoil their kids!"*

Not until they were on the highway did Phil break his silence. Sometimes—like now—she was embarrassed and humiliated that Alice was a witness to Phil's ugly moods.

"Get that shitty magazine out of the glove compartment," he told her.

"All right." She tried to brace herself for an outburst. *Phil had seen Frank's article.*

She opened the glove compartment and withdrew the magazine. Her eyes clung to the cover line dealing with Frank's article: *Man's Inhumanity to Animals.*

"Frank's magazine." She strived for casualness.

"What's the bastard trying to do?" Phil flared. "I always knew he was a card-carrying nut. All this shit about women not wearing furs."

"He belongs to some animal rights group."

"Every ten or twenty years some creep comes along and starts up with that crap. I don't want you to see Frank and Rhoda anymore."

"It's a free country, Phil. Frank has a right to say what he thinks." She understood that Alice was trying to divert Jesse's attention from their conversation. Even though he didn't understand, he was upset by his father's menacing tone.

"I hope the bastard croaks," Phil said viciously. "We don't see them anymore, you hear?"

Kathy was silent. No one could stop her seeing Frank and Rhoda. Along with Marge, they were her closest friends in this world. She had love and respect for Frank and Rhoda. So often she was shamed by the knowledge that she was enjoying a luxurious life style from the results of the killing of innocent animals.

"I remember Frank bragging back in Hamburg about how his father had driven an ambulance in Spain for the

International Brigade. A bunch of Commies," he said with contempt.

Kathy remained silent. Let him talk, she thought. Phil couldn't stop her from seeing Frank and Rhoda. He didn't have to know that she was seeing them.

Only minutes after they arrived at the house Kathy received a phone call from Irene Hale down the road. At last a young couple with one little girl and another on the way had moved into the neighborhood.

"I saw you drive up, Kathy," Irene said effervescently. "If I'd known you'd be up this weekend, I'd have sent Jesse an invitation. Tomorrow is Gillian's sixth birthday, and we're having a small lunch party. Would Jesse like to come?"

"I'm sure he'd love it," Kathy accepted for him. "What time would you like him to be there?"

With the party arrangements settled they talked another few minutes. Irene was upset that her longtime nursemaid—with her since Gillian's birth—was tired of New York winters and returning to her native Florida in two weeks.

"I feel so safe when she's here with Gillian," Irene said, sighing. "It's almost like having a member of the family moving away."

Off the phone Kathy alerted Alice to the party situation. Walking down the stairs to the lower floor, she heard Phil's voice. He was talking on the phone to his father about Frank and the magazine. He was going to be smoldering all weekend. She took off in the Caddy—kept at the Greenwich house now—to shop for a birthday present for Gillian.

Once she had found a suitable birthday gift, Kathy shopped for groceries. She'd brought along delicatessen and cold chicken from the city for lunch today. They'd have dinner at home tonight, she planned, but Phil would want to go out for dinner tomorrow night. Even out here he hated staying home on Saturday evening.

Turning into the driveway, she noticed the Peugeot was gone. She'd serve lunch for Jesse and Alice and herself now.

Phil could help himself from the refrigerator whenever he came back. The less she saw of him this weekend the better.

Alice told her that Phil had gone to play golf.

"He said he wouldn't be home for lunch," Alice added in her pleasant, noncommittal voice.

"Thank you, Alice. I'll put out lunch for us now. Why don't we have it on the terrace?"

Late in the afternoon Phil returned to the house. He seemed to have worked off some of his rage, Kathy thought in relief. After dinner she'd curl up on the living room sofa and read. She'd brought along the Saul Bellow book that everybody was raving about—*The Adventures of Augie March*. Phil would be parked in front of the TV in the den all night, watching baseball.

Earlier than normal she went upstairs to the master bedroom. The baseball game was continuing well beyond the normal ninth inning. Phil would be too satisfied with baseball and beer to reach for her tonight, she guessed.

With increasing frequency he was foregoing what he called the national Saturday night pastime. While she was relieved that he probably wouldn't be in the mood to make love tonight, she was ever haunted by his propensity to seek out other women. It hinted at a shortcoming in her as a woman.

Saturday morning was hot and sultry. As Kathy expected, Phil remained in bed until almost noon. He'd gotten out of bed to flip on the air conditioner, then had gone back to sleep. Now she heard the shower beating away in the master bathroom and reluctantly abandoned the Saul Bellow novel to go out into the kitchen to put up fresh coffee and bring out Phil's routine Saturday morning breakfast.

"Did you remember to bring up the nova?" he demanded a few minutes later, striding into the kitchen in his Brooks Brothers walking shorts and polo shirt.

"Right there." She pointed to the shining red slivers of smoked salmon on a plate on the sunlit breakfast room table. "And I put out bagels and cream cheese. Shall I heat the bagels?" Their weekly moment of domesticity, she thought bitterly.

"It's too hot," he dismissed, then frowned. "The house should be centrally air-conditioned."

She poured a cup of coffee for Phil and—as an afterthought—a cup for herself, and carried them into the breakfast room. *Why do I make a pretense of being a wife?* she rebuked herself. A wife shared her husband's life. She shared Phil's bed, and occasionally he indulged in his conjugal privileges.

"Are you playing golf today?" she asked, sitting at the table.

"Probably." He shrugged. "Look, would you drive into town and buy me a can of shaving cream and a razor? I'm giving up on my electric razor. It's making a mess of my face."

"Okay. I suppose you want to shave before you play golf?"

"That's the idea." He was attacking his breakfast with gusto.

"I'll drive Jesse over to the Hales', then pick up your shaving cream, a razor, and blades." Thank God, he'd shelved his rage at Frank. For now. Instinct warned her that Phil and his father would consider Frank's actions as high treason. "Do you need anything else?"

"No. And why can't Alice take Jesse to the Hales? Christ, they're like a block away."

"She has to dress and pack for her weekend at her sister's. I—"

"I forgot," he drawled. "You're playing Lady Bountiful again. How can we go out to dinner tonight?"

"I arranged for a baby-sitter. There's no problem."

Phil mentioned he wanted to go for dinner to a new seafood restaurant he'd discovered in a nearby community. It was informal; she wouldn't have to go through the dressing-up routine. He'd have a couple of drinks with dinner, come home and collapse in front of the TV. She'd settle herself in bed to read. It would be a comfortable, quiet Saturday evening.

Right on schedule, Kathy climbed behind the wheel of the car and waited for Alice to bring Jesse. How handsome he looked, she thought tenderly as she watched him scurry toward the car in his immaculate white shirt and shorts, happily clutching the gift-wrapped package in his hands. And he was so excited about starting first grade next week at the posh school where Rhoda taught.

She dropped Jesse off at the Hale house, then headed for the drugstore. On impulse she stopped first at a coffee shop. Not because she was hungry, but it was good to relax over a cup of coffee for a few minutes in anonymous surroundings. Phil could wait to shave.

She drove directly home from the drugstore, pulled into the garage and went into the house through the side entrance. She could hear Phil on the phone in the den. Probably talking with his father again about Frank and the animal rights group. No, he wasn't talking about that, she suddenly realized, halting to listen.

"Look, I don't want to be mixed up in this. I was told I could give you the information without being involved. The man's a second-generation Communist. His father fought with the Loyalists in Spain. *He brags about that.* His wife is no better than he is, and she teaches young kids at a private school—"

"Phil!" Kathy charged into the den. He was standing with the phone clenched in his hand, nodding as though the person at the other end could see him. *"Phil, what are you doing?"* Frank and Rhoda would lose their jobs!

"Get away from me!" he ordered through clenched teeth, one hand covering the mouthpiece. "Yeah, that's right." He'd removed his hand to continue the conversation. "That's the magazine he works for."

"Phil, don't do this!" Kathy gasped in disbelief and reached to pull the phone from his hands.

With one vicious gesture Phil slammed his fist against her face. She staggered, would have fallen if she hadn't grabbed at a chair. She was vaguely aware that Alice was standing outside the door, watching with her mouth ajar. She was conscious, too, of a pain at the bridge of her nose.

"You bitch!" Phil put down the phone and crossed to hang menacingly over her. "Don't you ever do something like that again!" Now he turned and stalked from the room. Alice had apparently retreated in alarm.

Kathy rose to her feet, trembling with shock. She reached a hand to her nose, discovered a warm trickle of blood running down the side. Phil's ring had ripped away a chunk of skin, she realized.

"Let me drive you to the hospital emergency room—" Alice came into the den with a wet towel in one hand. "That cut may need stitches."

"It'll be all right in a minute." Kathy reached for the towel. How could Phil do something so rotten? *He was destroying Frank and Rhoda.* Now—when Rhoda was pregnant and they'd just moved into a new, expensive apartment.

"You'd better sit down," Alice said anxiously. "Keep pressure on that cut."

"The ring dug into the skin," Kathy stammered, humiliated that Alice had seen Phil hit her. She struggled for calm. "It'll stop bleeding in a minute," she repeated.

"I'll bring you a glass of water." Alice's face reflected compassion for her, contempt for Phil. "Just sit still and hold the towel to your nose."

Kathy sighed with relief when Alice concurred at last that the bleeding had stopped.

"Your nose ought to be x-rayed," Alice said. "There might be a bone broken."

"No, I'm fine," Kathy insisted, and glanced at her watch. "We have to leave for the station. You'll miss your train."

"I'll take a later one."

"No, your sister will be worried. And I'm all right, Alice.

I'll drive you to the station, then I'll pick up Jesse. Please forget what you saw here." Tears stung her eyes. "Go bring down your valise, and we'll head for the station."

Kathy sat motionless, trying to deal with what had just happened. She had told Bella she would stay with Phil as long as it was good for Jesse. *But it wasn't good anymore.*

How could she allow her son to grow up in a house with a father who was so vindictive and rotten, who would betray her dear friends? Phil knew how red-baiting wrecked lives. Frank and Rhoda were fine, caring people, but he wanted to destroy them.

She would take Jesse and get out of this house. Out of Phil's life.

She would raise Jesse alone.

Chapter 22

Kathy drove Alice to the Greenwich station and returned to the house. Now she struggled to disguise the injury to her nose with makeup, though the swelling was a giveaway. Ever conscious of the time—because she was to pick up Jesse at the Hale house in twenty minutes—she began to pack for herself and Jesse. Grateful that spare luggage and a goodly amount of wardrobe was kept up here rather than at the apartment.

She packed one large valise with casual clothes, pulled a favorite winter coat from the cedar closet, and brought out a small valise to hold Jesse's clothes. Her diamond and sapphire necklace was in the apartment safe; it would have to stay behind.

She dragged the luggage out to the car and stowed it away in the trunk. Thank God, she always kept her secret savings account book with her. The balance wasn't large, but she and Jesse could survive on it for a year if she budgeted carefully.

She glanced at her watch again. It was time to go over to the Hales' to pick up Jesse. She'd drive into White Plains, then take a train into Manhattan from there. She'd leave the car at the White Plains station.

First of all, she must tell Rhoda and Frank what Phil had done. They had to be forewarned, though with the climate in the country as it was, she thought painfully, there was nothing they could do to clear themselves. Then she'd check into some small Upper West Side hotel for the night.

She couldn't stay in New York with Jesse, her mind warned. *Phil mustn't be able to find them.* They'd go to San Francisco. Marge was there; they wouldn't be alone.

But the company had a store there, she remembered in alarm. No matter, she determinedly dismissed this. San Francisco was a large city. Phil was there for a day or two twice a year. He'd never find them. She'd change her name. She'd be Kathy Altman from this moment on. She would never allow Phil to take Jesse from her. She and Jesse would begin a whole new life in San Francisco.

By the time she arrived at the Hales', the guests were beginning to leave.

"Alice is off for the weekend," she explained to Irene as nursemaids corralled their charges. "I'm sure it was a wonderful party."

"The kids seemed to enjoy themselves," Irene said happily, but Kathy was aware of startled scrutiny. Did her nose look that bad? "Would you like to stay and have coffee with me?"

"Thanks, but I have to run. Some friends are coming from the city," she alibied.

In the car she told Jesse they were going into Manhattan.

"We'll catch the train in White Plains. You'll like that, won't you?"

"Sure." His eyes were bright with anticipation. "What about Daddy?"

"He's staying at the house." She hesitated. "Jesse, how would you like to fly out to California to see Marge again?"

"Wow! But what about school?" All at once he was ambivalent.

"We'll work that out," she promised. Later she'd tell him that he was to go to school in San Francisco. Not today.

Weighed down with two valises and a coat over one arm, she managed to marshal Jesse aboard a New York–bound train. Part of her mind focused on entertaining Jesse while the other tried to plot their future. Phil would be sure she was going out to Borough Park, once he realized they were gone. He'd call Mom for sure. *Don't phone Mom. Not till later.*

She called Rhoda from Grand Central Station. Praying Rhoda would be home. When she was on the point of hanging up, Rhoda's voice responded.

"Rhoda, I can't say much because I'm in a phone booth in Grand Central." Kathy half-closed the door. She'd told Jesse to stand right there and guard their luggage. "I've left Phil. There's something I have to tell you before I check into a hotel. Could I—"

"You're not staying in a hotel," Rhoda interrupted softly. "Hop in a cab and get over here. And don't worry, Kathy, you're going to be all right." But Kathy sensed her anxiety.

Kathy and Jesse went through the station and out to Forty-second Street, and to her relief found a cab almost immediately. At Rhoda's apartment building she didn't bother ringing the doorbell. A small boy on his way out held the door for them and they headed for the elevators. She was glad that Rhoda and Frank lived in an elevator building now. The valises grew heavier, it seemed, with every step she took.

"Kathy, why didn't you buzz so Frank could come down to help you," Rhoda scolded and reached to hug Jesse. "Frank," she called over her shoulder. "Come bring in Kathy's luggage."

For a few moments they were caught up in greetings. Then after an exchange of sign language Frank prodded Jesse toward what was currently Frank's home office and would in a few months become the nursery, to see their new TV set.

"Try it out for us," Frank told Jesse enthusiastically. "We'll find a good program for you to watch."

"Kathy, your nose is all swollen—" Rhoda inspected her with sudden suspicion. "Did Phil hit you?"

"That's the least of it," she said, all at once exhausted. "I have to tell you—"

"First you're going over to the hospital emergency room to have that nose looked at," Rhoda insisted. "It may be broken."

"It's all right. It just throbs a little. Rhoda, I—"

"Later." Rhoda gestured for Kathy to wait while she left the room to go down the tiny hall. "Jesse," Kathy heard her say, "Mommie and I are going out to buy some ice cream. You stay here with Uncle Frank, okay?"

"Chocolate?" Jesse asked.

"Chocolate," Rhoda promised.

En route in a taxi to the hospital Kathy knew she'd have to wait for the privacy of the apartment to warn Rhoda and Frank about Phil's red-smearing. They talked instead about Kathy's going out to San Francisco.

"I want to get as far away as possible," Kathy said passionately. "And Marge is there. She'll help me find an apartment and to get Jesse settled in school." In a corner of her mind she remembered that Marge's saleswoman was leaving to get married. Maybe she could work for Marge.

At the emergency room Kathy's nose was x-rayed. There was, indeed, a fracture.

"We won't splint it. It'll heal by itself," the doctor in charge told her cheerfully. "And the cut will heal. It doesn't need stitches."

They stopped at a supermarket to buy chocolate ice cream, then hurried back to the house. Though she knew Jesse was safe with Frank, Kathy felt a need to be close to him.

"Look, if Phil calls, you don't know where I am," she cautioned as they rode up in the elevator. How was she going to explain their sudden move to Jesse? Was he going to be upset by this unexpected change in their lives? *But it was necessary.*

In the apartment Rhoda spooned out a lavish portion of ice cream for Jesse and carried it to him. She gestured to Frank to join her in the living room. Jesse was happy to continue watching TV with the added treat of chocolate ice cream.

"I left Phil because I caught him in a terrible act." Kathy's throat tightened as that image flashed across her mind. "If it wasn't for me, if you weren't my friends, this wouldn't be happening to you."

"What's happening?" Frank was bewildered. "You know we're happy to have you and Jesse here."

"I came into the house late this morning—" Kathy struggled to deliver her devastating message. "Phil was talking to somebody on the phone. He didn't mention any names, but I knew it was one of those hate-mongering groups. People who had something to do with *Red Channels* or *Counterattack* or something like that." What Max Lerner had called "the locust-plague of the democratic harvest." "He was telling them about your father, Frank, about the International Brigade in Spain. And he said your wife was teaching small children and—"

"Oh my God!" Rhoda was ashen. "Frank, I'll be fired!"

"We'll both be fired." Frank fought for calm. "It was that article, wasn't it?"

"Of course," Kathy whispered. "He and his father are livid about your animal rights group, and then Phil saw the article."

"I'll ask for maternity leave immediately." Rhoda was pale but defiant. "I don't want it on my job record that I was fired for Commie affiliations."

"So I'll be fired." Frank dropped an arm about Rhoda's shoulders. "I'll have time to focus on the book with no other interruptions."

"They'll attack the group now," Rhoda warned. "They'll go after every one of us. We're all caring people. We've signed petitions for human rights groups and contributed to the International Rescue Committee. Some of us even campaigned for Henry Wallace." She laughed derisively.

"And my father did serve with the International Brigade." Frank was grim. "That makes us guilty by association. That's all that's needed today. But this can't last. The country has to regain its sanity. Until it does, we'll survive."

The three adults masked their distress lest it be transmitted to Jesse. Not until they'd had dinner and Jesse had been put to bed on the convertible sofa in Frank's temporary office did they sit down to discuss their situation.

"I'll go in to the school Monday morning and ask for immediate maternity leave. They'll be pissed," Rhoda conceded, "but it'll go on my record as maternity leave and not dismissal."

"I'll sit it out until the magazine dumps me. If they're going to lose advertisers, you damn well know I'll be fired. But until that happens I'll stay put. Thank God, we've been saving for that house in the country. That'll see us through. Hopefully." He sighed, his face etched with frustration. "How did the country get into a shape like this?"

"Kathy, must you leave tomorrow?" Rhoda asked.

"By now Phil has probably already called my folks. He knows we're not there. He doesn't know where we are. He's going to be wild. Not because he's remorseful or pained at the thought of losing his wife. Because I dared to walk out on him," she jeered. "But what frightens me most, Julius is going to goad him on to try to take Jesse away from me. *I know this.*"

"And you mean just to disappear." Frank's smile blended comprehension with compassion.

"If I'm to keep Jesse, I have to." *Had* Phil phoned Mom and Dad? They'd be so worried. "Rhoda, please call my parents. Tell them Jesse and I are fine, but that I've left Phil. Say I phoned you from the airport. I'll write when I'm relocated. Tell her it's important that nobody knows where I am. She'll understand."

Rhoda phoned the Ross apartment. Kathy hovered over her as Rhoda talked with her mother, explaining gently that Kathy had taken Jesse and left Phil. Phil had called two hours ago, she gathered from Rhoda's response, and her mother had been mystified.

"Rhoda, why didn't she call *me*?" Kathy heard her mother's bewildered voice.

"She tried," Rhoda lied, "but your phone was busy. She had to board a plane in a few minutes, so she tried me next. As soon as she can, she'll call you. It's important that Phil doesn't know where she is," Rhoda emphasized. "Kathy's scared of an ugly custody battle. But she's all right, Mrs. Ross."

Rhoda talked with Kathy's father for a few moments, trying to reassure him. Finally she put down the phone.

"They're upset." Kathy's eyes searched Rhoda's.

"Not that you're leaving Phil." Rhoda astonished her with this admission. "Honey, we knew this was not an ideal marriage. Your parents are sensitive people—they could see that."

"I didn't call them because I was afraid I'd say too much," Kathy said. "And that Mom might be upset and repeat it to Phil. I can't leave until Monday because I have to go to the bank and close my private savings account." Rhoda knew about that account. "I didn't want it near the apartment. I went to a West Side bank. It's three blocks away."

"Phil won't come here, will he?" Frank was apprehensive.

"We just won't answer the doorbell," Rhoda shot back.

"He won't come. He wouldn't dare." Kathy smiled bitterly. "How can he? He'd be afraid you'd break his neck if he showed up here. He'll know I got the message to you."

"What about your diamond and sapphire necklace?" Rhoda was always practical.

"It's at the apartment. I don't dare go over there."

"Shall I go over and get it?" Rhoda asked. "I could tell the doorman you'd called me from Greenwich to bring something from the apartment."

"Forget the necklace." Kathy was brusque from anxiety. "I don't want to gamble on Phil's having been in touch with the building. I don't want him to know I'm here in New York, even for the weekend." She hesitated. "I'll have to write Alice and tell her I've left Phil. I'll tell her to get in touch with Irene Hale. Irene would love to have Alice for her kids. And I'll send her a check for three weeks' severance pay," she decided with sardonic amusement. "I have enough in the checking account to cover that." Phil would be livid when the bank statements came in and he found out.

Later, she promised herself, she would write Bella and tell her why she had left Phil. She'd send the letter to Rhoda and ask her to mail it from New York. Bella would understand.

Sunday afternoon Kathy phoned Marge in San Francisco and reported her situation.

"Kathy, that's the smartest move you've made in years," Marge approved, but she was somber. "What time does your flight arrive? I'll meet you."

"You can't leave the shop," Kathy rejected. "I'll take a taxi."

"I'll put my almost ex-saleswoman in charge," Marge said with an effort at humor. "Would you consider coming into the business with me? The shop can't afford a good salary yet, but—"

"Marge, I'd work for nothing!" Kathy said with a surge of anticipation. "I have enough to take care of Jesse and me for a year if I'm careful. I feel as though I'm about to be reborn. *Kathy Ross is back at last.*"

Chapter 23

"It's like I told you over the phone!" His eyes ablaze with fury, Phil spat the words at his parents. "I wouldn't have asked you to come into the city if I thought she was just sulking. She packed up and stormed out of the Greenwich house. She hasn't been at the apartment—I talked to the doorman. The little bitch walked out on me!"

"Let's go over this calmly," Bella ordered. "What exactly happened between you and Kathy yesterday?"

"We had a fight." He shrugged. "She's such a jerk about those friends of hers. You know, Rhoda and Frank."

"The bastard with the animal rights group?" Julius's face tensed ominously. "The one who wrote that fucking article?" He pointed to the magazine that lay on the coffee table.

"All right, you had a fight," Bella sighed. "Then what?"

"I left the house and went over to play golf. You know, a 'tensional release.'" He used his newest phrase. "I came back late in the afternoon, and she and the kid were gone. I didn't find the note until late in the evening when I went out to the kitchen for a beer. It just said, 'You'll find the car at the White Plains station.' That's all. Then I checked the closets. Some of her clothes were gone. Two valises were missing. I phoned Borough Park. Her mother said she wasn't there. I don't think she was lying. Kathy's stalling on telling her precious family. They'll probably think she's out of her mind to walk out on the sweet deal she's had for seven years."

"You get yourself the best damn divorce lawyer you can find," Julius ordered. "She's going to try to take you for fat alimony and child support payments." He frowned. "What about the diamond and sapphire necklace? Did she walk out with *that*?"

"No. I looked. The necklace is here." He ignored his mother's pained expression.

"First thing tomorrow morning you find yourself a lawyer. When her lawyer comes around gloating about a fancy divorce settlement, you be ready," Julius continued. "And what about the kid? She's got no right walking off with your son that way. It's kidnapping."

"You'll have a hard time proving that in court," Bella said drily.

"You don't let her get Jesse!" Julius rose from the depths of the burgundy velvet sofa. "That's my grandson. She can't take him away."

"Phil, what did you say that upset Kathy so?" Bella's voice was strained.

"For God's sake, Mother, are you taking her side?" Phil accused.

"It's not like Kathy to act on impulse," she said quietly.

"All I did was complain about Frank's writing that lousy article. I said, 'What kind of a friend is he to try to cut our throats?' And she started to rave about how she wouldn't let me talk about him that way. She started to punch me on the arm. She was like a wild woman."

"Hey, is something going on between her and Frank?" Julius demanded.

"There is nothing between Kathy and Frank but friendship," Bella lashed out. "I don't want to hear anything to the contrary from either of you."

"A hundred to one her lawyer will be calling you tomorrow or the next day," Julius predicted. "And you tell the son-of-a-bitch you're not handing over one dime of alimony or child support. And you'll fight for custody of your son."

"Don't use Jesse as a pawn," Bella warned. "You know he belongs with his mother."

"Who says so?" Julius challenged belligerently. "Why does everybody think the child should go with the mother?"

"How often does Phil see Jesse?" Bella taunted. "Half the time he's out of town, and the other half he's involved in the business or socializing." She turned from Julius to Phil. "Don't try to take Jesse away, Phil. He belongs with Kathy."

"Of course, she may come crawling back," Julius said with a devious smile. "When she realizes she's not walking off with fancy alimony and child support payments. In New York it's not that easy to get a divorce. Phil, you haven't given her any grounds for divorce?" Julius tensed in sudden suspicion. "She didn't catch you with some broad?"

"Dad, of course not." Phil managed a frown of reproach. Kathy couldn't nail him for adultery—he was always too careful for that. "What the hell does she expect from me? I gave her two beautiful homes—the apartment here and the house in Greenwich. She had the use of the family house in Southampton. Her own Cadillac, expensive clothes, jewelry. A housekeeper and a nursemaid. She never had it so good!"

"I've had enough for one day," Bella said abruptly. "I'm going to bed. Good night, Phil. And don't act like a jackass."

Julius waited until he heard Bella close the door to her bedroom before he spoke.

"Phil, you're sure she didn't catch you with some broad?"

"No way," he insisted.

"It's kind of a shame this happened." All at once Julius

seemed ambivalent. "I mean, you and Kathy as a couple brought in a lot of publicity for the company. Roz won't be happy about this." His eyes narrowed in speculation. "Would you take her back?"

"Hell, no!" Phil glared at his father. For publicity for the company the old man would do anything. "Not after what she's pulled. And I don't need her." He contrived to appear simultaneously hurt and boastful. "There are plenty of beautiful women out there panting to go out with me." Already he was envisioning himself as a sought-after playboy. "But let me tell you, Dad—" His smile was malicious and vindictive. "I'm going to make Kathy sweat. Before I'm through with her, she'll wish she'd never met me."

Though distraught about her own situation, Rhoda insisted on going with Kathy and Jesse to the airport. From a phone booth at Idlewild Kathy phoned her parents and haltingly told them what had happened in the past forty-eight hours.

"I'm all right, Mom," she insisted. "I'll be in touch with you soon. I don't want to say over the phone where I'm headed. I know I sound paranoid—Phil could hardly have your phone tapped—but he mustn't know where Jesse and I will be. I can't take a chance on his fighting me for Jesse."

"Kathy, do you need money?" her father asked when her mother relinquished the phone. "We'll wire you whatever you need."

"I've managed to put money away through the years," she reassured him while tears filled her eyes. No recriminations from her family. Only love and support. "You'll hear from me soon. And don't worry," she exhorted.

Kathy clung to Rhoda for an anguished moment before boarding her flight with Jesse. She knew the fears that had haunted Rhoda and Frank since she'd told them about Phil's actions. They all knew the devastation that afflicted those who were blacklisted. But now—before Jesse—she and Rhoda tried to hide their inner emotions.

On the plane Jesse was intrigued, as on other such occasions, by the excitement of takeoff. He was fascinated at being above the clouds. Normally she, too, enjoyed these moments, but today she was too anxious about the future to be aware of their surroundings.

Jesse couldn't understand why they were going to San Francisco just when he was supposed to start first grade — an awesome event in his young life. But as soon as possible she'd enroll him in school in San Francisco. So it wouldn't be a posh private school. Their life-style was changing.

Was she doing the right thing for Jesse? Now doubts tugged at her. How was she going to explain to him that he wouldn't see his father again if she could help it? Was it right to take him away from loving grandparents like her own parents and like Bella? Away from financial security?

She *had* to leave Phil, she told herself with fresh defiance. She couldn't let Jesse grow up exposed to Phil's thinking. Phil's ethics. And Phil had struck her. How could she be sure that, in a moment of rage, he wouldn't strike Jesse? No, this was the right—the only—path to take.

When they arrived at San Francisco airport and found Marge waiting for them, Kathy felt a rush of gratitude that she had such friends as Marge and Rhoda and Frank. Marge marshalled them through the terminal to the waiting taxis, talking brightly all the while about the success of the shop.

"Of course, I have nightmares about Fred and Cleo getting bored with the business and pulling out," she admitted. "I'm terrified at the way bills pile up. You know me, Kathy. I even had trouble managing my spending money in high school."

Marge told her that she had checked the public school system in her area. It was just a short walk from her apartment to an elementary school. Kathy could enroll him immediately.

"And you're in luck, Kathy," she said, clearly delighted at their presence in San Francisco. "I talked to Lee, and she's available to pick up Jesse after school and stay with him until you come home. I'm assuming you're coming into the shop?"

"Marge, I'm so excited about that." She wouldn't think about problems that lay ahead. She was going to enjoy being a whole person again. "I've got so many ideas I want to go over with you."

"On my own I'm scared most of the time. I won't be with you here, Kathy."

Within the next week Jesse was registered at school, Lee had become a warm, reliable part of their lives, and Kathy had a lead on an apartment just a block away.

On impulse—excited about the possibility of an apartment—Kathy took a few hours off from the shop to go to the beauty salon across the street.

"This is a new life, Marge. I want a new look." And she would feel safe from detection, Kathy promised herself, with a change in hair-coloring and hairstyle. She would no longer match the description of Kathy Kohn.

Marge greeted her with approval when she returned from the beauty salon. Her shoulder-length dark hair had been replaced by a honey-colored poodle cut.

"Kathy, you look about eighteen," Marge crowed. "I'm jealous!"

Kathy had insisted that the shop pay her no more than her predecessor. Over the weekend, at Marge's urging, she had gone over the shop's books. Though not an accountant, not even a bookkeeper, she could see that the shop was fighting to meet obligations.

"I can't convince Fred that we need to spend on advertising," Marge said in frustration while the two women lingered over Sunday breakfast and Jesse worked over the latest puzzle Kathy had bought for him.

"Suppose I loan the shop some money," Kathy said after a moment's hesitation. It was frightening to realize that all she had in the world was the few thousand she had brought with her. But she had grown up with budgets, she reminded herself. She and Jesse could squeeze through on her salary at the shop if she was careful. "We'll figure out where it'll do the most good."

"No." Marge was firm. "We can't gamble with that."

"It's not a gamble," Kathy pushed. "I believe in the shop."

They argued heatedly for a few minutes until Marge agreed to Kathy's investing money in advertising.

"That makes you a partner in the company," Marge said. "From my shares, so Fred can't complain about that."

Sunday afternoon, after an inner battle with herself, Kathy phoned home. Ignoring her mother's anxiety about the cost of the call, she talked with each of her parents and with Aunt Sophie for almost an hour.

"I can't take a chance on phoning again," she cautioned her mother. "Phil and Julius will pull any dirty tricks to get Jesse. I'll write care of Rhoda—she'll get my letters to you. And I want you to write me care of Rhoda. Mom, it has to be this way," she insisted when her mother began to protest. "I'm not being paranoid," she told her mother again. "I know Phil and Julius. I'm not concerned about a divorce or alimony or even child support. I just want Phil out of our lives, and this is the only way to do it."

"When will we see you?" Her mother's voice was forlorn. "You and Jesse—"

"You'll come out here," Kathy soothed, fighting off a torrential wave of homesickness. This wasn't like Hamburg. When could she go home again? "We'll see each other. I promise."

== Chapter 24

Phil sat opposite his father in the restaurant booth where they met for breakfast most mornings when he was in town.

"It's over two weeks," he said in exasperation. "Where the hell is she?" Not a word from any lawyer so far. Her parents pretended not to know where she was. He didn't believe *that*. "And you know what I found yesterday?" he asked with an air of martyrdom. "I got the statement for a checking account I set up in both our names. She gave Alice a check for three weeks' salary. And Alice went right to work for the Hales down the road from us in Greenwich. That was real bitchy."

"Kathy was always a bleeding heart liberal," Julius said contemptuously. "You knew that."

"Kissing cousin to the damn Commies." Phil dug viciously into a sausage. "She's no better than her 'red' friends."

"This is dragging on too long. Phil, I want you to find Jesse and bring him back home. I don't want my grandson raised by her."

"Dad, how the hell do I do that?"

"We hire detectives. She can't hide out forever. I don't care what it costs, Phil." He leaned forward, his face flushed in anger. "I want her to know she can't push us around this way."

"We don't have a lead! She's just disappeared into thin air."

"You hire the right detectives, they'll find her. And you keep your nose clean," he warned. "She may have detectives of her own out there looking for grounds for divorce. In this state she'll have to prove adultery."

"I'll be careful," Phil soothed. "Hell, she has no money for detectives!"

Unexpectedly Julius chuckled.

"What a dumb broad. She walked out and left a diamond and sapphire necklace behind."

Bella found a spot in the supermarket parking lot, and reached into her jacket for the grocery list. The new cook took to her bed after the first sneeze. It was difficult to keep help these days—she'd put up with Amanda's hypochondria. Once in a while, she didn't mind doing the grocery shopping or even preparing a meal.

She left the car and started toward the supermarket entrance. Wasn't that Alice just ahead?

"Alice?" she called out, her mind suddenly in high gear. Before Kathy walked out that way, she'd sent Alice a check for severance pay. Maybe Alice could fill in some of the gaps. "Alice?" Her voice louder this time.

Alice turned around.

"Good morning, Mrs. Kohn." She smiled but seemed oddly wary.

"Alice, may I talk to you for a moment?" Bella hurried to her.

"Of course, Mrs. Kohn." Still wary, Bella noted.

"We've heard nothing from Kathy since she left." Bella forced herself to appear casual. "I'm so worried about her. My son, well, he just said he and Kathy had a spat. I was wondering—I was hoping—do you know anything about that?"

"Mrs. Kohn, you don't want to know." Now Alice was agitated. "It's not a nice thing to talk about."

"Alice, I want to know desperately."

"He pushed her around," Alice said after a moment's hesitation. "I mean, he hit her."

"Oh, my God!" Bella felt sick.

"I was sure her nose was broken, but she refused to go to the emergency room at the hospital. She was always so sweet and thoughtful. She knew I had to make a train—she insisted on driving me to the station. I have to tell you, Mrs. Kohn. If ever she asks me to testify in court that her husband hit her, I'll be there for her. She's a fine young lady."

Kathy watched Jesse anxiously for signs that he was upset by the changes in their lives. School, she thought gratefully, was a terrific diversion. He hadn't even questioned her when she said they'd be in San Francisco for a while so he'd start school here. He was enthralled by this new experience. Once he'd asked when they were going home; but this was curiosity. He wasn't homesick. Not yet. *He didn't miss Phil.* He was used to his father's absences.

Three weeks after their arrival Kathy signed a lease on an apartment. To people in San Francisco she was Kathy Altman. Later Jesse might wonder about this. Thus far, he was unaware of the switch in names.

"Mommie, it's so little," Jesse said matter-of-factly when they moved into the apartment with the barest essentials of furniture. "Everybody here lives in little places." It wasn't a complaint, just an observation.

Kathy fell into a pattern now. Five mornings a week she took Jesse to school, then joined Marge at the shop. Lee picked him up after school and stayed with him until she arrived home. On Saturdays—a busy day at the shop—Lee took Jesse on sight-seeing trips about the city. Golden Gate

Park, the cable-car barn, the Aquarium, the Science Museum, Hyde Street Pier. Sundays Kathy devoted to Jesse.

Her mother wrote that a man had been asking questions in the neighborhood about her. *"Darling, nobody knows where you are, but I should tell you Phil has a private detective looking for you and Jesse."*

Kathy defiantly told herself there was no way Phil could track her down. This confidence was shaken when she returned on a mid-October morning from an appointment with a possible contractor for one of Marge's designs. She was barely inside the door when she froze in terror. Marge was talking with a man at one side of the shop, their conversation destroying her earlier high spirits.

"I'm sorry I can't help you, but I haven't heard from Kathy in months," Marge told the man. "You know how it is when there's so much distance between you. You lose touch after a while."

"Oh Miss," Kathy interrupted. Striving to sound casual. *Get him out of the shop.* "Would you have that beige cardigan in the window in a size 34?"

"Excuse me, please," Marge told the man and walked to Kathy. Beautifully impersonal, Kathy thought while her heart pounded. "I don't have it in beige in 34, but I have it in a lovely shade of blue. Would you like to see it?" No indication that she had ever seen Kathy before.

They played at the game of saleswoman and customer until the man left the shop.

"Marge, what'll I do?" Kathy whispered in panic. Her instinct was to pick up Jesse at school and run.

"Relax," Marge ordered. "We carried it off great."

Now the woman who had been browsing at a table of sweaters was ready to buy. Marge hurried over to make the sale. They'd fooled that private investigator, Kathy tried to convince herself. He'd believed Marge. How stupid of her not to guess that Phil would try to track her down through Marge. He knew how close they were.

"Look, you're not to worry about this," Marge scolded

her ten minutes later when they were alone in the shop again except for another customer trying on a skirt in the dressing room. "Phil contacted a San Francisco private investigator to make inquiries. I'm not surprised," she confessed. "But the guy will just write back to Phil in New York and say he had no luck."

"He scared the hell out of me," Kathy admitted.

"You were terrific. He never guessed a thing." Marge radiated confidence.

"The company has a store in San Francisco. Phil is out here a couple of times a year!" At odd moments she'd worried about this. "I could walk right into him one day!" She paled at the prospect of such an encounter.

"This is a city of 800,000 people, not counting the tourists. The chance of your running into Phil is microscopic. Look, we had a bad moment, but we were cool. I loved the way you jumped into action. That really got him out of here."

"I'm lucky he didn't have a photograph of me." Kathy shuddered. "I was five feet from him. I acted without thinking of that."

"He did have a photo," Marge told her and Kathy gaped in shock. "Sweetie, he had a photo of you with dark hair that swung down to your shoulders. He didn't recognize you."

"Now I understand." Kathy laughed. "Julius was looking for a bargain again. His bargain-basement P.I. was not very bright."

"Forget about it. You'll be okay here," Marge insisted. "Phil will check San Francisco off the list. And stop being scared," she exhorted. "We should celebrate. You've passed a terrific hurdle."

Phil grunted in rejection as the phone on his bedside table jangled, destroying the Sunday noon silence of the apartment.

"Oh shut up." He turned his back, but the phone continued to ring. Now he reached for it. God, he wanted to sleep. That little nympho he'd brought home last night couldn't get enough. "Yes," he barked into the phone.

"I saw you leave the party last night with that blond sexpot. How many times have I told you?" his father demanded. "You don't mess around with women until you're divorced from Kathy!"

"How can I divorce her when I can't find her?" Phil shot back. "And what am I supposed to do in the meantime? Enter a monastery?"

"You're out of town one week in four. Do what you have to do out of town, where nobody knows. I have this crazy thing in my head that tells me your bitchy wife is just waiting for you to slip up."

"Okay, I'll keep it out of town," Phil soothed. This was no time to start a battle with the old man. They were talking about transferring fifty percent of the company stock into his hands. "I just got horny last night."

"How was she?" Julius asked slyly.

"She couldn't get enough. That one could take on a whole army. I finally told her to go home."

"I called you because I've been thinking," Julius told him. "Put the house in your mother's name. The way real estate in Greenwich is rising it's worth a fortune. I don't want to see that crazy wife of yours trying for a chunk of it. And that company stock we've been talking about—"

"Yeah, I understand the papers will be ready by the middle of the week." Phil pulled himself up against the headboard. *He'd waited long enough for that stock.*

"I'm putting it on hold," Julius said. "If your wife is up to something, let her find you with your assets as low as possible."

"Dad, I don't think Kathy's got a private investigator dodging my heels." He tried to mask his exasperation. Damn it, he wanted that stock!

"You'll be out in San Francisco next month, right?"

"Right." After eight months of fighting him the old man

agreed it was smart to set up a concession in a top department store there. It wouldn't take away from the store—it would be additional revenue.

"I'm not sure I trust that two-bit detective agency we hired to check on her pal out there. You make a trip yourself to that shop the woman runs in San Francisco. See where she goes when she closes the shop. Something your mother said last night convinced me Kathy's involved with her."

"You think Mother knows where Kathy is?" Phil asked in astonishment.

"No. But she was talking about all those classes Kathy took at F.I.T. I got the feeling she's sure Kathy's working in the women's wear business. And where would Kathy turn if she needed a job and wanted to be in that field? Her bosom pal with a shop in San Francisco. Stay out there an extra couple of days if you have to, but you find her, Phil. You find her, and you grab your son and bring him home."

═ Chapter 25

Kathy walked hand in hand with Jesse along Grant Avenue, Marge and Lee in lively conversation directly behind them. She was pleased by Jesse's delight in this small adventure. He was entranced by Chinatown's colorful bazaars, the grocery stores with their displays of bamboo shoots, bean sprouts, dried fish, rows of glazed duck, by the apothecary shops that offered mysterious remedies. His eyes glowed with admiration for the painted silk lanterns swaying in the breeze.

To Jesse, the golden turrets, fanciful cornices, and pagoda tops of the buildings were part of a delicious fairyland. She was glad Marge had suggested they come down here for an early dinner, Kathy thought. This had been Jesse's introduction to Chinese dining. He'd been so serious when he tasted each unfamiliar dish.

"It's getting late for Jesse," Lee told Kathy. "Why don't the two of us go back to the apartment and let you and Marge have yourselves another hour or so to roam around?"

"Do we have to?" Jesse asked wistfully, but already he was fighting yawns.

"It's late, darling," Kathy pointed out. "And tomorrow's a school day." Magic words for Jesse. "I'll be home soon." Her eyes thanked Lee. It would be relaxing to spend an hour or so roaming about this fanciful city with Marge. "All right, Jesse?"

"Okay." Jesse was philosophical. "But can I have a cookie from the bakery there?" He pointed to a shop window displaying almond cakes, noodle puffs, and melon cakes.

"All right," Kathy agreed. "We'll go in and buy you an almond cookie."

With Jesse and Lee headed for home, Kathy and Marge strolled down Grant Avenue with the air of teenagers on an unexpected school vacation day.

"I love San Francisco," Marge confessed, "though as a New Yorker I feel like a traitor admitting it."

"There's only one thing that I resent here," Kathy said, her eyes reflective. "How can a city as liberal-minded and cosmopolitan as San Francisco keep the Chinese boxed in Chinatown?"

"Yeah." Marge nodded sympathetically. "It's so tough even for American-born Chinese to find apartments. We forget most of the time because it's not a problem we face."

"I worry about Rhoda and Frank," Kathy said. "When will this crazy red-smearing stop?"

"Have you heard any news about Frank's finding a job?" Marge knew that Rhoda was postponing all thought of job-hunting until after the baby was born.

"Nothing so far," Kathy reported. "He's sold an article to some low-paying magazine. That's not going to keep them going." She felt recurrent guilt over Phil's actions. If it were not for her, Phil would have lost touch with Rhoda and Frank; he would not have got them blacklisted.

Now they arrived at Little Italy, with its air of a Mediterranean seaside village that slithered from the heights to the water below. The area, dominated by Telegraph Hill and Russian Hill, was favored by the city's bohemians.

"Let's stop and have coffee here," Kathy said on impulse as they approached a sidewalk café.

"Great." Marge sighed nostalgically. "It looks like something back in Greenwich Village."

They settled themselves at a table and ordered pastry and espresso, both caught up in the convivial atmosphere created by the obviously bohemian patrons clustered about them.

"I feel so young here," Marge whispered. "Instead of an old bag pushing thirty."

They listened to the lively chatter at the table behind them, which hopped from books to painting to the Beats of Los Angeles's Venice West.

"I can close my eyes and think I'm sitting at a café on Bleecker Street," Marge said. "Remember that terrific Italian place that used to be right off Bleecker? The one with the sensational garlic bread? We used to go there on Saturday nights our last year in school—"

"Guido's?" a masculine voice suggested, and they both turned in surprise to the table at their right. "I was at school in New York for two years," the handsome bearded young man at the next table said reminiscently. "They served shrimp scampi and garlic bread that you could die for."

"Where did you go to school?" Marge asked.

"Columbia," he told them.

"I was at Barnard," Kathy said, feeling an instant rapport with him. He was about their age, she guessed. He seemed warm and sensitive and rather sad. "I graduated in '45."

"I was there in '42 and '43." His smile was electric. Kathy sensed he was lonely. "Then my mother's health started to fail, and I had to switch to Berkeley. Of course, she lived another nine years after that, but nothing would do but to have me within five minutes' driving distance." Now Kathy sensed bitterness. A demanding mother, she thought. "I didn't fight in Korea." A note of apology in his voice.

"Not everybody your age fought in Korea," Marge said dismissively.

"Remember the West End Bar?" His face lighted in recall. "Those were good years for me. Before I let myself get caught up in the guilt of the affluent."

"I went to Barnard, but we were hardly affluent," Kathy said. He was part of that new scene of bohemians who were disillusioned with the American dream, who considered it a disgrace to be affluent.

"I went to Hunter," Marge laughed. "You can't get less affluent than that."

"I'm fourth-generation San Franciscan and damn sick of the way the world's going. This rotten Cold War, the greed everywhere, the obsession for material things. We have to change, you know. Have you read Kerouac?" All at once he was reverent.

"I've never heard of him," Kathy confessed.

"He went to Columbia." Their new acquaintance seemed proud of this. "You're going to hear a lot about him."

Now they introduced themselves. He was Noel Bartlett. He had a sister who lived in New York and was furious with him because their mother had left him the family house, a mansion on Nob Hill, they gathered, though he was casual about this.

"My mother left the house to me because she knew I'd hang on to the old homestead. She knew Wilma would insist on selling it if she left it to both of us. Wilma stopped talking to me when the lawyers made it clear there was no way she could break our mother's will. The trust fund doles out a set amount of money for us every year for the next dozen years, then we share the principal. My mother figured by then we'll both have our feet on the ground."

Before Kathy and Marge left the café, they agreed to meet Noel when they closed the shop the following day. He was eager to show them a new bookstore that had just opened on Columbus Avenue. The first all-paperback bookstore in the country.

"It was opened by guys named Lawrence Ferlinghetti and Peter Martin. Ferlinghetti has a degree from Columbia, in addition to one from the Sorbonne," he pointed out with pride. "Columbia students do get around."

Kathy knew that she and Marge had discovered a real friend. She realized, too—though Marge frankly considered this a loss—that they would never have to worry about a romantic entanglement with Noel. He was candid about his homosexuality.

Kathy exhorted Jesse not to dawdle with his dressing.

"You don't want to be late for school," she warned while she stirred his cereal on the stove.

She glanced out the kitchen window. The morning fog seemed to swallow up the whole city. There were two kinds of fog in San Francisco. The ordinary kind, like today's, and the tole fog—low-hanging clusters of clouds that floated about in fanciful serpentine drifts and settled over only one segment of the city, leaving the rest gloriously sunny.

She switched on the kitchen radio, fidgeted with the dial in search of a weather report. It wasn't going to rain today, was it? In October you never knew when the fog might give way to a drizzle. The phone rang, and she instinctively tensed. When would she stop feeling defensive every time the doorbell or the phone rang?

She reached for the phone.

"Hello." Her voice guarded from habit.

"Kathy, don't get upset when you hear what I have to tell you," Marge urged. "We can handle this—"

"Handle what?" Despite her determination to be cool, Kathy knew her voice was strident.

"I was busy with the sketch pad last night so I didn't settle down to read *Women's Wear Daily* until too late to call you." Marge paused an instant. "Phil will be here in San Francisco this afternoon. Something to do with the company opening up a concession in addition to the San Francisco store."

"I have to get away!" Kathy fought panic. "Did *Women's Wear Daily* say how long he'd be in town?"

"He'll just be here for three days," Marge soothed. "But I don't think it would be a good idea for you to show up at the shop while he's in town. I'll call Melinda to cover for you." Melinda was a neighbor who helped out in the shop on occasion.

"I think Jesse and I are going on a short trip," Kathy said, her voice indicating to Marge that he'd just walked into the kitchen. "How would you like that, Jesse?"

"I have to go to school," he said reproachfully.

"I'll explain to your teacher that . . . that you've never seen the redwood trees. Jesse, they're the tallest trees in the world! We'll just be gone four days." A day extra, she promised herself, in case Phil extended his trip. *Why was her heart pounding this way? Phil wouldn't find them.*

Kathy and Marge discussed the most advisable destination. Kathy would rent a car, it was decided, and drive with Jesse to Monte Rio—crowded during the summer but sparsely occupied now. They'd have no trouble finding a place to stay.

"Even though it's close to San Francisco," Marge recalled, "it's kind of isolated. It still has that turn-of-the-century look. Phil wouldn't be caught dead there."

"We'll pack a picnic lunch," Kathy said, pleased that Jesse's eyes widened in pleasurable anticipation. "We'll be on the road before noon," she told Marge. "I'll call you tonight."

Phil took a taxi directly from the airport to the Palace Hotel. This was his first stay at the Palace, but he remembered the model from the shop who had sulked because he had taken her to a smaller, more private hotel for the night they'd partied together on his last trip out here.

What was her name? Something exotic. Sascha, he remembered, and felt the first tingle of arousal. Tonight he had a business dinner, but tomorrow night he'd entertain Sascha in a suite at the Palace. She wouldn't turn him down, he thought smugly. She knew he'd see to it that her salary went up if she was good to him.

As the cab pulled up before the elegant Palace Hotel at Market and New Montgomery, Phil reminded himself to phone Sascha before his dinner appointment. Tomorrow night with her would be the highlight of this trip. It had been a tough battle to persuade the old man to let him develop a concession deal, but already they could see signs that it was a new and profitable trend for them. Something else *he* was contributing to the company, he thought with satisfaction.

Settled in his top-floor suite, he phoned Sascha. She wasn't surprised to hear from him, of course—the shop staff knew he was arriving this afternoon.

"Phil, I can't wait to see you," she said in a throaty drawl.

"Tomorrow night, baby. I'm at the Palace." He heard her sensuous murmur of approval. "I'll call you and let you know when I'll be clear of business."

Later he played the gracious host to the two top executives of the department store that was taking in Julius Kohn Furs on a concession arrangement. The three men sat at a table in the glass-roofed Garden Court with its crystal chandeliers and stained-glass windows and, over a superb dinner, discussed their mutual project with soaring optimism.

He was relieved when their dinner meeting ended rather early in the evening. He was still operating on Eastern time. While preparing for bed he forced himself to map out his next day's schedule. In between business meetings he had to check out Marge's shop.

Damn, the old man was being a bastard about releasing the stock that was to be transferred to his name. He wouldn't feel secure until it *was* in his name. Brenda and Gail were seething that they'd never be part of the business. He wouldn't put it past them to try something funny.

He could hear his father's voice right now: *"You get a divorce from Kathy with no financial settlement or alimony, and you get back Jesse. Then—when I know she can't get her fucking hands on the business—I'll put the stock in your name.*" Fifty percent of the company. When their father went, the other fifty percent of the company stock was willed to *him*. Hell, he'd earned it.

Kathy waited until she was sure Jesse was asleep on one of the twin beds in their motel room before she phoned Marge. He'd sleep well tonight, she thought tenderly. He'd been awed by the huge redwood trees they'd seen in the state park, intrigued by the deer they'd seen feeding as they sought a spot to have their picnic spread. They'd stopped by the road to inspect a windmill. It had been a full, satisfying day for Jesse. He'd forgotten that he was missing school.

Now she reached for the phone, and dialed Marge's apartment. Marge answered immediately.

"Hi—"

"Jesse had a great day," Kathy reported. "Did Phil show up?"

"He was scheduled to arrive in town this afternoon," Marge reminded. "And he did. I called the Mark Hopkins, the Fairmont, and the Palace. He's registered at the Palace. I'll know when he checks out. Try to relax and consider this a vacation."

"He didn't come to the shop?" Kathy persisted. Needing reassurance.

"Sweetie, he arrived this afternoon. Knowing Phil, his first destination was the bar for a drink. If he comes to the shop at all, it'll probably be his last day in town."

"I can't keep running away every time he appears in San Francisco." Kathy strived to be realistic. "He's in town two or three times a year. But if he's talked to you and believes you don't know where I am, I'll feel safe."

"I'll give him an Academy Award performance," Marge promised.

"I'll call you tomorrow night. Oh, is Melinda available to fill in for me?" she asked in sudden concern.

"Melinda's all clear for the next ten days, and Phil is

scheduled to be in town for just three. *He won't find you.*
And even if he did, I don't think any court in the world
would let him take Jesse from you," Marge repeated for the
hundredth time.

"You're thinking logically. The world doesn't work that
way. With all their money and their connections, I can't
gamble on Phil's finding me."

"Are you staying there for now?" Marge asked.

"We'll be here. Let me give you the phone number. If I
don't hear from you before that, I'll call tomorrow at this
time."

After an afternoon conference with the manager of the San
Francisco shop, Phil decided to run over and talk to Marge.
The old man would be expecting a phone call tonight. With
the difference in time he'd have to get over to her shop
pronto, or it'd be too late to call New York.

"I'll meet you for dinner at Trader Vic's at 6:30," he
whispered to Sascha. "Be there."

He left Julius Kohn Furs, San Francisco, and took a taxi
to the 4-S Shop, near Union Square. She couldn't afford to
be on the Square, he thought with characteristic arrogance.
And what a stupid name for a women's store!

If it wasn't for the old man, he wouldn't be in such a rush
to track down Kathy. He was in no hurry for a divorce. Of
course, he missed the kid, he told himself with a temporary
surge of guilt. And until he cleared up this mess with Kathy
he wasn't going to see that stock in his name.

The taxi driver pulled up at the curb before Marge's shop.
Not bad-looking, he conceded, but shops like this were a
dime a dozen. She'd be lucky to stay alive with all the competition that was coming along these days.

He opened the door and walked inside, his eyes automati-
cally checking the staff. Marge—talking with a customer—
and another woman who was setting up a table display of
sweaters. The woman came toward him with a smile.

"I'm an old friend of Marge's from New York," he explained. "I'll just hang around until she's free."

"Phil!" All at once Marge spied him. "Be with you in a few moments." She was winding up a sale.

"Hey, the shop looks great!" he said when she came over to greet him. They contrived a light embrace. "How're things going?"

"Good," she told him with a breezy smile. "Is Kathy in town with you?"

"No." All at once he was irritated. Marge must know they were separated. "I thought you might know where she was."

Now Marge's smile faded. Her eyes seemed anxious. *Was she putting on an act?*

"It's been an awful long time since we've exchanged letters. You know how it is when you're so far apart." She paused, as though mentally debating. "I gathered you two had separated, but I figured it was just some spat and you'd made up by now. Some character came around here—I guess it was sometime last month—and he was asking questions about Kathy."

"She walked out with Jesse. We've been frantic to find them. She didn't even leave a note. I don't know what triggered her running off like that," he lied. He often asked himself if Kathy had talked with Rhoda about what happened. Wouldn't Rhoda have written Marge? The three women were thick as thieves. "It's as though Kathy and Jesse had just disappeared from the face of the earth," he said with an air of bewilderment.

"That's not like Kathy." Marge appeared upset. "And it amazes me that she didn't get in touch with me. We've always been so close."

"If you hear from her, will you phone me? Call collect," he said, turning on the slightly jaded Phil Kohn charm. She didn't know anything about Kathy—she was pissed that Kathy hadn't been in touch. "I'll be at the Palace Hotel here in town until Friday morning. After that, you can reach me in New York."

"I'm sorry, Phil. I can't imagine Kathy going off like that." She hesitated. Her face troubled. "You're sure she and Jesse went off on their own volition? They—they couldn't have been kidnapped?"

"Kathy didn't leave a note, as I told you," he said tersely. That cinched it. She didn't know anything. He was wasting good time here. "Just a scribbled memo that the Caddy was at the White Plains station."

"It's weird." Marge shook her head in disbelief. "If *you* hear anything, will you please let me know?"

"Sure thing," he promised. Now let him get the hell out of here. He had a heavy date for tonight.

The midday sunshine had given way to a dreary drizzle. Kathy and Jesse returned from sight-seeing to settle themselves in their motel room. Kathy with a magazine to read and Jesse with a new puzzle to put together. Even while she read, Kathy half-listened for the sound of the phone.

The jarring ring—when it came—sounded overly loud in the silence of their room. She picked up the phone on the first ring.

"Hello—"

"Everything went fine, Kathy," Marge reported, her voice jubilant. "He came here. We talked. He's convinced I don't know where you are. I suspect he believed I'm annoyed that you weren't in touch with me. You know, our being best friends for so long. You would have been proud of me. Like I promised, an Academy Award performance. And he's leaving on Friday morning."

"I'll drive home early Saturday morning," Kathy said after a moment. "Just to make sure he's gone." It was absurd the way her heart was pounding, just because she knew Phil was here in San Francisco. "Let's hope we've put this scene to rest."

*　　*　　*

Phil walked into Trader Vic's with an air of satisfaction that he was now on a first-name basis with the frontline staff. Every time he was in town he made a point of having dinner here at least once. It was becoming a kind of club for celebrities.

He'd made a very early reservation, not only because he was impatient for what he liked to call his "special dessert," but with an eye to avoiding anyone who might know him. Any friends, acquaintances, or business associates wouldn't arrive until 8 P.M. By then he and Sascha would be cavorting in the style he liked best in his suite at the Palace.

Walking into the nautical "Bali Hai" atmosphere of Trader Vic's, he thrust from his mind the gnawing reminder that his father was going to be furious that he had no lead on Kathy's whereabouts. Worry about that later, he thought in soaring high spirits. Tonight was for relaxing.

Sascha was waiting at the table for him. She was one of the few models he knew who could appear voluptuous with small tits and an almost flat rump, he thought. It was the way she moved.

"Hi." Her amazingly blue eyes were provocative against a perennial golden tan. She wore a flattering black sheath with the shorter skirt Dior had decreed last year and that women had rushed to adopt.

"Hi." He slid into his chair and a knee reached under the table to find hers. "You look good enough to eat."

"Later we play." She laughed in that throaty way that set his teeth on edge.

For a few minutes they concentrated on what to order. Both focusing on the Polynesian specialties. He could be happy with his life as it was, he told himself, with a wife conveniently off in the wild blue yonder. He could play with impunity. Why did the old man insist on getting back at Kathy before he turned over that stock?

Phil pretended to need swift service, and their waiter served them with commendable speed. Sascha scolded him when he rejected dessert as a time-waster. Still, he suspected, she was pleased that he was so hot to trot.

"We'll order dessert sent up to the suite," he promised. "If you still want it later." His eyes full of promise.

Once in Phil's suite they embarked on a passionate path to the bedroom. This was a chick who knew how to please a man, he thought in triumph while they dallied at the entrance to the bedroom. No doubts tonight that he'd be able to perform like an eighteen-year-old.

Sascha always wore sexy black lace underthings, he remembered while he helped her out of her bra. His hands fondling the tiny, huge-nippled breasts for a moment before reaching to release the hooks of her garter belt—all that she wore beneath her dress.

Her long slender fingers played with his hair—still movie-star lush except for the one thinning spot of which he was desperately conscious—while he dropped to his knees to guide her nylons down slender thighs and legs, his mouth nuzzling at her pelvis.

"Phil, let's go to the bed," she whispered. "Sweetie, I can't wait!"

"Okay, okay."

They were caught up in a crescendo of passion, moving to their ultimate destination with a matching frenzy when the phone rang.

"Damn it!" Phil grunted, freezing for a moment.

"Do you have to answer?" Sascha asked, her crimson nails digging into his shoulders, her body refusing to abandon its race.

"No," he said thickly. "Let him call back later." Knowing it was his father. "Let's get this show on the road!"

= Chapter 26

Kathy and Marge were in a festive mood when they headed together for the New Year's Eve party Noel was giving in his late mother's Washington Street mansion. Christmas business had been gratifying. Back from a month in the south of France, Fred and Cleo were impressed with the sales figures.

Kathy and Marge were hoping they were sufficiently impressed to put up funds for an advertising campaign. They plotted to discuss this with Fred and Cleo at Noel's party. It was Noel who cannily suggested he invite them. *"My parties are a real mix of people. They'll have fun. Sometimes that's the best time to get across a business message."*

In the few weeks since they had met at that sidewalk café in Little Italy, Kathy and Marge had become fast friends with Noel. He was bright, warm, intelligent. He was unhappy about the split with his sister Wilma, but he had no intention of giving her half-interest in the house, as she demanded. *"She'd have it on the auction block in a week."*

They knew that Noel had never held a full-time job in his life. He'd played at being an actor, a writer, an artist.

Most of the time he had been his mother's traveling companion on frequent jaunts to exotic places.

Noel had become their escort at the occasional diversions they allowed themselves. He treated them to a night at the San Francisco Symphony. Now it was a Friday night routine for Noel and Marge to come to Kathy's apartment for dinner, a festive occasion that Jesse enjoyed. Noel was so gentle and tender with Jesse, Kathy thought. The way David had been.

The Bartlett mansion was elegant without being intimidating. Kathy and Marge, along with Jesse, had been there for Thanksgiving dinner—prepared and served by Noel's staff of two. *"The terms of the will keep Curt and Greta on the job until they decide to retire. They're both in their middle seventies, but they love this house. They'll be here till they drop."*

Kathy and Marge arrived early. Despite their wealth and world-traveler status, Fred and Cleo were shy at being among strangers. And both women knew that holidays were trying periods for Noel. Despite his often irreverent remarks about her, he deeply missed his mother. He'd always made a point of spending holidays with her during the long years of her widowhood.

"You both look marvelous!" He greeted them with exuberant embraces and led them into what his mother liked to call the grand salon—a huge carpeted room with a grand piano at one side and a parade of six crystal chandeliers hanging from the high ceiling. The room had been cleared of its usual 18th-century furniture to allow for a change in decor. A pianist was playing a Cole Porter tune.

"Curt and Greta are setting up the most gorgeous buffet," Noel told them. "And Curt will do bar duty until midnight. After that we're on our own." Already Curt was behind the improvised bar.

"Noel, you've made it look like a Paris sidewalk café," Kathy said admiringly, viewing the lineup of small tables along one wall, temporarily adorned with prints by famous

French artists. Colorful tablecloths were spread on the tables, each table with a silver vase holding a single red rose. "You have a talent for these things."

"That's the story of my life," he flipped. "A collection of tiny talents. None of them big enough to be developed. That's one of the reasons I love you two. You're both talented, and you're working at it."

The first of the sixteen guests Noel had invited began to arrive. Sixteen, he'd pointed out earlier, because he loathed the habit of pairing off dinner partners "like Noah's Ark." Fred and Cleo were the last to arrive. Hurrying to welcome them—they'd met Noel at the shop so he wasn't a complete stranger—Kathy saw their wary glances about the room.

Noel's guests were an eclectic group. Kathy saw that Fred and Cleo would not be comfortable with Chris Logan, the talented young homosexual artist who followed Noel about with adoring eyes, nor with the Amazonian lesbian writer who was celebrating the sale of her first novel ten days ago. Noel had instructed Greta to lay four settings at each table except for one with five. That was deliberate, to allow Marge and her to sit alone with Fred and Cleo.

While gypsy-garbed fiddlers strolled among the guests, Greta began to bring huge platters of food to the buffet at one side of the room. When she signaled Noel that everything was in place, he clapped his hands together for attention.

"Chow time," he announced effervescently. "Let's greet 1954 with satiated tummies!"

It was incredible, Kathy thought with gentle amusement, that Fred and Cleo could be so traveled, so accustomed to money, and yet remain so unsophisticated. But they were enjoying themselves, she decided, while Cleo talked about the bargains she'd found in Italy on their last visit. To so many women, European cities were mainly a shopping mecca. Sight-seeing took second place.

She would have enjoyed the party immensely, Kathy told herself, if she and Marge were not so determined to persuade Fred to put up money for promoting the shop before he and Cleo took off again, this time for Palm Beach. For a moment she felt a touch of alarm. Probably Bella and "the girls" would be in Palm Beach, also.

But even if they should meet in that society whirl, Fred and Cleo knew her as Kathy Altman. Nor was it likely, she decided realistically, that talk about Phil's wife would enter their conversations. She must learn that she lived in an entirely new world now. Kathy Kohn was dead. Long live Kathy Altman.

"Marge tells us you came up with the title for the shop," Fred punctured her introspection.

"Not just the title," Marge said. "The whole concept of the shop. And it's working well. With some major promotion the idea could really develop big."

"We offer what appeals to the average young woman, and today they spend a lot of money on these items," Kathy added with studied casualness. Her eyes warned Marge against a hard-sell.

"You're sharp, Kathy," Fred approved. "I could see that right off."

"And I'd like to see us push more of Marge's own designs," Kathy pursued. "It's not as easy to manufacture on a small scale out here the way it is in New York, but we can do it."

"Kathy has an eye for what's commercial," Marge said. "I design and test it out on her. What she doesn't like, I change. I may complain and grunt a lot, but I know she's always right."

"No more shoptalk," Cleo ordered. "We're here to welcome in the new year." She gazed nostalgically at the strolling fiddlers. "Do you suppose they know 'I'm Falling in Love with Someone'?"

"I'll ask them," Marge said instantly.

"I love that song." Cleo beamed a sentimental smile in Fred's direction. "Fred used to sing it to me when we were courting."

As Noel expected of them, Kathy and Marge remained after all the guests—except for Chris, who was staying over—had left. While Chris went out to the kitchen to make coffee for them, Noel collapsed on a sofa in the small family sitting room along with Kathy and Marge.

"Well?" he demanded avidly. "Did Fred come across?"

"He said he'd think about it," Marge said. "Which means no."

"We tried," Kathy said ruefully. "He referred to promotion as 'Madison Avenue garbage.'"

"I can put up some money," Noel said after brief reflection. "You'll pay me back later."

"Can you handle that?" Kathy asked, remembering that his money was doled out annually. "I mean, we don't know for sure when we can pay you back."

"We'll live dangerously." Noel shrugged. "I'll bet I could borrow against the trust if I had to."

"I'm not sure Fred is going to be happy about this." But Marge was faintly defiant. Success had become an obsession.

"Look, you're running the show," Noel pointed out. "All Fred does is put up the cash, when he feels like it. Start your promotion campaign. Consider me available for your board of directors."

"Next year this time," Kathy predicted, her eyes aglow, "we'll be celebrating the opening of our second shop!"

In the weeks ahead Kathy and Marge found themselves in frequent consultation with Noel. They respected his promotional ideas, used some of them. As they had anticipated, the volume of business jumped. Now, too, they were striving to stress designs by Marge.

On a late evening in February, Frank called from New York to report that Rhoda had given birth to a daughter, to be named Sara Deirdre Collins. The following morning Rhoda phoned from the hospital, deliriously happy.

"The baby's done what Frank and I couldn't do. She's

brought the families together. You never saw prouder grandparents."

"How's Frank doing with the writing?" Kathy asked. Talking to him, she'd been so excited about the arrival of the baby that she'd forgot to ask.

"He has plenty of time to write," Rhoda said with rueful humor. "Of course, he's as upset as hell about the job situation, but he tries to push that aside when he's writing. He's sold a couple of articles to some small magazines. And I've applied to several private schools up in Westchester County for a fall teaching position. Let's face it, under current conditions I can forget about teaching in Manhattan."

They talked for a few minutes about the shop, and then Rhoda had to hang up because the baby had just been brought to her for a feeding. Despite their joy over tiny Sara, Kathy sensed, Rhoda and Frank were troubled about their lack of jobs. What Phil had done to them was unforgivable.

In April, Fred and Cleo came back to San Francisco. They would remain here until they left in June for a three-month tour of the Far East. Fred was amazed by the progress of the shop, though he grumbled when Marge talked about a move to a larger shop just off Union Square. But Marge and Kathy understood that he considered it part of his role to grumble. He had no intention of standing in their way.

"Okay," he told them shortly before he and Cleo left on their tour. "Go ahead and rent the store. I just hope profits go up enough to handle that crazy rent."

Marge had already negotiated the lease and made the large security deposit, which left their fluid assets minuscule. But Kathy and she were convinced this was the right move at the right time.

The shop had become an obsession not only for Kathy and Marge, but for Noel as well. He enlisted Chris's help in providing colorful posters for the windows and the walls of the shop. He developed offbeat promotions that brought in new customers. Kathy took on the often difficult job of seeing one of Marge's designs through from sketch pad to garment.

Though every waking moment seemed crammed with activity, Kathy was conscious of surges of homesickness. It was almost a year since she had seen her parents and Aunt Sophie, Rhoda and Frank, Bella. Twice she had sent a batch of snapshots of Jesse to Rhoda, with instructions to forward them to Bella. She knew Bella was sure to understand she didn't dare write, but the snapshots said Jesse and she were fine.

She was euphoric when her mother phoned to say that she and Kathy's father, along with Aunt Sophie, were considering flying to San Francisco for a week.

"None of us has ever flown," her mother said with a self-conscious laugh, "and of course, I'm terrified of planes. But Aunt Sophie says to see you and Jesse I can forget about being afraid. So if you think it's a good idea for us to come, make arrangements for us at an inexpensive hotel and—"

"Mom, no hotel!" Kathy rejected. "You'll stay here with Jesse and me."

"We'll stop off in Chicago for one day." Her mother was overly casual. "We won't even stay overnight."

"Why Chicago?" Kathy was alert to trouble.

"Just in case Phil is keeping track of where we go. Dad said I shouldn't tell you—you'd worry—but you should know. We're stopping in Chicago because some creepy private investigator has been asking questions again. Trying to check on our mail, the postman told us. You know Pete—he's been our postman for years. He told the man off. A couple of things like that happened. But if they see we're leaving town, and that man comes asking questions, they'll say we went to stay with a cousin in Chicago." Unexpectedly she chuckled. "Let Julius Kohn spend a bunch of money looking for you in Chicago."

Now Kathy counted the days till her family would arrive in San Francisco. It startled her to realize that Jesse had only slight recall of his grandparents and aunt, though she often talked about them with him. It was as though they were living in exile.

She had begun to accept Marge's assumption that she and Jesse were home free—that Phil and Julius had abandoned searching for her and Jesse. But that wasn't true. Julius had disliked her from their first meeting. Now he harbored a vendetta against her.

If Phil and Julius knew where she was, they'd try to grab Jesse. That was her constant nightmare. *Jesse would be terrified.* She felt sick at the thought of their taking Jesse, of what would become an ugly custody battle. Phil and Julius would make sure that it was.

Kathy took Jesse with her to the airport to meet the family, driving Noel's car at his insistence. *"Keep it for the week. Show your folks San Francisco."* Jesse was alternately excited and shy about the reunion with his grandparents and great-great-aunt. He was impatient as he waited for them to arrive.

At last the flight was announced. Kathy and Jesse stood hand-in-hand as disembarking passengers approached.

"Here they come!" Joy surged through Kathy as she rushed forward, caught up in the miracle of seeing them at last. "Mom—Dad—Aunt Sophie!" Her face was luminous with love.

"I can't believe this is Jesse," her mother crooned softly, knowing she must not overwhelm him at this first encounter. "You're so tall!"

"You must be in kindergarten already," Aunt Sophie guessed, knowing he was now a first-grader.

"I'm in real school. First grade." Jesse beamed.

"You still like puzzles?" his grandfather asked and extended a gift-wrapped box.

"Yes!" Jesse grinned. "Thank you." He hesitated an instant. "Thank you, Grandpa."

Her family's week in San Francisco seemed both incredibly short and yet packed with wonderful hours. But Kathy fought back tears when she saw them off at the airport. *When would she see them again?*

═ Chapter 27

On a late August day Kathy received a phone call at the shop from Lee.

"Kathy, I suppose I'm being morbid, but there was a news bulletin in the middle of my soap opera." Lee was addicted to the radio soaps. "When do you expect Fred and Cleo back from their tour?"

"In a few days. What was the bulletin?" Lee's air of anxiety infected her now. Though Lee didn't know Fred and Cleo personally, she knew about them, of course.

"A plane crashed somewhere over Ireland a few hours ago. There were some Americans on board. Kathy, they were part of some Far East tour."

"Fred and Cleo were headed for Ireland the last we heard," Kathy said, her heart pounding. "But there must be a number of Far East tour groups in operation this time of year. It's the high season. Let's don't jump to wild conclusions."

"When I pick up Jesse at school, I'll see if there's anything in the newspapers," Lee said. "If there's anything important, like a passenger list, I'll buzz you."

By late afternoon the tragic news had come through. All aboard the flight had been killed. Listed among the passengers were Fred and Cleo. For the first time—at memorial services several days later—Marge and Kathy met Fred and Cleo's son and daughter. Both were married and totally involved in their own lives.

"How could two such nice people have such cold children?" Marge whispered as they left the chapel. "Are you sure they weren't adopted?"

Five days later, when Marge was out of the shop, Kathy received a phone call from Fred and Cleo's son, Earl.

"Tell Miss O'Hara that it's important she contact me immediately. We have business to discuss," Earl said, his voice arrogant and disapproving.

"I'll tell her," Kathy said. The call was not unexpected, but dreaded.

When Marge returned, Kathy gave her Earl's message.

"He doesn't know anything about the women's wear field," Kathy tried to comfort her. "He can't take an active hand in the shop."

"He and his sister have probably inherited fifty percent of the shop." Marge was grim. "He can be a real pain in the ass." She was silent for a moment. "All right, I'll call him."

Marge set up an appointment to meet with Earl at the shop that same evening. She insisted that Kathy remain with her. The two of them listened in shock when Earl Palmer told them he expected Marge to buy him out—or he'd go to court to force a sale of merchandise and fixtures so that he could take out the fifty-percent interest that belonged to his sister and himself.

"I've gone through my father's records," he said tersely. "I know to the penny how much money he put into the shop. I want that back within six weeks, or I go to court."

Kathy and Marge were distraught. There was no way that Marge could raise that much capital. The move to the new, larger store had drained her liquid funds.

"What about a bank loan?" Kathy asked. Her own assets would not make a dent in what Earl Palmer demanded. "We can show a healthy situation, Marge."

"I'll try, but I doubt I'll be able to raise enough to satisfy him." Marge was pale and shaken.

"Go to the bank," Kathy urged. Marge had worked too hard to lose the shop now!

"And pray for a miracle. In six weeks," Marge reminded.

For the next three days Marge applied for loans at various banks. They recognized the shop was profitable. They offered loans but in far lower amounts than what Earl demanded.

"Talk to him about a lower first payment," Kathy told her. "Then spread the balance over a period of three years. You can swing that."

"I'll call him," Marge agreed.

Earl Palmer refused to discuss a delayed settlement. He insisted he wanted full payment within six weeks.

"I'm leaving with my wife on a trip to Italy in six weeks. Either you've returned my father's investment in the shop, or I turn the matter over to my attorneys. They'll proceed with the suit. My father was absurdly naive about his investments," he said with an air of contempt. "My sister and I are not."

Noel was outraged when they told him about the demands of Earl Palmer and his sister.

"They're taking advantage of the loose arrangement you had with Fred! You know damn well Fred wouldn't want to see you in a spot like this."

"I wasn't bright about the deal I signed," Marge conceded. "But who expected something like this to happen?"

"Look, you can't borrow enough to satisfy that stupid bastard, but I can raise that kind of loan against my trust fund." Noel's face lighted. "Let me take out the loan for you. You set up a new company with you and Kathy as partners. Kathy's a terrific asset. You pay off the loan over a period of five years."

"Noel, I can't let you do that," Marge protested, but her face was luminescent.

"All right, give me a ten-percent interest in the company and split the other ninety percent between you and Kathy," Noel said. "I've never in my whole life been anything but a dilettante. I think it would be great to work with you two. The three of us make a terrific team."

"Marge, it'll work!" Enthusiasm ignited in Kathy. It was not just that she would love being part of the business. Here was security for Jesse. "We'll go all out on pushing 'Designs by Marge,' " she pursued. "We'll promote your designs the way we've always been afraid to because of Fred."

"It's a tremendous gamble, Noel," Marge warned.

"We'll make it," Noel insisted, his smile brilliant. "Tomorrow I go to my bankers. They know their loan is safe if it's tied to my trust fund. Let's go out and celebrate. We're in business!"

Noel had been right. His bank was happy to extend the loan against his trust fund. Now he worked alongside Marge and Kathy in the shop—each of the three now assigned specific duties. Though the fall season was almost upon them, Kathy prodded Marge into designing a line of sweaters and skirts, and she roamed the city in search of shops that could manufacture for them in record time, raced about the area in search of materials that pleased both herself and Marge. With his keen eye for color and textures, Noel made up the third member of their "board of directors."

Their Christmas sales soared. Their only complaint was that they ran out of choice items before the peak season.

"We can't be so scared," Noel scolded at a Sunday business meeting at Kathy's apartment. "We have to show more faith in ourselves. We'll double our orders for spring merchandise," he said ebulliently. "I'll bet we could sell the original designs to other stores, too."

"Not in San Francisco," Kathy stipulated. "Maybe we could sell to a top department store in Los Angeles. Let's try that, hunh?" She gazed from Noel to Marge. "But in San Francisco, if they want a sweater or skirt that's a 'Design by Marge,' they have to come to the 4-S Shop. Let's build on that."

A month later—grateful that her wardrobe included a few designer outfits from her life with Phil—Kathy flew down to Los Angeles to show samples of Marge's small new collection to buyers of choice department stores. Her objective was to sign up one store to handle the line exclusively.

Kathy was elated when the second buyer pounced on the line with enthusiasm. She returned to San Francisco with an impressive order. Marge and Noel viewed her with awe.

"Kathy, how did you wangle such a large order?" Noel was entranced.

"Can we fill it?" Marge betrayed some misgivings.

"We have to." Kathy understood Marge's concern. This wasn't New York. They didn't have the Seventh Avenue "outside shops" at their command. There might be problems in receiving material in the quantities they'd need. "We'll deliver on schedule," she vowed. The challenge was exhilarating.

The three of them worked longer hours than ever in their lives, all dedicated to making a success of the shop. By spring of the new year Noel was already pushing Kathy and Marge to thoughts of opening a second shop. They were meeting their bank loans and putting money aside for future development.

With the Los Angeles department store asking for more merchandise, Kathy brushed aside Marge's alarm about their filling orders and opened up accounts in fashionable department stores in San Diego and Acapulco. She searched the metropolitan San Francisco area for contractors to handle their burgeoning business. She was intoxicated by the potential of both "Designs by Marge" and 4-S Shops Incorporated.

"What about a shop in Berkeley?" Kathy pursued at an after-hours conference on her return from Acapulco. "A small store on Shattuck Avenue. No," she corrected herself. "Later a shop on Shattuck Avenue. The next one should be Telegraph Avenue—catering to all those college co-eds."

They scheduled an August opening for the shop on Telegraph Avenue. Noel, ever charming and appealing to women despite his own sexual preferences, was to be in charge. They knew almost immediately that this shop, too, would be a success.

Kathy's family flew out from New York for a week's vacation, timing this to coincide with the opening of the Telegraph Avenue shop. Their pride in her brought tears to Kathy's eyes. Thank God for the telephone, she thought—at least they were able to talk once a week. Still, as much as she had learned to love San Francisco, she yearned to be back in New York, close to her family and friends.

"Kathy, I was so glad to hear that Rhoda has a teaching job at last," her mother said, and Kathy nodded in agreement. "She and Frank have gone through such a bad time."

"Frank's sold a few articles in the last year," Kathy told her. "And he keeps hoping his animal rights group will be able to afford to set up a paid staff soon."

Lee was enlisted to show Kathy's family the sights of San Francisco during the hours when Jesse was in school. She showed them the Golden Gate Bridge, Fisherman's Wharf, with its myriad restaurants, its Wax Museum and Maritime Museum, Coit Tower, and the Mission Dolores, the oldest structure in San Francisco. They rode on cable cars. Through dime-in-the-slot telescopes on Telegraph Hill they saw Alcatraz, the island barely a mile away that was home to famous San Quentin, where several thousand of the Federal government's toughest prisoners were incarcerated.

Kathy's mother and father and Aunt Sophie made a point of being at the apartment when Lee went to bring Jesse home from school. This was the high point of their visit—to spend time with him. In the evening Kathy took them and Jesse to dinner at Bardelli's, at Julius's Castle, high on the slopes of Telegraph Hill, with windows providing a breathtaking view of the waterfront, the Bay and the bridges.

As on the last occasion, Kathy felt desolate when her family left. The prospect of these separations continuing through long years was painful. But thank God, she thought, for Marge and Noel and Lee.

Marge had a casual social life with men that never developed into a serious relationship, but Kathy understood she was too wrapped up in the shop to be upset. Noel and Chris escorted Marge and her to the symphony, the ballet, and the theater at intervals. If Marge was seeing someone, then Noel and Chris and she were a festive trio.

Noel gave a party to welcome 1956. In many ways, Kathy thought, when the guests had left and only she and Marge and Noel and Chris remained, 1955 had been a great year. The shops were succeeding beyond their expectations. They'd had to hire additional help for both sites and were opening on Shattuck Avenue right after the new year. Kathy envisioned a West Coast chain from San Diego to Seattle in the not too distant future.

Chris went out to the kitchen to make coffee. Marge and Noel discussed Chris's imminent gallery show. Kathy was caught up in introspection. Tonight—in truth, the first hours of 1956—she felt a surge of homesickness.

Earlier she had phoned home to wish the family a happy new year. Then she had called Rhoda and Frank in Croton for the first greeting of 1956. There was so much she missed about New York, she thought wistfully. Winter snows, the new small theaters labeled Off-Broadway, the double-decker Fifth Avenue buses. Beaches where the water—unlike in San Francisco—was warm enough for swimming. And in New York they would have a much easier time with manufacturing, she remembered. A larger choice of materials. There was only one Seventh Avenue.

Always on New Year's she thought about David. Was he all right? Was he *happy?* Had he married that girl he talked about? Probably he was married and a father by now, she thought, remembering him with Jesse.

"Coffee, everybody," Chris called out exuberantly, walking into the room with a tray of mugs. He was so thrilled about his first gallery showing, Kathy thought with affection. At twenty-two, that was an achievement, even though it was being underwritten by Noel. "We've just ushered in what my crystal ball tells me will be a marvelous year for all of us," he entoned with mock seriousness.

"From your lips to God's ear," Marge said softly.

Their success, Kathy thought, was almost awesome, because it was happening so quickly. They worked hard and long, but so did many others. At recurrent intervals she marveled at their progress. At moments she was almost frightened by the way their sales were spiraling, as though disaster might lie just around a bend in the road.

January was a month of heavy designing on Marge's part. Kathy was ever enthralled to be part of this. Her ideas were always incorporated in Marge's sketches. She couldn't sketch or sew, but Marge said she had a wonderful eye for small details that made a garment special.

Guilty at having to leave Jesse behind—though she knew he was spoiled outrageously by Lee, Marge, and Noel in her absence—Kathy flew on a brief selling trip to Los Angeles and San Diego, and shortly after that to Acapulco. As before, she returned with impressive orders. But manufacturing problems escalated sharply.

After a week of fighting to organize a schedule that would meet their deadlines, Kathy ordered Marge and Noel to her apartment for an evening conference. With Jesse asleep they settled down over coffee to try to cope with their situation.

"There has to be a way to cope with orders," Kathy said with candid frustration. "As it is, I ought to try to set up department stores in Seattle and Denver."

"You know what I think?" Noel began with that low-keyed tone that usually indicated a discussion of major magnitude.

"What do you think?" Marge joshed.

"I think we ought to take off the blinders and admit we need to move our base of operation to New York. We need the facilities we can find only on Seventh Avenue. That is, if we're to keep building the company—and kids, it's ready to explode into a national organization. I can handle the West Coast operations. We'll all make trips back and forth three or four times a year. And you two will take care of the manufacturing out of New York."

"Noel, I can't go to New York—" Kathy's throat tightened. They all understood they couldn't work out of New York without her constant presence. *"You know my situation."* All at once she was trembling.

"Kathy, you can't go on killing yourself looking for contractors. Going crazy arranging for delivery of materials. And once we start missing deadlines, we'll be in serious trouble."

"After all this time—it's almost three years—Phil and Julius must have given up trying to track you down," Marge said.

"Phil might, but Julius is carrying on a vendetta. You don't know him the way I do." Kathy was agonized by the situation. The business couldn't stand still; it had to expand or slowly fall by the wayside. But how could she go back to New York? Gamble on Phil taking her into court over Jesse's custody? Or worse—and she felt cold at just thinking of such a possibility—physically carrying off Jesse at some vulnerable moment. "It would be too dangerous for me to show up in New York again."

"Look, it's a question of planning," Noel told her seriously. "New York is a huge city. You'll know how to avoid Phil. You'll always be one up on him because he won't suspect you're around."

"You've changed your appearance, changed your name. You won't move in Phil's circles. Like Noel said, you know

Phil's haunts—you can avoid them. We can set up offices well away from Julius Kohn Furs. You'll rent a house up in Westchester—the Kohns are in Greenwich and Southampton. What about a house up in Croton?" Marge pushed. "Near Rhoda's apartment. Lee will go along to New York with us—she'd love to. She has a younger married sister in Queens," Marge reminded.

"I'm scared." Kathy was fighting within herself now. She was passionately ambitious, aware of the logic of what they said. Could she handle this, being super-careful? She'd never set foot in Brooklyn—the family would come to her, she plotted. She'd keep a low profile both in the business and in Westchester. *Would it work?* She forever felt guilty at depriving Jesse of family. He was almost nine now, old enough to be aware of how alone they were. If she rented a house in Croton, Jesse could see Mom and Dad and Aunt Sophie regularly. That would make up for his not having the presence of a father. "I don't know," she faltered. "I'll have to give it a lot more thought."

During the spring school vacation, Kathy flew to New York with Jesse to scout for office space and a house in Westchester. She had appointments with real estate brokers in Manhattan and Croton. She was amazed to discover that American Airlines' new DC-7s flew from San Francisco to New York in seven hours and fifteen minutes eastbound—forty minutes longer westbound. When she and Jesse had flown out in 1953, the trip had taken three hours longer!

Still—despite Marge and Noel's conviction that she could lose herself in Manhattan—she felt a sickening trepidation as the plane approached Idlewild. The agony that brought on her flight to San Francisco was fresh again.

On the rare chance that her parents' movements were being followed, she'd exhorted them not to meet her flight. They'd made reservations for her at a small Upper West Side hotel, and would be waiting there for Jesse and her. She wanted to scream at Jesse for being so vocal in his delight at their arrival when what she felt was sheer terror. *Had she made an awful mistake in bringing him back to New York?*

They collected their luggage. A skycap carried the valises outside and found a taxi for them. Now joy at the prospect of seeing her family washed away her initial alarm at being back in New York. She watched the passing scenery with that special feeling of coming home after a long absence. Excitement kindled in her as the taxi drove over the Queensboro Bridge into Manhattan and headed west.

At the hotel she and Jesse were enveloped in the family's welcome. Her parents and Aunt Sophie knew this was not merely a visit but the first step in a return from exile. She hadn't told Jesse yet that they were moving back to New York. He thought this was just a visit plus business. She would make this work, Kathy vowed.

They left the hotel and went over to Tip Toe Inn for an early dinner. Her mother would stay with them in their suite while they were in town. Tomorrow she would inspect the office space the broker had lined up for her to see, and Mom would take Jesse to the Museum of Natural History. In the evening Dad and Aunt Sophie would come into Manhattan to have dinner with them.

The following day she would take the train up to Croton, be met at the station by the broker and shown several houses that were available as rentals. She would have a brief visit with Rhoda and Frank and tiny Sara before taking the train back into the city.

Kathy settled for office space on Madison Avenue in the low thirties. While the address was only a few blocks from Julius Kohn Furs, Kathy knew it was foreign territory to both Phil and his father. 4-S Shops Inc. would take possession on July 1st.

She rented a charming little house on East Mount Airy Road in Croton, set back behind a 400-foot dogwood-lined driveway that provided a maximum of privacy. On a whirlwind trip through the furniture department of B. Altman she ordered basic furniture to be delivered on their arrival in Croton.

Despite her original decision not to tell Jesse until the end of school that they were moving back to New York, she broke the news to him while they were aboard their return flight to San Francisco.

He sat in disturbing silence for a few moments.

"You mean I won't see Harry anymore?" Harry had been his "best friend" for the past year.

"Of course, you'll see him again," she soothed. "We'll go back on visits." He's upset, she thought. It wasn't good to uproot him this way. "Jesse, you'll love the house up in Croton," she said gaily. "We'll have a whole house to ourselves, with a huge deck, and almost two acres of land. Lee'll live with us, and Marge will have an apartment in town." Still, he seemed to be troubled. "With that house and all that land, maybe we could get a puppy." All at once Jesse's face was aglow. "How would you like that? He would be your puppy. You'll have to take care of him," she cautioned, relieved by his pleasurable reaction. *This would see him through the move.*

"Can I call him Harry?" Jesse asked.

"You pick him out," she promised, "and you name him."

"He'll be a collie, like Harry's dog!" Jesse decided effervescently. "We'll take pictures of him, and I'll send one to Harry."

Somehow, she must make this return to New York work, Kathy told herself yet again. Jesse needed the security of roots. They couldn't continue to run.

Chapter 28

The summer weeks were chaotic for Kathy both personally and professionally. She was grateful for Lee's presence in their lives. It was Lee who supervised their getting settled in the house, who found a congenial day-camp for Jesse. Lee was the family chauffeur. She drove Kathy to the Harmon station each morning for the commute into New York, and picked her up on her return.

The household now included the puppy Jesse had chosen at a Westchester animal center and named Harry, a rambunctiously affectionate mongrel of mixed ancestry—mainly collie and golden retriever, Frank had decided. It had been love at first sight for Jesse and Harry. Kathy, too, quickly succumbed to Harry's charms.

At disconcerting intervals Kathy was anxious about her presence in the city that harbored Phil, yet for most of the hours in the office she was so absorbed in work she might still have been in San Francisco. By the end of the summer—with Noel in New York for three days of consultations—Kathy brought up the subject of their hiring a publicity woman. She had learned the value of this from Phil.

"We stress our designer," Kathy said while she sat with Marge and Noel on the sprawling deck of the Croton house. "Marge, you'll always wear your own designs." Her mind flashed back to Roz, whom she'd disliked intensely but who had been so savvy about fashion publicity. "We've got to build a look for you. A new hairstyle, new makeup."

"Oh, God, you'll have me on television next." Marge grimaced in alarm.

"We'll hire a publicity woman with strong magazine, radio, and TV contacts," Kathy stipulated. "And you'll use just one name. Marge."

"Hildegarde and me," Marge flipped, but Kathy saw her awareness of what lay ahead of them.

By late fall their manufacturing was moving with a smoothness that elated the three stockholders of 4-S Shops Inc. Kathy made a quick trip to England to buy special fabrics. They were about to open their first Manhattan shop. She was negotiating with a major Philadelphia store to handle "Designs by Marge" on an exclusive basis. From the West Coast Noel was supervising the opening of a shop in Dallas and another in New Orleans.

Noel and Chris flew in from San Francisco to spend Thanksgiving weekend at the Croton house, combining business with pleasure. Kathy was euphoric at having the dining room table opened to its full capacity for this Thanksgiving dinner: her parents, Aunt Sophie, Rhoda and Frank and little Sara, now a few weeks short of her second birthday, but happy to be seated on a pile of pillows at the dining table, and Noel and Chris, along with Jesse and herself. Marge had gone to her family's in Brooklyn.

Lee was at her sister's house in Queens for Thanksgiving, but she'd insisted on preparing the turkey and seeing it into the oven before Kathy drove her to the station. Rhoda brought a pumpkin pie and a pecan pie, baked the night before. Chris had brought her a small painting of Jesse, done from memory.

After dinner they settled themselves about the spacious living room while Frank and Jesse made a joyous adventure of laying a fire in the fireplace grate and coaxing it into an orange-red blaze. Sara napped now in Jesse's bedroom.

"Jesse, if Harry gets any closer to the fireplace, we'll have roast dog," Rhoda teased.

"I want to take photos later," Noel said. "I have to try out my new camera."

"Noel, take one of Jesse and Harry," Kathy said on impulse. She'd send it to Bella. It was months since she'd sent a batch of snapshots to Phil's mother, she realized guiltily. Bella truly loved Jesse. How sad that they couldn't see one another.

For the dozenth time today her mind wandered back to Thanksgiving Day in Hamburg, eleven years ago. They'd had dinner late in the evening because this had been another working day for them. Phil had just arrived in Hamburg a few days earlier, and he'd come to the flat for dinner. He'd brought chocolate bars bought on the black market.

She'd given little attention to Phil at that Thanksgiving dinner, though the other girls, even Rhoda, had seemed fascinated by him. David monopolized her thoughts. She wore the brooch they'd discovered in a pawnshop in Berlin.

"This is a long way from Hamburg," Rhoda said reminiscently, and Kathy turned to her with a startled smile. Rhoda, too, remembered Thanksgiving in Hamburg.

"We had Spam instead of turkey," Frank recalled, "and canned cranberry sauce brought from New York. I wonder where the others are today—"

It was unlikely David would be celebrating Thanksgiving in Berlin, Kathy thought. But if he looked at the calendar and realized this was Thanksgiving Day in the United States, would he remember that Thanksgiving in Hamburg? Instinctively, she knew he would.

* * *

David was restless on the flight to New York. He'd debated over a month, since New Year's, about going to discuss the offer to set up his own research center in Manhattan. He wasn't making a commitment yet, he told himself. This was just to talk about what the group had to offer him.

His friends at the Institute thought he was out of his mind to consider leaving Berlin now. Its postwar recovery was sensational, the spirit of the city high. And here was none of the frenzy of such prosperous cities as Frankfurt.

The "Ku-Damm"—as Berliners called the Kurfürsten-damm—was lined with smart new shops, new theaters, fashionable hotels, bookstores, sidewalk cafés. At night, illuminated by myriad neon signs, the avenue exuded prosperity as well-dressed strollers thronged the area. On weekends shabbily dressed East Berliners sneaked into the Western Sector to walk on the Ku-Damm and stare in disbelief and fascination at the fine shops and their elegant merchandise. Glass-walled office buildings and cheerfully colored apartment houses had sprung up around the city.

It was weird, he thought, that as West Berlin prospered, he grew more uncomfortable living there. Perhaps because he knew that the rebuilding was financed by capital from the German government—which had confiscated all the worldly goods of the German Jews—and by the United States government, its former enemy. West Berlin's well-being was an affront to his memories of the Holocaust.

Of course, not all of West Berlin was flourishing, he conceded. It was a city, also, of rubble mountains—stark reminders of the war years. A hundred thousand families lived in rude shelters or on the streets. Unemployment was high. Many streets still had ruins.

It would be great to see New York again, David thought nostalgically. He'd been too wrapped up in work the last four years to accept invitations to participate in American medical conventions. He'd exchanged the usual two or three letters a year with Uncle Julius and Aunt Bella, but that was his sole contact with the States.

Jesse would be about nine and a half now, he guessed. He doubted that there was a brother or sister—Aunt Bella would have written if Kathy and Phil had had another child. He remembered his suspicions that Kathy and Phil's marriage was not a happy one. He hoped the situation had improved.

On this trip he would stay with Uncle Julius in the company's New York apartment. Aunt Bella was in Jamaica with Gail and Brenda for three weeks. He'd only be in town four days, just long enough for several meetings with the people involved in setting up the new research center.

He was conscious of a tremendous pull back to the States. And in this new position—if he accepted it—he would be able to schedule time to work on the book he'd long hoped to write. A layman's book on nutrition.

It wasn't only in the poor, backward nations that bad nutrition was taking a terrible toll. The middle and upper class and the rich often suffered, in the midst of such plenty, from the lack of a proper diet. Good health was the greatest gift in the world. The United States was the richest country in the world. But this wasn't reflected in health statistics.

As his uncle had arranged, the family limousine—with Wally at the wheel—was waiting for him at Idlewild. He was conscious of a flicker of excitement as they headed toward Manhattan, the winter sky bright with stars and a pale sliver of moon. He always had this feeling of coming home when he arrived in New York.

He'd surely see Kathy and Phil and Jesse while he was here. His throat tightened at the prospect. Seeing Kathy brought him both joy and anguish. It was always so wonderful to be in her presence, but he suffered such anguish in realizing that he could have spent his life with her if he had not been so neurotically caught up in the past.

That time when Jesse was ill with polio had been a precious period for him. He'd felt so close to Kathy. For a little while she and Jesse had been his family. Back in Hamburg he should have told her how he felt about her. *He shouldn't have stepped aside when Phil arrived.*

Watching the passing scenery with unseeing eyes, he remembered the night he'd asked Gretchen to marry him, and how later he had awakened in the night to see her standing by the window. He could hear her voice now.

"David, who is Kathy?"

"A girl I knew in Hamburg. One of our group. We were a team—"

"You talked about her in your sleep. I think you love her very much."

Gretchen was right not to have married him. He would always be in love with Kathy. Gretchen was married almost a year now. She was expecting her first child.

"You just missed a heavy snow." Wally's voice interrupted his introspection. "There's still a little on some of the side streets."

"Is it my imagination or have some new skyscrapers gone up since I was here?" They were approaching the Queensboro Bridge now, with the brilliantly illuminated skyline a dramatic vista.

"Yes, sir," Wally assured him with pride. "This city is really moving ahead."

Julius—in one of his smoking jackets that he thought gave him a cosmopolitan air—was waiting for him at the apartment.

"You must be starving," Julius said jovially when they had exchanged warm greetings. "Let's go out to the kitchen and dig into the delicatessen I ordered sent over from Reuben's. Nothing like their hot pastrami and corned beef."

While they devoured enormous amounts of food, washed down with ice-cold root beer, Julius boasted about Phil's success in the business.

"He's a real chip off the old block," Julius said with pride, and then his face tightened. "He deserved better than he got from his wife."

A coldness enveloped David.

"I don't understand, Uncle Julius."

"Didn't Bella write you? The little bitch walked out on him. My God, it was three and a half years ago!"

"I didn't know." David's heart was pounding.

"She walked out of the house in Greenwich without saying a word. Just took Jesse and disappeared. It's a terrible thing to deprive a man of his son," he said with self-righteous indignation.

"What happened? Why did she leave that way?" David was stammering. Reeling from this news.

"She was always a queer duck," Julius said contemptuously. "I never understood why Phil married her." His eyes narrowed as he gazed at David. "You knew her in Hamburg. Did she seem kind of unstable to you then?"

"Kathy was a fine, dedicated worker. Always compassionate and helpful. It's not like her to act on impulse." *What did Phil do to drive her away like that?*

"I've spent a fortune trying to track her down. Phil doesn't want her back. He wouldn't take her back if she came to him on bended knees. Not after what she's put him through. But he wants his son. I want my grandson." He glowered in frustration. "We haven't a lead. Her parents play dumb. They claim they don't know where she is, but I don't believe that for a minute. But hell, we can't keep a P.I. on their trail twenty-four hours a day year after year. Every once in a while we try again. We're getting Jesse back, David. I won't rest till that happens." Then he smiled. A devious glint in his eyes. "She walked out too fast to take anything with her. Even left her diamond and sapphire necklace behind. Cleaned out their joint checking account, but that wasn't a hell of a lot."

Settled in bed for the night, David knew sleep would be slow in overtaking him. The conversation with his uncle about Kathy ricocheted in his mind. Were Kathy and Jesse all right? She'd gone off without funds. Again, the question plagued him: what had Phil done that pushed Kathy to walk out?

It alarmed him that Kathy and Jesse were off alone somewhere. But like Uncle Julius, he couldn't believe that her parents were out of touch with Kathy. They'd always be there for her and Jesse, he consoled himself. She might not be living the luxurious Kohn life, but her parents would not let her be in want.

Would Rhoda know? They'd been close since Hamburg. But Rhoda would be afraid to tell him, afraid he might slip and alert Phil. Kathy wasn't asking for a divorce because she was afraid of losing Jesse, he surmised. And instantly he felt guilty at thinking of Kathy divorced and free to marry again.

On the following evening, after a day-long conference with the group he'd come to see, David was to meet Julius and Phil for dinner at Toots Shor's. Julius was there when he arrived. Phil was ten minutes late. He watched with a sense of shock as Phil strolled toward their table. The last time he'd seen Phil, he remembered, was that time in Paris. Already—a few weeks from his thirty-ninth birthday—Phil was losing his magnetic handsomeness. His body was that of a man who ate too much, drank too much, and never exercised.

"Hey, I hear you may be coming back to the Big City," Phil drawled. "Some fancy job being offered to you?" A hint of condescension in his voice.

"I'm considering it," David said quietly. "If I do take it, it won't happen for another year. I have to wind up my affairs in Berlin first, then stop over in Copenhagen for several months. But yes, it's fairly likely that I'll take the job." He hesitated. "I was sorry to hear about you and Kathy."

"It's rotten. I can't even get a divorce, and she's hanging on to Jesse."

"The kid's almost nine," Julius said, and David noted

that Phil didn't correct him. Jesse would be ten in June. "He needs a father in his life."

"You never thought she'd turn out to be such a bitch, did you?" Phil challenged.

"I hear you're doing great in the business." David avoided a reply. "Uncle Julius was telling me how well things are going."

Phil and Julius launched into a boastful discussion of their deals that continued until they paused to focus on ordering dessert. David intercepted Phil's furtive glances at his watch. He wasn't surprised when Phil decided to forgo dessert and coffee.

"You won't be mad, old man, if I cut out early, will you? I have a meeting with our new promotion people tonight. We're setting up a major campaign," Phil explained. "We're considering opening a shop in London."

"That sounds marvelous," David said. He'd lay odds Phil was meeting some woman. Was that why Kathy had walked out? No, he guessed. Kathy was bright—she probably knew long ago that Phil was philandering. That must have been just part of her unhappiness. "Good luck on the international scene." That would be how Phil would regard this newest expansion of the business.

David was relieved when Julius finally decided to leave the restaurant and return to the apartment. Over dessert and coffee Julius renewed his tirade against Kathy. Now— as Wally drove them back to the apartment—Julius switched to complain about the jittery state of the stock market.

"I don't like the looks of it. I got a gut feeling we're in for a recession. And a recession plays hell with the fur market."

David was grateful that it was sufficient to listen to Julius and appear impressed by his pearls of wisdom. His mind was in chaos over Kathy's disappearance. *His fault that*

Kathy married Phil. He should have declared himself. If he'd admitted he was in love with her, Kathy wouldn't have turned to Phil. *He knew what Phil was like with women.* Somehow, he should have intervened.

══ Chapter 29

With the business making increasing demands on her time, Kathy battled guilt that she wasn't a full-time mother, yet her own mother insisted Jesse was not suffering from her involvement in the growing chain of shops. Now each time she made a twenty-four hour trip to Philadelphia or Boston or Washington, D.C., her mother traveled all the way from Borough Park to Croton to have dinner with Jesse and Lee.

"He's becoming the most pampered kid in Westchester County," Rhoda teased her, but she knew Rhoda understood she was determined that Jesse should not feel himself lacking in love.

In late summer—when Kathy was exhausted from the daily commute plus side trips to their major stores—Rhoda and Frank tried to persuade her to take a week off to go to Montauk with them.

"You said Lee is going to spend a vacation week with her sister in Queens," Rhoda pointed out. "Come out with Frank and me and the baby. We've rented this big old house right across from the ocean. You and Jesse will love it."

"Isn't Montauk somewhere near Southampton?" she asked uneasily. But the prospect of a week in a house across from the ocean was enticing. Jesse was scheduled to spend that week of Lee's vacation with her family in Borough Park, in a hot, stuffy, crowded apartment. He'd loved the Southampton beach when he was little.

"Montauk is about thirty or forty miles beyond it," Rhoda guessed. "Nobody from Southampton is running up to Montauk. It's a fishing village—a whole other world from Southampton."

"You used to talk about the magnificent beach at Southampton," Frank reminded. "Wait till you see Montauk, without the social madness of Southampton but with a beach like nothing else in the world. Gorgeous sunrises, sunsets. You can walk for an hour and see nobody but sea gulls. Remember that time up in Wells Beach?"

"Frank, it was heavenly." Kathy smiled in wistful recall.

"This is more heavenly, and half the traveling time. Come on, give yourself a break."

"All right," she capitulated. Phil would never travel as far out as Montauk, she told herself. People went there to fish—or to cut themselves off from the rest of the world. That wasn't Phil's style, or his father's. And Jesse would love it. "When do we leave?"

At first sight Kathy fell in love with Montauk. Jesse, too, reveled in the stretches of empty beach, the domain of the sea gulls and a friendly pair of Labradors. He had a zest for living that brought joy to her. Together he and Harry romped joyously in the surf, Harry making a game of snapping at the waves as they rolled to shore, the two town Labradors often joining in the play.

Kathy liked the low Tudor buildings that were the local shops and the incongruous seven-story "tower" that rose behind the village green to remind the world that before the '29 stock market crash, Carl Fisher had plotted to make Montauk the Miami Beach of the Northeast.

On her third day in town Kathy knew she would buy a

house out here. It would be a runaway place when life closed in too frenetically about her, her refuge from the pressures of building a national chain of shops and a major designer—a house that looked down upon the Atlantic and that would be waiting for her every day of the year.

It was still a source of pleasurable astonishment that she was in a position to spend money this freely. To decide to buy a house and know that there was no financial problem. She had sent the family to Bermuda for two weeks last spring. She'd told Mom and Dad to scout around for a house in Borough Park. She coddled their guilt at this extravagance by assuring them it was a good investment for her. Her personal office had been redecorated to reflect the spectacular success of the business.

"You have to *learn* to enjoy money," Marge had told her good-humoredly. Marge had bought herself a sprawling apartment on the Upper West Side, which she predicted would one day be chic. Right now, its major attraction was the view of the Hudson from the terrace of her apartment. She drove to the office each morning in a new white Porsche. "Of course," she kidded, "you've got more experience at it than I have."

She'd had access to a luxurious life-style, Kathy conceded. But everything except her wardrobe—the furniture in the house, the restaurants they frequented, their vacations, their cars—were of Phil's choosing. She relished her new independence and her personal affluence.

Kathy returned to New York from Montauk refreshed and ready to face the fall business season. The 4-S Shops empire was creating much talk in the trade. Marge was the new hot young designer. The entrepreneurs—still in their early thirties—were highly promotable, though Ellen Somers, their public relations woman, was repeatedly reminded that Kathy was to remain in the background.

Months sped past. Kathy found the perfect house in Montauk and arranged to buy it. It was a low, sprawling contemporary in the Frank Lloyd Wright style, with a huge

deck that looked down upon the Atlantic. At intervals she
drove up for a weekend, trying to sandwich in time to furnish the new house. At school vacation between Christmas
and New Year's, she stayed there with Jesse while Lee went
off for a week's visit with her sister. She relished the views
of the winter ocean from her house—looking down from a
cliff. Her parents came for three days, then Marge, Rhoda
and Frank and little Sara for the long New Year's weekend.

Marge was making personal appearances at their growing
chain of shops, was interviewed for the national women's
magazines, and appeared on radio and television. In an in-
terview for *Vogue,* Marge ebulliently said that while basic
designs were hers, they were all embellished by her partner
Kathy Altman, hitherto known by insiders as the brilliant
business head behind the chain's spectacular success.

All at once Kathy became the subject of much curiosity.
Their publicity woman built up Kathy Altman as the reclu-
sive mystery woman of the 4-S chain. Marge and Noel were
delighted at the space they were garnering, not only in the
trade, but also in consumer publications, yet Kathy was
edgy about this.

"Kathy, relax," Marge exhorted at regular intervals. "All
the press knows is that Kathy Altman is a beautiful, highly
talented honey-blond with a poodle cut and an obsession
for privacy. Ellie makes a fetish of keeping your identity a
mystery except to the handful of people you work with in
the trade and those in our shops."

"I worry about a slipup," Kathy confessed regularly.

Then early in February what Kathy had fought to avoid
happened. The company had given a posh private party for
their Manhattan business associates. Noel had flown in from
San Francisco to attend. The press was not invited. But
three days later photographs taken at the party were published in *Women's Wear Daily.*

Kathy sat at her desk, cold and trembling, as she saw the
caption accompanying a group photograph: "Kathy Alt-

man, brilliant young executive of the 4-S Shops, in a rare public photo."

Kathy and Marge went into an anxious huddle.

"Look, you know Phil and Julius. They're only interested in what concerns the fur business," Marge tried to rationalize. "A thousand to one they'll both skim right past that photo. Phil may not even be in town. You know he spends a lot of time on the road. And you've always said the only thing Julius ever reads is the stock market report."

"Let me try and work from the house for the next week or so." Kathy knew it was the old "ostrich sticking its head in the sand" routine, but she needed to disappear for a while to hold on to her sanity.

"In two weeks we'll be in London and Paris," Marge pointed out. For the first time they were going over for the couturier shows.

"And Jesse will be with us." Kathy clung to this. She'd talked to the school about taking him away from classes for five days, and they'd agreed he was bright and able to handle this, and that a trip to Europe at his age would be educational.

"Kathy, maybe it's time to go public." Marge's voice was gentle. "To divorce Phil. Judges almost always give custody to the mother."

"Almost is not good enough for me," Kathy said tersely. "And with the Kohn money and connections they might manage to have the divorce brought up before a judge of their choice. I can't take that chance, Marge."

Nobody here at the office knew that she lived in Croton, she told herself. The word was that she had an apartment on the Upper West Side. Nobody even knew she had a son.

Only the tight clique of Marge, Rhoda and Frank, her family, and Noel in San Francisco knew about the house in Croton and about Jesse. Rhoda had arranged for Jesse's registration at the school. Nobody there connected Jesse's mother with Kathy Altman of the 4-S Shops.

She was safe, she told herself, unless Phil or Julius had

seen the photo in *Women's Wear Daily.* But she knew that
from now on she would be constantly looking over her
shoulder to see if some sleazy private investigator was trailing her from the office to learn where she lived.

Phil returned from his Montreal business trip in high good
humor. His stay in Canada had been expanded to include
two days at a ski lodge in the Laurentians, where he'd met
the attractive young model who most recently occupied his
bed. He was now on a fitness kick, designed to restore him
to his earlier image.

He settled in his office with a mug of coffee brought in
by his secretary and proceeded to go through the mail. Once
this was accomplished, he turned to the pileup of trade
newspapers neatly arranged at one corner of the desk.

He froze in disbelief at the sight of the photograph of
Kathy taken at the 4-S Shops party. She was fair-haired
now, and she'd changed her hairstyle—but it was Kathy.
He couldn't be in any phase of the garment industry without
knowing about the spectacular success of the 4-S chain.
He'd heard the name of Kathy Altman, of course, but he'd
never connected her with Kathy Kohn.

Excitement charged through him as he put the facts together. Kathy had joined Marge in the shops. She had hidden behind her aunt's name. *Incredible that Kathy could
have risen that way in the business world.* Resentment soared
in him.

He read the accompanying article. She was right here in
Manhattan. Jesse must be here. Kathy wouldn't send him
off to school.

He reached for the phone to dial his father's extension.

"Dad, the search is over," he said with exhilaration. "I
know where Kathy and Jesse are."

"I'll be right there!" His father's excitement matched his
own.

In minutes the two men sat across from each other in
Phil's office and dissected the situation.

"She has an unlisted phone number, and the office won't give out her address," Phil said. He'd had his secretary phone the 4-S offices to inquire about this. The devious ploy she'd contrived had failed.

"Kathy's assistant," he reported with sarcasm, "says she'll be out of town on business for the next three weeks."

"Shit!" Julius glowered. "How the hell did she push her way up like that? What did she know about business? So her father runs a two-bit candy store in Borough Park—what could she have learned from him?"

"She was forever taking classes at F.I.T.," Phil said grimly. "And sopping up whatever I told her about business in general. You remember how she sat in on a lot of our meetings with Roz."

"If she's out of town for three weeks, it'd be a waste of money to put a P.I. on the payroll," Julius said.

"I'll set up a deal as soon as we know she's back. I don't want to talk to her," Phil pointed out. "I want to find out where she's living, then I can go grab the kid. He's my son," he said triumphantly. "You can't be charged with kidnapping for taking back your own child."

"In the meantime," Julius told him, "draw a Dun and Bradstreet report on the company. We might come up with something."

Two days before Kathy and Marge were to leave for Europe, Noel arrived to supervise the main office in their absence. He was spilling over with pleasure at Chris's success. In December Chris would have a major gallery show in Manhattan.

"We'll throw a big bash for him," Marge promised. "Buy a Chris Logan painting and hang prints of it in all the 4-S shops. What do you think about that, Kathy?"

"I think it's great." She knew that both Noel and Marge were fighting to distract her from the ever-present fear that Phil was on her trail and would find Jesse and her.

"Relax and enjoy Europe," Noel urged her compassionately.

"Remember, Montauk is the closest I've ever been to Europe," Marge effervesced. "Or is Maine closer?"

Kathy had planned their accommodations on this trip to avoid the hotels where she had stayed with Phil. She took delight in Jesse's eager anticipation of seeing London and Paris. He had been too young to remember the earlier trips. This one he would remember.

They would fly on one of the last of the piston planes, Kathy thought whimsically. Everybody was talking about how the old DC-7s were to be replaced in the autumn by the revolutionary new jets that would carry nearly twice the number of passengers. But Jesse was always fascinated by flying—jet or prop would not matter to him.

They flew first to London. In the taxi that took them from Heathrow to the Claridge, Kathy was assaulted by memories of the earlier trip to London. Bella and Julius had traveled with them. That seemed another lifetime.

Kathy was pleased to be seeing London off-season. There were no hordes of tourists; their hotel was lightly populated. In their suite at the Claridge, cozy fires were laid in the bedroom fireplaces. Huge logs burned in grates in the downstairs rooms, despite the fact that Mayfair was considered to be a smokeless zone. Jesse was fascinated to see all the footmen in the public rooms wearing velvet breeches in the evening.

Since this was Marge's first trip abroad, and Jesse had little recall of their earlier trip, they contrived to see a few of the routine tourist sights between business appointments—mainly dealings with fabric houses. On their third afternoon in London they checked out of the Claridge to fly to Paris. Driving from Orly to the ultra-smart Hotel Meurice, which faces the Tuileries and the Seine, Kathy remembered how David had joined them in Paris for a day on that earlier visit. They had lunched at the Ritz, had dinner at Maxim's. In the afternoon she and Bella had gone

with David to the Louvre. She remembered how gentle—
how loving—he had been with Jesse.

All at once her heart was pounding. Did she dare call
David and ask him to join them in Paris for a day? It would
be so wonderful to see him. Did he know that Phil and she
were separated? *He must know.* Bella would have written
him.

As had happened many times in the past years, she felt
uncomfortable in not having written Bella to tell her why
she had walked out on Phil. Her only contacts with her
mother-in-law were the snapshots of Jesse she regularly
shipped to her via Rhoda. She remembered the time in Paris
when, in a moment of total candor, she said to Bella, *"I stay
with Phil for Jesse's sake. If the day ever comes when I think
it's not good for Jesse, I'll walk out."*

But how could she tell Bella that her son was a man who
beat his wife and betrayed his wife's friends?

At anguished intervals during that first day in Paris she
debated about calling David in Berlin. Would his wife be
upset if he came to Paris to see them? She and David were
old and close friends—he was family, Jesse's cousin as well
as Phil's.

She trembled at the prospect of David's coming to Paris
with his wife. She remembered the bow-shaped brooch she
and David had found in the pawnshop in Berlin. Would his
wife be wearing that brooch?

Finally, after Jesse had gone to sleep, she shared her ambivalence about phoning David with Marge.

"I keep asking myself if I should call him. It's tormenting
to be so close and not to see him." Marge had often heard
Rhoda and her talk about the months in Hamburg. Marge
knew there had been a special closeness between David and
her. "If it was Noel in Berlin and we were here in Paris,
I wouldn't think twice about calling."

"Kathy, call the guy," Marge told her. "If you go home
without seeing him, you'll forever regret it. There's no way

that seeing David will put you in jeopardy with Phil," she reasoned.

"I'll call in the morning," Kathy decided, light-headed with expectancy. "It's been so long since I saw him. It must be—" She squinted in thought. "Oh God, it's been five and a half years—that summer in Paris! Where did the years go?"

Kathy lay sleepless most of the night, falling into troubled slumber at the approach of dawn. She couldn't wait for the sound of David's voice, to hear him say that, yes, he could meet them in Paris for a day.

He wasn't angry with her for running out on Phil, was he? He knew her well enough to understand it would take something ghastly to push her to that. All at once she was anxious about seeing him. She knew his strong family loyalties. *Would he consider it disloyal to Julius and Bella to see her?* But however he felt, she had to know.

She waited until after breakfast to phone David. While Jesse and Marge discussed the sight-seeing that would be interspersed with business that day, she called the Institute in Berlin where David was on staff, worried that both her French and her German were rusty.

Finally she reached the Institute. "May I speak with Dr. David Kohn, please."

"Dr. Kohn is not here," the woman at the switchboard told her. Her voice was almost brusque.

"When do you expect him?" she asked, fighting disappointment.

"Dr. Kohn is no longer with the Institute," the woman said. "Not for quite a while. He left here to go to Copenhagen."

"Thank you," Kathy said politely and hung up. Trembling with disappointment.

David was living in another world. Their worlds would never meet again, she thought in raw anguish. Hadn't she realized long ago that the timing was never right for David and her?

$=$ Chapter 30

P hil was fighting yawns as he hurried into the restaurant to meet his father for breakfast. When was the old man going to stop this routine? Still leaving Greenwich at 5:50 A.M. five mornings a week. Expecting him here no later than eight. Hell, he'd earned the right to come into the office at 9:30 or 10—to bypass the breakfast shit.

He stared in surprise when he saw his father was not alone in their booth. The old man had dragged the P.I. here this morning. He slowed down as he saw the man rise from the booth. Whatever the old man said, the P.I. was pissed. He stared in recognition at Phil and strode past him without a word.

"What was that all about?" Phil asked as he slid into his seat.

"I just fired the bastard," Julius told him. "We know she's been back for five weeks now, and he still can't come up with an address." His father never referred to Kathy by name—it was always "she."

"I told you, Dad. We can't hire the creep for two days a week and expect results." His impatience surfaced despite

347

his intention of staying cool. "He's got to be out there every day until he comes up with what we want." The old man was always trying to cut corners at the wrong time.

"We're hiring somebody new. I got the name of this hot-shot guy. He's cutting our throats with his fancy fees, but I've had enough of this." He reached into his jacket pocket and pulled out a card. "Call him. Set up an appointment as soon as you can. We're nailing her."

The private investigator Julius wanted to hire stalled them for another two weeks, until he completed a current assignment. Then he went to work. Two days later he called Phil to report that Kathy took a train from Grand Central each night.

"She could be anywhere along the line. Tomorrow night I'll be on the train with her," he promised. "After that it should be a breeze."

Three mornings later he phoned to give them definite information regarding Kathy's address.

"She's in a house on East Mount Airy Road in Croton-on-Hudson. The name on the mailbox says 'Moses,' but she's living there. She picked up a gray Dodge Coronet and drove to the house."

"She could be visiting," Phil pointed out in irritation. Moses didn't ring any bells with him, but then he didn't know all of her friends. "How do you know she's living there?"

"I was back out there at 6 A.M. to follow through. She drove to the Harmon station a little past seven. She wore different clothes."

"Did you see a kid anywhere around?" Phil pushed. *This might be it.* "A little boy about nine. No," he corrected himself, searching his mind for dates. "He'll be eleven in June."

"They've got this long driveway—it must run back three or four hundred feet from the road. There's no way I can see into the house without digging up an excuse to get back there."

"Then find an excuse," Phil ordered. "Or park below, walk up in the dark. I want to be sure the kid's there."

"If he's around eleven, he'll be in school—the school year isn't over yet. I'll pull off on East Mount Airy a hundred feet or so past their driveway," the P.I. decided. "I'll let you know if the little boy lives there."

Shortly past nine the next morning, the new investigator called Phil.

"There's a little boy living there in the house," he reported. "I saw him get on the school bus."

"Great! I'll call you later in the day with further instructions."

Phil sat gazing into space for a moment. They knew where Kathy lived. She had Jesse with her. The name on the mailbox was a dodge. He tingled in satisfaction. The little bitch thought she was so smart.

He left his office and went to tell his father the news. He waited impatiently until Julius completed a lengthy call to London. He suspected it had been an incoming call. The old man would make a London call billed to them a short deal.

"Kathy's living in Croton," he said. "Jesse's with her. Now we have to figure out how to get hold of him and—"

"Back up, Phil," Julius rasped. "We've waited a long time for this. Let's don't mess it up. You want a divorce and custody of Jesse, right?"

"Right," Phil agreed. Actually, he wasn't so keen on full-time custody, he thought, but that was the road that would push the old man into turning over the stock. He'd do whatever it took. "So?"

"So let's see you go into divorce court with evidence that guarantees she won't walk off with any financial settlement, and that gives you custody of Jesse on the grounds that she's an unfit mother."

"That'll be rough," Phil warned.

"Look, any good-looking broad that's come up as fast as she has must have been in a lot of beds. We'll take our time, get enough to mess her up good, go into court. You get your divorce and Jesse. She gets shit. She'll be sorry she ever tangled with us." His eyes gleamed at the prospect of vengeance. "We'll see her face splashed across the front pages of the *News* and the *Mirror.* "

"You're talking about dirty scandal." Phil felt a tinge of unease.

"So what?" Julius chuckled. "You'll come out smelling like a rose, and she'll get what's coming to her. We won't rush, we know where she is. Let's just get the goods on her. It's the old cat-and-mouse game, and she's the mouse."

This summer Kathy drove out to the Montauk house on Thursday evenings, remaining until very early Monday mornings. Usually Marge went out with her, so the weekends could become working periods. Jesse, Lee, and Harry were in full-time residence. At intervals Kathy's parents and Aunt Sophie went out to stay with Jesse and Lee. Always Kathy was haunted by the fear that Jesse might be deprived of family.

"I'm keeping the house open all through the winter," Kathy told Marge as their small entourage headed back to the city the Sunday morning before the school season opened. "I've hired a local handyman to keep an eye on things. The thermostat goes on fifty-five degrees as soon as the weather turns cool. I won't have to worry about turning off the water that way." Involuntarily, she remembered this had been how she and Phil handled the Greenwich house once they moved into the Fifth Avenue apartment. "You said you'd be going out to Fire Island next weekend, didn't you?"

"I changed my mind." Marge sighed. "It's crazy. Every time I start to get involved with a man, I ask myself if he's interested in Marge the woman or in Marge the designer with *mucho* money."

"If you're mad about somebody, you'll forget that," Kathy predicted.

"I guess I'm more mad about career," Marge admitted. "And I resent the condescending attitude so many men take toward career women. If you're a woman and you have a brain, you're supposed to hide it. I've come too far, worked too hard to take second place."

"Amen," Kathy said softly.

In the fall the 4-S Shops launched another expansion. By the end of the year they would have shops in every major city in the country. In November Noel flew east for a weekend conference with Kathy and Marge at the Montauk house. Jesse was delighted to be spending that weekend with his grandparents and Aunt Sophie. It was a source of delight to Kathy that he felt so close to his grandparents and that there was an endearing relationship with his great-great-aunt.

"We're entering a new age of flying," Noel chortled as the three of them relaxed over espresso before the living room fireplace after hours of plotting their new business campaign. "Can you believe the new jets? They're bringing the whole world close together. Now you can jet to London for the weekend."

Did David ever fly to New York, Kathy asked herself. Was he married? He must be—he was seeing someone that time they met in Paris. Did he have a family? Why had he left Berlin for Copenhagen? These were questions that would never be answered for her.

In mid-November—when Kathy was planning a family Thanksgiving at the Montauk house—she received a phone call from Noel. He was close to hysteria. Three hours ago Chris had been killed in a freakish accident.

"Why, Kathy?" Noel mourned. "He's twenty-six years old with a brilliant career ahead of him. Why did this happen?"

At last off the phone with Noel—shaken and grieving—she called Marge, in Atlanta to make a personal appearance at their new shop down there. She knew that either she or

Marge must fly immediately to be with Noel. His sister Wilma and he were on bad terms. An aunt and several cousins had distanced themselves from him when he abandoned hiding his homosexuality.

"I can't believe it," Marge said in stricken tones while they talked about Chris's fatal accident—he had been killed by a falling chunk of granite from a downtown building. "We were already planning a big bash for his gallery opening next month."

It was decided that Kathy would fly out immediately, see Noel through the agony of Chris's funeral, and bring him back with her to New York. Marge would cut short her Atlanta trip and return to cover for Kathy.

Within hours Kathy was on a westbound flight. Distraught and haggard, Noel met her at the airport and took her home with him. She was grateful that Chris's parents were not barring Noel from sharing in the plans for the funeral. Unlike Noel's own family, Chris's family was understanding and compassionate about the relationship between the two men. Chris had loved Noel, and that made him special to them.

Kathy decided that the day after Chris's funeral she and Noel would fly to New York. She'd arrange for indefinite coverage at the West Coast offices. Noel would stay at the Croton house until he felt himself able to cope again.

From habit—even though his father was in Toronto on business—Phil stopped in for breakfast at their restaurant. He was restless, frustrated because Andrews—his father's fancy P.I.—was coming up with nothing on Kathy. And until the divorce went through, the old man was not going to put the stock in his name, he reminded himself. Suppose Andrews never came up with dirt on Kathy?

Maybe it was time to make a move on his own. There was one quick way to make sure Kathy agreed to a divorce with no alimony, no up-front settlement. All at once he felt a surge of excitement, of towering optimism. To hell with what the old man said—this situation called for a bold move.

If he grabbed Jesse, Kathy would sign anything, as long as he agreed to visitation rights instead of full custody. Hell, he had no time to raise a kid. His father was off-track on that point. He could handle this. Get hold of that old P.I. they had in the beginning. That one was always hungry. He'd check him out as soon as he got to the office.

When he located the old P.I.'s number, Phil dialed it. He reached the answering service.

"Tell him to call me as soon as possible," Phil instructed and gave his name and number. "Tell him it's important."

Forty minutes later the P.I. called him.

"I've got a job for you," he began.

"Your father told me to get lost," the man reminded, bristling.

"My father isn't in on this," Phil said tersely. "You want the job or not?"

"We can talk about it."

"Meet me in ten minutes at the coffee shop across from the office," Phil ordered. Not their regular place. He didn't want to be seen there with the creep.

Phil headed for the coffee shop, found a rear booth that was unoccupied. Why the hell wasn't the bastard here? His office—a hole-in-the-wall—was two blocks away. A few minutes later the P.I. arrived, looked around until he spied Phil. Somewhat belligerently he sauntered toward the booth.

"Sit down," Phil told him, and launched into his proposition.

"Let me get this straight." The P.I. was wary. "You're asking me to kidnap the kid?"

"I'm asking you to bring the kid to his father. I'll take it from there. Don't you think my son w nts to see me? Look, they can't charge us with kidnapping when my wife ran off with him that way. A father has rights."

"You say that. What's a judge going to say if we get

caught?" the P.I. shot back, but he was contemplative. "I could lose my license. But I know a guy who might be willing to pull it off for you."

For a few minutes they quibbled over money. A fee for his bringing in the man, a fee for the man himself.

"Okay, it's a deal," Phil finally agreed. "Set it up for tomorrow afternoon when the kid gets home from school. I'll fill in all the details."

Phil met the hired kidnapper at the southwest corner of Broadway and 40th at 2 P.M. sharp. They'd drive up together to Croton and wait for Jesse to arrive on the school bus. The guy was nervous, Phil judged, but hungry for the thousand-dollar payoff.

They picked up Phil's car, headed up toward the ramp and onto the highway. Traffic was light this time of day. The man was plying him with questions about the car. Probably the first time in his crummy life he'd been in a car that cost this kind of money.

"Look, suppose the kid don't wanna come with me?" he asked Phil forty-five minutes later, when they were minutes from their destination.

"You put a hand over his mouth so he can't yell, and you pick him up and carry him to the car," Phil said bluntly. "I'll be waiting there at the foot of the road. We won't run into many cars along East Mount Airy," he said with confidence. "Just get him into the car. Don't rough him up," he cautioned. "Tell him his father's waiting to give him a fancy present."

Phil consulted his watch. Timing was important here. Let them spot the school bus, follow it up that steep, winding hill. The school bus would stop to drop off Jesse. There was a four-hundred foot road up to the house. They'd catch him before he got there. Whoever was waiting inside for him couldn't hear the school bus arrive. The woman—probably the housekeeper—would think the bus was late today when Jesse didn't show up on schedule.

Phil drove slowly, watching for the bus. *There it was.* He

felt a rush of anticipation as he followed it along East Mount Airy. He dropped to a crawl when the bus stopped at a rural mailbox marked "Moses." A boy stepped down. Phil stared in disbelief. That was Jesse? God, he was as tall as Kathy!

"Get going," Phil ordered the man, trying to brush aside unexpected apprehension. "Play it cool. 'Your father is waiting down the road. He's brought you a terrific present.' "

"Yeah—"

Phil watched the tall, wiry figure push through the winter-bare bushes and onto the property. He could handle Jesse even if the kid put up a fight. Battling anxiety, Phil thrust open the car door and stepped out for a clearer view.

He frowned, swore under his breath. The creep was scared shitless. Why didn't he move? *Don't let Jesse get too close to the house.* Talk him into coming down to the car. Grab him if he balks.

He was moving in on Jesse now. Jesse saw him. They were talking. They were too far away for him to hear what was being said. Speed it up, jerk!

All at once a woman appeared on the deck. A rifle in one hand.

"Get away from him!" the woman yelled. "Get away before I fill you full of lead!"

Damn, the jackass had botched it! Phil slid behind the wheel of the car and started up the motor. Moments later the would-be kidnapper stumbled into the car. Gray with terror.

"You fucking idiot!" Phil snarled and stepped hard on the gas pedal. "You screwed up the whole deal!"

"You didn't tell me I might get shot," the man whined. "You said it'd be a snap."

"I'll drive you back to town," Phil told him. "Forget today ever happened." If the old man found out about this, he'd be pissed. They'd tipped their hand. Kathy would guess they were on her trail. Hell!

"What about my money?" the man asked defiantly.

"I'll give you fifty bucks for your trouble. And keep your mouth shut," Phil repeated. "You don't want to go up for attempted kidnapping." That bitch at the house hadn't seen *him*, Phil thought with shaky confidence. Nobody could prove anything.

Cold with shock, Kathy listened to Lee's report of the incident with the intruder while Noel and Jesse went out for Harry's last walk of the night.

"Harry didn't hear a thing," Lee told her. "He was fast asleep before the fireplace. But you would have died laughing if you saw me—" Lee was striving for a lighter note now. "There I was with that toy rifle Jesse's friend left here last night. I'm pointing it at him and yelling, 'Get away before I fill you full of lead!' That's what comes from watching those detective shows on TV."

Now Jesse and Noel came into the house with Harry, who insisted on greeting Kathy all over again, as though he had not provided a joyous welcome on their arrival half an hour ago.

"Jesse—" Kathy strived not to show her anxiety. "Tell me again what that man said to you."

"He said my father was in a car below, and he'd brought me a terrific present," Jesse said somberly. He had only vague recall of Phil, Kathy reminded herself. He'd accepted the fact that—like some of his friends' parents—she and Phil were divorced. "*Was* he there?" Curiosity stirring in him now, she thought with frustration.

"No, darling. It was just some bad person who knew I'd give him a lot of money to get you back."

"You mean like ransom?" Jesse was awed that he had been the subject of such an effort. "Wow!"

"Jesse, tomorrow's a school day. You take yourself off to bed," Lee ordered.

"But Mom just came home," he complained.

"And I'm here to stay," Kathy reminded. "Off to bed. We'll have breakfast together in the morning."

She waited until she heard Jesse close his bedroom door.

"That had to be Phil," she said tautly. "Oh Lee, if you hadn't been looking through the window!"

"I always watch for Jesse when the bus is due," Lee said.

"We have to move. I have to get Jesse away from this house—" He'd be upset at changing schools again, Kathy thought with anguish.

"Kathy, he won't try that again," Noel said gently. "He'll look for another angle."

"What?" she challenged. She felt sick at the thought of Jesse's being kidnapped by Phil. "This is what I've been afraid of since the day I left him."

"I don't know," Noel conceded. "But before he tries anything else, he'll pull back and reevaluate the situation. Don't let Jesse take the school bus anymore. Have him driven to school and picked up."

"Suppose he gets a court order!" Panic began to close in on her.

"For what?" Lee questioned. "He'll have to go into court if he's after custody. And if it comes to a court scene, you can fight him. Locate that woman you told me about. Jesse's nursemaid who saw Phil strike you. *You can fight this, Kathy.*"

"I'm scared," Kathy whispered. "And so tired of running."

"Sit back and let him make the next move," Noel said. "He's not taking Jesse from you. You'll fight, and you'll win in court."

"And Jesse will be put through such ugliness." Kathy closed her eyes in anguish.

"Jesse can handle this," Lee said firmly. "If it comes to court."

"Meanwhile, the three of us will watch over Jesse," Noel said. "There'll be no violent moves to take him away." His own grief had receded in his anxiety to comfort her. "And if you get served with divorce papers, we'll help you fight Phil. *He won't get custody of Jesse.*"

But how could she know what a judge would decide?

Phil was nervous about his initial meeting with his father, back from the Toronto business trip. Two days later he felt a new confidence. Earlier this morning he'd received a phone call from Andrews.

He left the Peugeot in the garage near the office and strode purposefully toward his regular morning rendezvous with his father. The plate-glass window of the restaurant steamed over from the sudden cold spell.

Normally he would have been pissed at Andrews calling so early in the morning, he thought as he walked inside. The aromas of bacon sizzling on the grill, coffee perking, bread browning in a toaster clothed him in an aura of well-being.

"Andrews will be here any minute," he told his father, and grinned as Julius's eyebrows shot upward. "He's got something hot to report."

"Like what?" Julius demanded.

"He didn't want to discuss it over the phone."

For a few moments they kibitzed with the waitress, then focused on their first coffee of the morning.

"Here's Andrews," Phil said, gazing at the entrance.

"Look, we don't let him drag this out into a big deal," Julius warned. "If it's hot, we go with it. We don't need him anymore."

"Dad, don't jump." Phil was testy. "Let's keep him until we have all we need."

"She's shacked up with some guy," Andrews reported when he was settled in the booth. "He's been there three days now—she leaves for work in the morning, but he stays at the house."

"Who is he?" Phil bristled.

"I haven't latched on to a name yet. That comes next." He reached into his jacket pocket and brought out a collection of snapshots. "Do you recognize him?" He handed some of the snapshots to Phil, others to Julius.

"Never saw him before," Phil said after a moment. *The little slut. Screwing around—with Jesse right there in the house.*

"What good do these do?" Julius challenged. "We need a picture of them in bed."

"I'm working on it," Andrews said, faintly hostile. "I can't bring them in for a photo session."

"We want incriminating shots of them," Julius emphasized, his voice telling Andrews that he was contemptuous of what the P.I. had brought them. "These will mean shit in court."

"I'm on it." Andrews was defensive now. "One thing at a time."

Kathy glanced up from her desk as Marge walked into her office and closed the door behind her.

"I just heard something I don't like," Marge said, dropping into a chair across from Kathy. "Some man has been floating about the office and asking questions of employees—"

"What kind of questions?" Kathy leaned forward in instant alarm. "About me?"

"That's the odd part. He's not asking about you. He's showing a photograph of Noel. He wants to know who Noel is." Marge paused. "He can't be somebody in our field. Noel's well-known."

"But he connected Noel with the business," Kathy said warily. Pieces hurtled together in her mind; her throat tightened as she considered the implications. "Marge, Phil knows about the business—that I'm Kathy Altman. And he knows Noel is living at the Croton house. Don't you understand?" Her face was drained of color. "Phil discovered Noel was at the house, but he doesn't know who Noel is. It's clear now. Phil has somebody trailing me to come up with something to take into court. *Phil thinks I'm having an affair with Noel.*"

"Honey, that's a bad joke." But Marge appeared upset.

"Phil couldn't grab Jesse, so he's trying another tactic. He's after evidence to take into court to fight me for custody of Jesse."

"How could he use Noel for that? You know the kind of stuff a husband has to bring into court if he's asking for child custody. Phil doesn't have that."

"I don't trust Phil and Julius. They'll have photographs doctored, make composites. You've read what sleazy investigators and lawyers do in divorce cases."

"Kathy, you're jumping to conclusions." Marge tried to be reassuring. "There must be some simple explanation for all this. For some reason some idiot must be out to blackmail Noel."

"Marge, Noel is very open about his life-style. They can't be trying to blackmail him."

"I'll go out to the house with you tonight. The three of us will sit down and try to figure this thing out."

"Instinct tells me Phil is behind this. He knows Noel is living at the Croton house. He doesn't know that Noel is gay, and he's sure Noel and I are having an affair. There're his grounds for divorce. It'll be awful for Jesse if Phil tries to use Noel in a custody battle. But we can't keep running," she said in pain. "Jesse will be twelve next June. We can't keep running until his eighteenth birthday."

"We'll talk about it tonight with Noel. After all," she said humorously, "Phil can't accuse you of having an affair with a man who's quick to tell anyone that he's gay."

"A lawyer would say he's bisexual. Or worse, nail me for being an immoral mother, exposing her young son to the attentions of an admitted homosexual." Kathy paused in anguish. "This all goes back to that group photo in *Women's Wear Daily.* Phil saw it, spotted me, hired a private investigator, and they've been on my trail ever since. And Jesse— my baby—will be the one who's hurt most of all."

══ Chapter 31

Noel listened soberly while Marge told him about the man questioning company employees. Kathy had shipped Jesse off to his room to do homework. Noel and the two women sat in the den before the fireplace, where flames enveloped a cluster of birch logs. Lee had gone to a movie with a local friend.

"He had a photograph of you, Noel," Kathy pointed out. "A snapshot."

"And somebody, of course, gave him my name," Noel guessed. "It was the natural thing to do."

"I suspect Phil is having me followed," Kathy was tense and tired. "And now he thinks he has evidence that I'm having an affair with you."

"You know what you have to do, Kathy." The situation had mercifully drawn Noel out of his despondency. "You have to beat Phil at his own game. Hire yourself a sharp private eye."

"Right." Marge nodded with conviction. "Kathy, you know Phil's always screwing around with some woman. It won't be hard to track down the current one—he's always in the gossip columns. You'll jump the gun on him."

"I feel so awful," Kathy whispered. "This seems so crude and shoddy."

"You get there first," Noel persisted. Compassionate but firm. "Ten to one he'll backtrack fast. And you'll live ever after without always staring over your shoulder."

"Suppose I don't get evidence against Phil?" Kathy recoiled from the situation the other two advised.

Marge chuckled.

"Phil leaves a trail behind him that any self-respecting bird dog could pick up. It's a matter now of pinning down the evidence and sending your lawyer to face Phil. A quiet divorce outside New York State—in Mexico or the Virgin Islands—and *no* custody battle. Everything out of the public eye. Jesse won't be hurt."

"It's important to move fast," Noel warned Kathy. "Stop Phil before he gets moving."

Phil sat hunched over his desk, fighting frustration while his father scowled at the snapshots Andrews had just presented to them, along with a hefty expense account.

"What the fuck's the matter with you?" Julius shouted. "So she's kissing a guy good-bye at the airport. What can we do with that? All this time and you can't come up with better?"

"I'm playing on a hunch," Andrews said softly. "Even with that damn mutt barking his head off, I've been close enough three or four times to look right into the house. No signs of any hanky-panky. They sleep in separate rooms. So I started thinking. The guy comes from San Francisco. 'Gay heaven.' So I've got somebody checking on him out there. I'll have a report in a few days."

"You mean he's a queer?" Julius glared at Andrews. "That'll screw up everything."

"We don't know that yet. But if we can prove he is, don't

you get the picture?" Andrews stared smugly from Julius to Phil.

"The little bitch!" Phil yelled. "She's keeping my son in a house with a gay guy! If he's touched Jesse, I'll break every bone in his body!"

"You get incontrovertible proof that he's gay," Julius ordered Andrews. "We'll go into court and blast her as an immoral mother. We'll get custody of Jesse. She'll be headlines in *Confidential* and all the tabloids. And don't drag your feet!"

When Andrews left, the other two men turned to discussion of business. Phil was elated because at last he could see himself holding the fifty percent of stock in Julius Kohn Furs. The old man couldn't stall anymore. In another five years, he reasoned, his father could be persuaded to retire. No more of the heated hassles that usually ended the way he wanted, anyway.

"Drive up to the house with me for the weekend," Julius said. "I want to go over the sales reports from the concessions with you."

"I'll drive up in the morning," Phil hedged. "I have a dinner party tonight. It's too important to cancel out at the last moment."

Julius gazed appraisingly at his son.

"You keep your nose clean from here on in," he ordered. "We don't want her going after your hide once she finds out what's up. Forget about being horny until the divorce and custody suit is settled. You'll need a sharp attorney, even when Andrews brings us in the evidence. But she's going to get shafted good," he said maliciously.

"I'm still not home free," Phil said. Not that he believed otherwise, but the old man was so smug all the time, he enjoyed needling him.

"Just about," Julius contradicted with a grin. "I've got a gut feeling this Noel Bartlett character is a real fruitcake, and that's all we need. She kept this guy in her house—left him alone with her young, impressionable son."

"I doubt that they were alone," Phil demurred. "Kathy must have a housekeeper. She's making a mint from the business." That rankled, both with him and the old man, Phil admitted to himself.

"Who's side are you on?" Julius flared. "If she kept a gay guy in the house with your son, you're supposed to be outraged. You made enough fuss when Andrews first mentioned it."

"I'll carry on in court," Phil promised. Now he was envisioning himself as the maltreated husband, the heroic father rushing in to save his son from possible molestation.

Julius pushed back his chair and rose to his feet.

"Come out to the house tomorrow morning," he said. "And remember, Phil, no fucking around until this is over. Don't give the little bitch ammunition to use against you."

As usual on Fridays, Wally arrived to pick up Julius by 4 P.M. in hopes of missing the rush-hour traffic at the Queensboro Bridge. Phil dallied at the office until past six. He had a dinner date with the gorgeous redhead—Debbie Matthews—who had worked as a temp in the office last week. Eighteen, fresh out of drama school, and ambitious as hell, he remembered complacently. She worked as an office temp three times a week and made theatrical rounds twice a week. Even these days anybody involved in theater fascinated him. And the temps used a lot of would-be actresses.

They were having dinner at that quiet French place on West 55th Street. Afterward they'd go to some cheap little hotel in the Times Square area. He wouldn't take a chance on bringing her to the apartment. This time the old man was right.

He was whistling as he left the building and hailed a cab. He didn't notice the man in a beat-up suede jacket and jockey cap who was following his progress with keen interest. In his mind he was already in bed with the gorgeous young redhead.

Twelve hours later he responded to a wake-up call from the switchboard operator.

"Thanks," he said briskly. "I won't need a follow-up call."

While Debbie slept contentedly beneath a clump of blankets, Phil showered and dressed. She knew he'd be away for the weekend, but he'd see her again Monday night. He scrawled a note and propped it up against the phone on the night table. He'd go over to the garage, pick up his car, and head for Greenwich. The old man would be champing at the bit if he wasn't at the breakfast table by 8:30.

When he arrived at the Greenwich house, he found his father at the breakfast room table, engrossed in the *New York Times.*

"Where were you last night?" Julius demanded. "I tried to reach you half a dozen times."

"I told you," he reminded nonchalantly. "I had a dinner party. A jet-set crowd." A new name had just been coined for what used to be called café society. The rich and the restless, who took one of the new jets for a weekend in London, for three days in Rio during Carnival season, to Paris or St. Moritz or wherever partying was at its height.

"I had a call from Andrews. He wasn't wasting time." Julius put aside the newspaper. "He's talked with his San Francisco contact. That Bartlett character, one of her partners in the business," he emphasized, "is a well-known gay. He's almost obnoxiously frank about it. Monday morning you contact that lawyer who handled Max Edelman's divorce—"

"Good morning, Mother—" Phil pushed back his chair as his mother walked into the breakfast room and greeted her with the expected filial kiss.

"Tell Amanda to get breakfast on the table," Julius told Bella. "And tell her not to be stingy with the lox."

"In a moment. Who's in need of a divorce lawyer?" Bella asked warily, sitting at the table.

"Phil, that's who," Julius said with an air of triumph.

"You've been in touch with Kathy?" Her face lighted.

"Yeah," Phil conceded. "We know where she is, but she doesn't know we know."

Bella gazed from Phil to Julius, eyes dark with suspicion.

"What are you two cooking up?"

"Phil's divorcing Kathy and gaining custody of Jesse," Julius told her. Exuding smugness.

"You can't take Jesse away from his mother!" Bella lashed out at him.

"What do you mean, we can't?" Julius challenged. "She walked out on her husband. She's living with some gay guy from San Francisco, with my grandson in the same house!"

"The guy's gone back to San Francisco now," Phil admitted, "but he stayed at the house for almost two weeks. We've got enough ammunition to guarantee me custody of Jesse."

"Jesse belongs with his mother," Bella said ominously. "Don't try one of your weird tricks." Her eyes swung from Phil to Julius. "You can't do this."

"We can, and we will."

"I doubt that." Bella was quiet for a moment. "Not considering why Kathy walked out."

"What do you know about that?" Julius challenged.

"I've talked to Alice. She works for the Hales now, down the road. She *saw* Phil physically mistreat Kathy. She's almost sure Kathy's nose was broken. And she'd be happy to testify on Kathy's behalf if ever the need arises." Bella spoke in even tones, but Phil sensed her inner rage.

"You damned *schmuck!*" Julius yelled at Phil. "You never told me you pushed her around! In front of the nursemaid, yet!"

"She goaded me into it," Phil defended himself. "You'd have lost your temper, too. And I'll bet Alice is bluffing. She didn't come in until I was leaving the room."

"Bluffing or not, she's willing to testify," Julius reminded. *"We don't want that."* He was shaken by this unexpected turn.

"Perhaps you can work out an amicable divorce," Bella suggested. "You do want a divorce?"

"You're damn right I want a divorce." Phil's face was flushed.

"But she doesn't get a cent," Julius warned. "That's one of the conditions."

"I know Kathy," Bella said quietly. "She wouldn't want a scandal for Jesse's sake. Tell me where she is, and I'll go talk to her."

"Phil won't give up custody of his son," Julius bellowed defiantly. "Maybe six months with his mother and six months with us—"

"I don't want Kathy going into court and saying I beat her up." How the hell could he have known Alice was there all the time? "How would that look to people?"

"Tell me where she is, and I'll go talk to her," Bella repeated.

"We don't have a home phone number," Phil hedged. *Everything was falling apart.* "We know where she lives, and that she's the CEO of 4-S Shops Inc. She's using the name Kathy Altman." Even his mother—addicted to big-name designers—recognized that, he realized in irritation.

"Kathy's the woman behind 'Designs by Marge'?" Bella's expression was a mixture of astonishment and pleasure.

"She was at the right place at the right time," Phil sulked. "And she learned a lot from me."

"All right, we'll have to wait till Monday morning," Bella said calmly. "I'll go to her office. We'll talk."

On Monday morning Bella drove to the Greenwich station to take the train into New York. She'd decided there was no need to bring Wally all the way out again to drive her in. She was eager to see Kathy, wistful that the reunion with Jesse would have to wait.

She had never forgiven Phil for what he had done to Kathy. He was his father's son, she thought in frustration.

Nor had she helped to establish her own values in him when he was growing up, she admonished herself.

Jesse would be different. He would grow up to be the man Phil should have been. Kathy must fight to retain full custody. But what judge would give Phil custody when the truth was out?

Let the divorce not become a notorious case. That would be horrible for Jesse. Kathy must meet with Phil, and they must work out something practical. Visitation rights every other weekend? She grasped at this possibility. How often would Phil—or Julius—want to give up a weekend to Jesse?

Her face softened as she envisioned the reunion with her only grandson. She cherished the snapshots Kathy had sent her through the years, knowing she must not share these with Phil and Julius. How sweet and understanding of Kathy to know how much these meant to her.

At Grand Central she took a cab to the building that housed 4-S Shops Incorporated. Her heart was pounding as she rose up in the elevator to Kathy's penthouse offices. The elevator door slid open, and she walked into the lushly appointed reception area.

"I'd like to see Kathy Altman, please," she said to the receptionist, who was inspecting her Givenchy suit and sable coat with infinite respect. The 4-S Shops offered sportswear for women less affluent than Bella Kohn.

"Do you have an appointment?" the receptionist asked politely.

"No, but please tell her I'm here," Bella said with quiet confidence. "Bella Kohn."

Moments later she was being escorted down a carpeted hallway to Kathy's office. The door opened and Kathy emerged.

"Bella!" Kathy held out her arms in joyous welcome. "Oh, how I've missed you all these years!"

Their arms about each other, they walked into the huge, multiwindowed office. Kathy closed the door behind her.

"Kathy, don't be upset that I've come here," Bella

pleaded. "Phil told me only Saturday morning that you were back in New York. That you're Kathy Altman. Darling, I'm so proud of you!"

"Bella, I'll fight to keep Jesse," Kathy said while they sat on the green velvet sofa that flanked one wall of her office.

"With Phil's activities that shouldn't be difficult," Bella said caustically. "But I've come to set up a meeting between you and Phil. The two of you have to—"

"He can't have Jesse," Kathy's voice was slightly strident. "I'm prepared to prove Phil would be a bad influence on him. I have photographs—"

"Kathy, I'm on *your* side. I talked with Alice long ago. She told me what happened. I was so upset—so ashamed of Phil. Meet with him, then let the lawyers work out the terms of the divorce," she urged. "Even if Phil insists on some weekend custody, we both know he's not apt to take advantage after the first few times. And make a point that Jesse sees his father at my house. I'll always be there." Her face was luminous. "I can't wait to spoil him."

"Bella, I'm scared." Kathy was flooded by doubts. "Julius is so vindictive, and he has friends in high places."

"I've told them Alice is willing to testify on your behalf—"

"Alice said that?" Kathy glowed with gratitude.

"Phil's terrified of having his image tarnished. You can handle him, Kathy. Just stand up and fight."

"I'll talk to my lawyer." Kathy was pale and tense. "He'll set up a meeting. But you tell Phil, Bella, if he starts any funny business, I'll call all the columnists and tell them he beat me. I can fight just as dirty as Julius and Phil Kohn."

Beautiful and elegant in a gray wool Dior suit and silver jewelry, Kathy sat with pounding heart in the posh law offices of Phil's attorney. Her own attorney was at her side and clearly irritated—as was Phil's attorney—that Julius was trying to take over the discussion of a prospective divorce for Phil and her.

"Look, Phil will go along with the divorce under the proper conditions," Julius said menacingly. "No alimony, no final settlement, and her written agreement to keep this confidential."

"Mr. Kohn," Phil's attorney interrupted, "will you please allow us"— he gestured toward the other attorney—"to conduct this meeting along productive lines?"

"There's no question of money involved." Kathy's eyes were blazing. "I'm perfectly capable of supporting myself and my son."

"Your husband is asking for joint custody," Phil's lawyer said cautiously. "Without his consent you took the boy away from the state in the fall of 1953 and—"

"There's no question of joint custody," Kathy's attorney said crisply. "We'll consider visitation rights at specified intervals. We—"

"You're being damned high-handed!" Phil ignored his lawyer's warning glance. "Keeping Jesse in the house with a gay guy. How do we know what happened?"

"Nothing happened, Mr. Kohn," Kathy's lawyer said tiredly. "Mr. Bartlett is a longtime family friend. And if you persist on this track, we must point out that we have evidence of your mistreatment of your wife, of your adultery on several occasions—"

"It's up to you, Phil," Kathy broke in, terrified and impatient but determined to face up to him. "A quiet divorce, or we'll both be splashed all over the tabloids. I'll do whatever it takes to retain custody of Jesse. *I won't let you have him.*"

"We have a witness to Mrs. Kohn's beating by her husband," her attorney picked up quietly. "Medical records that her nose was broken in the course of that beating. We—"

"Enough of that," Julius hissed, his face flushed. "Phil, tell them—you'll agree to give up child custody." Now he turned to Kathy's lawyer. "Arrange for a quickie divorce.

But Jesse spends one weekend a month with his father. Beginning next weekend."

"Dad, we'll be in Montreal next weekend," Phil mumbled. "At that convention."

"All right, beginning the weekend after that," Julius conceded. "But we want a signed statement that she'll never ask for a cent from Phil," he told Kathy's attorney. "And that what happened between her and her husband when she took off like that remains confidential. No leaks. Otherwise, we go to court."

"I'll sign it," Kathy said softly, exchanging a glance with her lawyer. "But visitation rights begin after the first of the year," she stipulated. "I need time to make Jesse understand what's happening."

Kathy sat back now and listened—trembling but triumphant—while the two attorneys worked out details. Julius was belligerent but quiet; Phil sulked. Visitation rights were to be exercised at the senior Kohns' home in Greenwich, as Bella had suggested. Because of Kathy's tight working schedule it was agreed that Phil would fly down to the Virgin Islands for the divorce.

By the second week of the new year she would be a free woman, Kathy exulted as she left the meeting with her attorney. No more fears of losing Jesse. Later she must deal with how to help Jesse past this new stage in his life, bound to be traumatic.

First Jesse would meet Bella—his other grandmother. He had some hazy memory of her. Bella would be warm and loving. She would be there when he met his father and grandfather. Knowing Phil, she doubted that he would be available to play the father role one weekend a month, but Bella was a loving grandmother, and Jesse would thrive under her spoiling.

Marge was in her office, waiting nervously to hear the results. She leapt to her feet as Kathy walked in.

"We won!" Kathy glowed. "It's over!"

"Call your mother and Rhoda," Marge ordered exuberantly. "Then let's go out to lunch to celebrate!"

"Marge, I feel as though I'd been reborn," Kathy said with an aura of joyous disbelief. "That there's a whole new world out there waiting for me."

Where was David now, she asked herself. How wonderful it would have been to share this day with him. But David was living in Copenhagen—and married.

== Chapter 32

Kathy spent the long New Year's weekend at Montauk, surrounded by those close to her. Her parents and Aunt Sophie—at the house for two days—were relieved and delighted that she was about to be divorced and that the constant fear of losing Jesse was behind her. Marge drove out with Rhoda and Frank and little Sara so they might celebrate this special New Year's Eve together.

"Remember New Year's in Hamburg?" Rhoda asked sentimentally while they sat at breakfast before an open fire in the huge country kitchen on the first day of 1959. "Can you believe that was thirteen years ago?" Rhoda's eyes rested tenderly on Frank. "If I hadn't gone to Hamburg, I'd never have met you."

And in Hamburg she'd met David, Kathy thought nostalgically. Perhaps it would have been easier if she had never met him.

On their return to Manhattan, Kathy threw herself more openly into the business. She gave interviews along with Marge, allowed Ellie to book her on radio and TV talk shows.

Kathy was relieved that—after the initial tense weekend in Greenwich—Jesse seemed to be accepting his father and grandfather. But when he returned from his weekend visits, he talked mainly about "Grandma Bella." On those weekends Wally drove to Croton on Saturday mornings to take him out to Greenwich and drove him back on Sunday afternoons, to ensure him time to do his homework for the next day's classes.

On the Wednesday before Jesse's May weekend in Greenwich, Bella phoned to say that both Phil and Julius would be out of town that weekend.

"Kathy, why don't you both come and spend the weekend with me?" she encouraged. "It would be so good to have a little time together."

"I'd like that," Kathy said after a moment's indecision. "Though it might upset Phil and Julius when they find out," she laughed.

"I don't particularly care," Bella confessed. "Jesse's my darling grandson, and to me you'll always be my darling daughter-in-law. Come. We'll have a great weekend—the three of us."

At the May weekend at the Greenwich house Bella persuaded Kathy to allow Jesse to come out to Southampton for the scheduled July weekend.

"Phil may or may not be there," Bella shrugged. "I'm his stand-in for visitation weekends. I'd love to have Jesse meet his cousins. The girls will be with me for two weeks in July while their parents fly out to St. Tropez. Then they leave for a month's tour of Europe with a school group. In time," she laughed whimsically, "he may even meet his Aunt Gail and Aunt Brenda and the uncles."

Now that she and Jesse could come out of the shadows, Kathy decided to move into Manhattan. She began to search for an apartment to buy. She treasured the hours when she could be with Jesse, and not having to spend two hours a day commuting would add to that time.

It was important to find an apartment before school

opened in the fall, she stressed to the real estate broker. She must join a synagogue, too, so that Jesse could begin to prepare for his bar mitzvah next year. Her father and mother were already planning the reception. Their pride in Jesse brought her recurrent pleasure.

The evening before Jesse was to go to Southampton, Kathy received a phone call from Bella to schedule the time for Jesse's pickup.

"Will ten o'clock be all right for Jesse?" she asked solicitously. "Wally has to take Julius into town for a meeting with some managers from the West Coast stores. He'll drop Julius off and shoot right up to Croton if that's all right with Jesse."

"Ten o'clock will be fine." Kathy hesitated. "Will Phil be there this weekend?" He'd missed the last two.

"He'll be there for lunch. He's got a present for Jesse— I suppose to make up for taking off after lunch." Bella's voice betrayed her irritation. "Oh, but good news, Kathy! Jesse will get to meet another cousin this weekend. David's coming out."

"David's here?" Kathy gripped the phone with such intensity that her fingernails dug into her palm. "In New York?"

"Why yes, didn't you know?"

"I know he'd left Berlin and moved to Copenhagen," Kathy said shakily. "I tried to call him when Marge and I were in Paris last year."

"He went to Copenhagen on some research project. He was just there for several months. I thought you knew. David's returned to New York permanently. He's head of a nutrition institute right in Manhattan. He's doing so well. Working too hard, as usual."

"I had no idea." All at once Kathy was cold and trembling. *David was here. Not just on a visit but to live.* "What persuaded him to come back? The new job—or his wife?"

"He's not married. He said they'd thought about it seriously, but he was sure it wouldn't work out. You know how devoted he is to his work. And he's writing a book based on his research. Isn't that exciting?"

"I'll tell Rhoda and Frank, they'll be so pleased. I'll give a little reunion dinner for us," she decided, her words tumbling over one another. "We were all together in Hamburg, you remember." *David wasn't married.* "Would you give me his phone number? I'll phone him after the weekend."

She and Bella talked for a few moments longer, then she put down the phone and tried to cope with her emotions. David was back in New York to live.

He must know she and Phil were divorced. *And he'd see Jesse this weekend.* Why hadn't he tried to call her? He probably wouldn't know where to reach Rhoda and Frank, but he could have called her.

She dialed Rhoda's number, was impatient when the baby-sitter responded. Rhoda and Frank were down in New York for a meeting of their animal rights group, the teenager explained. Kathy felt guilty that she so seldom attended, but she supported them with regular financial contributions. She *was* involved.

"Would you like Mrs. Collins to call you back tonight?" the baby-sitter asked. "It might be late."

"That's all right. Tell her to buzz me whenever they get in."

Kathy found it impossible to focus on her morning mail, opened by her assistant and placed in four piles—in order of importance—across her desk. It was late enough, she told herself. Call David. Be warm but casual.

"Kathy!" His voice was rich with tenderness. "How wonderful to hear from you! Aunt Bella told me you'd be calling."

"I just found out Friday evening that you were in town." She paused. "I was in Paris in February of last year. I phoned the Institute, and they said you'd moved to Copenhagen. I didn't realize that was temporary, that you were coming here."

"New York is home for me," he said quietly. "I've thought about you so often, Kathy. And about Rhoda and Frank," he added. "I should have called, but I couldn't bring myself to ask the family for your phone number. You're not listed, nor are Rhoda and Frank."

"Rhoda and Frank are living up in Croton," she explained. *He didn't know what Phil did to them.* "They have a darling little girl—she was five in February."

"How wonderful for them," David said wistfully.

"I told Rhoda and Frank you were here. The three of us would love to see you." She was talking too fast. He mustn't think she was pursuing him. "Would you mind making a trek up to Croton? I'm living up there until negotiations on an apartment in Manhattan are wrapped up."

"Just tell me when. I'll be there. And Jesse is great," he added. "So bright and handsome, as I knew he would be."

They arranged that David would come up to the house for a dinner reunion on Thursday. Jesse wouldn't be upset that she would delay going to Montauk until early Friday this week, she reassured herself. Her mother and Aunt Sophie would be up there with him and Lee.

"It'll be so good to see you all," David said, and she heard the anticipation in his voice. "It's bothered me so much that I couldn't reach any of you. But I gathered there was some hostility over the divorce. I couldn't ask Phil or Uncle Julius for your address or phone number—" Meaning, Kathy surmised, that Phil and Julius had made scurrilous remarks about her.

"Bella's been wonderful," she told him quietly. "Jesse just adores her."

It ever distressed her that Phil was a rotten father, but Jesse was surrounded by loving family that made up for that lack, she comforted herself: her family and Bella, Marge and Rhoda and Noel and Frank as surrogate aunts and uncles. And David, a cousin to be cherished.

Off the phone with David, she called Frank.

"That's great," he approved when she told him about the

dinner plans. "Rhoda and I can't wait to see David. Do you realize that we haven't seen him since Hamburg?"

On Thursday, Kathy left the office at shortly past one. She must give herself plenty of time to prepare dinner, she told herself. Rhoda would come over right after school to help. She'd searched her mind to remember preferences that David had mentioned in the past. Everything must be just right.

Last night she had made a seviche of shrimp and scallops—poached, because like herself David disliked raw fish. It was chilling in the refrigerator. She'd pick up the tenderloin of beef, ordered this morning, along with salad makings and vegetables. She remembered how David had praised the tenderloin at dinner at Maxim's in Paris. Rhoda had made a peppermint mousse—with slivers of Godiva chocolate—before going in to school this morning.

She was restless when the train ran five minutes behind schedule at an earlier stop. This was to be a relaxed, perfect day, with plenty of time to prepare dinner and to dress in leisure. She debated briefly about serving dinner on the deck, decided against this. Later they could have espresso on the deck.

She organized dinner planning. Trim the tenderloin and put it back into the refrigerator until time to go into the oven. Make the salad. Wash and scrape the baby carrots, clean and cut the mushrooms to surround the tenderloin. She jotted down each item on the kitchen chalkboard, then put the wine in the refrigerator to chill.

Should she have asked Martha, who came in five mornings a week to take care of the house, to come back this evening to serve and do the dishes afterward? No, that would have been pretentious. She and Rhoda would serve. This was a dinner for four very close friends. Those months in Hamburg, she thought nostalgically, had bound them together forever.

Rhoda arrived with the peppermint mousse.

"I brought an extra so we could try it out," she said ebulliently. "I remember what you said about using Godiva chocolate."

They paused to sample the mousse. Kathy labeled it superb. Together they set the dinner table, went out to cut red roses from the bushes that banked the huge deck on three sides.

"All right, go shower and dress," Rhoda ordered. "I'll do the salad."

"You're picking David up at the Harmon station," Kathy reminded. She couldn't bear the thought of seeing him for the first time after all these years at a public railroad station.

"I won't forget," Rhoda joshed. "I hope we recognize each other."

"You'll recognize each other," Kathy said confidently. "You might not recognize Phil after thirteen years, but David has hardly changed at all."

"Like you," Rhoda scoffed. "It's indecent that you still look about twenty-five."

"When's Frank coming?" Kathy was fighting against nervousness.

"As soon as the baby-sitter arrives. Later—when we're taking David to the station—we'll stop off at the apartment so he can see Sara. She'll be asleep," Rhoda conceded, "but I want him to see her. Now go shower and dress," she prodded. "I'll throw the tenderloin into the oven at the appointed time."

At Kathy's urging Rhoda left for the railroad station fifteen minutes earlier than planned.

"Sweetie, that train is never early," Rhoda laughed. "But I'll be there when David steps off it."

Moments after Rhoda left for the station, Frank arrived. He was in high spirits, eager to see David.

"I brought along a bunch of photos of Sara," he said proudly, reaching into a pocket of his slacks. Kathy remembered David's longing for family. He would have been such a warm, loving father.

When she heard the car coming up their long driveway, she walked impulsively onto the deck, her heart hammering, her throat tightening as she saw David emerge and walk to the steps that led to the deck.

"David!" Her face radiant, she moved to meet him with outstretched arms.

"Kathy—" He folded her close. They exchanged a light kiss. "You look marvelous. It's so great for us all to be together this way." Now he turned to Frank, who had followed her onto the deck. "Frank, it's like turning the calendar back thirteen years!" The two men embraced warmly.

The four of them went into the house. Frank opened a bottle of wine, and they toasted their reunion, the atmosphere electric with their lively reminiscences. Questions flew thick and fast as they tried to span the years.

Then Kathy went into the kitchen to bring the seviche to the table while Rhoda prodded the two men into the charming dining room.

"The shrimps and scallops are poached," Kathy told David as she placed the dish before him.

"You remembered." His eyes were bright with affection.

They talked about David's work at the Institute in New York and about Frank's writing and his projected book.

"Thank God, we survived the McCarthy period," Frank said, his eyes settling on Rhoda in bitter recall.

"You had problems with red-baiting?" David was astonished.

"My father drove an ambulance for the International Brigade in Spain. We had problems," Frank said grimly. "Rhoda was pregnant. We both lost our jobs. It was hell for a while." His eyes moved to Kathy. Hers pleaded for silence. She was all at once tense about discussing Phil's part in this. Later, perhaps. "Anyhow, that's all over."

Now Frank focused on the activities of his animal rights group, which elicited strong support from the others. This was like old times, Kathy thought, all of them emotionally involved in seeing the world become a better place.

Kathy talked about the business and the house at Montauk, all the while trying to assess David's feelings toward her. At truant moments, she thought, he betrayed himself. The look in his eyes was the look she remembered from Hamburg. He was still in love with her, yet she sensed he was holding back. *Why?*

At the end of the evening they agreed they must see one another soon.

"Why don't you all come out to the Montauk house next weekend?" Kathy invited. "We can drive up together Thursday night. There'll just be Jesse and me there. We have plenty of room."

"Super," Rhoda approved, and Frank nodded in agreement. "What about you, David?"

"I should be working Friday," he said slowly, but his eyes were wistful. "So I'll take an extra day off—I've been putting in long hours. I'd love to see Montauk, Kathy."

On the following Thursday Kathy arranged to have Frank drive her to the station in the morning. In the later afternoon he'd drive with Rhoda into New York, pick up David and her, and they'd head for Montauk. Sara was spending the weekend with Rhoda's doting parents. Marge was going to a house party in Southampton.

"I'd rather go with you guys," Marge said. "But I'm a woman on the prowl. Southampton is this week's hunting ground."

Kathy was glad that they were driving up on a Thursday evening rather than Friday—the traffic was less intense. David sat up front with Frank, both men engrossed in discussing world hunger, a subject close to the four of them. Kathy and Rhoda were content to sit in the back and listen to their conversation.

As always, Kathy was aware of a rush of exhilaration as they approached the village of Montauk, leaving the oppressive humid heat of Manhattan behind them. It was as though all her problems were thrust into the background for the time she would be here. She felt wrapped in serenity.

At the house the men carried their luggage inside, and then the four of them immediately took off for a late dinner at Gurney's Inn.

"It's a marvelous place," Kathy told David as they piled back into the car. "We'll have a perfect dinner with a perfect view of the ocean."

Dinner was a relaxing time, the ocean a symphonic background. Kathy was quietly euphoric at being in David's presence. By the time they returned to the house—the stars disappearing from the night sky—all four were yawning.

"I can't believe we're so sleepy," Rhoda said. "But that means we'll be up early tomorrow morning to enjoy the beach."

"You'll sleep till ten," Frank joshed. "We both do those times Sara is visiting grandparents," he told Kathy and David in humorous recall. "Sara's our non-failing alarm clock."

Kathy fell asleep moments after her head hit the pillow. Though she often battled insomnia, tonight the excitement of being with David plus the tang of sea air had induced slumber. But by 6 A.M.—daylight slithering through the division of her bedroom drapes—she was wide awake. The morning air was soft and cool.

She showered quickly, grateful for the damp warmth of the bathroom, then dressed in smokey-blue corduroy slacks and a blue Shetland pullover. She left her room, and mindful that the others were still asleep, walked with quiet steps down the hall to the huge kitchen, which had been redecorated to provide the cozy air of an old-fashioned country kitchen. A fireplace—bricked from floor to ceiling—had been installed at her direction on one wall so that it was possible now to have meals before a blazing fire.

She put up coffee, and walked out onto the wraparound deck to wait for it to perk. A dense fog enveloped the area, lending it an eerie air of being cut off from the rest of the world, the only sounds the cawing of the sea gulls on the beach below and the waves caressing the beach. When the aroma of coffee drifted out to her, she went inside, poured herself a mug of the steaming brew, and walked out onto the deck again.

"There's something wonderful about the aroma of coffee early in the morning—" David walked out onto the deck, a bright red sweater over his gray turtleneck shirt, a mug of coffee in one hand.

"Would you like breakfast?" she asked eagerly.

"Not yet. This is fine for now." He gazed down at the fog-drenched beach with obvious appreciation. "Isn't this beautiful?"

"Foggy mornings are one of my favorite times." All at once she remembered mornings in Hamburg, when fog rolled in from the sea, and David would say, *"Isn't this beautiful?"*

"Would you like to go for a walk on the beach?" he asked. "Once we've swigged down our coffee?"

"Oh, yes."

This was a special parcel of time, she thought: David and she isolated from everything by the fog. In companionable silence they drank their coffee, then left the house to walk down the seemingly fragile wooden stairs to the beach.

"The visibility can't be more than thirty feet," David guessed as they stood at the edge of the water and gazed out at the waves coming in to the shore.

"Someone was here before us," she laughed and paused to inspect the paw-prints of a large dog along the water's edge. The beach was untouched thus far except for these.

"He walked a while, then went in for a swim—" David pointed to where the prints disappeared into the water, then resumed twenty feet down.

"Harry does that," Kathy said. "Jesse's dog."

"You must have sensational sunrises out here when there's no fog."

"Breathtaking," Kathy said softly. "I stand on the deck and watch that glorious red-gold ball slowly rise above the horizon, and I'm bursting with awe."

They talked about Montauk and about Jesse, always skirting around any discussion of her divorce. Kathy knew David felt guilty at being here with her, as though it was a breach in loyalty to the Kohns. It always irritated her that he could feel such loyalty when it was undeserved.

They were approaching the house when Rhoda emerged on the deck and called down to them.

"Breakfast coming up! Blueberry pancakes and crisp bacon. And Frank's starting a fire in the grate. I woke him up—it's a sacrilege to sleep late out here!"

Later in the morning—the earlier fog lifting now and the temperature rising—Frank drove down to pick up a cluster of New York newspapers. With sun spilling over the deck they settled themselves on chaises to read, with mugs of fresh coffee conveniently at hand.

"I don't believe it!" Rhoda's voice punctured the companionable silence.

"Don't believe what?" Kathy looked up from the segment of the *New York Times* she'd been reading.

"Phil's married again! Some nineteen-year-old fledgling actress! It's here in Dorothy Kilgallen's column!"

"Let me see—" Frank reached over to take the newspaper from Rhoda.

"Bella must be upset," Kathy said after a moment of initial shock. She ought to feel *something*, but Rhoda might have been talking about two strangers. Whatever she'd felt for Phil was long dead.

"You won't have to worry about remembering when Phil has visitation rights with Jesse," Frank said sarcastically. "Not that he availed himself of his rights that frequently."

"Phil was never the doting father," Kathy conceded, and was all at once conscious of David's troubled expression. He was remembering that Phil had not been at the Southampton house when Jesse was there last weekend. "How would you all like to drive over to the Point later to see the Montauk Lighthouse at sunset?" Deliberately she changed the subject. "It was commissioned by President George Washington in 1790."

Over the weekend Kathy watched with ebbing hope for signs that David was relaxing with her. Endless times she glanced up to find his eyes resting on her, and she knew he was still in love with her. Why did he keep this invisible barrier between them, she asked herself in soaring frustration.

On Sunday morning Kathy awoke to the sound of rain on the windowpanes. While she dressed, she became aware of the aroma of fresh bread baking in the oven. Rhoda must have been up early. With a sense of anticipation she dressed and hurried out to the kitchen. Birch logs crackled in the fireplace grate.

"I've put up biscuits," Rhoda told her. "Frank adores waking up to the smell of bread baking in the oven. David started the fire," she said. "He went for a walk in the rain."

Within twenty minutes the kitchen radiated high spirits. David had returned from his walk and changed into dry clothes. Frank had awakened, dressed, and was stoking the fire. Rhoda had brought out a platter of country-style biscuits and was preparing to serve what she called her "empty the refrigerator" omelets.

Table conversation veered from nostalgic memories of less-appealing breakfasts in Hamburg to Frank's sobering recall of McCarthyism.

"It was a harrowing time for Rhoda and me. Thank God, it's over."

"We didn't shed a tear when Joe McCarthy died," Rhoda said, her eyes flashing with revived anger.

This was the moment to let David know what Phil had done to Rhoda and Frank, yet Kathy hedged. It would sound as though she were trying to absolve herself of blame for their failed marriage. She understood that Frank was saying nothing of this out of respect for her. But she was afraid to tell David that Phil had turned them in to the red-baiters. She knew his closeness to the Kohns—what he considered all that remained of his family. She couldn't risk antagonizing him.

Later in the afternoon the men carried the luggage out to the car for the return trip to the city. Kathy and Rhoda made the routine check of windows and faucets and electric range. All the while Kathy was conscious of the questions in Rhoda's eyes.

"Rhoda, stop looking like that," she exhorted. "Nothing's going to happen between David and me."

"Kathy, I see the way he looks at you—"

"He doesn't want a woman in his life," she said painfully. "It's too late for us. The right time was in Hamburg, and I muffed that. It'll never happen again."

═ Chapter 33

In September Kathy was caught up in the madness of moving from the Croton house into the huge, sprawling West End Avenue apartment. She was grateful for Lee's efficiency in handling much of this. She was relieved that Jesse liked his new school, the new apartment, and especially their closeness to the Hudson River and the yacht basin. She tried—futilely—to push all thoughts of David out of her mind.

Rhoda was in the process of tracking down a teaching job in Manhattan, to begin with the February term. When at the end of the month word came through that the job was hers, she and Frank began to worry about the availability of an apartment on the Upper West Side. Both Kathy and Marge offered to put them up until they could locate something.

Marge scheduled a small dinner party to celebrate Rhoda's new job and insisted that Rhoda invite David and Brian, now in New York again and working with Frank and Rhoda on fund-raising for their animal rights group.

"Call it a Hamburg reunion," Marge flipped. "I may not have been there with you, but I feel as though I was."

"Marge, I know what you're doing," Kathy said bluntly over luncheon with her and Rhoda on the day Rhoda came into New York to sign her job contract. "David's all wrapped up in his work. That's the way he wants it. There's no room in his life for me."

"For a woman who can be so aggressive in business," Rhoda sighed, "you give up awful fast when it comes to a man."

"Invite him for dinner," Kathy agreed, "but remember, we're only longtime friends. He's over forty and set in his ways; he feels his job can satisfy all his needs. I'm not throwing myself at his feet."

Dressing for Marge's dinner party, Kathy changed three times before she reluctantly conceded this wasn't a fashion show. A dinner with old friends. She was eager to see Brian, who drifted in and out of their lives at three- or four-year intervals. Hamburg had drawn them together forever.

The last to arrive at Marge's new penthouse co-op—also on what she good-humoredly called the unfashionable Upper West Side—Kathy was swept up in the convivial mood that permeated the group. Marge's cook-maid had prepared a superb dinner. The conversation jumped from topic to topic in the manner Kathy enjoyed. And as before she often glanced up to find David's eyes dwelling on her.

When at last they decided to call it an evening, David offered to see her home, a few blocks distant. Rather than bother with a taxi, they walked. The night was crisp and cool, with a hint of autumn already in the air. Yet despite a beautiful closeness between them, Kathy was conscious of that same invisible wall.

"Would you like to come up for coffee or a drink?" she asked when he walked her past the doorman to the elevators.

"I know tomorrow is Saturday, but I have to go in to the office," he said regretfully.

"I'll be at my office, too. We're two workhorses, David," she laughed.

"It's been a great evening."

Why did he look at her like that, and yet keep her at a distance?

"We must do it again soon," she said casually.

He kissed her lightly on the cheek and waited for her to enter the just-descended elevator.

On a mid-October weekend—with Jesse en route in the Kohn limousine for Greenwich—Kathy decided on impulse to drive to the house in Montauk. She was tired and tense and frustrated at the futile encounters with David. She'd leave right away, come back tomorrow night, she plotted.

Within thirty minutes she was at the garage and waiting for her Mercedes to be brought down from an upper level. She drove a Mercedes because of Marge. *"Darling, you have to drive a Mercedes to keep up your image of the 'successful career woman.'"*

When Phil returned from the Virgin Islands and she knew they were divorced, she had been euphoric. For a little while. She should be so happy, she rebuked herself. She was free of Phil and Jesse was legally in her sole custody. The business was fantastic. She shouldn't need any more than that. Life wasn't meant to be perfect.

When she had driven past the endless miles of cemeteries in nearby Queens, she began to notice the splendor of the scenery—the trees a glorious medley of dark red, brown, and golden leaves. It would be a beautiful weekend out at Montauk, she thought, and all at once her heart was pounding as she envisioned sharing this with David.

Give them one more chance, Kathy told herself, exulting in this decision. She pulled off at the next gas station with a public telephone, called David. There was no response at his home phone, but she caught him at the office.

"I know it's a last-minute call, but it's so marvelous up

here. I thought you might enjoy getting away from the city. There's a train at—"

"I'll drive up," he said quickly. "I went to hell with myself and bought a car ten days ago. Just give me directions."

He expected Jesse and Lee to be at the Montauk house with her, she realized. She'd explain that Jesse was with Bella and Lee was spending the weekend with her sister. She was being brazen, yes, but at thirty-five she could afford to be, she thought with shaky bravado. *She was giving them one last chance.*

She stopped along the way to shop for food, watching the clock because instinct told her David would waste little time getting on the road. Her mind was alternately assaulted by hopes and doubts. Would she drive David away forever when he understood she had deliberately arranged a weekend alone with him?

When she pulled into the garage at the Montauk house, she was conscious of the familiar magic. The ocean was choppy beneath a magnificent October sun—seeming to match her own chaotic emotions. The stretch of beach before the house was deserted except for a cluster of sea gulls. The houses on either side—gratifyingly distant from her own—were unoccupied this weekend.

She hurried about the house, opening up windows, putting up a pot of coffee, debating about their luncheon menu. Belatedly—out of cowardice, she admitted to herself—she concocted a story to tell David. Rhoda and Frank were supposed to drive up, too, but she arrived at the house to hear that they were having trouble with the car and couldn't make it.

She set a table on the deck for luncheon, though the wind made it necessary to anchor napkins beneath the plates. She relished the quiet, unbroken except for the sound of the ocean.

She felt a surge of excitement as she heard a car turn into the driveway. She went onto the deck to welcome David.

"Hi!" She stood in the sunlight with the wind blowing her hair about her face and reveled in the pleasure she saw in his eyes. "Was I wrong about the day?"

"It's magnificent," he agreed, running up the steps to the deck. "I'm so glad you called me."

"Rhoda and Frank had to turn back on the road—some trouble with the car," she lied.

"That's rough luck—" But for a revealing instant she saw the glint of excitement in his eyes.

"You're probably starving. I have lunch ready. Let's have it on the deck." As always when she was nervous, she was talking too fast.

"The coffee smells marvelous. Remember the garbage we usually drank in Hamburg?"

"Remember the coffee in Berlin?" She laughed shakily. It was almost as though they were there this moment. "At the Hotel Adlon?"

"I've thought about that day so many times," he said quietly.

They sat down to lunch on the deck. Kathy was confident that before this day was over David would make love to her. He was fighting against it, out of his absurd sense of loyalty to the family. *Because the man he called "Uncle Julius" would not approve.* But what they felt—and the circumstances—would break down that wall between them, she promised herself.

After a leisurely lunch they walked on the beach.

"I'll bet the water's warm," Kathy said and impulsively reached down to untie her sneakers and kick them off. "Shall we wade?" she challenged him.

"How can we not?" he laughed, caught up in her mood.

The day sped past. There was no question of going out for dinner. While Kathy prepared small miracles with pasta, a marinara sauce, and a tossed salad, and garlic bread was warming in the oven, David was absorbed in coaxing a blaze into being in the kitchen fireplace. There was a tacit understanding in their minds that this weekend belonged to them.

They ate before the fireplace, caught up in memories of the early weeks in Hamburg, before Phil had arrived. Kathy was aware of David's nearness, waiting for him to reach out and pull her into his arms. It was as though he were slowly building up his resolve to do this.

Together they cleared away the dishes, loaded them into the dishwasher. They stood face to face while the hum of the dishwasher blended with the sound of the rough waves crashing against the shore.

"I have to keep reminding myself that you were Phil's wife," he said unevenly, but his hands were at her waist.

"*Were,* David," she emphasized. "That's behind us now."

"Oh, Kathy, how can we deny ourselves at a moment like this?" he whispered.

"We don't, David. We don't," she said urgently.

Her arms closed in about him as he drew her close and brought his mouth down to hers.

"This is so wrong," he said painfully when their mouths parted at last.

"David, how can it be wrong?" she protested. "It's what we both want."

He lifted her off her feet and carried her into her bedroom. Outside the brisk wind was increasing to storm proportions. The sun had retreated behind darkening clouds. While the elements roared into a Wagnerian crescendo, Kathy and David abandoned themselves to emotions long kept imprisoned.

"Oh, Kathy, Kathy—"

They left the bed to watch the storm over the ocean, and then made love again. It would be a night she would forever remember, Kathy thought, no matter how many nights they had together in the years ahead.

She awoke in the morning and was immediately aware that David was not beside her. In childlike alarm she thrust aside the comforter and left the bed. She paused, a smile lighting her face. David was making coffee in the kitchen. She slid her feet into slippers and reached for a robe.

Last night's storm had subsided. Sunlight poured into the house. She walked down the hall and into the kitchen. David looked up with a brilliant smile.

"We'll have coffee, walk on the beach, then I'll make breakfast for us." His eyes were tender, yet she sensed he was troubled.

"I'll go dress," she said. *Why did David look like that?*

They walked on the beach with mutual joy, and returned to the house for breakfast. Yet she knew instinctively that deep within himself David was unhappy. He couldn't be upset because she had once been Phil's wife? That was another lifetime. *Phil was married again.*

Not until after breakfast, while they lounged on chaises on the deck, did David tell her what was troubling him. It was as she had suspected.

"How can I explain to Uncle Julius and Aunt Bella about my feelings for you?" he asked in quiet torment.

"You don't *have* to explain." She struggled to remain calm.

"In the eyes of the family I'm siding with you against Phil. To them this is wrong. And Uncle Julius has been so good to me."

"Oh David, wake up!" Her voice was involuntarily harsh. "Julius Kohn is a monster."

"Kathy, don't say that," he rejected. Shocked by her outburst. "He and Aunt Bella took me in when I had to run from the Nazis. They—"

"Julius Kohn swindled you out of a fortune!" Kathy's longtime rage erupted. "He's never done anything for anyone except himself. He—"

"Kathy, you can't say that about Uncle Julius!" David stared at her as though he had never seen her before. "He took me into his home when my parents sent me out of Germany. Without him I would never have gotten through college and medical school."

"David, how can you be so blind?" Kathy fought against exasperation. "You owe him nothing. You—"

"Uncle Julius and Aunt Bella are my family—all that remains of generations of Kohns. *I owe them my life.*"

"Bella is a warm, sweet woman, and I love her," Kathy told him. "But I can't bear to see you swearing loyalty to a man who deserves only your contempt."

"I'm sorry." His face was cold and set. "I can't stay here and listen to you talk this way. I'm driving back to New York."

Kathy's face was ashen as she stood at a window a few minutes later and watched David pull out of the garage. This time it was over for them forever. There was no turning back.

= Chapter 34

Kathy was at her desk by 8 A.M.—a common occurrence at rush business periods—because she had awakened before six after a night of broken sleep. She had come early to the office in a determination to push out of her mind the calamitous conclusion to what had seemed a perfect weekend with David.

She struggled to focus on business. In a burst of exasperation she left her desk to brew a cup of instant coffee. *Why had she behaved so stupidly?* All these years she'd managed to keep her silence, even while she fumed at David's misplaced loyalty. A few careless sentences, and she'd destroyed everything between them.

At close to nine Marge arrived. She and Marge were almost always the first to arrive, the last to leave. But they had a dedicated staff, she thought with pride. In a crunch everybody pitched in to get the work done.

"You were carousing yesterday," Marge drawled. "I called you three times and you didn't answer."

"I went out to Montauk," Kathy said somberly. "Come in and let me tell you my tale of woe."

Marge listened sympathetically while Kathy talked about the reunion with David and its ultimate outcome.

"Marge, it's fate," Kathy said painfully. "I should know by now."

"Bullshit," Marge scolded. "It was a landmark occasion—you and David had your first fight."

"The first and last," Kathy said with a towering sense of loss. "I tried—I was aggressive—but I screwed up."

"David's too bright and sensitive not to wake up to the truth," Marge comforted. "He'll think things through and know you're right."

"When?" Kathy challenged. "When I'm ninety?"

"Men can be jugheaded," Marge conceded. "All this talk—all the articles now about how women are coming into their own at last—but what guy wants to hear about it? To the average male any woman with brains is a queer duck. And a successful woman is either an affront to their manhood—or the pot of gold at the end of the rainbow."

"Forget the lot of them." Kathy opened a folder and pulled out a report. "Let's figure out our spring promotion for the Atlanta and Palm Beach stores."

David checked his watch as he changed into a fresh shirt for the evening. He was tired from the sixty-five-hour weeks at the office and would have preferred to have dinner and collapse with a book. Still, he knew he couldn't turn down his uncle's request to fill in as his aunt's escort to dinner and the theater tonight.

Uncle Julius and Phil were entertaining out-of-town buyers, he recalled. Not even hard-to-get theater tickets would stand in the way of business. The three of them were alike in that, David told himself. Their work came before all else.

But he had been tense and insomniac since the weekend at Montauk five weeks ago. He'd flown off the handle that way because he'd been so uptight about an experiment that was driving him up the wall. But how could he stand by and let Kathy vilify Uncle Julius that way?

He reached for a topcoat—the November night was cold—and hurried from the apartment. Aunt Bella had suggested meeting him at the restaurant, but he insisted on picking her up at the company apartment where she was staying for a few days. Part of his European childhood, he thought humorously.

Bella was waiting for him, beautifully dressed as always and wearing her trademark diamond necklace.

"I felt guilt at Julius's drafting you this way," she said while he held her sable coat for her, "but then I remembered how hard you work and that you probably need a night of relaxation."

Wally was waiting downstairs with the limousine to drive them to the Colony. He would return in time to drive them to the theater. Seated at their table David and Bella focused on ordering dinner. Then Bella launched into talk about Jesse, whom she obviously adored.

"I never thought I would be a fatuous grandmother," she mocked herself good-humoredly. "I wasn't that way with my granddaughters. But there's something about Jesse. He reflects the love and understanding Kathy has lavished on him through the years. I'll never really forgive myself for raising my kids the way I did. But Kathy isn't making my mistakes."

"Jesse's special," David agreed. *Kathy* was special. He'd known that since those days aboard the ship that took them to Hamburg.

"I'm absolutely disgusted with Phil's new wife," Bella confided. "Not just because she's the same age as two of his nieces, but because she doesn't give a damn about Phil except for what he can do for her career."

"A lot of young women today are obsessed by career," David said softly.

"Kathy has a career, and a damn successful one. But she's a fine human being. I don't know how Phil could have treated Kathy the way he did." For a moment her face was taut with grim recall, then, unexpectedly, she chuckled. "It was the biggest shock of Julius's and Phil's lives when Kathy left Phil without taking her diamond and sapphire necklace. I told Phil if he gives Kathy's necklace to his new wife, I'll never speak to him again."

"I—I was shocked when I learned Kathy and Phil had broken up."

"Kathy married the wrong Kohn," Bella said softly. "She deserved better." Her eyes met his with warmth and compassion.

Aunt Bella knew, he thought. How had they given him away? She knew, and she approved.

"I've always found my own diamond necklace a great consolation prize." David was grateful that she was diverting the conversation. But her message was clear. She saw nothing wrong in his loving Kathy. "The others don't know it, but I've willed my necklace to Kathy. Julius was so proud of having bought the diamonds as stones from a young Jewish refugee back in 1937—" She paused and David tensed, a pulse suddenly throbbing at his temple. "He was so smug because he'd bought them at a fraction of their worth. But you know Julius and his bargains—"

David was cold with sudden, bitter comprehension. *Those were the diamonds his father gave to him through the barbed wire fence at Salzburg.* Kathy had been right. She had tried to make him understand, and he had walked out on her.

Kathy forced a smile while Jesse talked enthusiastically about the school trip that was to take place today, but the aromas of food were making her faintly queasy. She always waited until around ten for breakfast, brought in routinely by her assistant, but she made a practice of having a "wake-up" cup of coffee with Jesse and Lee before leaving for the office. This morning she abandoned the coffee after a few sips.

"You look like you could do with some sleep," Lee

scolded. "You haven't stopped yawning since you sat at the table."

"I feel as though I could sleep around the clock," she admitted.

"But you won't," Jesse guessed. "Mom, the office won't fall apart if you stay home and sleep this morning."

"Don't tempt me," she laughed and pushed back her chair. "Enjoy the school trip, darling."

The cab that picked her up each morning was just drawing up at the curb when she walked out of the building. Seated in the cab she leaned back and closed her eyes. It was ridiculous to feel so tired. Was she coming down with a virus? She had no time for that, she thought querulously. Then—with dizzying suddenness—suspicion took root in her mind.

That was ridiculous. *She couldn't be pregnant.* But of course, she could, her mind taunted. Occasionally she was late, she told herself—that meant nothing. But being late and feeling this way was unnerving. She glanced at her watch. Please, no traffic tie-ups this morning. She needed to talk to Marge.

She waited impatiently at her desk for Marge to arrive.

"Marge!" She hurried from her desk to the door as she saw Marge appear in the hallway.

"Let me dump my coat and get some coffee—" Marge was already pulling off her coat.

"Now," Kathy said agitatedly and beckoned Marge into her office.

"What's up?" Marge asked in alarm while Kathy closed the door behind her.

"I think I'm pregnant." Marge knew about the weekend with David. "Of course, it may just be early menopause—"

"At thirty-five?" Marge scoffed, her face aglow with tenderness. "Sweetie, call David!"

"I can't," she hedged. "Besides, I'm not even sure."

"Go for a pregnancy test." Marge was practical. "You'll know tomorrow morning."

"Don't tell a soul," Kathy warned. "It's probably nothing." Yet deep inside she prayed that she *was* pregnant. That she was carrying *David's baby.* Somehow, she would manage her life.

"Get on the phone with your doctor," Marge ordered. "Tell her to send you for a pregnancy test. Neither of us can survive more than twenty-four hours of uncertainty!"

The following morning Marge was waiting with her to make the phone call to her doctor's office.

"Marge, I'm scared," Kathy whispered, her eyes focused on her watch. Her doctor had told her to call at 10 A.M.— she would have the lab reports. "Maybe I'm not pregnant. Maybe it's an ulcer, or cancer."

"Call," Marge said matter-of-factly. But Kathy knew that she, too, was anxious.

Kathy dialed and waited. Moments later she was speaking with her doctor.

"The test was positive," the doctor said briskly.

"That means I'm pregnant?" Kathy asked shakily.

The doctor chuckled. "That's the usual assumption. When you've calmed down, call my secretary and make an appointment."

She'd have the baby out in San Francisco, Kathy plotted. Noel and she would switch locales for a few months. But she showed so quickly, she remembered in panic.

"She said yes?" Marge prodded as Kathy stared into space.

"I'm pregnant," Kathy said. "What will I tell Jesse? What will I tell my parents?"

"You'll worry about them later. Tell David!"

"I can't. He hates me now. This would be like a shotgun marriage."

"Kathy, you tell David. You're giving him the greatest gift in the world—his child."

"But he hates me," she said in anguish.

"He doesn't hate you. You upset his image of Julius. One

of you has to make a move, and I don't think it's going to
be David."

"I can't do it, Marge—" But in her mind she was waver-
ing. Remembering his longing for family. His tenderness
with Jesse. That night in Montauk they had brought his
dream into reality. *She was carrying David's son or daughter.*
Their child. "I'll try to call him. Just get out of here and
let me think about it."

Ten minutes later she was on the phone with David.

"David, I've felt so awful about what I said to you up
at the house," she apologized, her heart pounding. "It's
haunted me ever since."

"You were right, Kathy," David rushed to reassure her,
and she heard the joy in his voice that she had made this
overture. "I was wrong. Bella made me understand. But I
didn't have the guts to call you after the way I'd behaved."

"Come up to the apartment for dinner tonight," she
urged. "Jesse will be so pleased to see you, too."

"What time?" he asked gently.

Kathy sat through dinner in a pleasurable haze. After dinner Jesse went off to his room to do homework. Lee cleared
the table and stacked the dishes in the dishwasher, then disappeared into her room.

"I'm so *glad* you called me," David told Kathy while they
walked into the living room. "I've been such an idiot—"

"Have you seen the view from this front window?" she
asked, all at once nervous about confiding her news. "We
can see all the way across the Hudson to New Jersey."

"I only want to see you," he said, reaching to pull her
close.

"David, I'm pregnant," she whispered, her face radiant.

"Kathy—" His eyes searched hers. "Our baby?"

"Are you questioning that?" She clucked with mock reproach, knowing he was in shock.

"This is the most wonderful moment in my life." His
voice was reverent. "I can't believe this is happening. We'll

be a family." All at once he was anxious. "We'll get married immediately."

"It'll have to be a civil marriage," Kathy reminded. "I don't have a religious divorce."

"The father of a colleague is a judge up in Connecticut. We can have him marry us," David said.

"I'll need a few days to break the news to my family," Kathy said. "About the wedding," she laughed. "A week later I'll tell them about the baby. Oh, David, we've waited so long!"

Two limousines carried the wedding party to the judge's home in Connecticut. Kathy's parents, Jesse, her aunt Sophie and Bella in one. Lee, Marge, Rhoda, Frank, Sara, Noel—who flew in from San Francisco for the occasion—with David in the other.

Kathy chose a gray velvet suit for the wedding, to highlight the jeweled bow that David would give her the moment she was his wife—as Alex Kohn's mother had urged him to do generations ago. At her suggestion the bow now hung from a silver chain.

Her face luminous with happiness—all those she loved surrounding her—Kathy stood with David before the judge. This marriage, she told herself with joyous confidence, would endure forever. In a brief but lovely ceremony the judge married them.

"I now pronounce you husband and wife."

Kathy lifted her face to David's. Tenderly he kissed her, then reached into the pocket of his jacket to pull forth the jeweled bow, restored now to its original splendor.

"From my great-grandmother to her new great-granddaughter-in-law," David murmured and dropped the chain to which the bow was now attached in place about Kathy's throat. "At last it's home, my love."

"How beautiful!" Kathy's mother leaned forward and inspected the jeweled bow with admiration after warm embraces were exchanged.

"Where did you get that?" Aunt Sophie stared with an air of disbelief, then reached to turn over the bow, where initials had long ago been inscribed.

"Kathy and I discovered it in a pawnshop in Berlin almost fourteen years ago," David explained. "I recognized it instantly. It's a family heirloom."

"Kathy said your family was from *Russia.*" Sophie was pale and trembling.

"Aunt Sophie, does it matter?" Kathy was bewildered by her aunt's agitation. "David's great-grandmother and great-granduncle were furriers in St. Petersburg. His grandfather was born there, but—"

"But Alex had to run from St. Petersburg after Czar Alexander II was assassinated," Sophie picked up. "He went to Berlin. He became a medical student—"

"Aunt Sophie, how do you know this?" Kathy was astonished.

"I know the jeweled bow." Sophie's voice was strong with conviction. Her face radiant. "It was a brooch when Alex gave it to me. It had been especially designed as a wedding gift for his mother, with her initials on the back. When Alex had to run from St. Petersburg, his mother gave it to him and told him to keep it for his bride—"

"Aunt Sophie, you loved David's grandfather—that was the man you told me about." Tears filled Kathy's eyes.

"My father insisted that I couldn't marry Alex then, I must go to America with my parents and sisters. I returned the pin to Alex, to keep until we were reunited. I never saw Alex again. I never stopped loving him."

"This marriage was meant to be," David said gently and leaned to kiss Sophie on the cheek. "Kathy and I are fulfilling the dream you shared with my grandfather. At last, the jeweled bow has come home."